MW00529292
come true...

A HIDEAWAY FOR LOVE

Ben's body was warm against hers in the chilly attic. Emily pressed closer to him, the better to feel the strength of his body straining toward hers. He bent lower, his lips caressing the length of her neck and trailing down the fabric of her bodice as he bent down. His arm caught her behind the knees, lifting her in his arms as easily as a child. Slowly and carefully, he made his way down the steps. He needn't have carried her. She'd have gone willingly on her own.

With the toe of his boot, he nudged open the bedroom door, catching it with his heel before it could make any noise. Slowly he pushed it closed. He still held her close against him while he locked the door.

"Emily," he whispered into her soft hair. "I want you, Emily. I want you now. Don't make me wait. . . ."

HOME FIRES

LINDA SHERTZER

DIAMOND BOOKS, NEW YORK

This book is a Diamond original edition, and has never been previously published.

HOME FIRES

A Diamond Book / published by arrangement with the author

PRINTING HISTORY
Diamond edition / December 1992

Cover appliqué illustration by Kathy Lengyel.

For information address: The Berkley Publishing Group, 200 Madison Avenue, New York, New York 10016.

ISBN: 1-55773-823-8

Diamond Books are published by The Berkley Publishing Group, 200 Madison Avenue, New York, New York 10016.
The name "DIAMOND" and its logo are trademarks belonging to Charter Communications, Inc.

PRINTED IN THE UNITED STATES OF AMERICA

10 9 8 7 6 5 4 3 2 1

To
Melinda Metz, my editor,
who encouraged me to start this;
and to
Cynthia and Rhonda,
Mika and Renae,
who gave me moral support until
I finished it

CHAPTER ONE

"I CAN SPIT FARTHER THAN YOU CAN."

"Can not."

"Can too."

With a mixture of horror and fascination, Emily Shaw watched the two bickering children. They were seated with their backs to her at the edge of the platform of the deserted depot. They swung their sun-browned legs rhythmically, their bare heels making hollow, ringing sounds against the large tin milk cans beneath them. Apparently, they didn't know she was watching their unusual contest.

"You think you're so darned good," the one child continued.

"Know I am," came the confident reply.

In spite of her shock over the subject of their dispute, Emily found herself smiling at such a bold display of confidence.

"Well, let's see you do it, then," one child demanded, poking the other in the ribs with a bony elbow.

Taking up the challenge, the other clapped a grubby, tanned hand down upon the crown of the battered straw hat, reared back, and expectorated into the dusty street. It fell just short of the left front hoof of the bay mare tied to the ring of the wrought-iron hitching post. The child gave a proud tug at the straps of the blue denim overalls.

The mare shook the flies from her twitching black-edged ears, setting the brass rings and buckles of her harness to jingling. She shifted her weight from one hind foot to the other. The shafts of the buckboard creaked slightly with her weary movement. Other than that, Emily saw no indication the horse had any qualms about being used for target practice.

"Not bad," the challenger conceded grudgingly, head cocked, as if examining the other's handiwork to gauge the degree of difficulty of this next move.

An equally grubby tanned hand reached up to the owner's hat. Instead of being tightly clamped down, the straw hat was briskly ripped off. To Emily's surprise, two long, black plaits tumbled down the child's back. Now freed from any burdens that might hinder her performance, the girl spat forcefully.

"Oh, shoot!" the other exclaimed. She tore her own hat from her head and slammed it down beside her in frustrated defeat. A set of plaits, equally as long as her competitor's, fell to her waist. Strands of sun-lightened blond intertwined with the golden brown tresses. "I didn't believe Nelly when she told me you'd beat Jimmy Lindstrom yesterday. Guess I owe her that stick of licorice after all. And it's all your fault!" She laughed and gave her companion a playful push.

The dark-haired girl laughed and shoved her back. "Didn't your pa teach you not to gamble?" she scolded.

"Didn't yours teach you not to spit in public?" the other quickly replied. She gave her friend a push that sent them both toppling over.

The two little girls dissolved into a squealing pile of arms and knees and elbows as they wrestled on the platform. Suddenly detaching herself, the dark-haired girl snatched up her friend's discarded hat, jumped down from the platform, and sprinted away.

"Hey! Wait for me!" her friend cried. Springing to her feet, she grabbed the remaining hat. Then she, too, disappeared around the corner of the depot. The little girls' squeals and giggles faded into the distance.

Emily sighed and looked around her. Now that the children were no longer there to entertain her, she was struck with the realization of just how alone she was in this strange town.

When she had first arrived, she had been busy retrieving her baggage. After her two brass-bound, black leather trunks were safely deposited beside her, she'd watched the passengers who had descended with her. Cheerfully and very noisily, family and friends had greeted them one by one and immediately carried them off to the comforts of hearth and home.

She had lifted her head, turning her neck this way and that as she searched among the people, trying to find the gentleman who was supposed to meet her. Ebenezer Cameron was not only Emily's brother's senior law partner, he was also George's brother-in-law.

When Emily had received the letter from the law offices of Cameron and Shaw, informing her of George's sudden passing, and the fact that she was now her ten-year-old niece's legal guardian, she took some small comfort in envisioning Mr. Cameron as regally bewhiskered, pompously plump, and endearingly condescending—much like the lawyer who had handled her father's estate. Now, having observed some of her fellow travelers by rail into the rustic Iowa countryside, she feared Mr. Cameron might instead sport patched overalls, chew tobacco, and have notoriously bad aim when it came to hitting brass cuspidors.

In spite of the fact that she had no idea what the man really looked like, she'd searched for him in the crowd. She had sent a telegram notifying him of her arrival. Even if she could not identify Mr. Cameron, he should be waiting for her. The fact that she was standing at the depot looking for someone might be his first clue as to who she was.

She continued to wait while groaning workmen loaded large sacks of corn into boxcars. The sweet, dusty smell reminded her of the bin of cornmeal in the kitchen of her own elegant townhome in Washington Place in Baltimore. It also made her realize just how hungry she was.

A sudden shift in the direction of the wind brought another more acrid, and infinitely less pleasant, odor to her nostrils. Huge, smelly hogs grunted their protests as they were prodded out of their pens in the crowded stockyard and loaded into the slat-sided stockcars. Whatever small semblance of an appetite she might now retain, Emily decided it was *not* for pork.

The loud clanging of the brass bell startled her. With a wheezing of steam and a grinding of iron wheels, the train pulled out of the station.

Now that everyone else's business had been taken care of, maybe the stationmaster could take the time to help her locate Mr. Cameron, or at least give her directions to his office. Emily looked around the depot for the stationmaster. Unfortunately, no one claiming that responsibility could be found.

At the edge of the platform ran the railroad tracks, and beyond that the stockpens. Now that the livestock had been loaded, no one remained, not even an old sow.

On the other side of the depot, across the street, there were people going about their daily business. Emily was not used to approaching strangers for help, and these people were too far away, and looked far too busy, for her to seek help from them. She didn't think she should leave her baggage unattended, either.

The only conveyance left at the depot was the abandoned

buckboard. Emily scrutinized the placid little bay mare. At the circus she had once seen a horse who could count, but she didn't think this horse, or any other, would be very good at giving her directions to Mr. Cameron's office. The tiny grin this image brought to Emily's lips quickly vanished in the face of her growing concern at being virtually abandoned.

She removed a precisely creased yellow sheet of paper from the small pocket in the side of her slim skirt and reread the sparsely worded telegram. No, she decided as she carefully refolded the paper and replaced it in her pocket, she had not been mistaken. Mr. Cameron was supposed to meet her here at the depot at half past two. She looked down at the small silver watch hanging from the chatelaine pinned to the bodice of her gray wool traveling suit. Two fifty-seven, exactly—and still Mr. Cameron made no appearance.

Well, lawyers were busy men, Emily reasoned. Maybe he had been unavoidably detained, but he might at least have had the courtesy to send a clerk, or even a small boy, with a message.

A nagging worry crept into Emily's thoughts. Ebenezer Cameron was her sister-in-law's *older* brother, although how much older she couldn't recall. Emily's own brother had been almost ten years older than she, and a friend's half-brother had been nearly twenty years older. Sarah's brother could easily be fifty years old. And, in Emily's limited experience, she had observed that senior law partners were usually not young men.

Suppose Mr. Cameron had not forgotten her? Suppose the poor old gentleman had had a stroke or had fallen down in his home and was unable to rise? Emily had not spent the past eleven of her twenty-five years caring for her aging parents without gaining some knowledge of the calamities that befell the elderly.

Suppose Mr. Cameron was dead! Who, then, would help her to settle her brother's estate and enable her to make a secure home for her orphaned niece?

Emily paced the deserted platform. The heels of her boots tapped against the weathered wood and echoed in the stillness of the crisp autumn air. She was tired from the long, tedious journey in the stifling atmosphere of the railroad car. Her muscles ached from sitting for so long, all the while being jostled unmercifully as they rattled along the rails. She was hungry and worried, and she was becoming more upset by the minute.

Through the long years of her parents' illnesses, she had learned to hide her emotions. But if someone didn't help her soon, she thought she'd begin to cry, right here, right now. She drew in a deep breath and gave just the tiniest sniffle.

"Can I help ya, ma'am?"

The drawling voice startled her. Emily turned to the wiry little man who had managed to appear behind her without making any noise at all. His rheumy blue eyes peered at her over the gold-rimmed spectacles perched at the end of his broad nose, which somehow managed to end in a sharp point. The stiff white collar stood away from the wrinkled skin of his scrawny neck two full finger-widths all the way around. Tufts of white hair stuck out above his ears from both sides of the black peaked cap he wore. He blinked, and Emily realized how much the man resembled an owl. However, the small brass plate across the front of the crown of his hat declared him to be the stationmaster.

At last the man had decided to make an appearance! Where had he been when she first needed him? Why had he kept her waiting so long? What did he know of the elusive Mr. Cameron?

"Been waiting long, ma'am?" he asked.

"Only since the train arrived, almost an hour ago." She

tried to answer as calmly as possible. She refused to allow anyone to see her unruffled. And, really, she conceded, the stationmaster had his own duties to perform. This poor soul wasn't to blame for Mr. Cameron's negligence. It was Ebenezer Cameron she was angry with.

The stationmaster pulled his gold-plated watch from the pocket of his black broadcloth vest, which he wore over a red plaid flannel shirt. He flipped the watchcase open. He stared at the bold little face and frowned, then held it out farther and farther until the gold chain pulled at the fabric of the pocket, threatening to turn it inside out. Then he lifted it to his ear for a moment. Still not satisfied, he held the watch out again and gave it a few good thumps on the back with his bony forefinger. He held it to his ear once more, this time smiling and giving a satisfied nod.

"Trains don't always run on time," he commented dryly.

"Apparently the people don't, either," Emily could not help but remark. "I was supposed to meet—"

"Folks can only go as fast as the trains'll take 'em," he answered with a philosophical shrug of his bony shoulders. "And the trains can't go without the folks."

"But I was supposed to—"

"Ya got to get ya a real good watch like this one here," the stationmaster continued, oblivious to her problem. He held his watch out for her inspection, hefting it up and down just to prove to her how worthy a timepiece it was.

"Very nice," Emily noted politely, grinning at his obvious pride in the cheaply made watch. "However, there is nothing wrong with *my* watch, either. It's exactly quarter after three."

"Naw! Not yet. See, ya set yer watch to the last station clock, didn't ya?"

"Certainly. Why not?"

"I knew it." The wiry little stationmaster nodded sagely.

"See, what's noon to them ain't noon to us—yet," he explained. He looked upward, extended his arm, and pointed a bony finger straight up into the clear blue sky. "It ain't noon till the sun's directly overhead, right? And the earth keeps moving 'round, right?" His swung his stiff arm jerkily, marking the angles of the sun. "So the sun is always directly overhead someplace different at some different time." He tipped his head in the direction from which the train had just come. "Them down thataways, they're 'bout fifteen minutes ahead of us. Understand, ma'am?"

His watery blue eyes peered at her intently, as if he were hoping she'd get it the first time, and he wouldn't have to go through his taxing explanation all over again.

"I understand," Emily said with a resigned sigh. She'd never traveled out of Baltimore before. No wonder she hadn't thought of this. She began to adjust her erring watch.

"Don't feel bad, ma'am. Nigh on to everybody makes the same mistake at first. Really messes up the train schedule, though," he grumbled. "What they oughta do is divvy up the country—make everybody in one section follow the same time till they get to the next section. I keep telling 'em at the central office that's what they oughta do, but nobody never listens to *me*," he ended with a forlorn shake of his head. He looked up at her again, frowning with concern. "Is yer watch set right now, ma'am?"

"I suppose so. Thank you for clearing that up for me." Perhaps she was a bit early. It still didn't change the fact that Mr. Cameron was now very late.

Apparently satisfied that he'd completed his duty, the stationmaster snapped his watchcase shut and replaced it in his pocket.

"Excuse me, sir," Emily said quickly. She was afraid he would run off again before she had the opportunity to have her other questions answered. "Please. I was supposed to meet a Mr. Ebenezer Cameron here at—"

The little man jumped as if jarred awake from a fitful sleep. His red-rimmed eyes grew wider, emphasizing his resemblance to an owl suddenly exposed to daylight.

"Are *you* Miss Shaw? Mr. George's sister?"

"I'm Emily Shaw," she answered.

"Aw, darn!" he exclaimed. "We plumb forgot ya!"

Emily was not surprised.

The stationmaster quickly turned and disappeared around the back of the depot. Emily despaired of ever seeing him again until she heard him holler, "Ben! She's here!"

So Mr. Cameron *had* sent someone, Emily thought, her faith in the dependability of the legal profession just slightly restored. It was this "Ben" who was to blame for her distress and discomfort. Most probably, he was a filthy, irresponsible little urchin like the two she had so recently observed—dawdling along the way instead of attending to his errand promptly. Well, she'd be sure to inform Mr. Cameron of the boy's unreliability. Mr. Cameron would give the little scoundrel the scolding of his young life.

The stationmaster skittered into sight again, pattering excitedly back and forth across the edge of the platform. Emily decided he had suddenly transformed from an owl to a little banty rooster.

"Ben, Ben!" he cried frantically to the man who appeared from behind the depot.

So "Ben" was not a boy, but a man, Emily revised her assumption. Most probably he and the stationmaster had been whiling away their time in the local saloon while she paced the depot.

"Ben, we plumb forgot," the stationmaster called. "That lady ya was supposed to meet is here. Been here quite a while, too."

"Oh, shoot!"

Emily heard the man give a low moan of disgust. So that was what he thought of his responsibility to her!

Ordinarily Emily would never have been brave enough to confront this lazy good-for-nothing. She would have let Mr. Cameron handle it. But *he* was not here—and she had taken more than she could bear. She intended to give this shiftless scoundrel a piece of her mind.

Summoning all her courage, she moved closer to the three steps at the edge of the platform that led down to the dusty street. As the stationmaster scurried out of the way, Emily could at last see the man called Ben—or at least part of him.

He carried a large sack toward the buckboard. Slung across his shoulder, the sack hid his face from her. All Emily could see of the man was his bare, sun-bronzed back and the denim jeans that hung low on his narrow hips. In spite of the coolness of the day, rivulets of sweat trickled between his shoulder blades and ran together in the channel in the center of his back to disappear at the base of his spine and down into his jeans.

Emily swallowed hard. The stableboys, their handyman, the workmen in the city streets, even on the hottest of days, always kept their clothing on in public. Never in her life had she seen a man's naked torso—until this man. And there was so much of him! From the broad swells of flesh at the top of his shoulders, all the way down to—my gracious! She could see the two slight dimples in the small of his back. If those tight denim trousers of his slipped any lower, the next thing she imagined she would see was—why, she felt faint at the very notion! But she didn't swoon. She only continued to stand and stare at the man and the way he moved.

The sack he carried was heavy. Emily could tell by the way his muscles bunched and rippled under his smooth skin.

Yet he lifted it with seeming ease and dumped it onto the rear of the buckboard.

He lifted his broad-rimmed hat and wiped his arm across his brow. His hair was a soft, golden shade of brown—made all the lighter in places by streaks burned in by the sun. Even the dark hairs on his sinewy forearms glinted blond.

He replaced his hat and turned to face her. Her eyes still affixed to his body, she couldn't help notice the fine scattering of hair between his—have mercy! Emily felt her throat contract in a surge of excitement, which she quickly fought down. The man had flat brown nipples, and a broad chest, and a concave stomach—complete with a small, oval navel revealed by the low-slung jeans. Oh, if her heart didn't slow down, she was afraid it would stop beating altogether!

Emily managed to urge her gaze up his chest, past the firm squared chin and straight nose. He raised his hand to push his hat farther back on his head and looked directly at her. Was it because his face was as deeply tanned as his body, or was it because the sun shone on them, or did his pale blue eyes actually glow?

All intentions of scolding *this* man as if he were a naughty child quickly fled her thoughts.

"I suppose you're ready to leave now, ma'am." The corners of his eyes crinkled as he grinned at her.

"Yes," she managed to mumble while giving her head a slight nod.

"Are those yours, ma'am?" he asked. He raised one long arm to point behind her.

The man could have been indicating two hogs that had gotten loose from the stockyards, wandered up onto the platform, and had somehow managed to open her trunks and slip into her nightgowns, Emily thought, and she would have acknowledged their ownership. Unable to take her eyes from his in order to turn to see exactly what he was pointing at, she merely nodded again.

"Well, let's get them loaded up, then," he said, rubbing his gloved hands together as if preparing them for work.

His long legs carried him up the steps of the platform two at a time. He passed so close beside her that Emily could feel the heat of exertion emanating from his body. He smelled of dust and hard-working sweat, of green corn and old leather. Some new feeling inside, which Emily refused to name, made his earthly scent more heady for her than any city man's carefully concocted cologne.

She couldn't help notice that he was watching her, too. His eyes lost none of their brilliance in the shade of the depot. His gaze slid over her figure with such bold appraisal that she felt as if he had actually seized her with both hands and run them up and down the length of her body. She quickly turned away from him to hide the warmth that rose from her bodice, up her neck, and spread over her cheeks.

He dragged the large, heavy trunks to the edge of the platform and swung them into the back of the buckboard to rest beside the sack. Emily was still watching him, and he knew it. His eyes met hers and held them as he slowly pulled the rough leather workgloves from his strong hands and tossed them into the back of the buckboard.

He reached for the blue cotton shirt that had been carelessly tossed over one wheel. He swung the shirt around behind him, then leisurely stretched each long arm into a sleeve. He shrugged his shoulders as he fit the garment over his body. The pale blue shirt turned dark where it clung to the sweat on his bronzed skin, delineating each swell and curve of his muscles.

Emily watched him, barely daring to breathe.

"Begging your pardon, ma'am," he said. One eyebrow

moved just slightly with a teasing lift. He turned his back to her and proceeded to button his shirt.

She silently moaned. After subjecting her to such a wanton display of flesh, why was he now deliberately trying to be so coy?

Still, she continued to watch with fascination as his sun-browned hands reached behind him to jam his shirttail into his jeans.

He turned and moved slowly to the bottom of the steps. "Any time you're ready, ma'am," he said.

"I've been ready for some time now," she answered.

She hoped her tone of voice held the appropriate note of disapproval for his having kept her waiting. Then she saw the crooked grin he flashed her. She had been referring to going to her brother's home, but she felt a strange fluttering in her breast when she thought that might *not* be what *he* had understood her to mean.

"My apologies, ma'am. I should have been minding the time," he said.

She began to feel a bit more relieved.

He extended his hand up to her. Emily was so surprised by the man's courteous gesture that she almost failed to respond. His polite offer of assistance seemed out of place with his rugged appearance and his previous behavior.

She reached out reluctantly and placed her hand in his. Through her thin black gloves, she could feel the warmth of his strong fingers steadying her as she descended the three rickety steps.

When she reached the bottom, he did not release her hand, but continued to escort her to the right of the buckboard.

Emily grasped the thin iron rail running around the top of the seat and placed her foot on the small, oval cast-iron step. Her grip on his hand tightened as she pulled herself up. The vehicle was higher than she had judged, and in her slim skirt she began to teeter precariously. She stiffened as she felt his hand upon the small of her back, assisting her to rise the rest of the way. Quickly she released his hand and sat on the hard wooden seat. Even though her skirt gave every outward appearance of being neat and orderly, she busied herself with nervously brushing at invisible wrinkles.

Ben untied the mare, then gently urged her to back up. ''Easy, Annabelle,'' he said, smoothing his hand over her reddish-brown neck. Throwing the reins over the mare's head, he sprang up into the buckboard and remained standing.

Emily turned to watch him towering over her, then quickly turned away again. Surely, there was more fabric in Iowa. His jeans did not have to be cut *that* tight!

Ben turned toward the rear of the buckboard. Raising one hand, he placed two fingers in his mouth. He then emitted the most piercing whistle Emily had ever heard. Even the horse started at the volume.

His whistle brought an equally shrill response from the other side of the depot. The squeals and giggles grew louder as the same two grimy little girls appeared, approaching the buckboard at a run.

Emily was surprised to see them hoist themselves into the rear, then settle in, facing backward. Why in the world were the children coming with them?

The child with golden-brown plaits punched the dark-haired girl's shoulder. ''Darn, you're good!''

At first Emily supposed they had been involved in another expectorating contest on the other side of the depot. She was relieved she hadn't witnessed that one.

''Wish I could learn to whistle like that,'' the brown-haired child lamented, jerking her thumb in Ben's direction.

Emily knew it was none of her business. Still, she

couldn't resist gently reprimanding the little girls with the old saw her grandmother was so fond of repeating to her whenever she had misbehaved as a child. "A whistling woman and a crowing hen both come to a no-good end."

The two little girls threw Emily a sidelong glance, then turned and stared wide-eyed at each other. Their hands clasped tightly over their mouths, they both doubled over in silent laughter and simultaneously sank out of sight behind Emily's trunks to at last giggle aloud.

Emily could feel the man beside her, staring at her. "Is there a problem?" she asked him.

"Not at all, ma'am." Ben jerked his gaze away from her. She watched the corners of his mouth as he struggled to pull them down, to keep himself from laughing at her, too.

"Did you work for Mr. Shaw?" she asked. She hoped he had. Then perhaps she could say something that would reinforce her position as his employer now.

"Oh, he tried to tell me what to do from time to time," Ben answered with a careless shrug of his broad shoulders.

She should have figured as much. The man was a complete reprobate. On the other hand, she still might have some control over him.

"Then I take it you work for Mr. Cameron now?" she asked.

Ben chuckled. "Oh, he's even worse than Mr. Shaw."

No use in even trying any further, Emily surrendered with a sigh. She heard the two little girls giggling, unseen, behind her. Oh, she'd be so glad when this trip was finally over, and she and her niece were safely back in Baltimore. She'd never been without someone to look after her. She longed to reach the security of Mr. Cameron's office, to be shown the comfortable safety of the home her brother had established here for his family, to at last have the chance to meet her sweet little niece, Meggie.

"Get along, Annabelle." Ben slapped the reins over the mare's back. The buckboard lurched forward.

"Welcome to Winterset, Miss Shaw," the stationmaster called cheerily after her departing figure.

Emily felt as if she ought to offer some sort of farewell. Under the circumstances, considering their brief acquaintance and his limited service, she believed a polite nod might be enough.

"See you later, Sam," Ben said to the little man.

"Ya take care now, Ben," Sam cautioned with mock concern. Holding his hand out to shade his eyes, he gazed off into the cloudless sky. "Looks like there might be a storm a-brewin'."

"Thanks for the warning," Ben replied with a wry grin. He waved a long arm in response. "I think I can handle it."

"I'd bet on ya." Sam was still chuckling as they drove away.

CHAPTER TWO

THE BUCKBOARD ROLLED DOWN THE STREET, past a saloon and a general store. They passed a small shop that displayed not only a red-and-white-striped barber pole out front but also a large wooden tooth hanging over the door, indicating the barber's skill as a dentist as well. The storefronts gave way to a blacksmith shop, then a church and rows of large houses, set far back on wide green lawns.

Emily looked with anticipation at each house, but Ben continued to drive on. The town turned to farmland. Neat whitewashed clapboard homesteads and spacious red barns dotted the vast expanses of golden fields. Stands of trees in shades of red and gold and green edged the river's meandering course.

"Where are we going?" Emily asked. She was alone with two little tomboys and a strange man who kept eyeing her in a very familiar way. Her anticipation was beginning to turn to panic. She raised her chin—as if that would give her the courage she needed! "Ben," she stated as calmly as she could, "you're supposed to take me to Mr. Shaw's house. I thought my brother's house was in town."

"It is. Just not *that* town," Ben answered with a small chuckle. "We're going to Bidewell."

"But my brother's address said Winterset," Emily insisted.

"Mine does, too. But there isn't a post office in Bidewell yet, so we all just put Winterset on our mail. It's easier that way all around."

"I suppose so." Emily nodded her agreement with their system. If everyone in town were like Sam the Stationmaster, they couldn't bear too much confusion.

As the houses became spaced farther apart, the road grew bumpier. The buckboard rumbled along, tossing Emily from side to side. The low slat at the end of the seat prevented her from being thrown completely off the edge. But what was to prevent her from colliding with Ben's strong shoulder and slim hip on her other side? Emily slid closer to the edge of the seat and gripped the low iron handrail to prevent herself from bouncing around any more than she already did.

She glanced down at the seat. Did the man *have* to take up almost the entire bench as he guided the horse slowly down the long country road? Was he deliberately trying to come nearer to her? He had propped one foot up on the board across the front of the wagon and stretched his long legs out in front of him. He rested his elbows easily on his knees. Did his callused fingers have to look so strong as he held the leather reins? And did those blasted jeans have to mold so close to the firm muscles of his thigh?

The buckboard hit another deep rut and gave a bone-jarring jolt, sending Emily too far over the side. Ben's strong hand quickly seized her wrist, pulling her back before she completely lost her balance and fell headlong out of the wagon.

"Thank you," she said, giving a deep, relieved sigh.

"If you weren't sitting so close to the edge, you wouldn't have almost fallen," he quietly pointed out to her. His eyes darted invitingly from her face to the wide empty space on the seat between them.

For heaven's sake, Emily chided herself, it wasn't as if

this were the first time she'd gone for a drive with a gentleman. She'd gone with a few friends of the family—businessmen like her late father, lawyers like her late brother. Why did only this dirty, sweaty farmhand make her want to keep her distance from him by the plain and simple fact that she wanted so badly just to touch him again? Emily had no intention of closing the gap.

He still had not released her wrist. She hadn't given it much thought before, when he had kept hold of her hand as he led her to the buckboard and helped her to climb up. But this time their quick movements had caused the sleeve of her dress to slip up just enough to allow Ben's warm fingers to encircle her bare wrist.

"Thank you," she repeated. Mentally she scolded herself for allowing her voice to shake as she spoke. How could her throat betray her so—revealing the quaking feelings this man caused in her? As she tried to pull her hand away, she added, "I don't think I'll fall off now."

He quickly opened his fingers, releasing her. Her skin still seemed to tingle where he had held her. She restrained her impulse to rub away the sensations his touch had left—as if she ever could. Trying to avoid meeting Ben's gaze, Emily looked at the land spreading out before her.

"Don't worry. It's not too much farther," Ben assured her.

"I hope not," Emily said. "I'm anxious to meet my niece."

The two little girls suddenly popped up from behind the large trunks. They were still giggling and whispering behind their grubby little hands.

They certainly should have been taught, as she had been, to use better manners when adults were speaking, Emily thought. But, recalling the girls'—and Ben's—reaction when she had admonished them for whistling, this time she decided she'd be better off holding her tongue and saving herself a good deal of embarrassment.

"Hush back there," Ben ordered.

The little girls quieted immediately. Instead of sinking back behind the trunks, they propped their elbows up on them and knelt there, grinning.

"Don't you know your own niece?" Ben asked Emily. His brows were raised in disbelief.

"Unfortunately, no," Emily admitted.

"You've never seen her? Not even a photograph?" He pushed his hat farther back on his head, as if his own surprise had knocked it loose. "I find that hard to believe."

"My brother met a girl who'd come from Iowa to attend the Mount Washington Female Academy in Baltimore," Emily explained. "She was very pretty. And pleasant, too."

"I'm glad to hear you thought so," Ben said. When she turned a puzzled look to him, he pursed his lips and commented sagely, "It's good for sisters-in-law to get along."

"I hardly know," she said sadly. "I mean, I only saw Sarah three or four times, and I liked her very much right from the start. But that was eleven years ago, and I was only fourteen. Then Sarah returned to her hometown to make arrangements for their wedding, and George moved out here. I had hoped, when I was older, to have the chance to visit them, to get to know Sarah better, but"—a note of regret tinged her softening voice as she added—"I never saw either of them again."

After a moment Ben asked, "Why didn't you come out for the wedding?"

He was watching her closely, waiting for her answer. She felt unnerved. His probing questions and penetrating blue eyes caused her to unearth feelings she had long left buried.

"My parents were older when I was born. My mother had

been an invalid since I was just a little girl,'' Emily finally managed to answer. ''She never let me . . . I couldn't leave her,'' she amended. ''And after Mother passed away, Father became a virtual recluse. When he became seriously ill, I was so busy caring for him until he passed away last year . . . and then, with all the time it took to settle his affairs . . . I never really had time for . . .'' She was unable to finish her excuse, even to her own satisfaction. Why had she almost revealed the omissions of her past to a total stranger?

They rode in silence for a while. Suddenly Ben smiled and pointed ahead. ''See, I told you it wasn't much farther, ma'am.''

It wasn't much of a town, either, Emily decided. ''This is Bidewell?'' she asked aloud, trying to keep her disappointment from showing in her voice.

''Yes, ma'am,'' he answered proudly.

A tiny little general store, with the pretentious name of Randall's Emporium, and five large houses stood on one side of the road; six similar houses stood on the other side. The houses were beautiful and neatly kept—all except the last one coming up on the left.

''What a mess.'' Emily's astonishment caused her to voice her thought.

Emily was so absorbed with the dilapidated house that Ben had almost driven completely through Bidewell before she noticed.

''Why aren't we stopping?'' she demanded abruptly. ''Why aren't you taking me to my brother's house? What's wrong?''

''Nothing, ma'am.'' His voice sounded as if he thought her silly for even thinking such a thing. He smiled and his eyes twinkled, yet Emily couldn't help but believe there was a certain veil over their brightness—almost as if he were hiding something.

Emily began to worry even more. "Then please take me—"

"I'd rather not take you to Mr. Shaw's house, ma'am. Not yet," Ben said hesitantly. "We're going to my farm instead." Once again his eyes swept her body appreciatively. "I thought a lady like you might want to freshen up first."

Oh, how she wished he would stop looking at her that way. She was getting very tired of blushing!

"I want to go to my brother's house," Emily insisted.

Ben cleared his throat, as if stalling for time before he answered. "Your brother's house, it . . . well, it needs just a little fixing up first, ma'am."

Suddenly putting two and two together, Emily twisted in her seat to better view the receding ruined building. Her knee bumped against Ben's outstretched leg. Quickly she drew back. She had been appalled at her own wanton desire to touch him again with her hands. She never imagined that other parts of her anatomy might make contact with him!

Obviously Ben was not as unnerved by the accidental contact as she was. He reined Annabelle to a halt so Emily could get a better view of the deteriorating structure and the overgrown lawn spreading up to a rickety front porch.

"That is *not* my brother's house," Emily stated emphatically.

"How would you know?" he asked, a mocking gleam in his eye. "I thought you said you'd never been here before."

Her head craned forward. Her green eyes were wide with surprise and horror. "George would *never* have allowed his home to go to ruin like this."

She continued to stare at the house, shaking her head. Suddenly she turned to him. Her eyes narrowed skeptically and her lips twitched as she fought down a grin. "All right, Ben. I realize this is probably some silly little tradition in your town, playing tricks on all the naive newcomers. But the joke is over. Please take me to my brother's house."

Ben looked directly at her. She had seemed such a mousy little thing at the depot. He almost smiled at the tiny spark that managed to peek through her staid exterior. But if he did, in the state she was in, would she try to bite off his head? In a low, deep voice he very slowly told her, "This *is* Mr. Shaw's house, ma'am."

Emily continued to peer into the depths of his eyes. He wasn't laughing at her. He wasn't even smiling. Emily felt a horrid chill that came with the realization that this man must be telling the truth. What reason did he have to lie?

She shook her head, as if that would chase away all the cobwebs that clogged her thinking. What had begun as the simple task of retrieving her niece was turning into an increasingly complicated process.

"Come on, ma'am," Ben said. He slapped the reins across Annabelle's back. The mare snorted, shook her head, and began to move again down the road. "I'll take you out to the farm to tidy up, get something to eat, calm down a bit. . . . Then maybe tomorrow—"

"No," she insisted. "I appreciate your kind offer, Ben, but I *must* see Mr. Cameron—immediately."

After seeing the terrible condition of the house, Emily realized, with a sinking feeling in the pit of her stomach, that instead of relying on Mr. Cameron for help, she'd have to tell him that his service was unacceptable and that she'd seek the advice of another lawyer.

"George always claimed Mr. Cameron was so intelligent, so sensible," she murmured, half to herself. "I can't believe Mr. Cameron has allowed this to happen. My brother *trusted* him. How *dare* he neglect my brother's business!"

"Ebenezer Cameron did *not* neglect your brother's business," Ben told her sternly. His cool blue eyes, warmed by the amber light of the setting sun, had begun to smolder with well-controlled anger.

Pressed to the limit of her endurance, Emily finally snapped, "Oh, how would you know? And what concern is it of yours anyway?"

Ben twisted his firm lips into a wry grin, but his eyes still watched her intently. "Because *I'm* Ebenezer Cameron."

Emily stared at him, speechless. "No. You can't be," she managed to say at last. "You're . . . you're Ben."

"E—BEN—ezer," he repeated, very slowly and distinctly, as if he were clarifying things for Annabelle the horse instead of for her.

He had the most self-satisfied smirk on his face. Emily was seized with the urge to smack the grin right off his face—and shove him out of the wagon in the bargain!

"You *can't* be Ebenezer Cameron," she insisted. Her visions of the potbellied middle-aged lawyer were rapidly displaced by her memories of Ben's long, tanned body, not to mention the unsettling feelings he stirred within her. "You don't *look* like a lawyer."

"What does a lawyer look like?" he asked. Once again his eyes swept her body. Even if Emily didn't know what a lawyer looked like, this man was certainly making no bones about wanting to know exactly what *she* looked like—every inch of her!

"Why didn't you say so in the first place," she demanded, angry at her own chagrin, "instead of letting me make a complete and utter fool of myself?"

Still grinning, he shrugged his shoulders. "You were doing such a good job, I hated to stop you."

"Mr. Cameron—"

"Ben," he corrected.

"*Mister* Cameron. If this is how you've taken care of my brother's house, I hate to think of what's happened to my niece!" Her confusion and impatience—and her growing concern for Meggie—made her voice louder and more high-pitched than usual. Emily had been taught *never* to raise her voice. She took a deep breath and regained her calmness and control. "It looks as if I've arrived just in time. Why, if things were allowed to continue like this, Meggie might be running wild like . . . like *those two*."

She gave her head a sharp backward nod in the direction of the two little girls, who had long since ceased their giggling and were now listening intently to every word Emily had to say.

"What's wrong with *those two*?" Ben demanded. His blue eyes bored into her, as if daring her to find fault with the children. He pulled the brim of his hat down in front, as if that would accentuate his frown.

Emily hesitated just a moment. Her concern for her niece, whose welfare was now her duty, overrode her natural reserve. Still, her nervousness caused her to stammer as she said, "Just . . . just look at them. How could two little girls get so filthy?" She gestured toward the children, hoping that would distract Ben's piercing gaze from her. It didn't.

"Didn't you ever get dirty as a child?" Ben asked. Then his eyes swept her body once again, and he shook his head. "No. I don't suppose *you* did."

Emily bristled. Of course she'd gotten dirty making mudpies when she was a very little girl, but that was before . . .

She quickly stopped. Once already she had almost risked letting Ben pierce her facade. She wouldn't do it again.

"They've been playing outdoors all day," Ben said.

"It'll all wash off anyway. What harm could a little honest dirt do?"

Emily opened and closed her mouth a few times, trying to think of an answer. Finally she said, "I only know *I* certainly wouldn't want *my* niece to participate in the disgusting spectacle I witnessed between those two this afternoon."

Ben at last allowed his gaze to slip from her for just a second. Emily was grateful for the reprieve. His eyes narrowed as he looked at the girls and demanded of Emily, "What was that?"

"A . . . a spitting contest," Emily finally managed to say. She hoped the tone of her voice conveyed to him the complete revulsion with which she viewed the entire activity.

Suddenly a wide grin spread over Ben's face, and his eyes danced with laughter. "Was that all?"

"All? Two little girls . . . spitting?" She was more than a little upset that he didn't seem to share her disgust. In exasperation she clenched her fists in her lap. "Oh, how could I expect you to understand?" she grumbled.

Ben started to chuckle. "Who won?"

"What difference does that make?" she demanded, dismayed that he would even want to know. "It's *still* a disgusting habit. . . ."

"Who won?" he insisted.

"Honestly, Mr. Cameron," Emily declared indignantly. "The way you're acting, one would think you had bet a lot of money on the outcome."

Ben made no comment but only looked as if he would repeat his question. Emily sighed with resignation. With a wave of her hand, she indicated the dark-haired little girl.

Ben's gaze darted to the other child. "Oh, shoot, Frannie!" he exclaimed.

The child with the light brown hair shrugged her shoulders and smiled at him apologetically. "Sorry, Pa. I did my best."

"Yeah, I know you did. You always do," he said with a little more consolation in his voice.

"*She*'s your *daughter*?"

Ben nodded.

With a conscious effort Emily closed her gaping mouth. She wondered how she ever could have missed the resemblance between the man and the little girl. As she examined the dusty man seated beside her, and recalled his careless disregard of being prompt and the way he had fooled her about his identity—not to mention his wanton display of flesh—she thought she really should have known that his offspring would be just as wild. Still, her remarks had been awfully rude.

She managed to summon up enough presence of mind to apologize. "I do beg your pardon, Mr. Cameron."

"Ben," he corrected her again. "And don't think anything of it, ma'am. Because, you see, the other one," he said, pointing to the little girl with the dark plaits and giving what Emily thought was a very wicked chuckle, ". . . is your niece, Meggie."

"Meggie?" Emily stared in disbelief. The grubby little girl gave her a broad grin, displaying two front teeth that were much too big for the impish little heart-shaped face. "Margaret Susanna Shaw," Emily pronounced her niece's full name, just to make sure there was no mistake. She was almost desperate enough to consider demanding proof in the form of a baptismal certificate.

There was no mistake. Once she actually bothered to really look at the child, Emily could not mistake the dark brown hair—so like her brother's, so like her own. There was no mistaking the blue eyes, either—the main feature she remembered about her sister-in-law, Sarah.

"Oh, for heaven's sake! My own niece, participating in a *spitting* contest!" Emily wailed.

Ben shrugged his shoulders. "She won."

"I'm sure that's something she'll want to tell her grandchildren about," Emily replied sarcastically. Then she threw a worried glance back toward the little girl still sitting in the rear of the buckboard. "Oh, what must Meggie think of me now?"

Before anyone could answer her, Ben turned the buckboard off the main road and up a little side road. He pulled to a stop beside a tidy clapboard farmhouse. The two little girls scrambled down, splashing through puddles as they ran toward the front of the wagon where Emily sat. Meggie stood there, grinning up at Emily, waiting.

As soon as Ben had rounded to her side and handed Emily down from the buckboard, Meggie threw her long, scrawny arms around her waist.

"I'm so glad to see you, Aunt Emily!" she exclaimed, giving her an extra hard squeeze before dashing off, with Frannie in tow, both giggling loudly once again.

Emily breathed a deep sigh of relief. She turned to Ben and said hopefully, "How sweet. Perhaps she didn't hear the awful things I said about her after all."

Ben rubbed his hand over his squared jaw. Emily could see his broad shoulders shaking in his effort to hide his laughter. "Oh, I think maybe she did," he said, nodding toward the front of her dress.

Emily glanced down at the smears of brown mud dotting the front of her gray wool traveling dress. Meggie had gotten even with her after all, the little urchin! Emily shook her head and sighed. Still, she grudgingly had to admire the child's spirit.

"Come on, ma'am," Ben managed to say in spite of his continued laughter. "Let's get you into the house and clean you up."

Emily nodded. "I'd appreciate it if your wife would—"

"I'm a widower," Ben said quietly.

"Oh, I am sorry," Emily managed to murmur. She really was sorry for him, and for his daughter. On the other hand, this certainly accounted for the unconventional behavior of the two little girls.

"My mother'll see to you," Ben added. He motioned her toward the house.

As they rounded the corner of the house, the spacious farmyard came into view—along with a most unusual sight right in the middle. Wide-eyed, Emily stopped in her tracks. "What in the world is that?"

The sturdy keel and curving ribs of a large boat, silhouetted in the waning light of day, stuck up toward the sky. "It . . . it looks like . . . it's a boat!"

"It's an ark," Ben corrected.

"Is it yours?" She was almost afraid to ask, and equally afraid of the answer she might get.

"Of course not." Emily's relief was short-lived when Ben added, "It's my brother's."

"What's it doing here? We're miles from any water deep enough to . . ."

"Oh, he's got his reasons, I guess," Ben answered. He gestured toward the farmhouse, indicating their destination.

Before she could follow his lead, Emily heard a man's voice call out, "Hey, Ben!"

Emily hadn't noticed the man before. He climbed down from the skeleton of the ark and made his way toward them. She was tempted to slip behind Ben for protection.

"Hey, Noah," Ben answered.

"Noah?" Emily repeated.

"My brother."

"Of course." She should have known.

"You must be Miss Shaw," Noah said, smiling. He was as tall as Ben, but his arms and legs were a good bit scrawnier. His eyes were a grayer shade of blue than Ben's, but they were shaped the same and crinkled in the same way when he smiled at her. "Pleased to finally meet you."

"Nice to meet you," Emily answered weakly. She was still having a little trouble taking her eyes from the boat.

"Nice piece of work, ain't it?" Noah asked. He slipped his thumbs between his suspenders and the little potbelly hanging over the top of his jeans and rocked proudly back and forth.

"Very interesting," Emily responded. Feeling that this comment was inadequate, she added, "It's so . . . large."

"Has to be. But I figure she'll handle whatever comes along."

"I'm sure it will." Emily kept waiting for Ben to say something, or to suggest that it was now time to go to the house. Getting no help from him, Emily felt compelled to say something more. But what does one say to a man with an ark? "Ah . . . where are your animals?"

"Ain't got no animals . . . not yet."

"Then why are you . . ." Emily hesitated. It seemed somehow rude to ask him exactly why he was going to all the trouble to build an ark without any animals. On the other hand, she just *had* to know! "Why are you building an ark when you have no animals?"

"Well, you see, God figures I got enough on my hands just building this thing," Noah answered readily. "He's left the collecting to somebody else. And someday, that somebody's gonna show up, with all the animals we'll need."

"I see," was all she could manage. Too many concerns for her niece were running through her head for her to think about a big silly-looking boat, built by a man named Noah, sitting in the middle of an Iowa farmyard.

Worse yet, the man was Meggie's uncle! What of the rest of the Cameron family?

Emily recalled Sarah as such a sensible, intelligent young woman. Ebenezer was a well-respected lawyer, if what George had claimed was true. Her own thoughts on Ben Cameron had nothing to do with intelligence or respect, she realized with a sudden flush of her cheeks. Still, she couldn't help worrying that insanity might run in the family. She could only hope that while Meggie had inherited the Cameron eyes, she had inherited nothing else from them.

Finally, much to Emily's relief, Ben said, "I don't know about you two, but I can smell Ma's soup simmering all the way out here. Come and eat now, ma'am."

Ben led her through the opening in the whitewashed rail fence and up the red brick walk. In spite of the approaching cold weather, several pots of bright red geraniums still splashed their color up the three steps leading to the freshly whitewashed porch.

The door swung open wide. Before Emily could enter, a squirt of tobacco shot past her to land in the clay flowerpot on the top step.

"T'baccy's good for 'em," the wiry little old woman said. She winked at Emily. Her eyes were as blue as the bright flowers that dotted the calico dress she wore. Her hair was as white as her crisply starched apron.

"I didn't know that," Emily answered, still staring at the remarkable distance the old woman had managed to cover.

"Come on in. Make yourself at home," she invited. She seized Emily's hand with her gnarled fingers and pulled her into the house. "I'm Dolly Cameron."

"Pleased to meet you," Emily mumbled. She hadn't needed an introduction. It was easy enough to see the family resemblance here, too. It was also easy enough to figure out who had taught Meggie and Frannie how to spit.

"Oh, I saw what that little rapscallion did to you, Miss Shaw," the sprightly old woman declared. "Shame on you, Meggie!" Her bright eyes shot the girls a warning glare. "Let's tidy you and that pretty dress up right away, Miss Shaw. Ben, bring the nice lady's trunks in meanwhile."

"I don't want to impose," Emily protested. "I really had intended to stay with Meggie at my brother's house."

"Not tonight you don't," Dolly said.

From her seat on the bottom step of the long staircase, Meggie mumbled, "Not ever!" to Frannie, but specifically loud enough for Emily to hear.

"Not when I've made my best chicken soup and johnny-cakes for you," Dolly said, ignoring Meggie's sulking.

Although Emily spoke to Mrs. Cameron, she looked directly at Meggie and, with what she hoped was a tone of reconciliation, said, "I'm really afraid I don't know much about my niece at all. I hope we can get better acquainted."

Meggie grimaced. She turned to Frannie and poked her in the ribs. Before anyone could stop them, the two little girls had made their escape through the front door.

"I got the spare room all set for you, Miss Shaw." Dolly led Emily up the steep staircase and down a narrow hall. "There's a pitcher of water for you there, and a sponge, too," she indicated as she got Emily settled into her room.

After the door closed tightly behind Dolly, Emily turned up the wick on the coal oil lamp. She unfastened the buttons and removed her mud-splattered jacket. She poured a bit a water into the washbowl, then dipped one end of the sponge into the cold water and began to dab away the mud.

Ben made his way across the yard to the buckboard to retrieve Emily's trunks. He grinned at the sight of Meggie and Frannie, running a game of tag around Noah, who was splashing off the day's grime at the iron pump to the side of the house and occasionally splashing the girls, too.

He knew his mother had tried her best. Ever since Sarah had died six years ago and George had taken to drink, Ma had been raising Meggie like her own—just like she had raised Frannie when Betty had died giving her birth.

Sarah and he had turned out just fine, Ben decided. So had Noah, sort of. But Frannie and Meggie *were* grimy, he realized. If it weren't for the long plaits hanging down their backs, a person would hardly know they were girls. And he did want his daughter and niece to grow up to be the kind of ladies their mothers had been.

Maybe Miss Emily Shaw—with her dark curls arranged neatly beneath that silly little hat, and her green eyes wide and bright with all sorts of imagined worries, and her fashionable gray suit fitting so tightly in all the right places—maybe she was right. Maybe she *had* arrived in Bidewell just in time. Maybe Emily Shaw *was* lady enough to tackle those two. Hadn't she already tried to scold Meggie for her whistling?

Ben grinned as he shouldered the heavy trunk. He couldn't help wondering what it contained. More little gray dresses—neat and prim as the lady herself? And for underneath? A petticoat—of nothing less than white silk for this lady. With lace, meticulously handmade in candlelight by cloistered nuns in some French convent, no doubt. A frivolous contrast to the starkness of the lady's exterior—or just the real Miss Shaw, hidden under layers of confinement, layers just waiting to be cast away?

Startled by his own preoccupation with Miss Shaw's underthings, Ben grinned wider. It had been a long time since he'd met a woman he wanted to have those kinds of thoughts about.

He was still grinning—and still allowing himself some carefully controlled daydreams about Emily Shaw—when he entered the house. He could hear his mother in the kitchen, with her wooden spoon clattering over her enamel pots and pans, no doubt showing Miss Shaw her pride and joy, the new black cast-iron stove from Sears and Roebuck that he'd had shipped to her all the way from Chicago.

He mounted the stairs and continued down the hall, toward the best spare bedroom, where his mother intended Miss Shaw to sleep.

His head bent low beneath his burden, Ben pushed the door open and swung the large trunk onto the floor of the room.

He wasn't winded from carrying the heavy trunk. It was the sight of Emily that pulled the breath right out of him.

She wore only her skirt, nipped in at her tiny waist, and a thin white chemise that covered her corset. The stays pushed her soft white breasts up into two delicate mounds. The white lace at the top of her chemise skimmed across her creamy flesh. Ben was seized with the desire to run his fingertip along the edge of the delicate lace, brushing it gently aside to tenderly touch her warm breasts.

"Mr. Cameron!" she exclaimed. She dropped the wet sponge to the floor and snatched up her jacket, clutching it defensively to her bosom.

Even though she tried to hide behind her jacket, her protective gesture only pushed her breasts closer together, accentuating the soft swells of flesh. He never took his eyes from what he could still see of the deep crease between her breasts.

"Sorry, ma'am," Ben mumbled. "Didn't know you were in here. Really, I didn't."

He stumbled over the rag rug as he backed toward the

door. Like a bumbling adolescent, he silently cursed himself. As if you'd never seen those things before.

"I'm really sorry, ma'am," he murmured again as he closed the door. Once the door was shut, however, Ben found he still couldn't shake the image of her from his mind.

When she'd first arrived at the station, although he couldn't see her, he'd been listening to all her complaints to Sam. He'd thought to tease the prudish little old maid with a shocking view of himself. Now he'd been accidentally treated to a view of Miss Emily Shaw that he'd bet the farm no other man had ever seen. Things were different when the tables were turned.

Had it really been so long? he wondered. Had he really kept himself so busy, since Betty's death, with his family's farm, and with his own law office taking care of other people's problems, that he'd almost forgotten what it felt like to be a man again, with the need to touch a soft, beautiful woman? With the need to touch Emily.

CHAPTER THREE

DOLLY'S CHICKEN SOUP AND JOHNNYCAKES WERE delicious. And while she slurped from her spoon and, from time to time, wiped her mouth on her sleeve, Emily decided Dolly herself was a pleasant woman. Had it been just the two of them, seated for an afternoon tea, Emily might have enjoyed the visit in spite of herself.

It was a bit more difficult to sit calmly at the table with Noah when she was always wondering if the slightest patter of rain might send him running for his boat.

It was even more difficult to sit between the freshly scrubbed Meggie and Frannie and enjoy her meal when the two of them kept eyeing her with suspicion.

But it was virtually impossible to sit across from Ben now that he had seen her the way no man had ever seen her—not even Dr. Wisner in the whole time he'd treated her for that awful cold that had plagued her all winter when she was fourteen.

Emily was relieved when supper finally ended.

Noah rose from the table. Walking to the window, he pulled back the calico curtain and peered up at the lowering sky.

"Got to be hitting the hay," he said, heading for the door in a hurry. "Looks like rain. Tomorrow's gonna be a busy day."

Emily stared after him as he left in a rush. She wondered exactly who all he was planning on taking in his boat, and if she had arrived too late to find a place on board—just on the off chance Noah was right.

"Noah's got his own cabin behind the barn, right next to his ark," Ben explained.

Ben didn't seem too alarmed, Emily noted with relief. Neither did Dolly and the girls. Maybe there wasn't anything to worry about after all—yet.

Dolly rose and began to clear the table. Meggie and Frannie excused themselves—politely, much to Emily's surprise—and started carrying empty serving plates into the kitchen.

"Please let me help you, Mrs. Cameron," Emily offered, lifting her bowl and Meggie's from the table. She'd never scrubbed a dish in her life, but she'd do anything not to have to stay in the same room with Ben Cameron now.

"No, no. You're my guest," Dolly protested, taking both bowls from her. "Why don't you go out for a little fresh air instead?"

Emily thought she might appreciate some fresh air right now. Then Ben rose and headed for the door that led from the dining room to the entrance hall. Emily lingered at the table, still looking for something to take back into the kitchen. Being with Ben in the brightly lit parlor might have been bearable, but the thought of going with him, alone, into the darkness, caused her to quiver inside, and not from fear of the dark.

"Don't know how much longer this nice weather'll last," Dolly warned. "I'll stay in here and make sure those two little varmints get settled into bed. I set great store by book learning, Miss Shaw. And tomorrow is a school day."

Meggie and Frannie began to moan.

"Hush now." Dolly sent the girls a look that quickly

quieted them. She turned to Ben. "Don't know what's gotten into them lately. They never complained like this last year."

"I'll talk to them, Ma," Ben offered, glancing toward the kitchen door where the girls had disappeared.

"You think I can't handle that pair? Now go on, you two, get out of here!" Dolly scolded good-naturedly. "I hate to have folks doing nothing but watch me work!" With several quick waves of her gnarled hand, she shooed them both out the front door.

The door closed behind them, blotting out the pool of yellow light that had spilled over their feet and across the gray porch floor. The beam shining from the dining room window faded as Dolly, her work there finished, trimmed the wicks of the lamps.

Emily made her way out of the shadows under the roof of the porch to stand at the railing. Placing both hands on the banister, she looked out over the farmyard. The sun had set long ago. Now she could not even see the huge skeleton of Noah's would-be ark.

"It's so dark out here," Emily whispered, as if speaking in a normal tone of voice was somehow out of place in the silent darkness. "And so quiet."

"Then you're not listening right," Ben replied, also in a whisper.

He stood behind her, so close that Emily believed she could feel him, almost as if his callused hands or his warm body were actually touching her.

"I—"

"Shh," he whispered, placing one finger over his lips. He lowered his hand and placed it on her shoulder. Leaning closer to her, he said, "Listen." His breath was warm as it passed across her ear and over her cheek. She could feel strands of her hair catch in the stubble of his chin. Could he really be standing that close?

Emily couldn't hear a sound for the thundering of her heart in her ears.

Gradually she recognized the chirps of the crickets, slowing in the cooling autumn air. From the barn, an owl called out his ceaseless question "Who?"—to be answered by his mate, who knew no more than he.

"I guess I'm used to the city lights. It's . . . it's so dark out here, I can't even see your face," she managed to state.

"Funny," he said. His hand upon her shoulder gently turned her to face him. "I can see you real clear, ma'am."

"Your . . . your eyes are more accustomed to the dark. . . ." She tried to offer him a logical explanation but completely lost her train of thought as she looked into his eyes.

"There's light out here, Emily," he said.

And there was, she was forced to silently agree as she saw the gleam in his eyes. For just a moment she felt a longing to acknowledge that gleam with an answering smile.

No! she firmly told herself. That's *not* why I'm here. I have responsibilities. . . .

"Well, yes, there *is* the moon," she said suddenly, and rather too loudly, disturbing the peaceful evening mood. She sidestepped and slipped her way along the rail. Quickly walking to the far side of the porch, she poked her head out from under the overhanging roof and peered up into the sky with intense interest. "And now that you mention it, I do believe that, as my eyes have become accustomed to the darkness, why, I can see all sorts of stars. . . ."

Hearing Ben's boots slowly treading toward her, Emily clutched at the watch hanging from her bodice and turned it up to her. She didn't think for one minute that she was fooling Ben. No one could have seen the pale little enamel face in the dark. Still, she exclaimed, "Just look how late it is! Please, you really have to excuse me. I've been traveling all day, and the thought of my bed right now is very appealing."

"Yes, it is, ma'am," Ben agreed as he watched her retreat back into the farmhouse. "Very appealing indeed."

"Aunt Emily, we thought you were gonna stay in bed forever!" Meggie exclaimed as Emily descended the stairs at what she considered a very early hour the next morning.

"Now, girls, don't pester." Dolly waved her wooden spoon as a warning.

"But *we*'ve been up for hours," Meggie boasted, glancing about at Frannie and Dolly and including herself as well in the energetic trio. "Uncle Eb and Uncle Noah have been up even longer."

Emily felt she ought to make some reply, at least to show them that she really was awake this morning, even if she didn't feel awake yet. Her long journey had been very tiring. She had spent a restless night in the unfamiliar bed, sleeping fitfully, dreaming of Ben. She was disturbed further by the fact that, when she awoke from time to time, Ben was still on her mind.

Even now, in the bright morning light of reality, the passionate nature of these dreams, both sleeping and waking, was too vivid for her to risk comment on Ben. Emily merely said, "Your Uncle Noah must be a very hardworking man."

Dolly made a noise that was halfway between a snort and a laugh and shook her head. She beat her long-handled wooden spoon hard against the side of the cast-iron pot in order to shake off the globs of the bubbling oatmeal she'd been stirring.

"C'mon! Come with us!" Meggie called her invitation. She held out her hand for Emily to take.

Meggie's blue eyes were bright with excitement. Perhaps the child had forgotten Emily's disapproving words. Or perhaps Dolly, or even Ben, had spoken to her about her manners. Either way, it didn't matter. Emily was glad that Meggie wanted to include her in whatever activity she was planning.

"Where are we going?" Emily asked eagerly.

"Chores," Meggie explained in a tone of voice that indicated Emily certainly should have known better. "We've all got chores to do before breakfast."

"Couldn't we have breakfast first?" Emily offered tentatively.

"Nope. There won't be no breakfast if we don't do our chores. C'mon." She scooped up a small wicker basket from the kitchen table and, swinging it at her side in a wide arc, approached Emily.

With Meggie on one side and Frannie on the other, they each seized a hand and pulled Emily toward the door.

"We're searching for eggs," Meggie explained as she led Emily around the farmyard. "Sometimes the hens get loose from the coop and lay their eggs in the most *unusual* places."

Frannie nodded her solemn agreement.

Emily found herself ducking under bushes and stepping high to surmount the low fence around the herb patch at the back of the house. Oh, what she wouldn't do to earn the love and trust of her niece! She followed the girls as they slipped in and out of the frame of Noah's boat. Noah was hammering furiously and hardly seemed to notice them at all.

They had already found enough eggs for everyone's breakfast. Considering some of the remote places where Meggie had already led her, Emily didn't think there were too many more unusual places to look for eggs. Certainly none could be more unusual than inside the frame of Noah's ark. Still, Meggie and Frannie kept looking.

"There's this one hen," Meggie continued. "Lays the best eggs in the whole county."

"Prizewinner, she really is," Frannie agreed.

"It's kind of a family tradition that our guest gets her egg for their first breakfast here. And we want *you* to have it," Meggie said.

Emily's heart swelled with the joy that Meggie seemed to have accepted her at last.

"It's also tradition that *you* got to find it," Frannie added.

Recalling how she'd only been able to follow Meggie and Frannie uselessly around during the hunt, Emily chuckled. "I'd starve before I found that egg."

"No, you won't. We wouldn't want you to starve," Meggie said. "We'll make it easy for you. That hen is so peculiar"—Meggie pointed to the small shed that stood behind the large pigsty—"she'll only lay her eggs up on that roof."

"But I could never reach that high!" Emily protested, viewing the roof with alarm.

"Oh, sure you can," Frannie assured her.

"We'll help you," Meggie offered.

Placing the basket of eggs in a safe tussock of grass at the bottom of one fence post, Meggie and Frannie wrestled down a long plank that had been leaning against the side of the shed. They slid it along the top of the fence surrounding the pigsty until it reached the other side, making a neat little bridge.

"There!" Meggie exclaimed triumphantly, placing both grimy little hands on her hips. "Now all you got to do—"

"I think I understand," Emily said. She didn't want Meggie to think she was uncooperative or disagreeable, but she really didn't believe she was going to be able to do this. Why, she hadn't done any climbing on fences since they'd sold Grandmama's farm so long ago. . . . Emily shook her head, chasing away the memories.

"What if you girls went up there for me?" Emily asked, making one last desperate attempt to avoid this terrible task.

"But then it wouldn't be *tradition*!" Meggie insisted.

Emily gave a deep sigh of resignation. She concentrated on climbing up the narrow fence rails until she could get a good purchase on the wider board. Her balance was precarious enough. It certainly didn't help any when Ben suddenly appeared from around the back of the barn.

He leaned his long frame against the red barn siding and crossed his arms over his broad chest. She almost slipped when his blue eyes met hers. The man was grinning at her and shaking his head from side to side, very slowly.

So, he didn't think she could climb this fence, did he? Did he think she was that clumsy? Well, maybe she wasn't the most graceful, most athletic person in the world. But she'd show him she was no coward, either, she thought with a proud little sniff. Still, she first checked to be certain her skirt had not lifted to an immodest height before taking the last step that put her atop the board.

"We know you can do it!" Meggie and Frannie called their encouragement up to her.

Grasping the edge of the roof, Emily began to make her way along the board. With each step she took, the board rocked and rattled against the top rail. She could see now that the board was severely warped. There was no way it was going to lay flat and allow her to pass easily. Well, there was no stopping now. Emily gripped the edge of the roof even more tightly.

Not daring to take her eyes from her careful study of

where to place her feet, Emily felt around in the tin gutter spouting for the elusive prize egg.

"Are you sure she laid one here?" Emily called down to Meggie.

"I saw her up there earlier this morning, just a-flapping and a-clucking," Meggie assured her while Frannie echoed her reply.

Emily continued her search. The odor rising from below was far worse than her memory of the acrid stockyard scent. It was a wonder there ever were any little baby pigs, she marveled. How *did* pigs stand each other?

She was in the middle of the board now, directly over the center of the sty. She continued to feel around in the drain spout. Ben was still grinning and shaking his head at her. She still hadn't found that egg, but she was more determined to find it now than ever, just to show Ben she *could* do it!

Suddenly the board teetered again, rocking back and forth. Standing in the center, there was no way for her to stop it, or for her to steady herself. Abandoning her search, she gripped the edge of the roof with both hands and hung there while the board settled down again.

Feeling it was safe again to move, Emily released one hand and began to make her way to the other side. Egg or no egg, she was getting off this board! But as soon as she set one foot in front of the other, the board began to wobble uncontrollably once more. Quickly she grabbed the roof again with both hands.

There she was, she thought with a deep sigh as she clung to the rough wooden shingles, stuck in the middle of a wobbly board, over the middle of a pigsty, in the middle of a farm in Iowa. How in the world had events led her to this sorry state?

Once again she looked over to Ben. He was still shaking his head, but he had stopped grinning. He was watching her with what Emily could almost believe was a great deal of concern shadowing his pale blue eyes.

She didn't need his unnerving gaze to upset her further. Emily quickly averted her eyes to look down at the board. Only a few more steps and she could get down. Slowly she began to move again.

The board miraculously lay still and flat. Encouraged, Emily released her death grip and, supporting herself with one hand on the gutter, began to make her way across the pigsty. Suddenly the board began to rock uncontrollably. Her grip gave way.

''Ben!'' Emily cried as she sailed through space to land flat on her bustle in the pigsty.

Meggie and Frannie squealed with laughter. The pigs squealed, too, and skittered to the far side of the pen. They stood bunched there, snorting and grunting their unanimous disapproval of Emily's intrusion.

''Oh, shut up, all of you!'' Emily angrily ordered the pigs. ''I know you don't want me here—and I don't want to be here!''

Meggie scooped up the basket of eggs from its place of safety and headed for the house at a run.

''Gramma! Gramma! Aunt Emily fell into the pigsty!'' she cried, with what seemed to Emily to be much too obvious delight.

''Oh, look at this mess!'' Emily wailed. She had landed on her bustle and her elbows. Her dress was completely ruined, but thank heavens the muck she had landed in was too thick to have splattered much.

She tried to rise now without pushing herself up with her hands. She was very sure that she didn't want to dip her hands in what she knew she was sitting in. But each time she tried to rise, the muck beneath her sucked her back in.

Ben was the only person available to ask for help, as far

as she could tell. "Oh, don't just stand there," she called to him as she surveyed the mess around her. "Help me out of this. Please!"

She waited for what seemed a very malodorous eternity for Ben to show up. She couldn't see him from where she sat, but she could just imagine him—his long, lean body still relaxing against the barn—grinning at her and shaking his head.

She looked up from the mess she was in. Ben was not standing nonchalantly at the corner of the barn, as she had expected. He was already at the fence, leaning his elbows on the top rail and watching her intently.

When he saw her turn to him and try to rise, he grinned. "Got a problem, ma'am?"

Damn that man! Emily fumed. One of these days she really was gong to smack that crooked grin off his face. She hesitated a moment, toying with the tempting thought that, if she *did* hit him now, maybe she *should* set her hands into the muck first.

Ben reached over and began rocking the crooked board back and forth. "Couldn't you see the thing was warped?" he asked.

"I am *not* in the lumber business!" she snapped. She was still struggling to rise and still having no luck.

"Well, neither am I, but I never thought it took a college degree to tell a straight line." Then he seized the plank with both hands, drew it toward him, and leaned it back up against the shed beside the sty.

"You should chop that thing up for kindling," Emily told him.

"Then Meggie and Frannie wouldn't be able to use it again."

"Again?" she demanded, once more struggling to rise,

and once more plopping back into the muck. "Do you mean they've done this before?"

"Yes, ma'am." He nodded.

"There's probably no prizewinning hen, is there?"

"Sure there is!"

Emily eyed him skeptically. "Well, I'll bet she doesn't lay her eggs up there, does she?"

"No, ma'am." He shook his head.

"Then this was all a deliberate trick?"

"Yes, ma'am," was all he answered. What else was there to say?

She glared at him. "Did you have a part in this?"

"Of course not!"

"But you *knew* about it! And you just stood there and watched and let them do this to me!" she fairly screamed in exasperation and anger. She was so angry, she thought if she stayed here any longer, the muck around her would begin to boil. "How *could* you?"

Ben reached up and pushed his hat farther back on his head. "Frankly, ma'am, I never thought you'd be dumb enough to fall for their tricks."

Emily sat there for a moment, struggling to regain her lost composure. At length, through lips so tightly compressed that she had difficulty enunciating clearly, she demanded, "Get me out of here. Now!"

Ben hoisted himself to the top rail of the fence, then slipped down into the pigsty. His boots made grotesque sucking noises as he picked his way toward her through the crowd of snorting pigs.

Ben's blue eyes glinted in the morning sun as he laughed more heartily. He towered over her, blotting out the rays of sunlight as he bent down to extend his hand to her. "I wasn't sure you'd want me to help you."

"Right now I'd be very grateful for your help." With a wry smile she added, "Even if you *are* laughing at me."

Emily took his hand. She felt the muck pulling at her again, but Ben reached down to take her other arm. His strong grasp easily lifted her.

"I'm not laughing at *you,*" he told her. It was true; he had stopped laughing at her. He held her close to him, making certain she was steady on her feet. "Are you sure you're all right? You did take a pretty nasty fall."

He ran his hands gently up and down her arms, taking care to avoid the patches of muck on her elbows. With his light touch he never could have determined if any of her bones were broken, but he certainly was causing all sorts of disturbances with her vital organs.

No, she assured herself, it was only her anger and embarrassment and physical exertion making her heart beat faster and her breath come in short, ragged gasps. It couldn't possibly be because his coarse brown linsey-woolsey shirt was opened at the throat, giving her just a small glimpse of the broad chest she had seen so much of yesterday, and which was now so close to her that she only had to raise her hand to touch him, if she dared.

"I'm not a doctor, but I think you'll survive," he said.

His voice was soft, Emily noted, as if he were trying to be kind. Still, every now and then, a little chuckle escaped, leaving Emily no doubts as to how he *really* viewed this incident.

"Come on, Emily." With one hand on her back, he gently tried to guide her to the gate in the fence, her means of escaping from the pigsty.

She took a step and teetered as the mud sucked at her shoes, threatening to unbalance her and send her sprawling back into the muck. The ooze seeped up around the ankles of her shoes and leaked in over the tops. The muck pulled at the hem of her dress, and even now threatened to drag her down again.

She grasped at the sleeve of his shirt. It offered little help as she continued to slip.

He eased his arm about her shoulders and held her tightly to him.

For support, Emily told herself as she clung more closely to him. But the slippery mud only made her stumble more. Her unsteadiness certainly couldn't be because of the firm muscles she could feel rippling under the coarse fabric of his shirt.

"Let's get you back to the house, ma'am, and I'll give you a bath. . . ."

She stared at him.

"I mean I'll get you a bath. . . . I'll get Ma to . . . Oh, hell. Let's get you cleaned up." He suddenly bent down and scooped her up into his arms. His boot heels sucked at the mud again as he carried her to the fence and deposited her safely on the other side.

The pigs grunted contentedly, as if they were glad to have her gone.

Dolly promptly chased the still giggling Meggie and Frannie out of the house.

"Get on over to Noah's," she told Ben when he set Emily down on the front porch. She wouldn't even allow him to come into the house. "One of you smelling like this is bad enough. I can't stand two, and I can hardly send Miss Shaw over to strip down at the pump, now, can I?"

"Guess not," Ben answered.

His eyes twinkled when he looked Emily up and down in her ruined dress. Emily had the feeling he was trying to picture her stripped down at the pump, and not having too hard a time doing so.

Dolly did her best to heat enough water quickly so that Emily could have a bath and still not be late for her appointment at the law office in Winterset.

After sponging off in the tub set in front of the big cast-iron stove, Emily retreated upstairs to put on other clothing.

She eased herself into her combinations, tied on her hose and garters, and slipped on her shoes. She fastened her skirt, then picked up her jacket from where it lay upon the bed. The sunlight streamed in her window. The birds outside sang a much cheerier song than the mournful hoot of that old owl last night. Emily made her way toward the window.

It had been so dark last night that she couldn't see a thing. But this morning, from her second-story window, Emily could look out over the farmyard and the surrounding countryside as far as the eye could see. It really was a very beautiful land.

She looked down into the farmyard below. Ben stood at the pump, stripped to the waist.

He'd made enough of an impression on her yesterday afternoon at the depot, seeing his bare chest like that. His appearance hadn't changed any, she noted—the same firm tanned muscles, the same scattering of hair. Strange how the sight of him now—after he had come so close to her in the moonlight, after he had held her in his arms so closely in, of all places, a pigsty—should cause a flutter deep down in her stomach and an ache in her chest, just longing to have him hold her again.

The September morning breeze was chilly, Emily decided. Certainly that could be the only reason her nipples suddenly tensed and pressed impudently against the soft silken fabric that covered her.

Quickly she turned away from the window and put on her

blue wool jacket. She'd only come here to get her niece. What in the world was Ben Cameron doing to her?

While Emily was glad that her unexpected need for a bath had not delayed their departure for school, Meggie and Frannie were not quite so happy. Ben hustled them all into the buckboard and drove them into Bidewell, making Annabelle trot all the way.

He pulled them to a halt in front of the Shaw house.

"Where's the school?" Emily asked, looking about. She knew she hadn't seen one during their brief ride through town yesterday, and she doubted that they'd been able to erect a schoolhouse overnight.

"Right behind the house," Meggie said. After snatching up their lunch pails from the back of the buckboard, she and Frannie headed through the backyard of the large house.

"But there's only a cornfield behind . . ." Emily said, puzzled, as she tried in vain to follow them.

"It's Old Man Pendergast's cornfield," Meggie answered as she ducked into the first of many evenly spaced rows. "All we have to do is cut through it. It's lots easier in the winter once the shocks are cut down—but nowhere near as much fun."

"Take care you don't get lost in there," Ben warned.

"Oh, shoot, Pa!" Frannie protested. "Me and Meggie know this field like ticks know Rover." She waved to her father, then ducked into the cornfield right behind Meggie.

Emily stared at the space in the solid wall of browning corn stalks where the two girls had disappeared. She knew she couldn't stand there all day. Sooner or later she was going to have to go inside her brother's house.

As much as she had wanted to come here last night, now that the moment when she would actually see the place had arrived, she found herself increasingly reluctant to go inside.

''Come on, ma'am,'' Ben said. He held his arm out behind her, not actually touching her, but as if he were shepherding her toward the fold. ''It used to be such a pretty house,'' he said. His gaze moved across the long porch that stretched all the way across the front of the house, then traveled up past the tall second-story windows, to the carvings hanging from the eaves of the roof like ornate wooden icicles. ''It's a shame for you to have to see it like this, but I guess we can't put it off any longer.''

Emily silently nodded and allowed him to lead her toward the house.

''Anyway, I guess things always look better in the light of day,'' Ben said.

''Not necessarily,'' Emily commented, eyeing the house. She picked off a peeling fleck of white paint from the banister as she walked up the rotting porch steps.

Ben pulled a long, thin brass key from his pocket and unlocked the front door.

''Ordinarily, ma'am, I'd be gentlemanly enough to hold the door and allow you to enter ahead of me,'' he said with a mischievous smile. ''All things considered, however, I think I'd best go first.''

From the quick glimpse she had of the dark, musty interior, Emily saw no reason to argue with him on this point. She followed him inside.

So this was George's house. Emily looked about, trying to see as much as she could in the semidarkness of the closed house.

The floorboards in the vestibule creaked with each step they took. Emily coughed to clear her throat of the dusty air.

Ben had already made his way into the parlor to the right. He drew aside a moldering red velvet drapery and pulled open the lacy curtain. After unlatching the window, he tried to raise the sash. The wood creaked in protest and refused to budge an inch, even under pressure from Ben's strong arms.

"Well, ma'am, some fresh air might be what this place needs right now, but I don't think we're going to get it from this window."

He moved on to one of the identical windows that flanked the hearth and opened out onto the side of the house. This window was more cooperative. He not only managed to open it completely but unlatched the dark green shutter and opened that, too.

A brisk September breeze fluttered the lacy curtain and caused the heavy velvet drapery to sway slightly. The sunlight dappled through the yellowing leaves of the oak tree outside, sprinkling splotches of variegated brightness on the darkened carpet.

Emily made her way around the sofa toward the mantelpiece. She lifted one of the small frames and studied the three faces peering up at her.

There was Sarah, looking a little different than Emily remembered her, with her hair pulled up into a neat matronly knot, instead of falling long and loose down her back the way she had worn it before she married. She looked so thin and pale, except for the two flushed spots on her cheeks, and her eyes looked so tired.

There was Meggie as a baby, her dark ringlets peeping out from under the little lace cap tied under her tiny chin with a slender ribbon, her large eyes staring at Sarah instead of the camera.

There was George. How she missed him! He'd been ten years old when she was born. Her first clear memories were of him riding her about the parlor atop his shoulders, her pudgy fingers securely twisted in his dark hair. Oh, how

Mother had scolded and then taken to her bed with the vapors. Dear funny George. How she missed him still!

Emily reached up to wipe the tear from the edge of her jaw. How had it gotten all the way down there? She hadn't even noticed she was crying.

"Ma'am." Ben's voice was soft and low as he came up behind her. "Are you all right, Emily?"

"I'll be fine," she assured him.

Ben reached out to take the picture from her hand. As his fingers folded about the frame, he froze. He stood behind her, silently studying the faces with her. Then he began to replace the frame on the mantel.

Emily quickly laid her hand atop his to stop him. She withdrew a small linen handkerchief from her pocket and began to obliterate the fine gray coating of dust that covered the mantel everywhere but the three small spots of dark mahogany where the little feet of the picture frame had stood.

"Don't do that," Ben said.

"Why not?"

"Don't you know, if you clean one thing in a room, it makes everything else start looking so bad, you have to keep cleaning until everything is done?"

Emily was surprised. Why should he care about her housekeeping habits? She looked up at him, puzzled.

He was grinning at her again. Still, she could see his eyes looked just a bit more moist than usual. Gently she returned his smile.

"I don't think removing a little dust could possibly make one single other thing in this room look any worse than it already does," she told him softly.

"Well, you've probably got a point there, ma'am." Ben watched her with what Emily could almost believe was a mixture of curiosity and—strangely enough—anticipation.

''But you don't have to do it all today, you know. You've got a long time ahead of you to make this house a nice place for you and Meggie to live.''

''Live here?'' Emily repeated, then gave a little laugh. ''Oh, no. You're mistaken, Mr. Cameron. I only intend to have the house fixed up enough so that I can sell it. I haven't come to live here. I've come to take Meggie back to Baltimore with me.''

CHAPTER FOUR

"YOU DON'T MEAN THAT. YOU CAN'T WANT TO sell this house and go back to Baltimore,'' Ben insisted.

He looked confused—a natural reaction, Emily thought. Maybe he hadn't been expecting her to leave with Meggie so soon. He looked very disappointed, too, she noticed with just a little surprise. Maybe he hadn't been expecting her to leave with Meggie at all.

''Why do you want to take Meggie away?'' he asked.

''Why would I *not* want to take my niece back home with me?'' she countered, frowning with puzzlement.

Emily was unable to bear the inexplicable pain she saw in Ben's eyes. She turned away and quickly glanced about the neglected room.

Now that she was no longer distracted by the intensity of his gaze, she was able to continue speaking. ''My brother named *me* as Meggie's guardian.''

Even though she did her best not to see him, she knew he was still watching her. He was still listening to every word she said, and that made her very uneasy.

She took a deep breath, as if trying to draw in courage as well as oxygen. ''I intend to do my best for my niece,'' she said. ''I've already had my lawyers make arrangements to enroll Meggie in an excellent private school in Baltimore. . . .''

"Do you think she hasn't had the opportunity to go to school here?" Ben demanded. He swung his arm behind him, as if indicating the farm they had just left. "You just saw for yourself this morning how my mother—and I—insist that both girls go to school every day."

"But she'll be able to attend concerts and visit museums. . . ."

"Well, maybe she can't get those things in Bidewell," Ben conceded. Then he lifted his head. Emily saw his broad chest expand with pride. "But we have concert halls and museums in Iowa, too. We're not all just pigsties and cornfields, you know."

"Yes, of course," she said more softly. Ben was right, and she knew it. Still, she felt there must be *something* Meggie could not get in Bidewell, something which Emily alone could offer her niece. "I'll give her a secure family life. . . ."

Suddenly Ben's clear eyes changed from the hazy blue of disappointment to a darker shade.

"Do you think Meggie hasn't had a good family life here?" he demanded in tightly clipped syllables.

Emily was startled—and just a bit frightened. Ben was managing to keep his obvious anger well under control—so far. She realized she didn't really know this man well enough to be left alone with him here. Who knew what he might do next?

She didn't think he'd actually hurt her. He didn't seem like that kind of man. But there was just something so *physical* about him, something that disturbed her very much. Who could predict what he might actually be capable of if pushed too far?

Emily realized with dismay that perhaps in challenging Ben Cameron, she had bitten off far more than she could chew.

Suddenly she didn't want to be alone with him. Slowly she began to inch her way toward the front door.

"After Sarah passed away, I think my brother did the best he could," she answered. Now, at what she considered a safe distance from him, she paused by the door. She moved her hand in a tiny gesture meant to indicate the entire unkept house. "I think it's fairly obvious it wasn't good enough."

Ben's long legs carried him swiftly across the room to stand before her. He folded his arms over his chest, waiting. Oh, how she wished he wouldn't do that! It made the fabric of his sleeves pull more tightly across the finely etched muscles of his arms and accentuated the bold expanse of his firm chest. He was doing it deliberately, of course—just to distract her from making all the fine points that would win for her this argument. And he certainly was succeeding!

"Do you think you can do better?" Ben challenged.

"Yes, I do." This time Emily stood her ground in the doorway.

She was used to leading such a quiet, peaceful, sheltered life. She had never had to argue with anyone before, not even her brother. The emotional effort it took to stand up to this forceful man seemed to be draining her physically.

For Meggie's sake, and somehow, strangely, for her own sake, she knew she must not back down. She raised her chin and stared at him defiantly. Then, unexpectedly, he lowered his gaze to study her lips.

She couldn't stop herself. Her own gaze wandered down the smooth tan of his cheek to rest on his lips. In contrast to the other tense muscles of his face, his lips looked soft and vulnerable. For just a moment she wondered if they felt as inviting as they looked. Her own lips suddenly tingled with the very thought of touching his.

She quickly turned away from him and began to make her way across the rickety front porch. Then, fearing that he might view her exit as a retreat, she made herself walk much more slowly down the crumbling brick walk toward the buckboard.

Ben was persistent. "A woman alone, raising a child," he said as he followed her down the walk.

Emily couldn't decide whether the tone of his voice was one of derision or exasperation. His apparent show of contempt for her mothering instincts made her all the more determined to convince him of her ability to raise her niece on her own.

He shook his head, then said in an unexpectedly softer voice, "Don't you think your niece needs a father's influence, too?"

"Meggie has had a father's influence," Emily pointed out as she stopped beside the buckboard.

What she'd seen of this house, and of Meggie's behavior, so far, was beginning to make her fear that George's influence had not been a very strong one. But she would *never* voice her doubts about her own brother—especially not now, especially not to this critical man.

"I agree that a father has a very strong effect on a child's life. But a certain refining, feminine influence from a mother is absolutely necessary, too—especially for a young girl."

"Do you think *you're* the only person who can provide Meggie with that feminine influence?"

The vision of Dolly Cameron spitting into a flowerpot flashed into Emily's mind. A valid point to make in favor of taking Meggie back with her, she noted. But when she looked into Ben's eyes, dark with unsettled emotions, she decided it might be wisest at this point not to anger him any further with personal remarks about his mother. After all, she was going to need a ride to the farm to collect Meggie's and her things, and then back to the depot to escape that wretched farm and the peculiar people who inhabited it.

"I'm sure Dolly—and all of you—have done what you could to raise Meggie properly," Emily said in a very slow, very calm voice. She was even bold enough to hope her tone sounded very condescending to Ben. "But *I'm* in a position to give Meggie so much more, once I take her back to Baltimore with me."

She turned her back to him and tried to climb up into the seat of the buckboard without his help. It was *very* important to her, just now, to be able to do *something* without Ben's help.

Drat this skirt, she silently cursed as it caused her to teeter for just a second on the cast-iron step of the buckboard. Too quickly Ben's strong hand reached out to support the small of her back and give her just the extra lift she needed to rise into the seat.

Oh, she was upset enough already! Why did he have to touch her? Why did the slight pressure of his hand on her back have to make her feel so warm all over? She'd come here for her niece. She hadn't come searching for feelings she'd never experienced before, feelings she wasn't sure she wanted to know.

After all the emotional turmoil of her mother's, and then her father's death, her life was settled now, peaceful, orderly. Having Meggie come live with her was going to make enough of a difference. The last thing Emily needed now was a man to complicate matters—especially a man like Ben Cameron. All she wanted to do was take Meggie away from this wild, earthy place and retreat back into her safe, civilized haven in Baltimore.

Ben rounded the buckboard, untied Annabelle's reins from the hitching post, and swung himself up into the seat beside her, all without saying another word. He clucked his tongue and rattled the reins. Annabelle took off for town at a trot.

Emily noted the lace curtains at the front windows of neighboring houses falling back into place as they passed.

Then, as if he could bear his own silence no longer, Ben shook his head and insisted, "Meggie needs to stay *here,* with her *family.*"

Emily's heart sank when she heard him. He wasn't going to let this go, was he?

"I *am* her family, Mr. Cameron," Emily said, staring at him defiantly. Her jaw was tightly set. Her hands were balled into fists in her lap. This newfound courage—even belligerence, she noted with surprise—where was it coming from?

"So am I," he answered quietly.

As he determinedly returned her stare, Emily noted with a sad, sinking feeling that his warm blue eyes were no longer even dusky with anger. They had grown icy cold, as if he had no more emotions.

Had he buried them all deep inside? she wondered. Was he preparing to keep them safe so they would not be hurt in the coming fight? Or had he put them away because he was so coldly calculating that he didn't use his emotions in battle? That thought made Emily shiver.

"I'll fight you every inch of the way for Meggie, Miss Shaw," he warned her. "I'll use every legal means I know."

"You have no legal means, Mr. Cameron," she said, stressing his formal name only because he had used hers. Her green eyes burned with a determination to equal his. "My father's . . ."

She stopped herself. Her father had been dead for over a year now. They were no longer her father's lawyers.

"*My* lawyers in Baltimore have examined my brother's will, and it's as sound as a new dollar," she stated confidently. "Meggie is legally *my* ward and *my* responsibility. You'll *never* take her away from me."

"We'll see, ma'am."

It was bad enough when he had gone back to calling her "Miss Shaw." But Emily couldn't explain her disappointment to hear him call her "ma'am." It had sounded so nice last night when he had whispered "Emily" in her ear. No man outside of her family had ever called her "Emily."

But Ben reached up and pulled his hat lower down over his eyes. The raucous bickering chatter of the crows in the fields and the steady *clop-clop* of Annabelle's hooves along the dirt road were the only sounds as they rode the rest of the way into town.

Out of the corner of her eye Emily glanced at Ben. His lips were pressed together tightly with determination. He held himself ramrod straight, as if fearful of allowing the slightest weakness to show. Both feet were planted firmly on the weathered floorboards, and his knees were barely inches apart.

Emily noticed the gap between Ben and her was much, much wider than it had been on their arrival in Bidewell.

She noted the way his callused fingers gripped the reins and the way the denim of his jeans stretched over his legs, just like they had yesterday afternoon. She blushed when she acknowledged that she missed the feel of his firm thigh pressing against hers as she had been jostled back and forth on their first trip.

No, she scolded herself, drawing her wandering thoughts back to where they belonged. She shouldn't think about Ben that way. She shouldn't be thinking of him at all!

* * *

Ben pulled the buckboard to a halt in front of a two-story yellow brick building. Silently he helped Emily down, then escorted her inside.

He stomped up the narrow flight of stairs ahead of her. Just like a spoiled little boy, Emily thought. She almost could have laughed at the petulant way he acted. But when he swung the dark mahogany door open with a crash, she realized he was indeed a man—a man far more to be reckoned with than any bad-tempered little boy.

The young woman who sat hunched over a large desk, flipping nervously through piles of papers, jumped up when Ben entered the room, spilling a cascade of papers to the floor. When she looked up, startled, her big blue eyes behind her gold-rimmed spectacles appeared even larger than normal. Her wispy white-blond hair was pulled back into a tight bun at the nape of her neck, but rebellious strands had escaped to stick out above each ear. She reached up to push her spectacles farther up on the bridge of her nose. Emily thought she resembled a little baby owl.

"Morning, Mr. Cameron," the little owl-lady said. Emily had expected a high-pitched screeching voice, in keeping with her appearance. She was surprised to hear her speak softly, and rather breathlessly.

Ben mumbled some sort of reply.

"Mr. Taylor's waiting," the owl-lady tried again to make some effort at communication with her boss.

Ben nodded again. Then, almost as an afterthought, he grunted some sort of an unintelligible reply.

Well, at least we're making some progress, Emily noted. She toyed with the idea of calling him a spoiled child and laughing in his face, or calling him a complete jackass and kicking him in the shins.

Emily looked about her. Dust motes floated in the musty air, glinting in the rays of morning sunlight streaming through two tall narrow windows. She breathed in the scents of well-waxed woodwork and dusty leather-bound volumes. The pages of the legal papers crackled as the little owl-lady sorted and stacked them on her cluttered desk.

Two glass-paneled doors opened off the high-ceilinged waiting room. One was lettered in gold with "Ebenezer Cameron, Esquire" across the frosted pane. The other door bore no markings at all.

Had that been George's office? she wondered. She threw a sidelong glance at Ben. He certainly hadn't wasted any time removing her brother's name from the door, had he?

"This is your office?" Emily asked.

Ben silently nodded.

She pointed to the blank door. "Was that George's?" she asked.

Ben nodded again.

"I suppose now you're going to sulk like a child until I leave." She whispered, so as not to further embarrass him because of his rude behavior in front of his employee. Although why she should care, she didn't know. The owl-lady seemed completely used to such temper tantrums.

"No," he answered. "I never sulk. I just haven't had anything to say to you."

Emily felt a twinge of disappointment. He'd seemed to have had plenty he wanted to say to her last night, she recalled.

He pushed open the sturdy swinging mahogany gate in the rail that separated the offices from the waiting room. She waited on the other side until he came through, then followed his lead toward the unmarked door. She was a little surprised that he should take her to this door instead of his own.

"And do you have something to say to me now?" she asked.

Ben nodded.

"And what is that?" she asked. She was angry enough with him already. Having to pull every bit of information out of him like a dentist extracting teeth was only irritating her more.

Ben tapped on the wooden frame of the door with the knuckles of his hand. "Mr. Taylor?" he called, twisting the knob and pushing the door inward. Then he turned to Emily and said, "Miss Shaw, this is Mr. Taylor. He'll be handling your business during your stay."

With that, Ben spun around on his heel and strode toward his own office. He closed the door behind him with a bang. Emily was left staring after him.

"Miss Shaw?"

Emily turned to Mr. Taylor. The slim, dark-haired young man had risen from behind his desk, and was smiling at her.

"Miss Shaw, so glad to meet you," Mr. Taylor said, quickly coming around the desk. His chocolate-brown eyes held a look of deepest sympathy. "Please accept my condolences on the recent loss of your brother."

Before Emily could thank him, his mobile face suddenly broke into a wide, welcoming grin. He eagerly seized the red leather wing chair and pushed it in Emily's direction. "Won't you have a seat?"

Emily thought that, in his enthusiasm, she was lucky he hadn't tried to pick her up bodily and put her in the chair. This ridiculous picture snapped her out of her surprised and hurt state. She closed her gaping mouth and returned the young man's smile.

"Thank you, Mr. Taylor," she answered, seating herself in the comfortable chair. "Please excuse my confusion. I wasn't aware that my brother's law offices had taken on a new partner—so new, in fact, that they haven't even had the chance yet to paint your name on the office door."

Mr. Taylor began to chuckle. Then his youthful face quickly took on a more staid expression—one he apparently felt his newly exalted status warranted.

"No, Miss Shaw," he said, seating himself at his desk. Then he leaned forward and whispered, "Not yet, but, confidentially, I have my aspirations."

"I'm sure you'll achieve them someday," she commented politely. "But I'm still a little confused. I was under the impression that Mr. Cameron was handling my late brother's affairs."

She was also more than confused. She was surprised, and just a bit angry, that her brother's business should be left in the hands of a mere associate. She refused even to consider the possibility that she might be disappointed that she wouldn't be dealing directly with Ben.

"I can assure you, Mr. Cameron has the utmost confidence in my abilities, as did your late brother," Mr. Taylor quickly added.

"I'm sure they did. Please, I didn't mean to offend you, Mr. Taylor."

"Oh, no offense was taken," he assured her.

"Then, if you please, may I just sign whatever papers are necessary for the sale of the house and my brother's share of the business?" Emily said. She didn't try very hard to keep the note of weariness from her voice. "Then I can get my niece and we'll be leaving."

Mr. Taylor's ears and cheeks turned a bright crimson. He drew in a deep breath. "I'm afraid it's not going to be that simple, Miss Shaw."

Emily's heart sank to the bottom of her chair, where it churned like an ice floe breaking up after a spring thaw.

Emily heard the door of Ben's office open and close much more quietly than it had before. Well, she thought, thank goodness the man has finally come to his senses.

Through the thin glass of the door to the waiting room, Emily could hear Ben moving about—back and forth, back and forth. Oh, why couldn't the man sit down and get to work so that she could concentrate on what Mr. Taylor was saying!

She had never really had much of a head for business or figures. That was why she had lawyers, to handle those kinds of things. It was difficult for her to take in everything that Mr. Taylor told her. He had a genuine ability to drone on and on, talk his way round about a question, and still say absolutely nothing of worth.

Emily's visions of the pompous yet competent lawyer handling her brother's estate disappeared completely when confronted with the eager, youthful Mr. Taylor. She had thought to find endearing pomposity, but instead she had apparently found endearing incompetence.

Emily spent several hours of the morning, sitting in his office, listening. From what she could glean from their conversation, the law offices themselves were on fairly solid financial ground. Emily had fully expected them to be. But she was very surprised to find that her brother not only owed a good deal of money on the mortgage of his house, and that he had even borrowed on his savings, but that several of the records of these various transactions were missing.

She had thought George was doing so well. How could he owe the bank so much money? And how could some of his records be missing? Why hadn't the bank kept better accounts?

"If you could just manage to pay—"

"I wish I could, Mr. Taylor," Emily said with a sad shake of her head.

She really wished she could. She wished George had let his family know he was having problems instead of trying to work it out alone. Then things might not have come to this. Their father would have helped him quickly and easily. As for Emily, her hands were tied.

"All my capital is invested. The allowance I receive from the interest is certainly generous for anything I might want, but I can't touch the principal. . . ." She shrugged her shoulders helplessly. "I couldn't afford to pay George's debts and still be able to maintain my own home in Baltimore."

To compound the trouble she was having concentrating on the problems of her brother's estate, she could still hear Ben roaming noisily around on the other side of the door. What in the world was he doing? Moving every tall bookcase and heavy table and leather chair from one end of the waiting room to the other? All he did was pace back and forth, back and forth, in front of Mr. Taylor's office door. Why couldn't the man have some consideration for the work they were trying to do in here? Why couldn't the man keep his distance from her?

"I'm really very sorry, Miss Shaw," Mr. Taylor apologized for about the hundredth time. "You came all the way out here, and we still don't have anything ready for your signature."

"I was coming anyway, for my niece and to collect my brother's things. But I really don't understand why there should be a problem, Mr. Taylor."

"Oh, oh, it's no problem," he answered quickly, shuffling through the papers on his desk. "I wouldn't want you to think we were incompetent or something."

Recalling the beleaguered little owl-lady and her sea of papers in the waiting room, Emily said, "I understand how these things might be misplaced, Mr. Taylor, but . . . well, I still don't understand. . . ."

"If you could just manage to stay a little longer in town . . ." he suggested.

"Stay?" she repeated. "Here?"

"Yes, ma'am. For just a little—"

"*Must* I stay—here?" Emily's eyes grew wide with horror at the very thought of a prolonged stay.

"It shouldn't take us that much longer," he reassured her, trying very hard to resume his air of competence. "I feel sure it's only a matter of a few hours of diligent search to find the missing papers. When you told us you'd be coming to get your niece, we thought we'd save some time and have you sign the papers while you were here. I'd hate to think you had traveled all the way from Baltimore. Then, once you left, we would find them, and have to send them to you. Such a waste of time and money," he said with a shake of his head.

Emily realized with alarm that she was actually nodding her head. She couldn't possibly be consenting to stay here. Perhaps she was so tired her bobbing head meant she was dropping off to sleep. Yes, that must be it. On the other hand, she hadn't slept that badly last night—no matter how her dreams of Ben had kept her awake.

It certainly couldn't be because she was actually agreeing to stay the extra time in Bidewell. Where on earth would she stay? George's house didn't look livable. She had no intention whatsoever of staying on that wretched farm with the kind but crude Dolly, and the slightly loony Noah, and especially with the very disturbing Ben Cameron.

Emily gave a weary sigh. "I suppose I can make some kind of arrangements," she said. "I *do* still own the house, don't I?"

"Well, actually, it belongs to the heir of George Shaw—which, of course, is Meggie. And you, as Meggie's guardian, hold it in trust for her. But just for the time being, I'm sorry to say, unless those payments can be met,'' Mr. Taylor answered. ''I can find out for just how long the bank is willing to—''

''No, thank you, Mr. Taylor. Please don't put yourself to all that trouble.'' Emily decided it just wasn't worth listening to Mr. Taylor any longer to find out. Probably by the time he had figured everything out, she and Meggie would be on their way back to Baltimore, where she could have her own *competent* lawyers look into Meggie's inheritance.

Emily realized that, after several hours in the law office, she had still accomplished absolutely nothing. She rose abruptly. Mr. Taylor dropped the stack of papers he had been shuffling and sprang to his feet. She began to move toward the door.

Emily could think of many words to describe Ben Cameron, but stupid was not one of them. Then how could he not know that his silhouette was clearly defined against the glass of the door in the bright noonday sunlight. Was the man eavesdropping on every word she said? Didn't he have some kind of respect for the privacy between a lawyer and his client?

Mr. Taylor pulled the door open. Emily stood face to face with Ben. It must be her imagination, she decided. It would be impossible for this irritating man to look the least bit guilty, even when caught red-handed in his crime. Unless he were feeling guilty for another reason? What *had* happened to her brother's money, and his papers? she wondered.

''Have you come to offer your expert legal advice, Mr. Cameron?'' she asked.

''I'm not sure you'd take it, Miss Shaw,'' he answered, grinning at her. Apparently he had recuperated very quickly from any guilty feelings he might have.

''I'd take it if I thought it would help me,'' she replied.

"And you don't think I'm trying to help you?"

"I thought that you'd already made your position on that matter perfectly clear, Mr. Cameron," she said.

"Yes, I suppose I did," Ben said. "Well, then, are you ready to go home, Miss Shaw?"

"Yes, I am," she answered. "Unfortunately, Mr. Taylor tells me I'm going to have to stay *here* just a little longer."

"Oh." He sounded surprised, but somehow Emily had the feeling he wasn't. From the gleam in his eye he actually appeared to be very happy.

"I have to do some more work in town this afternoon. . . ."

"I hope you'll be searching for my brother's missing papers," she interjected.

Ben pressed his lips together for just a moment. "We'll *all* be doing our best," he answered. Then he extended his hand toward the door, leaving no doubt in Emily's mind that he was inviting her to depart. "I've made arrangements with Noah to take you back to your brother's place."

Emily had always appreciated horses. They were such beautiful animals. Useful, too. Without horses, how would people travel, or deliver milk, or entertain themselves? But she had never really given much attention to individual horses, until now.

She would never be able to fully express her gratitude to Annabelle for getting her to her brother's house safe and sound. Noah certainly never could have done it alone.

Noah rested his elbows on his knees as he held the reins. Emily could hardly describe what he was doing as "guiding" the horse.

He'd been clean and cold sober this morning when she left the farm. Now he reeked of hard liquor and had trouble sitting up straight—and it was barely past noon! It was too early in the day to start drinking. How could he have gotten so drunk so quickly? What in the world could have caused such a change in Noah?

"I know ye're in a hurry t' git back t' the farm," he said.

"Well, no, actually," Emily admitted. "I mean, yes. . . ."

Noah looked up at the sky. "Yep. Me, too. Looks like more rain."

More rain? she wondered. She knew it hadn't rained last night. Heaven knows, she'd been up enough not to have missed even a shower. She looked up. There wasn't a cloud in the bright blue September sky. She was really starting to worry about Noah.

Emily was also very angry with Ben. The man hadn't seemed concerned in the least when his brother showed up at the law offices smelling like a distillery. How could Ben allow her to travel home with a man who could barely sit up and hold the reins in his hands? How could he and Dolly subject two impressionable little girls to a man with Noah's obvious weakness for hard liquor?

She was very worried for Meggie, too. The longer Emily stayed in Bidewell, the more she was convinced that she needed to take her niece far, far away from here—immediately!

"We . . . we could go jus' a teeny bit fas'er, ma'am, if ya wanna git home fer lunch," he offered. Then he belched loudly.

"No, no," Emily quickly responded. "I'm not all that hungry."

She was starving! She'd lost so much time this morning, after Meggie and Frannie's little trick had necessitated another bath and a complete change of shoes and clothing. She'd had time for only a single, fresh-baked biscuit and a cup of coffee for breakfast. It was already past noon, and she hadn't eaten anything in town. Her stomach grumbled.

But she'd never admit it to Noah and risk having him run Annabelle and the buckboard off the road at a gallop.

''Are you certain you won't let me drive?'' she offered one more time.

''No, no, ma'am,'' Noah insisted, clutching the reins more tightly to him. The pull on the reins would have made another horse veer to the right, but Annabelle continued toward her destination with single-minded purpose, never even breaking stride. Emily was very glad that Annabelle knew the way home.

Emily decided to try a different tactic. ''You know, Noah, I haven't driven since . . . since I was a little girl,'' she said. ''There was a pony cart at my grandmother's farm. It's been so long, but you know, I'd really like to try my hand at the reins again, just to remember how it was—if you don't mind.''

''No, no,'' Noah insisted. He was beginning to lean to his left. ''Ain't right fer a lady t' be drivin' when there's a perfec'ly capable, able-bodied man t' do it fer her.''

Emily sighed. She had serious doubts about Noah's capability in this condition. She would just have to put her trust in Annabelle.

Noah leaned farther to his left. Another inch in that direction and he would topple over and out of the buckboard. Should she grab him now, she wondered, and appear very forward, touching a man she barely knew? Or should she wait until he had actually begun to fall and take the chance that she would be quick enough to catch him before he tumbled completely out?

Suddenly Noah snorted and pulled himself upright just in the nick of time. He belched loudly. ''I'll tell ya, ma'am,'' he said. ''This here drivin' sure makes a man thirsty.''

Emily considered the unkind notion that Noah would find sitting in a church pew made him thirsty.

She looked ahead up the road, hoping for Bidewell to appear. Getting Noah out of this buckboard, and getting some coffee into him, couldn't happen too soon.

At last the neat little whitewashed houses of Bidewell came into view through a stand of yellow-dappled, white-striped beech trees. She glanced over to Noah. He was sitting perfectly upright. She breathed a sigh of relief. Maybe they would make it after all.

Then Emily saw a sight that brought more fear to her heart than her first ill-fated encounter with Meggie, more fear than this unpredictable ride with Noah, almost more fear than her argument this morning with Ben.

Lined up along the brick walk on the front lawn of George's house were all the good ladies of Bidewell, each wearing a beaming smile and carrying a plate or a crock of some sort of homemade concoction in outstretched hands.

CHAPTER FIVE

OH, WHAT A FINE FIRST IMPRESSION TO MAKE! Emily silently groaned as she viewed the line of curious ladies.

She glanced at Noah. He still smelled badly, and he was leaning toward the left again. At least he wasn't leaning on her! What an awful impression that would make on the ladies!

She could only hope that Noah would be able to leave her at George's house, and then at least take the buckboard out of sight beyond the bend in the road before he fell out of it completely.

Even more than that, she hoped the good ladies of the town did not think that she herself drank, just because she was seen in company with Noah!

If only she could just lower her head and pretend she didn't see them. Then she and Noah could ride on past and come back later, after the ladies had all grown tired of waiting and gone away.

Suddenly Dolly Cameron spotted them and began to wave furiously. "Yoo-hoo!" she called. "There she is, ladies!"

Oh, no! How could Dolly do this to her? Emily wished she could slither down under the seat and disappear. There was no escaping the ladies now.

As she sat cringing in the wagon, suddenly her heart went out to Dolly. When she organized this impromptu little welcoming party, how could she have known what an awful state her younger son would be in? How embarrassed the elderly lady would be to have her friends see Noah this way.

Since Emily was the one the ladies obviously wanted, for a brief moment she considered hopping from the moving buckboard as it passed in front of the house so that she could distract them. Then Noah could continue on and be far down the road before anyone noticed his pathetic condition.

But Noah reined Annabelle to a halt directly in front of George's house. The mare was so used to continuing on to the farm that Noah had difficulty stopping her. He pulled back so hard on the reins that he almost flipped backward over the seat.

Emily gritted her teeth and began to climb down from the wagon.

"No, no, le'me help ya," Noah insisted.

"*You*'re the one who needs help," she whispered. "Go home and get some sleep!"

"No, wait!"

As she slid from the seat, Noah reached across to stop her. His reactions were slowed by the whiskey. He grabbed for thin air and fell flat on his face on the wooden seat.

Emily fought hard to subdue the flush of embarrassment that rose up her cheeks. Then she turned a beaming smile to the welcoming committee descending upon her.

"Well, now, just in time for lunch," Dolly said. "That's Nola Lindstrom, Erma Conrad, Wilhelmina Robbins, Iris Hannigan . . ." She continued around the circle of smiling faces.

"How do you do?" Emily replied automatically. She knew she would never remember a one of their names or faces. She was upset about the news of her brother's financial problems. She was disturbed by Noah's inebriated state. She was furious with Ben for opposing her in her plans for Meggie. She was in no state just now to bother with trivial social pleasantries.

"C'mon, c'mon," Dolly insisted. Balancing the cake plate on one broad, work-worn hand, she seized Emily's elbow with the other and began to lead her up the walk. "Come and meet the other ladies."

Emily glanced back at Noah. Inch by inch, with his arms firmly braced beneath him, he was slowly propping himself back upright.

Dolly just shook her head as she watched Noah's slow progress. When he had finally succeeded in sitting upright again, she breathed a deep sigh. Emily wondered if it was a sigh of embarrassment or a sigh of relief.

"Af'ernoon, Ma. Ladies." He shook his head, as if to clear away the cobwebs, and threw the ladies a proud smile.

And rightly so, Emily decided. In his condition, sitting upright *was* quite an accomplishment.

"C'mon, Annabelle," he said, and then hiccuped. "Lesh git back t' town." He had enough trouble keeping his balance, much less trying to turn the buckboard around in the middle of the road, but somehow he managed—or did he owe his success all to Annabelle again?

He shouldn't be going back to town anyway, Emily thought, where there were taverns and readily accessible beer and whiskey. He should be going home for some strong hot coffee. Why didn't Dolly say something? He might be a grown man, but she was still his mother. Her own mother certainly wouldn't have hesitated to tell Emily exactly what she had done wrong.

"Oh, don't worry about Noah," Mrs. Lindstrom assured her.

''But he's so . . . inebriated,'' Emily finally found the courage to point out.

''It's Friday,'' Dolly explained. ''Noah *always* starts drinking on Friday.''

But when Emily had first met him, Noah had been stone, cold sober. If he always started drinking on Friday, yet she had seen him sober, there must be some point in the week at which he stopped drinking, she reasoned. Eagerly she wondered how soon that would be.

''He'll be just fine,'' Dolly said as she reached out to pat Emily's hand.

''The Lord watches out for fools and drunks,'' Mrs. Robbins added sagely.

''He must be taking special care of Noah then,'' the wizened Mrs. Lindstrom remarked.

Emily was surprised that they all seemed to take Noah's drinking problem as quite usual. Well, she supposed every place needed a town drunk. But it was very difficult to accept the fact that the town drunk was your own niece's uncle.

''We're so happy to have you in Bidewell,'' Mrs. Robbins said. ''Why don't you invite us inside for a spell, and we can get to know you.''

''The house really isn't ready for visitors. . . .'' Emily began to protest.

''Nonsense,'' Dolly said. ''It's lunchtime, and everyone needs to eat.''

Mrs. Lindstrom, holding a jar of pickles tucked into the crook of one arm, seized Emily's elbow with the other hand. Trapped between the two formidable ladies, Emily was propelled up the brick walk.

As if they were afraid she would escape from their curious scrutiny, the ladies did not release Emily until she reached out to turn the tarnished brass knob.

Emily wanted to just send the ladies away with the excuse that she simply wasn't receiving today. Then the aroma of the delicacies the ladies brought drifted to her nostrils. They *were* going to feed her. Why shouldn't she let them in? Oh, how could she be such a slave to her physical needs? she moaned as her stomach growled. She willingly turned the knob.

"Now, just leave everything to us," Dolly declared. She shooed Mrs. Conrad and Mrs. Robbins off to what must certainly be the kitchen. "Why don't you sit and chat with Mrs. Hannigan and the others?"

The neat young woman with thick blond braids coiled about her head led the way into the parlor.

"Oh, I see you've already been here!" Mrs. Hannigan exclaimed ingenuously.

As if they hadn't all been watching earlier today, Emily thought with exasperation. She felt a flush of remembrance when she saw the window that she and Ben had inadvertently left open in their rush to get away from each other, and from the memories that this house held, and from the unpleasant future that circumstances were forcing upon them.

Dolly laid a white cloth over the round table in the center of the circle of chairs. The other ladies busied themselves with pulling open the dusty draperies or flipping off dust covers and folding them into the corners.

After they had arranged themselves around the table, Mrs. Hannigan uncorked a jug of cider and poured a measure into pale green glasses.

"We're so pleased to finally meet Mr. Shaw's sister," Mrs. Hannigan said. "He was . . . well, he really was a nice man—really."

"Noah thought a great deal of him," Mrs. Lindstrom interjected with a sly smile.

"And Sarah was so sweet," Mrs. Hannigan added quickly. "It was a pleasure to have her for a neighbor. I can remember all the fun we used to have when they first came here—she and George, and Ben and Betty, and my Robbie and me."

So Ben's late wife had been named Betty, Emily noted—although she still couldn't figure out why she should be bothering to take note of Ben or anything about him. How long had they been married? she still couldn't stop herself from wondering. And what had happened to Betty?

Mrs. Robbins entered the parlor carrying a plate of thick ham sandwiches. She was followed by Mrs. Conrad, bearing the cake plate. They all helped arrange the plates and bowls on the table. Mrs. Lindstrom opened her pickle jar and placed it in the center of the table, as if they were so fine they deserved a place of honor.

"I declare," Mrs. Hannigan continued with a tittering little giggle. "Ben can still make me laugh."

"Oh, he's a real charmer," Mrs. Lindstrom said with a hearty chuckle. "I swear . . ."

"Oh, Nola, don't swear," Mrs. Robbins scolded.

"Oh, c'mon now, Wilhelmina," Mrs. Lindstrom leaned over the table and whispered loudly. "Them big broad shoulders and them big blue eyes of his—well, they're enough to make even a saint swear—and I ain't no saint! Seems to me like my old eyes are starting to be able to see through things, 'cause it don't matter what he's wearing, no matter how much I look, all I can see is them shoulders—bare!"

Emily didn't think the age or condition of a person's eyes had anything to do with the knack, as she seemed to be developing that uncanny ability herself.

"Anyway, I've seen *you* peeking at him, too, when he works in his yard," Mrs. Lindstrom accused. "Are you tired of Mr. Robbins by now? Eyeing Ben up for yourself, are you?''

Mrs. Robbins's fair complexion flushed. ''Nola! How you talk!''

''I'm old,'' Mrs. Lindstrom pointed out. ''I can talk any way I want.''

Mrs. Robbins busied herself with doling out generous portions of everything.

''Eyeing him up for that homely daughter of yours then, eh?''

''Pearl's just going through an awkward stage, Nola,'' Mrs. Robbins defended her offspring. ''Just like your Clara did.''

''Well, don't go calling for the preacher yet,'' Dolly cautioned. ''Ben ain't been interested in nobody since Betty died.''

When did Betty die? Emily found herself wondering. She didn't want to ask. She wouldn't want any of these ladies to think she was actually interested in Ben herself. She wasn't interested at all. Really, she wasn't.

''Yes, it's so sad to think how they've all gone on to their reward now—except for Ben and me.'' Mrs. Hannigan gave a deep sigh.

Much too deep, Emily decided on an impulse. Almost as if what Mrs. Hannigan were sighing for wasn't the good times passed, but something else she wanted even more and didn't have—yet.

As if you should care whether she gets him or not, Emily scolded herself, a little more harshly than she ordinarily would have done.

After all, it was no business of *hers* what Ben Cameron and the ladies of Bidewell did. *She* would be gone from Bidewell soon—very soon. Even though George and Sarah, Mr. Hannigan, and Betty Cameron were now gone, they had made some small difference just by being here. But when *she* left, they would all go on with their lives—as if she had never been here at all, Emily found herself thinking sadly. Even worse, if she returned to Baltimore without Meggie, once she was dead, it would be as if she had never existed at all.

"Well, we're glad to have you here now," Dolly reassured Emily. She passed a piece of cake to her. "It'll be good to have a woman in this house again."

"Yes. Sarah was such a *good* housekeeper," Mrs. Hannigan agreed, pouring Emily more cider. "She had a real green thumb, too, when it came to her flowers, although no one could ever guess it from the way the place looks now. . . ."

"Oh, hush, Iris!" Dolly growled.

"Well, it *was* a pleasure to have her for a neighbor," Mrs. Hannigan insisted.

Emily began to feel a certain sense of inadequacy. Glancing about the dusty parlor, she recalled the forlorn state of the garden, too. She hoped they weren't expecting her to single-handedly bring this place back to its former tidiness. She had no idea where to begin, and even if she did, she certainly was going to need some help. Still, she supposed she ought to at least give the impression that she was willing to try.

"I really would like to see this house put to rights again," Emily finally managed to summon up the nerve to say. "I was wondering if any of you would know of someone I could hire as a cleaning lady. . . ."

The ladies broke out in tittering laughter. "A cleaning lady? Hire a cleaning lady?" they chattered, sharing knowing looks with their neighbors.

"Well, I suppose the place could use a good gardener,

too,'' Emily said, not wanting them to think that she wouldn't give the outside of the house equal care.

Mrs. Lindstrom laughed a wicked cackle. ''We're *all* gardeners here. Most of us just have gardens that are a couple hundred acres bigger than you're used to. But what do you need a gardener for? Isn't your husband coming out here to farm, too?''

''Oh, I don't have a husband,'' Emily said quickly. She drew in a sharp breath as all eyes riveted to her. The ladies waited, holding their breath, in anticipation of what she was going to say next. Emily knew with dread certainty that this had definitely been the wrong thing to say.

''Why, Dolly,'' Mrs. Robbins said, eyeing her suspiciously. ''You never said a word. . . .''

''You never asked.''

''Are you widowed, too?'' Mrs. Hannigan ventured cautiously.

''I . . . no, I . . .''

''Did the slimy varmint desert you like my first husband—may he burn in Perdition—did to me?'' Mrs. Lindstrom demanded.

''I still say you should have shot him in the back when you had the chance,'' Dolly whispered rather loudly.

''No, I . . . I'm not married,'' Emily finally managed to squeeze into the conversation.

''Oh, a single lady,'' Mrs. Hannigan said. The warm and friendly smile that had lit her pretty face turned as flat as cardboard.

Mrs. Lindstrom laughed. ''Even though Emily *is* a fair bit older, I'm sure she and Pearl'll become good friends,'' she said to Mrs. Robbins.

''I'm sure they will,'' Mrs. Robbins answered, as if the next expected event would be pigs flying overhead.

''And she'll be moving right in on the other side of Ben

from you, Iris,'' Mrs. Lindstrom continued. ''Won't that be cozy?''

''Just wonderful,'' Mrs. Hannigan declared, without a trace of enthusiasm.

''Just awful!'' Meggie's mournful cry rang through the vestibule and into the parlor. The boom of the door hitting the wall behind accented her words like a big bass drum thundering through a parade. ''I hate her!''

''I don't blame you,'' Frannie said.

Oh, Lord! She's talking about me, Emily thought with a sharp twist of anguish in her heart upon hearing Meggie's harsh words. And in front of all these ladies! It was bad enough she had hurt Meggie's feelings when she first arrived. Did the entire town have to know how miserably she had failed in her first attempt at being an aunt?

''Why did she have to come here in the first place?'' Meggie demanded angrily, slamming her schoolbooks down on the bench in the vestibule.

''Well, ladies,'' Mrs. Lindstrom declared. She rose to her feet, snapped the lid of her pickle jar shut, and tucked it back under her arm. ''I think we've had a lovely welcoming party for *Miss* Shaw, but the menfolk'll be wanting supper soon. . . .''

''Oh, really, do we *have* to go?'' Mrs. Hannigan tried to say.

''Mine always comes home hungry and cantankerous as an old bear with a sore foot!'' Mrs. Robbins said.

''Once, just once, I'd like to punch her. Or put a tack on her chair, or a worm in her apple, or . . . or gunpowder in the stove,'' Meggie continued to issue her unseen threats.

Dolly leaned over and patted Emily's hand. ''Sometimes it takes 'em a while to get used to it,'' she advised.

''Sometimes,'' Mrs. Hannigan whispered ominously in Emily's other ear, ''they never get used to it—ever.''

Emily swallowed hard at Mrs. Hannigan's dire warning. She managed to murmur words of thanks as she accompanied the departing ladies to the front door. Passing in front of the brooding Meggie and her little shadow, Frannie, the ladies were gone as quickly as they had descended upon her. Only Dolly remained.

"Oh, Gramma! I hate her! Can I go home with you?"

"Hush! That's no way to talk in front of company. Anyway, I'm not going straight home," Dolly said. "I've got to stop by Mrs. Robbins's for her recipe for apple dumplings with cream sauce. She'll never give ya the whole recipe, but I think I can figure out what ingredients she's left out this time." She glanced back and forth between the girls. "Course, ya can still come with me if ya'd like—and play with Pearl."

"No, thanks!" Meggie answered quickly. "All she ever wants to do is fix my hair all funny and put bows and stuff on it. My day's been awful enough already."

Dolly shrugged. "Suit yourself," she answered. "Why don't ya just stay here till Ben comes?"

Meggie frowned and shrugged. Dolly patted Emily on the shoulder as she quickly went out the door.

Frannie had deserted her friend for the sandwiches and pieces of cake the ladies had left in the parlor. Emily was left alone in the vestibule with a sulking Meggie.

Meggie kicked at the foot of the sturdy banister. Emily could see one big tear trickling down her soft pink cheek. She wished she could think of something to say or do which would ease Meggie's hurt. She was beginning to realize, much to her dismay, that she didn't know much about children at all. If she did, she certainly would do her best to help Meggie now. She glanced back to Frannie, who was enjoying herself in the parlor.

"Would you like some cake, Meggie?"

"No, thank you."

"I'm so sorry, Meggie. Is . . . is there anything I can do?" Emily asked.

"No," Meggie mumbled.

Emily felt a little relieved. Meggie could have told her to leave town on the next train—or to take a leap into the path of that oncoming train. Maybe she wasn't personally to blame for Meggie's unhappiness after all.

Feeling her lighter heart more capable of comforting Meggie, Emily moved toward the little girl and placed her hand on her shoulder.

Meggie turned her tear-stained face up to Emily. With the back of her grubby hand, she smeared away the damp little lines that ran down her cheeks.

At least she didn't pull away from me, Emily noted with increasing relief.

"What's wrong, Meggie?" Emily repeated.

"She failed her spelling test," Frannie announced through a mouthful of cake as she came into the vestibule. "Again."

"You've failed your spelling test twice?" Emily repeated.

"No."

"No, she failed it three times," Frannie answered.

"Quit it, Frannie." Meggie punched at her friend.

"Hey!" Frannie jumped out of the way.

"Well, you don't have to be so gosh-darned honest!" Meggie hissed.

"Meggie, school has only been in session for three weeks, hasn't it?" Emily asked.

Meggie nodded.

Hoping to cheer Meggie, with a weak little laugh, Emily continued, "Well, that's good, or else you'd have failed four or five tests by now."

"Oh, she has."

"For crying out loud, Frannie!" Meggie shouted. "Why don't you just shoot me where I'm standing?"

"Four or five?" Emily repeated.

"Math and geography, too," Frannie said.

"If she fails one more test, Miss Bloom says she's going to make Meggie sit on this tall stool in the corner, with a really dumb-looking pointy hat on her head and . . . Ow! Stop poking me," Frannie exclaimed.

"Well, I warned you."

"Miss Bloom is your teacher?" Emily asked. Suddenly things were becoming clearer.

"I hate her!" Meggie cried.

Emily was relieved to realize that Meggie had been referring to Miss Bloom and not to her. She wished the other ladies of the town could know that.

"Miss Ida Bloom!" Meggie spat out the name as if it were a snake crawling down her tongue. Her little hands were clenched in two fists held tightly at her sides. "What a pickle! What a miserable, dried-up old prune! Smelly as a polecat. Ugly as as warthog. Mean and nasty as a serpent."

"Gee, Meggie," Frannie interrupted. "If you could spell those words you just used, you wouldn't be in the fix you're in now."

"Isn't she a good teacher?" Emily asked.

"Well, she's . . . well, I don't know," Meggie answered. "All I know is, Ol' Lady Bloom is *mean*!"

"How old is she?"

"Old. Really old," Meggie answered. "Even older than you."

Emily wasn't sure if this was an insult or a compliment. "Did you hate her last year, too?"

"No. Last year I had Miss Mueller. I really liked Miss Mueller, but she left to get married." Meggie slapped her arms at her sides and wailed, "Oh, why did she have to leave? Why did they have to hire mean ol', ugly ol' Ida Bloom to take her place?''

Emily placed her arm farther around Meggie's shoulder to comfort her.

''There, there,'' she repeated the words soothingly, just like Grandmama had done when Emily had felt bad when she was a little girl. ''Do your best for just a little while longer. Pretty soon you won't have to suffer through another one of her classes.''

''You're taking me out of school?'' Meggie squealed with delight.

''Lucky dog!'' Frannie exclaimed.

Meggie turned to Emily and threw her long, thin arms around Emily's waist.

''No, no,'' Emily quickly corrected her niece. ''You *have* to go to school. You wouldn't want to grow up ignorant, would you?''

''I . . . I guess not.''

''Of course not,'' Emily said confidently. She was pretty proud of how she was handling this problem, if she did say so herself. ''I'll see to it that you go to a nice private school—with excellent teachers—nice, pretty, young teachers. You'll learn so much more, once I get you back to Baltimore—''

''Baltimore!'' Frannie exclaimed. Cake crumbs shot out of her mouth.

''Baltimore?'' Meggie repeated. ''I can't go there!''

''Yes, you can. I'm taking you home.''

''I *am* home,'' Meggie insisted.

''I'm taking you to my home—*our* home now. It's a very nice home. . . .''

''I'm not going!''

''But—''

''I won't leave!'' Meggie insisted.

Emily could feel the floorboards quivering with the force of Meggie's feet stamping angrily upon them.

"I won't leave Gramma and Uncle Noah and Uncle Eb! I won't leave Frannie!"

Meggie kicked the banister hard one more time, then turned and kicked the table just for good measure. Emily was afraid she would be the next target, but Meggie turned and sped out the door.

Emily, dumbstruck, stared after Meggie for just a moment.

"Meggie, wait!" she cried, following her out onto the porch.

But Meggie had already left Emily and Frannie both far behind. She sprinted across the front lawn, then sprang over the weedy little patch of dead flowers that separated George's house from Ben's.

"Meggie!" Emily tried to call once more, but the little girl was already across Ben's neat and spacious lawn and into the next yard.

"Where's she going?" Emily asked Frannie.

"Mr. Hannigan's house."

Emily suddenly had a sick feeling in the pit of her stomach. She watched helplessly as Meggie pounded up the front steps. The pretty blond widow bustled out onto her front porch to greet her.

Mrs. Hannigan held out her arms, and Meggie fell sobbing into them. Mrs. Hannigan patted Meggie's dark curls, smoothing her ruffled hair back to its usual luster. Mrs. Hannigan went inside and reappeared with a plate of freshly baked sugar cookies and a glass of cold milk for Meggie. Emily watched with growing sadness and wished it were she who could be making all the nice little gestures that Mrs. Hannigan made to comfort her niece.

She'd only been trying to do what she thought was right. How could things have turned out so wrong?

Ben pressed his thumb and forefinger into the little hollows at the sides of the bridge of his nose. He looked up wearily from the papers he had been reading. He rose and, placing both hands in the small of his back, leaned backward. He rolled his head from side to side to loosen his stiff neck. He shrugged his shoulders, then extended first one long arm and then the other out to his sides as far as he could reach. He was stiff from sitting too long. He felt like he'd been reading all day.

The sun had moved around to the other side of the building, and its warm rays stretched across the clutter on his large mahogany desk. He reached into this pocket and pulled out his watch. Flipping the top open, he listened to the little chimes sounding in time to the rhythmic tick in his palm. Five-thirty. He slipped his watch back into its pocket. He *had* been reading all day. It was definitely time to go home.

He still felt as if he hadn't accomplished anything in the entire eight and a half hours he'd been sitting there. He'd searched all his files. He'd had timid little Lottie search through all the files behind her desk in the waiting room and all of George's old files in the office Mr. Taylor was using—twice. He still hadn't found any additional papers regarding where all George's money had gone.

Worse yet, he'd been over George's will again and again, and he still came to the same conclusion every time. Emily's lawyers were correct. George had named his sister as Meggie's legal guardian. There was nothing he could do to change that. And there was nothing he could do to stop her from taking Meggie away from them.

Lord, how he was going to miss that little girl! he thought

as he stretched his long arms into his suit coat. You could grow pretty fond of another person in ten years.

It would be hard to imagine life without Meggie. She was such a lively little thing, always pulling shy Frannie into things that she never would have thought of getting into on her own.

Like this morning, he remembered with a smile. Oh, Frannie would readily go along with Meggie's plan, but she never would have had the gumption to think up a rotten trick like that to play on Miss Shaw by herself.

The smile faded from Ben's face and he frowned. It was a shame Miss Shaw had come to take Meggie away, and he might never see them again—either of them. What was Frannie going to do without her best friend? And what was he going to do with the rest of his life? There had to be a way to get Emily to let Meggie stay. For his daughter's sake, he told himself, he had to find that way.

Ben chuckled remembering just how perfectly Emily had fallen into their trap. He really had thought a city-bred lady like her would have been more wary. Had Emily really led so sheltered a life?

She was so light in his arms, even with her clothing bogged down with pig muck, as he had lifted her from that pigsty. She felt so soft held closely against his chest. For just a second the image flashed into his mind of Emily in her sheer lace-trimmed underthings held just as closely up against his bare chest as he reached up to untie the smooth, pink ribbon. . . .

Ben suddenly jerked himself out of his contemplation. He figured it was normal for him to feel upset with the thought of Meggie going away. But he realized that it was the idea of never seeing Emily again that really bothered him.

There was something left unfinished between them, Ben

felt certain. And there was more to it than just the unsettled argument about Meggie this morning.

It was the way he had felt when he helped her into and out of the wagon. It was the way he had touched her on the porch last night, and the way he had held her in that gosh-awful pigsty. It was the way he had felt when he had seen her in her soft silken underclothes.

He didn't even need to touch her to know that there was more to why he wanted Emily to stay than just the fact that he would miss his niece when she was gone.

Somehow, he had to convince Emily to stay in Iowa. Somehow he had to convince her that Iowa was a wonderful place to live—and to raise a child.

CHAPTER SIX

"MISS SHAW? EMILY?" BEN CALLED AS HE OPENED the door. "I've come to take you home—um, back to the farm."

Emily sat alone on the sofa in the parlor, watching the sky darken and the sliver of the new moon rise behind the big oak tree at the side of the house. She'd been feeling just a little melancholy, thinking of the good times her lively brother and his beautiful wife must have had in this house. What joy the birth of little Meggie must have brought to them. How sad to think it had all come to an end before its time.

"Hey, the house looks good," Ben said cheerfully as he stepped into the parlor.

She looked up at him, hoping that her mournful thoughts didn't show in her eyes. She didn't want him to know she was unhappy, especially when he sounded so happy. Why should he be? Had he found some means of repudiating her brother's will? Was he happy because he had found a way of taking Meggie away from her? That was nothing special. Mrs. Hannigan had already done that.

But Ben just stood there in the center of the parlor, nodding his approval. He never said a word about George or Meggie or the will.

The sparkle in his blue eyes was so charming, and the

smile on his face was so infectious, Emily decided, that she had no other choice but to lose her fears and smile back.

Maybe he had realized there was nothing he could do to stop her after all, and at least had the good grace to let them part with no hard feelings on either side. She thought that was a good idea. Somehow, the thought of leaving Bidewell, and of leaving Ben angry, was very disturbing. She quickly shook away the fleeting regret that leaving Ben at all was disturbing her.

"Good?" she repeated, trying very hard to make light of her melancholy thoughts. Her eyes were wide with disbelief, but the corners of her mouth curved in a smile. "You think the house looks good? Have you seen that kitchen?"

"Not lately."

"I was appalled!" She rose, as if, sitting down, she couldn't begin to show just how horrified she really was. "The other rooms might be dusty, but at least they're usable."

"Well, you know menfolk in the kitchen," Ben said with a laugh and a seemingly helpless shrug of his broad shoulders.

"Men? It looks like *bears* have been living in there! What in the world was George doing?"

"No, the place looks good, real good," Ben repeated, as if he hadn't heard her question—or as if he was ignoring it. Hooking his thumbs into the tops of his jeans, he circled the room, his head tilted up to examine the ceiling. "Have you been cleaning all afternoon?" He turned around and smiled directly at her.

She still couldn't figure out why he was so happy. Did he think she'd been doing this because she'd changed her mind about staying?

"No, of course not," she answered.

"Oh. What a shame," he said.

Emily detected a definite note of disappointment in his voice.

"After I cleared away what the kind ladies of Bidewell left this afternoon, I spent a few hours wandering around the house. Of course, there's only so much tidying and sorting and poking around in drawers and closets that a person can do without having to actually start cleaning, and I have no intention of—"

"But it looks like you did something," Ben insisted, moving past Emily toward the mantel.

Oh, what was it about this man, Emily silently demanded, that continually made him have to pass so close to her whenever he wanted to get by? Was it some miscalculation on her part that always put her between where Ben was and where he wanted to be?

He picked up several of the small picture frames and ran his fingers over the smooth, clean wood of the mantel. "You *have* been dusting," he accused with a short laugh.

"I found an old cloth in the kitchen," she admitted. "I came back in here, thinking I'd just finish up what we . . . what I started this morning."

Ben had replaced the clean picture frames and moved to the open window. "Well, let's get this window shut for the night. We wouldn't want any little furry critters paying you a visit, would we?" The narrow rope screeched against the small metal pulleys, and the wooden sash thunked against the sill as Ben lowered the window.

"I think quite a few little furry creatures have already set up housekeeping here," Emily said with a laugh.

"Hmmm." Ben's brows lowered over his eyes, and he rubbed his chin with exaggerated slowness, as if trying to impress Emily with how hard he was thinking. "Well, the way I see it, we'll have to get you a nice tabby or two to evict your furry houseguests."

"I don't intend to be here long enough to need—"

"Meggie sure likes cats," he added, giving her a meaningful nod.

Emily just smiled. She was too tired to get into a discussion with Ben about cats. Silently she decided that hiring the mouse-hunting tabby would have to be the next tenant's responsibility.

He pulled the draperies closed, then came back to stand beside Emily. "Weren't you listening to me?" he demanded.

He placed his feet apart and rested his knuckles on his hips, as if preparing for a confrontation. Then he took another step closer to her. His brow furrowed, but the charming twinkle remained in his blue eyes. His mischievous smile wasn't threatening, only teasing. Why, then, did her heart pound in her ears and her arms tingle at the very thought that he might touch her again?

"I warned you about too much cleaning."

"Yes, you did," Emily recalled. With a wry twist of her mouth, she also recalled that he had warned her about a few other things, too, such as his determination to take Meggie away from her.

Her body no longer tingled with the need to have him touch her again, but her heart still beat a heavy rhythm—not from excitement but from her apprehension that they would have to repeat this morning's argument again this afternoon. She took several steps back from him.

"So . . ." Ben said in a long, drawn-out voice. He took a step or two away from her, as if contact between them was something he, too, wanted to avoid. "So you're cleaning. You've decided to live in Bidewell after all?"

"No, not at all," Emily said quickly. "But, considering the state the law offices are in, I don't think Mr. Taylor or your secretary—or even you, Mr. Cameron—are going to find my brother's papers very quickly."

"We *are* trying, Miss Shaw," he assured her. His blue eyes appeared so earnest, how could she not believe him?

"I'm sure you are," she replied in a voice that shook just a little from his nearness and her own nervousness. "But since you won't be working on Sunday, to all intents and purposes, I'm stuck in Bidewell until at least Monday afternoon, *if* I can get a train out then."

"Is Bidewell so terrible a place that you're in such a hurry to leave?" He took a step closer to her again.

"Not really," she admitted. This time she did not back away.

"You know you can stay at the farm for as long as you need to," Ben said.

"Mr. Cameron—Ben. Please try to understand. I know your mother's been very kind, and I do appreciate it," Emily said. "But she probably wasn't expecting me to be here this long, either. I really can't impose on her for a prolonged stay."

"Ma doesn't mind having you," Ben insisted. "In fact, I think she enjoys having another woman around to talk to again."

Recalling her enthusiastic welcoming party, Emily smiled and said, "It looked to me as if your mother already has a lot of friends to talk to."

"Friends aren't the same as family," he said. He reached out to place his hand on her shoulder.

Her heart took a giant leap. She forced herself to remain standing—very, very still. What she really wanted to do was raise her hand to touch his strong arm and lean her head to the side so that her cheek brushed the back of his hand.

Instead, in a voice that sounded much too breathless for her liking, she reminded him, "I'm not family, Mr. Shaw."

"No? Well, of course, if *you* think you're not . . ." he said softly and dropped his hand back to his side.

Emily felt the intense need to move away from him again, before she did something incredibly stupid, like actually reaching out to take his hand and following through with her first impulse. "And since I'm stuck here, I might as well stay in a house I own—at least I own it for the time being," she added.

Why was she explaining this to him? He knew all about this, didn't he? As a matter of fact, she decided, he was probably the one who had engineered this entire scheme, just to keep Meggie here.

Ben pulled his watch from his pocket. "Well, look at the time! Are you ready? Ma's waiting supper, and Noah's waiting out in the buckboard, and I'm starving and can't wait!" He laughed at his own joke, a little too loudly to be truly enjoying himself.

"Is Noah still . . . you know . . . drunk?" Emily asked cautiously.

Ben chuckled. "What do you think?"

Emily didn't want to tell Ben what she really thought. Instead, she asked, "Is Noah driving?"

"He wasn't when I left him."

"I hope he hasn't changed his mind," she said with a little laugh to hide her nervousness.

"Oh, there's nothing to worry about when Noah takes the reins," Ben assured her. "It's Annabelle that really does the leading."

Emily nodded as she went out the front door. She had understood that from the first.

"Now, where are Meggie and Frannie?" Ben asked as he closed the front door behind them.

Emily sighed. "Meggie . . . well . . . right after school

she went over to talk about . . . her schoolwork with Mrs. Hannigan.''

Well, technically she wasn't lying. Mother had always taught her never to lie.

''Frannie stayed for a little food, then she, too, deserted me—for Mrs. Hannigan. I . . . I think they're both happier there,'' she reluctantly admitted.

''Well, I guess that's to be expected,'' he said philosophically. Was he really trying to comfort her? ''After all, they've known Mrs. Hannigan all their lives. Tell you what. Why don't you make yourself comfortable in the buckboard while I go fetch them home?''

Emily climbed onto the buckboard with Ben's help. For some reason, tonight, she didn't mind that he helped her. As a matter of fact, she secretly enjoyed the comforting feel of his strong hand on her arm.

She peered over the seat. Noah was curled up in the back on a pile of empty feed sacks. He was lying so still, Emily had to ask, ''Is he dead?''

''Sleeping.''

''How can you tell? It looks as if he's not even breathing.''

''Because if he were dead, he'd probably smell better.''

In spite of herself, Emily chuckled. ''Well, if you haven't been able to get coffee into him, I suppose sleep is the next best thing.''

Suddenly Noah began snoring peacefully. With this reassurance, Ben left Emily to find his runaway daughter and niece.

Emily didn't want to appear too curious, but she just *had* to know what Ben, Frannie, and Meggie were doing at Mrs. Hannigan's. She twisted around in the wagon seat. She watched Ben's long, muscular legs carry him over the lawns toward Mrs. Hannigan's house.

In the lowering twilight Emily saw Meggie and Frannie come dashing out of the house to throw themselves into Ben's arms. From the way Mrs. Hannigan came out of the house, Emily fully expected to see her do the same.

Instead, the pretty little widow sat in a long wicker sofa on the porch and patted the place beside her, inviting Ben to join her. Emily blinked with surprise when Ben actually sat down. Wasn't he the one who was so hungry? Wasn't he the one who didn't want to be late for Ma's supper?

Ben and Mrs. Hannigan began to have what was apparently a cozy little chat. Meggie and Frannie chased each other around the yard in the twilight, squealing with delight.

Emily turned to face forward. They all made a lovely little tableau of family life in the country, she thought with a sour twist of her lips. The only thing missing from the picture was a calico cat curled up in Mrs. Hannigan's lap, or a lazy hound dog sprawled out at Ben's feet—or maybe a big, friendly, black and white cow with limpid blue eyes standing right between them.

Noah's snoring grew louder. Emily's stomach began to growl. The sandwiches and cakes the ladies had brought had all been delicious, but that was a long time ago. Emily had been working hard and had not eaten anything since. What in the world was keeping Ben?

Emily continued to sit and wait. She glanced down at her watch. She was growing increasingly impatient. Why was getting home soon not so very important to Ben now?

Her curiosity overcame her caution and good manners. Emily turned again in her seat. She watched Mrs. Hannigan as she laid her hand lightly upon Ben's strong shoulder. No doubt she was saying just the right things to him, too, just like she had done for Meggie.

Not like me, Emily thought morosely. I'm always saying

the wrong thing and making not only Meggie but Ben angry with me as well.

Recalling bits and pieces of the ladies' conversation this afternoon, Emily wondered how long Ben's wife had been dead. How long had Mr. Hannigan been gone? She knew Mother would have scolded her if she had dared speak such unkind—not to mention lascivious—thoughts, but Emily couldn't help wonder just how cozy Ben and Mrs. Hannigan's chats had become.

On the other hand, Dolly had said that Ben hadn't been interested in another woman since Betty had died. On the other hand, Ben had seemed *very* interested from the way he had spoken to her on the porch. Obviously, Dolly was missing something important here.

Emily hadn't thought anyone could see her in the twilight, in the buckboard out by the road three houses down. In fact, she was counting on not being noticed. But Mrs. Hannigan saw her. She turned to Emily and waved to her enthusiastically, and continued to wave persistently until at last Emily waved back. All the while Mrs. Hannigan's other hand never left Ben's shoulder.

Oh, Emily could see her just fine—just the way she knew Mrs. Hannigan had wanted her to.

Frannie sat quietly at the supper table, eating her meal. She looked as if she wanted to say something—anything to break the awful silence enveloping the dining room like a dense gray cloud. But Emily knew Frannie wouldn't have much to say without her friend.

Meggie sat silently, slowly pushing her mashed turnips around in a circle on her plate.

"Don't play with your food, Meggie," Dolly said. "And for gosh sake's, eat something."

"Not hungry," Meggie mumbled.

Dolly shrugged and looked to Ben, who silently repeated her gesture. As a matter of fact, everything Ben did, he did silently, never taking his eyes from Noah.

Dolly recited apple recipes to Emily throughout the entire meal. She had to speak loudly to be heard over Noah's occasional snoring. After each one she added comments regarding which ingredient had been left out when the recipe was given to her, and how she had figured out what it was.

Emily had no idea there were so many things beside sauce and cider and pies that a person could do with an ordinary apple. While Dolly made everything sound delicious, Emily had the distinct impression that Dolly was reciting her lines without much interest. The real object of her concentration was Noah, sitting beside her at the table.

Leaning his elbow on the table beside his plate, and resting his chin in the palm of his hand, Noah had managed to prop himself up in front of his dinner plate. But he barely touched his ham or the aromatic cabbage. He only made holes with his fork in his mountainous pile of mashed turnips and sat there grinning vacuously into space.

Suddenly Noah snorted loudly. His elbow slipped and his face plummeted directly into his portion of fresh-made applesauce.

"Uncle Noah fell over again!" Meggie and Frannie cried with glee.

"Oh, consarnation!" Dolly grumbled. "I hate when this happens."

Giggling madly the whole time, Meggie and Frannie jumped up from their chairs and dashed around to Noah's side of the table. Each girl stood on one side of him. They seized his shoulders and hauled him upright again. The girls held him while Dolly wiped off his face with her apron.

Emily sat watching the entire episode with horror. How

could they take this as such a commonplace occurrence? How could they allow Meggie and Frannie not only to witness such sorry behavior, but to actually help Noah out of it?

Ben pushed back his empty plate and rose from the table. "I'll take him back, Ma," he offered.

"You'll stay with him?" Dolly asked.

Emily glimpsed the deep concern in her bright blue eyes. Maybe she had underestimated Mrs. Cameron.

"You know I will, Ma. C'mon, ol' boy," Ben said to his brother very loudly, as if trying to break through the heavy coating of alcohol that soaked his brother's brain.

Emily watched as Ben slipped his arm under Noah's and lifted him from his chair.

"I c'n mak' it m'self," Noah protested softly as Ben guided his brother's staggering feet over the polished hardwood floor and out the door.

Emily watched Meggie close the door after them. Ben was gone to spend the night watching over Noah.

After she and Dolly and the girls had cleared away supper, Emily went out onto the front porch. She needed to be alone in the darkness and the silence, just to be able to concentrate on finding a solution to the problems that had sprung themselves on her since her arrival in Bidewell.

The moon was bright through the clouds. There was a little chill to the air, but it was still very pleasant out.

Emily glanced over to the small house behind the barn—barely big enough to hold two rooms, but big enough for Noah, she guessed. Ben was over there, probably seeing to it that Noah got tucked into bed without another drink.

It was better that Ben stayed out there instead of in the same house with her. Tomorrow night she would be staying in George's house—a much better arrangement—much safer, certainly. Even though she was very angry with the man, whenever Ben was near her, no matter what else she tried to think about, all that insisted upon coming to mind was how much she wanted to touch him and how much she wanted to feel his arms around her.

On the other hand, she *did* want to talk to Ben. She needed to talk to him. Not in his law office, where the formal atmosphere came between them. And not in George's house, where raw emotions were likely to surface. She thought it might be easier to talk to him here on the farm, where things were peaceful and quiet. Maybe here she could keep him calm and make him see things her way.

"Morning, Aunt Emily," Meggie whispered. Frannie echoed her greeting just as softly.

Emily halted her progress into the kitchen. Was this some new trick they had thought up to play on her? She stood in the doorway, examining them all for signs that would give away the joke.

Ben sat silently at the table, sipping black coffee from a thick brown mug. He never said a word, but smiled his greeting and motioned for her to enter the kitchen.

"Morning," Dolly called softly from her place at the large black stove. "Pour yourself a cup of coffee and have a seat."

Dolly's whispered greeting gave Emily more hope that this was not a trick. Dolly would never take part in such a demented scheme, she felt certain. Or would she? After all, she was the one who had apparently organized her ill-fated little welcome-to-town party yesterday afternoon. And while Ben had not taken an active part in Meggie and Frannie's little pigsty trick yesterday morning, he hadn't done anything to prevent it, either. Maybe the whole family was crazy like that. Emily worried for Meggie even more.

"Flapjacks'll be ready in a minute," Dolly told her.

Pretending to be very, very surprised, Emily threw a teasing glance at Meggie. "What? No eggs for breakfast this morning?" she asked in a normal tone of voice.

"Shh!" they all hushed her.

"No, that's only for your *first* breakfast here," Meggie answered, again whispering. She leaned closer to Frannie, as if sharing a secret, and said in a voice much louder than the whisper she had used earlier, "First, and should have been *last*!"

"Do you have a sore throat, Meggie?" Emily asked. Although she was feeling fine, and still had her doubts that this was not some sort of a trick, she spoke in a whisper just like the others. "We could go into Bidewell. I'll bet Randall's Emporium sells horehound drops, and maybe we could get you—"

"No, I'm just fine!" Meggie asserted. "I'm only whispering 'cause Uncle Noah's sick."

"Oh." Emily wasn't surprised when Noah, red-eyed and disheveled, stumbled into the kitchen and collapsed into the chair beside Ben. Placing both elbows on the table, he rested his head in his hands.

Dolly placed a plateful of flapjacks in front of Emily. Emily looked to Noah and said, quietly, "I thought you'd be a pretty good carpenter. I had hoped you'd be willing to help me but . . . well, I guess asking you to help me today at George's house would be out of the question now."

Noah let out a low moan.

Dolly laughed without real humor and returned to her hot griddle.

What about getting Meggie to help? Emily wondered. She watched her niece dig into the tall stack of flat, golden-brown flapjacks oozing with molasses and melting butter that Dolly had just set down in front of her. Meggie would just as soon burn the house down with Emily in it as help her to tidy it up.

And Frannie? Well, if Meggie asked her, she would certainly be there to light the match.

''What about Ben?'' Dolly suggested. Her back was still turned to Emily as she continued to flip flapjack after flapjack off the griddle.

What about Ben? Emily wondered. She glanced over to him. His strong, callused hand was wrapped around the mug. In his faded denim jeans, and with his muscles showing through his red plaid flannel shirt, he looked just the man for the job.

He looked up from his plate to Emily. One eyebrow was raised as if he were waiting for an answer—or a question. He had certainly heard his mother volunteer his help, even whispering. The man wasn't deaf. But he only continued to sit there, eating flapjack after flapjack, as if he had heard that Dolly was intending not to make them ever again, and never said a word.

Well, if he couldn't volunteer, she wouldn't ask him, Emily decided stubbornly. She wouldn't give the awful man the satisfaction of even thinking she needed his help.

Determined not to give Ben a second thought, Emily ate her flapjacks.

''Dolly, are you sure there's no one I could hire to—''

Dolly spun around. ''You stop that talk right now,'' she ordered, shaking the spatula at her. ''That's what got you into trouble yesterday with the ladies—well, part of it. People round here don't go hiring nobody to do work they're perfectly able to do on their own.'' She turned back to her griddle and flipped the bubbling flapjacks over to brown on the other side.

''But I'd be willing to pay . . .''

Dolly's wrinkled lips were pressed into a deep frown. "You still don't understand, do you?"

Emily opened her mouth to speak. She could certainly understand if only someone would explain it to her.

"Is that the way you do it back East?" Dolly asked. "Always having to pay somebody to get your work done? Don't you have friends and neighbors you can call on?"

"Well . . ." Emily wasn't sure.

She supposed on the farms outside of town, and maybe in some neighborhoods, people all got together to accomplish some communal tasks. But Father had always paid workmen to do various jobs for him. And with Mother being an invalid, Father had few friends to the house—and Emily had had even fewer. Emily couldn't even begin to imagine her father's friends, wearing their black evening clothes and stiffly starched white shirts, with their big smelly cigars and silver-tipped canes, helping to clean a house or weed a flowerbed.

"No, not really," Emily answered.

Dolly sighed and shook her head. "Then maybe it would be better if you did go back to Baltimore . . ."

"Gramma!"

"Ma!"

Emily turned suddenly with surprise. She could not tell whose voice sounded more horrified—Meggie's or Ben's.

"I intend to, Mrs. Cameron," Emily said. She rose. "I guess I'd better get started, then. Thank you for your hospitality."

Before she reached the kitchen door, Emily stopped. She turned in the doorway. "I don't suppose I could get a ride into Bidewell."

"We'll take you into Bidewell," Meggie offered eagerly. "Won't we, Uncle Eb?"

Putting down his coffee cup, Ben rose and headed for the

door, passing close by Emily. He smelled of coffee and shaving soap. She drew in a deep breath, savoring the mixture.

''Sure, Meggie,'' Ben answered.

He placed his hand on her shoulder. Was he trying to push her out the door? Emily wondered.

''Come on, Miss Shaw,'' he said. ''We'll take you into town.''

''And leave her there,'' Meggie commented loudly to Frannie.

''Oh, you're staying there, too,'' Ben told her.

''In a pig's eye I am!''

''Just overnight,'' Ben suggested. ''Frannie could stay, too.''

Meggie and Frannie studied each other. Obviously, Frannie was waiting for Meggie's decision.

''Well, all right. But one night's all I can take,'' Meggie warned him.

''One night'll be enough,'' Ben agreed.

A wave of futility swept over Emily as she once again looked up at her brother's house. How in the world was she going to get this place looking good enough to sell all by herself?

Before she could turn around in the buckboard to ask for their help, Meggie and Frannie jumped down and escaped over to Mrs. Hannigan's house. Their little legs carried them over the browning, leaf-strewn grass as fast as they could go.

''Well, I suppose those two will be no help at all to me,'' Emily said to Ben as he came around to her side of the wagon.

''I'll talk to them . . .''

''No,'' Emily quickly refused his offer. ''Your mother

was right. I can't hire help for something I should be able to do myself. And if they won't volunteer, either, then I'd just as soon not have any of them." She glared directly at Ben.

"Suit yourself," he answered.

There was not a trace of guilty feeling in the man's voice. Well, of course not. The man didn't think he'd done anything wrong.

"I'll be right next door if you need me."

"Thank you," Emily answered because it was the polite response she had been taught to make. It certainly didn't mean she was going to need him. In fact, she'd make very certain she didn't.

Emily watched Ben from her own front walk as he disappeared into his house. She might have known he'd find something else to do—something that didn't include her.

Noah was apparently too hung over even to help himself get out of bed. Meggie and Frannie had deserted her. She believed she had even succeeded in alienating the crude but usually pleasant Dolly. Once Ben had closed the door to his own house next door, Emily felt truly alone. Not even the movement of the lace curtains in front windows up and down the street could alleviate her feelings of loneliness.

When she looked up at the big house so badly in need of whitewashing, and looked at the weed-strewn garden, she felt a sense of complete helplessness as well.

Emily pressed her lips together. She was *not* helpless. As much as she had doubted she could do it at first, she had made the train trip out here alone to get her niece. What other things might she be able to do on her own if she really set her mind to it?

Emily stood there, contemplating the house. It wouldn't take much to pull up a few of the weeds that had taken over the garden. Even if the house still needed painting, a neat garden might make the place look just a little more appealing to a prospective buyer. Ben had left his sturdy leather work gloves in the back of the buckboard, she remembered. She turned back to the wagon.

She hesitated. Ben hadn't been in a hurry to volunteer himself. Would he mind her requisitioning his gloves? Well, he wasn't using them, Emily decided. And if he had been so set against her using them, he should have stayed around to tell her so, shouldn't he? Of course he would have, she decided. She leaned over the side of the buckboard to pick up the gloves.

The leather was soft and pliant from much use. Emily turned them over and over, noting how the leather had already molded itself to the form of his hand. It wasn't very hard for her to imagine how the cool leather would turn warm when Ben's hands were in them. She almost did it—then stopped herself, with shock and horror at the strength of her own impulses—just before she placed the worn glove against her breast.

She drew in a deep breath as if to clear her head. Then she took several of the empty feed sacks that had, not long ago, served as Noah's pillow. She folded them over several times, then placed them under her knees as she knelt by the weedy little flower garden between her house and Ben's.

Weeding was definitely not the type of work that required a great deal of concentration, Emily decided. And from the direction she was facing, it was very easy for her to look up occasionally to either Ben's house or Mrs. Hannigan's.

No one came in or went out of Ben's house. If the buckboard wasn't still there, Emily might even believe he'd gone into town or back to the farm.

Emily could hear the sounds of the girls playing, but couldn't see them. They were probably in Mrs. Hannigan's backyard—with Mrs. Hannigan. Emily twisted her lips, wishing that the girls could find as much fun in being with her.

After a while, Emily looked down the row with pride. She hadn't been working that long, and already the flowerbed was looking much nicer. Of course, it would look even better if there were some nice chrysanthemums in there, to add a splash of color to the autumn garden, instead of all summer annuals, which died right after the first hard frost. And if she could get some daffodil bulbs and plant them before the frost hit, this spring she could have . . .

Emily stopped herself before her silly daydreams went too far. She would be back in Baltimore with Meggie, watching her own bright yellow daffodils and creamy white dogwoods bloom next spring.

"Ouch!" Emily yelled as something sharp bit into her ankle.

She turned quickly to see several fat hens scratching in the discarded grass and dirt behind her for whatever bugs she had unearthed with the weeds. But one silly biddy thought Emily's ankle looked like a tastier portion.

"Ouch! Stop that!" she yelled, shooing away the hen with a wave of her soft work glove.

But the stubborn fowl was not about to miss out on what she obviously considered delicious fare. She continued to peck at Emily's ankle.

Emily sprang to her feet. "Go away! Ouch! Go away!"

When she saw the glove was doing no good, Emily decided she had no other choice. With the toe of her shoe, she tried to nudge the persistent old biddy out of her garden, back into its own yard.

"How *dare* you!" Mrs. Hannigan shrieked with high-pitched indignation as she pounded down her front porch steps and began her trek across Ben's lawn. The blond braids she usually had wrapped around her head fairly bristled out behind her and her pale face had become pink with anger. "How dare you try to kill my chickens!"

Oh, just what I need! Emily thought with exasperation. *Two* cackling old biddies pecking at me.

CHAPTER SEVEN

"HOW DARE YOU TRY TO KILL MY CHICKENS!"

''Kill your chickens?'' Emily repeated, still sidestepping the aggressive hen. ''Ouch! What are you talking about?''

She didn't want to kill Mrs. Hannigan's—or anybody else's—chickens. In fact, after spending a good part of yesterday morning chasing all over the farmyard for an elusive egg, which didn't even actually exist, Emily didn't want to have anything to do with feathered creatures again for a long time.

''I saw you kick her!'' Mrs. Hannigan called angrily as she swiftly made her way across Ben's front yard.

''I only tried to push her out of the—ouch!'' Emily continued to try to dodge the chicken's sharp beak—unsuccessfully.

''Just who do you think you are, Miss Shaw?'' Mrs. Hannigan demanded.

''Well, I—ouch!''

''You come waltzing into town, thinking you can take over George's house, and buy people to do your work for you, and take our little Meggie away from the people who love her,'' Mrs. Hannigan accused.

She had come all the way across Ben's yard and now stood with the flowerbed safely between her and Emily. Hands on her hips, Mrs. Hannigan glared at her.

Emily tried to meet her gaze, glare for glare. It was hard to do when she had to keep dancing around, trying to avoid the persistent hen.

"And now you think you can abuse someone else's livestock!"

"Mrs. Hannigan," Emily tried to say in as calm a voice as she could muster while still suffering the occasional well-placed peck from the angry hen. "I was just minding my own business—ouch!—trying to weed the garden—"

"Well, that just shows how much *you* know. You can't weed the garden without expecting the hens for company." She turned to the chickens and, in a high-pitched, singsong voice, said, "You all just love your little bugs and worms. Don't you, girls?"

Emily recalled elderly Miss Vogt, who had lived next door to them when she was a child in Baltimore and who had talked to her little yellow pet canary, but Emily had never met a lady who talked to a flock of speckled chickens.

As useless as she felt it was going to be, Emily made one more attempt at reason. "Mrs. Hannigan, I—"

"Don't you know how to share, Miss Shaw?"

Without a moment's consideration Emily declared, "No, Mrs. Hannigan, I don't!"

She'd come to Bidewell for her niece, not for arguments. But since she'd been here, she'd already had three—in only two days. Enough was enough!

"This is my yard and I won't share it with your nasty chickens," Emily told her. "And if I see even one of them over here again, I'll just have to assume that you want to share them with me—and I'll have a nice big pot of chicken soup!"

Emily took a step forward, scattering the noisy hens.

"Oh!" Mrs. Hannigan, her arms outspread and flapping, quickly tried to gather up her wandering flock.

As she watched Mrs. Hannigan trying to herd all the squawking, flapping hens back to her own yard, Emily was struck with the woman's resemblance to the plump little chickens. She knelt down and, still chuckling softly to herself, continued her weeding. She couldn't resist looking up just once more to see how much progress Mrs. Hannigan had made across Ben's yard back to her own house, back where she belonged.

The smile fell from Emily's face. Mrs. Hannigan was standing there, talking to Ben. Well, not just talking, actually, Emily noticed as she watched. Mrs. Hannigan's pert little mouth was drawn up into a quivering bow, as if she were struggling mightily to keep her tears in check. Every now and then she would point in Emily's direction. Luckily, Emily always managed to lower her head before Ben looked over, just in time to pretend she was so absorbed with the weedy flowerbed that she couldn't be bothered with anything else.

Keeping her head down, Emily peeked up. Mrs. Hannigan covered her face with her hands. Her small shoulders began to shake.

Emily had very little experience with men, but she knew by intuition what would, without fail, bring out the protective instincts in a man—especially toward a woman he cared for very much.

She frowned and pressed her lips tightly together as she watched Ben envelop Mrs. Hannigan in his long, strong arms. Just to comfort her, she was sure he was telling himself.

Emily ground her teeth with disappointment. She had thought Ben intelligent. How could he fall for Mrs. Hannigan's tearful trick just as easily as she had fallen for Meggie's and Frannie's eggie one?

While he continued to comfort the weeping Mrs. Hannigan, Ben suddenly looked over to Emily. This time she was not quick enough to lower her gaze before she saw the look of disgust in his eyes—disgust for her!

Just how much of their argument had he seen? And how far from the truth was the version Mrs. Hannigan was telling him?

Ben had gone inside his own house when they'd first arrived. Best to leave Emily on her own for a while, he decided, even though he intended to keep an eye on her—just in case. That woman had a real knack for getting herself into trouble. But he'd wait, and watch. When she'd realized how much she really needed his help, maybe then she'd be ready to accept him.

He stood at the front window of the parlor, sipping black coffee from his thick white cup. He held the cup close to his face, savoring the warmth and aroma of the brew on this cool autumn morning.

He shook his head as he watched Emily bending over her dormant garden. Sure, he knew that the ladies all thought those bustles made them look so pretty. Personally, he thought they looked silly. Somewhere, under all that steel wire and cotton padding, there was the form he preferred—the form of a soft, pliant, and very real woman.

Ben watched Emily's bustle, and the soft derriere he knew was hidden beneath it, stuck up in the air as she knelt over her garden. He began to chuckle. She wiggled back and forth with the effort of yanking up the stubborn weeds. His blue eyes narrowed as his gaze became more intense as he mentally stripped away the unnecessary layers of clothing. His breathing became deeper and his grip tightened around the coffee cup. A warmth in the pit of his stomach intensified to match the heat of the cup in his hands. Or maybe, considering the way he felt just watching her, it was the heat of his body keeping the coffee hot.

Suddenly, from the corner of his eye, he spotted Iris Hannigan stomping across his lawn, heading directly for Emily. The smile faded from his lips.

No one had ever called him a coward, but he'd sooner eat live worms than get involved in a fight between two women. He'd watch from a distance, he decided. But he'd stay just close enough to be able to go for Doc Perkins, if he had to.

But Ben was in for quite a surprise. Of all the outcomes he had imagined for this situation—several of which included freely flowing blood—Iris scurrying off defeated wasn't one of them.

He put his coffee cup down on the windowsill and wandered over to look out the open front door, curious to see what would happen next.

Iris had herded her chickens halfway across his lawn when she spotted him in the open doorway.

Too late now, he thought. Now he'd have to go out onto the porch and walk down the front steps. Now he'd have to listen to her whining complaints.

"Oh, Ben!" she wailed. "What an awful woman she is!"

"Who?" He saw no harm in playing dumb just this once.

"Miss Shaw, of course."

"Oh. Do you really think she's so bad?"

"She tried to kill my chickens," Iris offered as evidence, as if that alone were enough to warrant Emily's immediate lynching. She looked up at him sadly with her big, round blue eyes. Tears were already welling up in them.

Darn, he wished she wouldn't do that! It was awful hard to be logical or tough with a woman weeping into her hankie right in front of you.

"I need my chickens, Ben. Without their eggs, how will I ever support myself?" she whimpered. Her full bottom lip started to quiver. "I'm just a poor, lonely widow, with nothing to call my own but my house and my chickens—and the lumber mill. I mean, it's not like I have a husband anymore to take care of me. . . ."

Suddenly she covered her face with her hands and began to emit loud wailing noises.

Oh, how did women know exactly what pitch to hit that would irritate a man's ears the most? Ben wondered. Since turning around and walking away would only further aggravate the situation, there was nothing else to do to protect his hearing but hold her in his arms—to muffle the sound.

Ben held his arms outstretched to Iris, who readily snuggled into his embrace. Yes, the sound of her piercing sobs, muffled by the fabric of his shirt, was a little less irritating. He raised his eyes heavenward with relief. Then he glanced over to where Emily still knelt, engrossed in her garden. He stifled a sigh. What a darn shame it wasn't Emily he was holding in his arms right now.

Of course, if it were Emily instead of Iris, he'd hold her much closer. He'd want to feel her soft, round breasts pressing against his chest. He'd press closer to her, too, so she'd have no doubts about his feelings for her. And she wouldn't be crying.

"I said, a poor widow like me has got no one else to look out for her," Iris repeated in a voice much louder than the first time she'd said it and Ben had missed it.

"Well . . . well, did you try to explain that to Miss Shaw?" he asked, a little befuddled at being snapped out of his forbidden daydreams so fast. He wasn't even sure that he was urging Iris to explain to Emily, but it seemed a safe thing to say, all things considered.

"I didn't get the chance. I was afraid she might come after *me* next."

Ben frowned. He was having a lot of trouble picturing Emily killing a bunch of chickens in cold blood, much less threatening Iris.

"She's just not . . . not very friendly," Irish complained. She pulled her handkerchief out of her sleeve and sniffled into it.

Ben didn't think too many people would be very friendly if they had been unjustly accused of the attempted murder of the neighborhood fowls.

"She didn't seem too happy when we all paid her a call yesterday afternoon. She's made no effort since to come see any of us," Iris continued to number Emily's sins. "She really doesn't neighbor much."

"Miss Shaw's not used to the way we do things around here. Just give her time," Ben suggested.

"Time?" Iris repeated. She lifted her head from Ben's chest and glared up at him. "She said she had come out here to get Meggie and then was going right back to . . . I don't know. Wherever it is she came from." She waved her hand around in the air like she didn't know—and really didn't care. "How much longer is this woman going to be here?"

Ben had no idea what answer to give her. If he said Miss Shaw would be staying for a while, Iris wouldn't be happy and he probably wasn't telling the truth. But to say that she was leaving as soon as possible—well, that was something he'd rather not think about.

"It still wouldn't hurt to be nice to her while she's here, would it?" Ben suggested. "I mean, then she'd go back to Baltimore telling everyone how nice the people of Bidewell are."

Iris eyed him skeptically. Oh, shoot! He didn't think she'd fall for that, but at least he'd tried.

Then, much to his surprise, she grudgingly agreed, "Well, I'm willing." She dabbed at the corners of her eyes with her handkerchief. ''After all, no one ever called *me* inhospitable.''

''I never heard them,'' Ben admitted with absolute truthfulness.

''But she really has to learn not to harm other people's valuable property.''

The corners of Ben's mouth pulled down in disgust. It was over and done with. Wouldn't Iris leave this matter alone? While she dabbed at her eyes again, he quickly looked over to Emily and was startled to find her staring back. Before he could change his expression, she turned away from him.

Too late, he told himself. Did Emily think his look of disgust was intended for her? He'd have to talk to her, explain things—and do it right away. He released his embrace and quickly backed away from Iris.

''Well, what if I talk to her about that?'' Ben volunteered. Not too eagerly, of course. He wouldn't want Iris, or anyone else, to start thinking something existed between Emily and him that really didn't. On the other hand, he did want to talk to Emily again. Alone. And not just about chickens.

Emily stood and brushed the brown pieces of dried leaves and dead grass from her skirt. To tell the truth, she hadn't tried very hard to stay neat. She was getting a strange kind of satisfaction from ruthlessly yanking up the dirt-covered roots of weeds, and probably a few flowers, too, to notice where her knees were. She was too busy mulling over the scene she'd just witnessed to bother much with where she was tossing her weeds.

''Emily,'' Ben said softly to get her attention.

The clump of weeds landed on the toe of his boot.

Emily looked up, surprised. She had been so engrossed in her task that she hadn't even heard him approach.

"Sorry if I startled you," he said. He grinned at her as he shook off the dirt. "Can we talk?"

Emily lifted her eyebrows with feigned surprise. "What about?" she asked in an unnaturally casual voice.

"Um . . ." Ben hemmed and hawed and finally suggested, "Chickens?"

Emily pursed her lips, then reluctantly rose. She drew the dirty work gloves from her hands. She held the gloves out to him.

"I hope you don't mind my borrowing them. I thought, since you weren't using them, *someone* ought to use them to get some work done around here."

"Not at all," Ben answered casually, even though the irritation in his pale blue eyes was clearly evident. Why did she have to be so darned independent-minded for a woman? he thought. When would she finally realize that she needed his help? He tucked the gloves into the back pocket of his jeans. "Now, about these chickens—"

"I hope you told her to keep her awful animals to herself." She picked nonchalantly at a few bits of dried grass still clinging to her skirt.

"No."

"Well, you should have. They don't belong on my property."

"You still can't go around threatening to kill other people's chickens," he reminded her.

"You really believe all the awful things she said about me, don't you?" Emily accused angrily.

"Well, not . . . I mean, I guess . . . Aw, Emily . . ." If he said no, then why was he here to talk to her? And if he said yes—oh, brother, was he in trouble!

"I might be city-bred and not understand a lot of the things that go on out here in the country," Emily said. "But at least give me credit for having some common sense!"

"I do, Emily," Ben said. "I do, but . . . you have to learn that, out here, people's animals are very important to them."

"People's animals are important to them in Baltimore, too, Mr. Cameron," she said coldly. "I don't come from a different planet, you know."

"Well, while you're here, would you at least try to be a little more . . . well, *tolerant* . . . of the chickens?"

Emily smiled with mock sweetness. "Certainly. It should be very easy, too, as I won't be here long at all."

Ben knew that. She'd made it clear again and again. But it still caused a certain ache when she brought it up to him one more time.

They stared at each other in silence for a moment. Then Emily said, "You know, it's not all *my* fault. Did Mrs. Hannigan also tell you that her awful birds tried to eat me?"

He held his mouth shut tight as he tried to stifle a laugh and ended up snorting through his nose instead. "I don't think there's much danger from that," he tried to point out as gently as possible and still keep from laughing. He coughed and rubbed his hand across his mouth to hide the next escaping laugh better than he had the first, but with even less success. "After all, I haven't seen the Wild West Show exhibit any man-eating chickens lately." He couldn't stop the full-blown laughter which burst from him.

"Oh, go ahead and laugh while I'm trying to be serious," Emily scolded. "Do chickens get hydrophobia? Look! I might even be bleeding!"

She was so upset, she didn't even stop to think of the consequences. She lifted her brown wool skirt just high enough to show Ben the damage that the silly chicken had done to her stocking, and the skin underneath, around the top of her shoe.

Balancing on one foot on the uneven grass, with the other

one lifted to better show her injuries, Emily began to teeter. Ben reached out to steady her at the same time she reached for him. She grasped his arm as he caught her and tumbled into his embrace.

"I'm sorry you got hurt, Emily," he said softly as he held her in the safety of his arms.

"So am I," she muttered crossly, still concentrating on her injuries. Then she looked up into his eyes.

He was too close, too strong and warm. He made her feel so dizzy standing near him that she thought she would fall all over again.

She made just the tiniest move away from him, but she felt his embrace tighten, drawing her ever closer to him, preventing her escape. It felt good to be this near to him—so good that she wondered why she had ever wanted to escape him in the first place.

She lifted her face to look into his eyes. His voice was soft and low, as light as a breath across her cheek as he held her in his arms.

"I don't want to see you hurt, Emily."

If he didn't want to see her hurt, why was he playing this awful game with her emotions? Why was she suddenly toying with the idea of staying just to be with him when she knew that Ben only wanted her to leave Meggie in Bidewell and then take herself far, far away?

Why was she letting him hold her like this right on her own front lawn? From behind the lace curtains in each front window, the eyes of every lady in Bidewell were probably fixed on them this very minute.

What would those ladies think? She should slap his face right now, shouldn't she? But somehow, when she thought of touching Ben's face, it wasn't with a swift, violent motion—and it wasn't with just her hand. How could she be having such feelings about a man she barely knew?

"I don't want to see *Meggie* hurt by all this," she replied. Slowly and very reluctantly she pushed herself away from his warm, broad chest. This time, to her disappointment, Ben didn't try to hold her.

She quickly stooped down and gathered up the feed sacks. She moved toward the house, hoping that Ben wouldn't follow. She felt more than just a little disappointed when he didn't.

"Chickens!" she grumbled as she shut the front door tightly behind her. Heaven forbid any of the miserable creatures should get into her house. Then that horrible Mrs. Hannigan might accuse her of kidnapping, too. And Ben would probably volunteer to serve as the prosecuting attorney.

"Men!"

She slammed the folded feed sacks down on the bench in the vestibule. She wasn't sure whether she was more upset with Mrs. Hannigan or with Ben. She didn't even want to have to think about it, because she already knew which choice she would make. Iris Hannigan she could ignore, and when she left Bidewell, she could forget her. With Ben, she knew she could do neither.

Either way, she was so upset, she couldn't just sit around. If she really did intend to stay here, even for a day or two, she had to do something about this house.

She peeked cautiously into the cluttered kitchen. With a slight shudder she decided that room could wait until last.

She did find the pantry, with its empty shelves, and a broom closet, complete with several long-unused aprons, a dried-out mop, and a well-worn broom.

She shook out an apron. Poor dear Sarah's apron. What a shame she wouldn't be using it again to tend to their cozy home. Emily tied the frayed and faded ribbons around her waist. Pushing up her sleeves, she set to work.

She looked into the parlor. The window was shut, and she couldn't open it again herself. The air would be almost unbreathable once she started moving the dust around, but she had no intention of calling on Ben to open the window for her. She'd rather suffocate than let that man think she needed him.

Instead, she went into the dining room. She straightened the chairs around the large cherrywood table. How could the dark red-brown wood have gotten so battered? How did the blue and white striped damask seats get so torn and stained? Why did the cushions smell like beer and dill pickles and—was that chocolate? Emily decided she really didn't want to know and went upstairs.

At least she could get several of the bedroom windows open by herself. She felt so pleased with her accomplishment that she began to rip the coverings off the beds to give the mattresses a good airing. She hung the stale sheets out the window.

She pushed down on the edge of the mattress. Well, it certainly wasn't as soft as her mattress at home. It wasn't even as soft as she would have expected to find in George's house, but it would do for a night's sleep—or two. It would have to. She just hoped she wouldn't be here much longer than that.

Emily looked around. There wasn't much more she could do up here. The only thing left was to go back downstairs and attack that kitchen.

The kitchen door unlocked easily enough, but the door screeched when she opened it. A puff of fresh autumn air blew bright gold and red leaves around the backyard, then gusted inside, chasing the stale, musty odors from the room.

She tested the pump at the large steel sink. With just a little encouragement the water began to flow clear and cool.

After pushing all the trash out the back door and stowing

it in the dustbin, She swept the floor and dusted off the large table in the center of the room. Now there was only one job left. No matter how disagreeable it might be, it was something that had to be done—and there was no one but Emily to do it.

She eyed the big black cast-iron stove that stood attached to the back wall of the house by a huge black pipe. The grate at the front of the stove seemed to be baring its teeth at her in a wicked snarl, challenging her to take him on. The four skewed lids lay like the half-opened eyes of some menacing black ogre, watching her to see if she would take up the terrible task. Emily had the eeriest feeling that if the stove weren't attached to the wall by the pipe, it would jump up and devour her, just like a ferocious monster suddenly unchained.

Slowly she knelt down in front of the stove.

"I can't believe it!" Meggie exclaimed from the back door. "She's really going to do it."

Frannie stood, silently shaking her head.

"Well, she fell for our egg trick," Meggie said. "How smart can she be?"

Frannie continued to shake her head in amazement.

Emily grasped the handle. She hoped, when she opened the oven, that no little furry things would jump out at her. Slowly she eased the door open. Metal grated loudly against metal, but at least nothing came scurrying out. Emily felt relieved that she hadn't had to jump back screaming and make an even bigger fool of herself in front of her niece than she already had. She hoped nothing dead was lying in the dark inside, just waiting for her to pull it out.

"I'm cleaning the stove, Meggie, so that you and I can have a nice dinner here tomorrow," Emily explained.

"*We*'re having Sunday dinner at Gramma's house," Meggie said.

Frannie nodded her confirmation.

Meggie eyed Emily cautiously as she came into the kitchen, followed by Frannie. ''We *always* have Sunday dinner at Gramma's house, right after church.''

''Always,'' Frannie echoed.

''Well, I'm not so sure that's a good idea right now,'' Emily said hesitantly.

''Why not? Gramma's a good cook,'' Meggie asserted. She perched herself atop the kitchen table and wrinkled up her little nose. ''Better than *you.*''

That most probably was true, Emily admitted to herself, but she'd never let Meggie know. That would hardly inspire much desire in the child to eat here with her.

''How do you know?'' Emily demanded with a feigned air of competence. ''You've never tasted anything I've cooked.''

''But I like having dinner with Frannie and Gramma and Uncle Noah and Uncle Eb,'' Meggie insisted.

But there weren't any drunken uncles at this house, Emily longed to point out. She wasn't sure what condition Noah would be in by Sunday, and she didn't want to take any chances on subjecting Meggie to Noah any more than she had to. She had to watch out for her niece's welfare.

There wasn't any Ben Cameron in this house, either, Emily added. She had to watch out for herself, too.

''They're my family,'' Meggie pointed out.

''Well, Meggie, I'm part of your family, and you're just going to have to get used to having dinner with me, too,'' Emily said.

Upset that, after all her efforts, Meggie was still reluctant to be with her, Emily stuck the broom into the oven with a little more force than she probably should have. Ashes and cinders flew out.

Meggie pursed her lips. She swung her legs out in front

of her and rocked back and forth. "You really intend to cook in there?"

"I do." Emily was very determined to succeed. She had to prove to Meggie—and to Ben—that she could make a good home all by herself.

"You really know how to cook, huh?"

"Do you like pot roast?" Emily asked.

"Sure. Is that what you do best?"

"Probably," Emily answered. Since it was the only thing she had even the faintest idea how to cook, it might very well be what she did best.

"Pa didn't do much cooking," Meggie said.

"I guess not. He didn't do much cleaning, either, did he?"

Emily poked the broom into the back of the oven again, trying to look very casual about her reputed cooking abilities. This time the broom refused to come out.

"Oh, no."

"Is it stuck?" Meggie asked. A smile slowly crept across her face.

"It certainly looks like it is."

Meggie looked at Frannie and nodded. "Yep. Same thing always used to happen to Pa, didn't it?"

"Sure did," Frannie agreed.

Emily turned and frowned skeptically at Meggie. "I thought you said he didn't cook much."

"Well, he didn't. Didn't clean the oven much, either. But when he did, the broom would always get stuck on something back there. Pa always said he was going to get around to fixing it, but I guess he won't now. . . ."

Meggie's voice trailed off. It was the first time since Emily had been here that she'd mentioned the fact that her father was no longer with them. Emily didn't want to make her niece any more sad than she already sounded, so she just continued to pull at the broom.

"That won't work. Only one way Pa could ever get it out," Meggie said, her voice still a bit hesitant at the mention of her father. "You got to stick your arm way, way back and unhook it."

"But my arm's not long enough," Emily protested. "I'll have to stick my whole head in. . . ."

"Nope." Meggie shook her head. "Ain't no other way to get it out."

"No other way," Frannie echoed.

"Trust me. I watched Pa do it lots of times. It's real easy—once you get in there."

Emily grimaced. What did she know about stoves and ovens and brooms? She took a deep breath and stuck her head into the dark mouth of the beastly black stove.

Reaching far back, she found the small, irregular hook in the cast iron that had caught the string that tied the bundle of broomstraws together. Meggie was right. It *was* easy to undo. She hadn't been trying to fool her after all. Maybe things between them were improving.

Emily began to back out of the oven.

"Ouch!" she cried as something scratched the back of her head. Briefly she wondered how in the world that nasty chicken had gotten into her stove. She laughed at her own silliness. Then ashes flew up her nose and down her throat, and she began to cough.

She tried to back out once again, but this time, whatever it was that had scratched her had now latched onto several curls and hairpins and held her fast. She couldn't go any farther into the oven or she'd bang her forehead against the back. She couldn't move backward without ripping her hair out. She was stuck.

"What's the matter, Aunt Emily?" Meggie asked.

"I'm . . . I'm stuck."

"You're kidding."

"Why would I joke about a thing like this? Do you think I enjoy having my head in the oven?" Emily demanded.

"You're really stuck. Really, really stuck!" Meggie was fairly whooping with glee.

Emily could hear the table thumping with what could only be the motion of Meggie bouncing up and down on it with a certain morbid excitement. Even without seeing her, Emily knew Frannie was also enjoying her predicament.

"Yes. My hairpins are caught on something, I think," Emily admitted. She was growing increasingly angry. "Now, you've got to tell me. How did your father get out of here?"

"I don't know. It was just the broom. *He* never got stuck in there." Meggie was laughing so hard that Emily was having trouble understanding her. "He . . . he never . . . never wore hairpins!"

Meggie laughed so hard, Emily heard her roll off the table. She fully expected to hear a second thump following, as Frannie usually imitated everything else that her cousin did.

"Meggie," Emily called sternly, hoping to snap her out of her silliness. "Get me out of here!"

"I don't know how, Aunt Emily," she gasped through her laughter. "Really, I don't!"

Emily tried to reach up behind her, but the oven wasn't large enough for her to move around in. She couldn't get her arms up and behind her to unhook herself.

"Help!" Emily began to cry out for anyone to hear. With her head encased in the thick cast-iron oven, all her cries for help were muffled. Meggie and Frannie were laughing so hard, Emily didn't think anyone would hear her above their noise anyway. And even if they heard her, who would come to her aid?

If Mrs. Hannigan knew Emily was stuck in the oven, she'd probably start looking for kindling.

And Ben? If he was in his own house, he couldn't hear her. Even if he did hear her, would he help her get out or help Mrs. Hannigan search for firewood?

She doubted that Noah would come staggering by. And if he did, in his condition, would he even be able to find the oven door, much less free her?

Emily certainly knew she couldn't count on Meggie or Frannie. Those two would push her farther into the oven, if they were ever able to stop laughing.

She really was stuck in this blasted oven. She wondered how long a person could go without food and water. How long would it take before someone found her desiccated corpse stuck in the oven and gave her a decent burial? Or would Ben Cameron make sure her body was shipped back to Baltimore, just to get her out of Bidewell for good?

Suddenly Ben's voice thundered through the kitchen. "What have you done now?"

Emily wasn't sure if he was scolding Meggie or her. All she knew was that she was kneeling here with her behind stuck out, and that Ben Cameron was getting a very different view of her from anything he'd ever seen before.

CHAPTER EIGHT

BEN ENTERED A VERY CHANGED KITCHEN FROM what he was used to at George's house. He couldn't decide if it was the fact that the room was now relatively clean, or if it was the two little girls rolling on the floor convulsed with laughter and the screaming lady with her head stuck in the oven that made the difference.

"Meggie, did Aunt Emily fall for another one of your tricks?" he demanded.

"No, no! We didn't play any tricks this time," Meggie said through her laughter. "I swear! Honest, Uncle Eb. Her hair's caught on something we can't reach."

"I'll bet you didn't try very hard, either, did you?"

Meggie just shrugged and gave him a hopelessly incompetent look. Then she poked Frannie in the ribs, and the two of them set to laughing again.

Ben grimaced and stepped over the two giggling little bodies. He stood beside Emily and tapped her on the back to get her attention.

"You can stop screaming now," he told her. "I'm here to help you."

"Get me out!"

"No, no! Leave her there!" Meggie cried.

"Can't do that, Meggie," Ben said. "All the noise she's making, she's liable to scare Mrs. Hannigan's chickens so bad they'll never lay another egg.'' He bent down over Emily. ''And we wouldn't want to disturb Mrs. Hannigan's chickens now, would we?''

''Very, very funny,'' Emily said dryly. ''If I had my way, those chickens would be in this oven with a couple of dumplings right now, instead of me. Now, get me out of here.''

Ben turned about, surveying the situation—not to mention appreciating the wonderful view he had of Emily's tiny waist and softly rounded behind.

''Get me out of here now!'' she insisted when he didn't move as fast as she apparently thought he should.

''My, my,'' he said, chuckling. ''Aren't we testy today? Especially for somebody who looks like she needs help pretty bad.''

''Get me out of here,'' she said in a much less demanding tone of voice. ''Please, Ben.''

''Well, since you said 'please' . . .''

He knelt down beside her. He took a deep breath. This wouldn't be so hard to do if he hadn't watched her kneeling in her garden and thought those wicked things about her. All those same notions came rushing back at him now, filling him with a desire to kneel beside her and do more than just unfasten her hair.

Meggie and Frannie had managed to control their laughter just long enough to get up from the floor and come to stand as close beside him as possible, the better to see what he was up to.

The opening into the oven wasn't that large. He had to press his body very close to Emily's. Trying to feel his way to where she was caught, Ben eased his fingers up her back and over the soft, smooth curve of her neck.

He couldn't reach far enough. Almost losing his balance,

Ben placed his hand on Emily's back for support and scooted closer to her on his knees.

''Sorry, Miss Shaw,'' he said.

Of course, he really wasn't sorry for being able to touch her soft, warm body once more—but he could hardly tell her that, could he?

Oh God, she felt good so close to him. He felt his jeans growing tighter. He turned his body to face the oven, away from Meggie and Frannie, whose curious little eyes were watching everything he did with great interest. He was glad Emily was caught and couldn't turn around to witness his embarrassing condition, specially since it was all her fault.

He brushed his fingers over the little tendrils of hair that had been torn loose from her hairpins. He fumbled around her ear and brushed his hand across her temple, almost poking her in the eye with his finger.

''No, no. I'm caught at the back of my head,'' Emily said.

''Sorry. I just can't seem to find where,'' Ben said. He was going to have to pay more attention to what his fingers were doing—and less attention to other parts of his body—if he was going to get Emily loose from here.

''Please get me out of here,'' Emily said. She coughed again. ''And hurry.''

Ben stretched farther. ''You really are stuck, you know.''

''I know,'' Emily responded wearily.

''Only one thing to do then,'' Meggie pronounced with an air of undisputed authority.

''Just one thing,'' Frannie agreed.

''Got to cut her hair off.''

''Only thing,'' Frannie said with a very emphatic nod.

''I'll go get Mrs. Hannigan's scissors,'' Meggie readily volunteered, already heading out of the kitchen door.

''Don't you dare!'' Emily cried from the black pit of the oven.

''Oh, don't worry, Aunt Emily,'' Meggie said. ''I know she'll be real happy to lend them.''

''I'll just bet she will,'' Emily grumbled from inside the oven.

Meggie and Frannie dashed out the door, intent on their peculiar mission of mercy.

''Don't worry,'' Ben said. He gave Emily's back a reassuring pat, trying to soothe her. But, oh, Lord, have mercy! How he wanted to run his hands up and down her back and cup her soft bottom in his hands, and press her close to him.

Calm down, Ben, he told himself. But right now his body was in no mood to listen to reason.

''I'll do my best to see that we don't need to cut,'' he promised her.

As if to prove that he was sincere, Ben grunted loudly with the effort it took to stretch his arm to the back of the stove. If only Emily could know that it took an even greater effort to keep himself calm while kneeling so close to her. Especially now that the children were gone, now that he and Emily were alone and he could allow himself to think freely about how good she felt to him—and what he'd like to do to her to make her feel this way.

''Darn!'' he cursed as he missed freeing her once again.

Emily coughed again. ''Please hurry,'' she pleaded. ''Before the girls come back with their scissors.''

''Don't worry,'' he repeated his reassurance to her. ''If they have to cut your hair, I'll make sure they only take off a little where it most likely won't show. Or maybe you can rearrange your hair some new way to cover the bald spot. Or if all else fails, buy a new hat.''

''That's what I like about you, Ben,'' Emily said. ''You're so resourceful.''

''I'm doing my best for you, Emily,'' he said. ''Because,

to tell the truth, I really don't care much for bald-headed women.''

She chuckled. ''Have you met many?''

''None that I cared to keep company with. At least, not for long,'' he answered.

Would she take that to mean that he might care to keep company with her as long as she kept all of her hair? Ben wondered as he continued to run his hands over her silky tresses, searching blindly for the snag.

He could imagine running his hands through her hair, released from its pins. Her face would be turned to his instead of hidden from him. Instead of kneeling in front of an oven, he would be stretched out beside her—and she naked and all atremble—in a giant featherbed.

He hoped Emily understood what he meant. His body certainly did.

''I'm sorry, but it can't be helped, Emily,'' he warned her. Then he laid his hand on her back and reached farther into the oven.

He could hear the sound of her breathing, and the wild thumping of her heart beating within her lovely little body. Ben pretended he was exerting himself a great deal and moaned audibly.

With this last stretch, Ben's fingers finally found the entrapped lock of hair. After a few more fumbles in the dark, he found the place where her curls had hooked onto the spur of iron and quickly freed her.

''Oh, thank heavens!'' Emily cried.

She backed out of the oven so quickly that her elbow just missed ramming Ben sharply in the groin.

''Oh, rats! She's loose!'' Meggie cried with disappointment. She stood in the doorway, a large pair of scissors dangling from her fingers. ''Aw, Uncle Eb, I still say you should've left her in there. Or at least given us a chance to use these.'' She brandished the scissors in front of her like a well-honed blade. Then she shrugged with disappointment. ''Oh, well. C'mon, Frannie.'' Meggie and Frannie turned around and headed outside again.

Emily drew in a deep breath of relief and sat back on her heels.

''Oh, thank you!'' she exclaimed. ''It's so good to be out of that oven.''

''And not a lock of hair is missing,'' he said, grinning at her proudly. Then his grin slowly faded as his eyes took on a deeper gleam. ''Glad I could be of help,'' he said softly.

Yes, he told himself, he certainly was glad he'd been able to help her, and at the same time get to touch her again. He was glad he'd been able to dodge her elbow, too. If not, in his condition, he'd have been singing soprano with Mrs. Robbins in the church choir tomorrow morning, instead of his usual baritone.

Emily raised her hands to her hair and began patting it back into place. Her dark hair was whitened by the ashes, which puffed out in little clouds and sifted down to her shoulders.

As Ben knelt before her, he couldn't help but smile. All her fussing wasn't doing her hair one bit of good, but the way she raised her arms sure made her breasts jiggle nicely.

''You look awful pretty like that,'' he said. He hoped his voice sounded gentle to her. Inside, he knew very well his voice was husky with pent-up longings.

''Pretty? You think I look pretty—now?'' She laughed a different kind of laugh. It wasn't the same kind she'd used before to show that she hadn't believed a word he said, or just to be polite. It was almost a young girl's giggle, as if she'd never been complimented like that before.

Ben nodded. He lifted his hand and smoothed his finger down the bridge of her nose, rubbing out a small streak of soot left there. He really didn't do much good, as her whole face was smudged with gray ashes.

His finger paused on the tip of her nose, then slowly moved across her cheek and down her slender jawline, erasing soot as he went along.

"I'm sure it does my complexion good to have my face smeared with ashes," Emily said. "I don't think I'll ever come clean."

"Sure you will," Ben said. He kept stroking her cheek with his thumb and wished he had the nerve to do more.

Oh, she probably thought he was rubbing off the soot. Without a mirror, how could she know her face was now fairly clean? Without being able to read his thoughts, how could she know that he was doing this just because he liked to touch her?

"As a matter of fact, I wouldn't be surprised if you couldn't clean yourself up real nice by tonight." As he spoke, Ben's blue eyes moved slowly up and down her figure.

Emily laughed. "Am I so dirty that you think it'll take that long just for me to make myself presentable?"

"No, no!" Ben answered quickly. He was glad to be talking with Emily when it didn't look as if their conversation was going to turn into an argument. He didn't want to risk saying anything that she might take as an insult. Lately, he seemed to be getting pretty good at saying the wrong things to women.

"The Lindstroms," he began. "Maybe you met the wife today. Nola?"

Emily nodded. "Who could forget Nola? And her pickles?"

"Every autumn they have this party," Ben explained. "Hire a couple of fiddlers to play and everything. All the ladies bring cakes or something. I thought maybe, if you'd like to come . . .''

''I . . . I don't really know any of these people, Ben,'' Emily said hesitantly. ''And the Lindstroms aren't expecting me. . . .''

''There's always room for one more at the Lindstroms'. Their place is pretty big.'' His blue eyes slowly swept her body. ''Anyway, you're such a little thing, you don't look like you'd take up much room.''

Just the space between him and the mattress when he was propped up on his elbows, he thought, was all the room she'd take. Yes, he bet she'd fit there real nice and comfortable.

His gaze drifted from her body up to her soft green eyes. He saw the little worries and uncertainties peeking through, and blushed when he thought of how he'd been dreaming of taking shameless advantage of her—and making sure she enjoyed it.

''Anyway,'' he continued with a shrug of his shoulders, ''as long as you have to be in town tonight, you might as well have some fun.''

''But I don't have anything to—''

''Oh, you don't have to worry about your dress,'' he interrupted quickly.

''Just like a man not to worry about his clothing, even for a party,'' Emily scolded with a little shake of her head. ''I did bring several extra dresses.''

''I know. I carried in your trunks—both of them.''

''But I still don't have a cake or anything else to bring.'' She gave a brief nod in the direction of the stove. ''I don't think this thing would cooperate with me so I could have something ready by tonight.''

''You don't have to worry about that. Ma's bringing her special cake. You can come along with us.''

''Us?'' Emily asked cautiously. It had seemed a harmless enough invitation at first. Suddenly she was viewing it with increasing dread, waiting to hear the rest of the guest list.

''Ma and the girls, Noah and me,'' Ben replied.

Knowing Noah would be coming in his sorry state was reason enough for her to hesitate. She held her breath, waiting for Ben to include Mrs. Hannigan's name. If she was coming with them, going to this party wasn't such a good idea after all.

She had to say something soon. Ben was kneeling there, smiling at her. His blue eyes danced with anticipation. Then, much to her relief, he never added another name to his list.

''Yes, thank you, Ben,'' she answered at last. ''I'd like to go very much.'' On an impulse she added, ''On one condition.''

Ben frowned. ''Meggie was right. I should have left you in the oven.''

Her eyes opened wide in shock.

''It might have kept you humble, so you wouldn't think you were in any position to make bargains with me,'' he finished with a grin. Then he eyed her skeptically. ''What's your condition?''

Emily couldn't imagine what possessed her to do it. Seeing him kneeling so near to her, she couldn't help herself. Maybe it was because she was grateful to him for having rescued her from the mouth of the black iron beast. Maybe it was the way the sunlight shone through the window onto his finely lined jaw and pale blue eyes. Maybe it was just because his body was close enough for her to touch and so she did. Emily reached out to lay her fingertips lightly on his cheek.

''Do you think you can get yourself cleaned up by then, too?'' she asked, brushing away a smudge.

Before she could move her hand away, Ben had reached

up to hold her fingers against his cheek. His blue eyes gazed into hers with such intensity that Emily was grateful the stove had no fuel in it, or he would have set it ablaze. His other hand moved up to rest on her shoulder. His gaze traveled down her cheek to her lips. Slowly, very slowly, Ben drew her closer to him.

"Uncle Eb! Uncle Eb!" Meggie cried as she fairly flew back into the kitchen. "Mrs. Hannigan needs you."

Ben released Emily's hand at the same time she pulled away from him. Picking up her broom, she turned and continued cleaning the large black stove.

"What's the matter with Mrs. Hannigan now?" Ben asked, still keeping his back to the girls. He loved his daughter and niece very much, but they had the worst darned timing!

"She sent us to tell you she needs some help with . . . some things," Meggie replied. She shrugged her little shoulders, as if all these adult concerns were too complicated for her young brain to worry about the details.

Ben reluctantly rose to his feet. Oh, Lord, have mercy! When a man was interrupted like that, what was he supposed to do to adjust his straining jeans? Either way he turned, someone was sure to see him. Thinking quickly, he began dusting his hands off on the front, then the seat, and then the front again of his jeans. He pulled his shirttail out of his jeans and wiped his hands on the edges. Safely covered, he breathed a little more easily. By the time he got to Iris's, he'd have calmed down enough to tuck his shirttail neatly back in.

"Oh, all right," he answered wearily. "Tell her I'll be right there."

Ben turned to Emily, still kneeling at his feet. He reached down and brushed away one last little smudge on her forehead that he had missed before. "I'm looking forward to this evening," he whispered. Then he moved away.

"Oh, yeah, Aunt Emily . . ." Meggie turned back as an

afterthought. "Mrs. Hannigan says she'd be real happy to lend her scissors again any time to cut your hair."

"Or my throat," Emily muttered.

Emily started a fire in the big black stove. She pumped up several pots of water from the sink and heated them. Then she quickly bathed off all the grime from her encounter with the now tamed stove.

Ben, assisted by Meggie and Frannie, brought her trunks from the farm to George's house. They also brought enough things of Meggie's for a few days' stay, and of Frannie's just for overnight.

Meggie clomped up the stairs and, completely bypassing the room Emily had chosen, stormed into her old bedroom. She plopped into the chair by the window and glared out at the gold leaves, which fluttered a last wild dance before falling to earth.

Frannie, on the other hand, was constantly underfoot. She flitted back and forth between several of Emily's large, drumlike hatboxes and the first large black trunk.

Burdened under the last of Emily's trunks, Ben couldn't see where he was going, and Frannie was paying no attention at all to where she was going.

"Shoot, Frannie!" Ben declared as he stumbled into her. "Are you all right? One of us is going to get hurt. Make yourself scarce, girl!"

Frannie darted across the hall to Meggie's room.

"There's the last of it," Ben said as he lowered the trunk to the floor.

Emily watched the way the muscles of his back strained through the shirt, and the way his jeans rode his slim hips, and the way the denim conformed to his narrow buttocks.

He turned to face her before she could move her eyes to

some less tempting view. ''If there's anything else you need . . .''

I need to touch you again, Emily thought. She wanted to touch him so badly her fingers ached.

She was so shocked by her own sudden, impulsive longing that she turned quickly from him to begin toying with the strings of one of her hatboxes. She could feel the hot flush rising up her cheeks and hoped that Ben couldn't see it.

''No, nothing right now,'' she answered in a voice that shook from her sudden passion and her own surprise that she would experience these feelings so acutely. ''You've done enough . . . been very helpful, I mean.''

Instead of untying quickly and easily when she pulled one end, the darned strings twisted into an impossible knot. She picked at it for a bit, even though she knew the effort was futile. Still, it gave her a chance to calm down.

Feeling more composed, she was able to face him again. ''Thank you very much, Ben. And thank you for bringing Meggie's things, too. I know she didn't want to come.''

He opened his mouth to say something. Before he could utter the dread thought that she knew he was thinking, Emily quickly acknowledged, ''And I know you didn't want to bring her. That's why it was especially kind of you to allow your daughter to stay with Meggie. Sort of ease the transition, you know. . . .''

Ben nodded. ''I want to make it easy on Meggie.'' He glanced down at the floor, as if reluctant to say what he was thinking. ''I want to make it easy on you too, Emily.''

''Easy for me?'' she repeated, frowning. ''You've fought me every inch of the way. When did you decide you wanted to make this easy for me?''

''Well, let's say less painful then.''

"Less painful?" That phrase was no better. "You still think I can't do this, don't you?"

"It's not that. But it's not easy raising a ten-year-old. Or an eight-year-old, or even a two-year-old," he warned her. He grinned, as if remembering the things that had made Frannie's upbringing difficult and finding that they weren't so terrible now after all. "Of course, I don't have any firsthand experience beyond ten, but, remembering Sarah growing up, I don't suppose twelve or fourteen is any easier, either."

Emily's eyes narrowed. She nodded with the dawning realization of what Ben was up to. She could feel her cheeks begin to flush again, not from desire for Ben, but from her growing anger. Her voice was growing louder and rising in pitch.

"You think after having these two for a few days, I won't want to take Meggie back with me. That's it, isn't it?" she demanded.

"That's not it, either, Emily," Ben protested. "I just think you need to . . . to give it a little more thought before you go running off—"

"I am *not* running off!"

"You know what I mean."

"Yes, I do," she said.

She understood Ben very well. Why couldn't she understand herself as easily? she wondered. One minute she could hardly restrain herself from running her hands all over the man's body. The next, she couldn't wait to punch him in the face. Why did he have this power to upset her entire world? And why didn't she have more ability to resist him?

"We've been over this before. I thought you'd accepted this. But one way or another, I *am* taking Meggie . . ."

Suddenly she stopped. She drew in a deep breath and

deliberately tried to lower her voice. She wouldn't want Meggie and Frannie to hear her yelling like a fishwife.

"I don't really want to argue with you, Ben," she said. To her own relief, she found she sounded much calmer.

Then he took a step closer and said softly, "I don't want to argue with you, either."

Quickly she backed away from him. It was bad enough that she was having these feelings about him just looking at him from across the room. Heaven only knew what might happen if he came too close in this bedroom. She might forget all her proper upbringing and good intentions.

"You have helped me a lot today, Ben," she said hesitantly. "And I'm very grateful. And I wouldn't want to spoil the party you were kind enough to invite me to tonight. Why don't we . . . see if we can declare a truce?"

She looked up at him hopefully.

Ben grinned. "Sure. We'll see if you can stop yelling at me for twenty-four hours."

"If *I* can stop screaming?" she repeated, very loudly. "Why don't we see if you can stop doing things to irritate me?"

Suddenly Ben began to laugh. "I think I'm on my way to winning already."

"Don't count your chickens before they're hatched, Mr. Cameron," she warned him in a much more quiet tone of voice, just to avoid further trouble.

"I won't. I've seen what you do to chickens." Ben smirked back at her. "Why don't you let me help you open the trunks. That could be a good start to our truce."

"All right," Emily agreed.

Ben unlatched the large brass clasps on the black leather straps. At the sound of the snap Frannie appeared in the doorway. Apparently, her curiosity had gotten the better of her. Still, Meggie had not appeared.

Frannie ran back to Meggie's room and called, "Meggie! Meggie, you're going to miss it."

She got no reply.

Ben flipped open the heavy lid, to be confronted with several layers of soft, silky pink things. He knew there were several layers there because he could see straight through the top one.

"Oh, I think you can handle this on your own now," he said, backing away. No one had ever called him a coward, but the way he felt about Emily, he wasn't sure he could trust himself. Knowing that what he was looking at had identical counterparts under what Emily now wore, he didn't want to stay around long enough to prove himself right.

"See ya, Pa," Frannie called after Ben as he descended the stairs. She'd never figure out grown-ups. Pa always told her don't run down the stairs or you'll fall and break your neck—and there he was, doing just what he had told her not to.

Frannie hurried into Meggie's room.

"Come *on*! She's unpacking now," Frannie announced. "You should see this stuff!"

"I've seen her things," Meggie mumbled. She even refused to look at her best friend. "Nothing special."

"No, not all of it," Frannie hesitated. "She's got two big trunks. Gramma ain't never had that many things to wear in her whole life. Or Mrs. Hannigan. Or maybe even Mrs. Lindstrom."

"Sure they have."

"Not all in one place," Frannie said. "C'mon and see." She reached out to grab her cousin's hand, but Meggie pulled away.

"I'll see more than enough of her things when she takes me away to go live with her," Meggie said gloomily. "I don't need to see it now."

"Suit yourself." Frannie gave in a with a shrug of her

little shoulders. "I'm going." She ran back into Emily's bedroom—quickly, so she wouldn't miss anything else.

"Traitor!" Meggie mumbled angrily.

Frannie was very interested in rummaging through Emily's personal belongings. She held her gold and pearl earrings up to her own small pink ears and peered at herself in the mirror above the recently dusted dresser. She tried on the gloves, so big for her little hands that the fingers flapped loosely every time she wiggled them.

Emily couldn't help but laugh at her enthusiastic antics. Encouraged by Emily's reaction, Frannie found herself lifting hats from their boxes, putting them on her head, and strutting around the room like a grand lady.

Emily unfolded her dresses, skirts, and jackets onto the lumpy featherbed. What in the world was she going to wear to this party? She wanted to make a better impression on the ladies than her first one. Even more, she wanted to look especially nice for Ben.

She had always dressed nicely because—well, because it was the proper thing to do. Father could easily afford it. Mother had insisted upon it, even though they rarely had visitors. Emily found it an odd and certainly very pleasant notion that she was actually worried about dressing to please a man—a particular man. A particularly handsome man.

He'd seen her grimy from train travel and covered in pig muck. He'd also seen her when she was barely dressed at all, she recalled with a slight blush. She needed to wear a special dress to make herself look elegant when Ben whirled her around the dance floor. She wished she'd brought some of the other, truly nice gowns still hanging in her wardrobe at home. Oh, well, she'd have to make do with what she had.

Frannie had settled down cross-legged on the floor in front of the bed, quietly watching.

From the corner of her eye Emily noted Meggie, lingering

in the doorway, apparently drawn by Frannie and Emily's laughter.

"Well, what will it be?" Emily asked. She held up her two evening gowns, hoping to get a helpful opinion. Even though the girls didn't appear to know much about fashion, she hoped this might be a good way to try again to become friends with her niece. She held a pale green satin gown under her chin and turned around in front of them. "Which one do you like best?"

"Well, it's really nice," Frannie began, "but nobody—"

"She means it's really nice, Aunt Emily," Meggie said, poking her cousin in the ribs as she took a seat beside her on the floor. "But nobody would pass up that other one . . . wow!"

"This one?" Emily asked. She carefully laid the green gown back on the bed and picked up a much more elaborate gown of royal blue velvet.

"Oh, yes!" Meggie exclaimed. "That's the one!"

"Yes, that one," Frannie chimed in.

Emily frowned. "Do you really think . . . ?" She stopped herself in midsentence. Meggie was actually showing a friendly interest in her. She didn't want to do anything that might spoil this new, and favorable, way in which Meggie was responding to her.

"Oh, yes."

"It's not too heavy for this time of year?" she asked.

"No, no," Frannie said, apparently caught up in the festive spirit of preparing for the party. "The Lindstroms' big old ba—"

"Ballroom." Meggie cut Frannie off short with another poke in the ribs. "The Lindstroms' big old ballroom is always drafty and cold," she continued. "This'll be perfect."

Emily held the dress up under her chin and measured with her hand approximately how far down her bosom the neckline came. After all, if she'd be dancing with Ben, she had to figure out just how much of her she should show. Of course, even by accident, he'd already seen quite a lot.

"But, it's not too . . . daring, for the country?" Emily wondered aloud.

"Oh, no," Meggie said again. "As a matter of fact, I wouldn't be surprised if that wasn't the prettiest gown there tonight."

"I mean, I wouldn't want to dress inappropriately," Emily continued, still unsure. "And embarrass myself."

"Oh, don't worry, Aunt Emily. We wouldn't dream of letting you do that to yourself."

"Of course not," Frannie agreed.

"I don't even know why I packed this," Emily said, more to herself than to the girls. "I don't usually wear such low-cut gowns."

"It's just perfect," Meggie insisted. "See, this way, even if it's chilly in the ballroom, once you start into dancing, and get to sweating . . ."

"Meggie, a lady never sweats," Emily quickly corrected her.

"Right, Aunt Emily. And they don't whistle, neither."

"Emily!" Ben exclaimed when she greeted him at the door.

The soft fuzz of the dark blue velvet made a sharp contrast to the smooth whiteness of her breasts. The dress was cut so low, Ben could see almost all of the creamy fullness that he still pictured in his mind as he lay in bed alone at night, and daydreamed about most of the day, too.

"Is that what you're wearing to the dance?"

"Don't you like it?" she asked. The bright smile quickly fled from her face.

Ben's mouth opened and closed a few times with no sound coming out, like a fish out of water gasping for oxygen. "I like it," he finally said. "I like it a lot. But . . . but, well, aren't you going to be cold in that?"

"Meggie and Frannie said it was—"

Ben grinned and nodded his head. "Yeah. I should've known they'd think it was a wonderful gown for tonight."

"Don't you?"

Ben gave just a tiny little chuckle. "Oh, Emily, I think it's a wonderful gown for *any* night."

The beaming smile returned to Emily's face. As she moved toward the door, Ben picked up her wrap from the bench and placed it about her shoulders. Taking her by the hand, he led her down the rickety front porch steps and the uneven brick path to the waiting buckboard.

Ben's hands were warm and strong. The path wasn't that bumpy, and it wasn't so dark out that she couldn't see her way. Still, it felt good to have him take care of her.

It was going to be a wonderful evening, she just knew it. She felt that Meggie, and even shy little Frannie, in spite of their silliness this afternoon, had become much friendlier to her when sorting through her gowns.

Ben was more pleasant to be with, too—now that they had called this uneasy truce. She was looking forward to dancing with him, just a dance or two. She wouldn't mind being close to him again, swaying their bodies in time to the rhythm of the music, even if it was in a brightly lit ballroom with a crowd of people gathered around. She was really looking forward to feeling his strong arms wrapped around her again, and not just carrying her out of a pigsty!

When she looked at the seat of the buckboard, she felt a glimmer of concern. A rough wooden bench wouldn't do her velvet skirt any good. And what kind of party were they going to, anyway, that they would go in a buckboard? Although, as she recalled, she hadn't seen a carriage in their yard. Maybe they didn't own one. After all, they were just plain farmers.

She allowed Ben to help her up. Dolly was sitting at the other end of the bench, carefully balancing a cake on a plate on her lap. Emily gave her a cheerful smile as she sat down.

"Ya look real . . . fancy," Dolly said.

"Thank you," Emily answered. She couldn't see Dolly's gown under the voluminous shawl the elderly lady wore. "You look very nice, too," she responded anyway.

Dolly just nodded. "Is that what all the ladies back East are wearing?"

"Well, yes. Yes, it is."

Dolly nodded again. "I figured."

Noah and the girls were sitting in the rear of the buckboard. It was too dark to see them, but she could hear them swinging their legs off the back, and singing just as loudly as they could. "Oh, Buffalo gals, won't you come out tonight, come out tonight, come out tonight?" What they lacked in talent, they made up for in enthusiasm—and volume.

Ben's firm thigh pressed against Emily's as they bounced along toward the Lindstroms'. There was no chance of getting away from him this time, Emily thought. She could hardly move over and push Dolly off the seat, could she? And, to tell the truth, she really didn't want to get away from the firm warmth of his body.

The Lindstroms' brightly lit farmhouse looked so cheerful, Emily began to feel a little foolish for the nervousness and uncertainty that had been creeping over her the closer they came to the party. But when Ben drove the wagon past the house and around to the barn at the back, Emily's mouth began to gape just as Ben's had done earlier when he first saw her at the door.

"It's in a barn," Emily stated.

CHAPTER NINE

"WELL, OF COURSE IT'S IN A BARN. WHERE ELSE would a dance be?'' Dolly demanded.

Emily didn't know who to glare at first—Ben or Meggie. What in the world was she going to do with her satin dancing pumps on a dirt floor strewn with straw and hay and who knew what else? How would her blue velvet gown fare with all the chips of straw floating through the air? And how could she bear the sharpness of the various animal aromas that were sure to be wafting from the stalls?

''No one told me it was in a barn,'' she said very slowly, so that neither Ben nor Meggie would think they had fooled her once again.

''Well, I thought you'd have enough sense to figure that much out on your own,'' Ben said with a chuckle, as if he were really surprised that she hadn't. Not for one minute did Emily actually believe that he was. ''After all, there's no other place in Bidewell big enough to hold this kind of party except a barn.''

Emily understood the logic behind his words, but she still glared at him. She'd never been to Bidewell before. *Somebody* should have told her.

Ben jumped down from the buckboard quickly, as if trying to get out of range before she took a swing at him—and oh, she was sorely tempted. What was he trying to do? Embarrass her so much in front of everyone that she'd quit Bidewell in such a rush that she'd leave Meggie behind?

Ben tied Annabelle's reins to the long pole set on two shorter posts that served as a hitching rail in front of the barn. Then he came around to the other side of the wagon to help Dolly with her cake.

"Here, hold this, please," Dolly said. Before Emily could respond, she thrust the heavy cake plate into her hands, then let Ben help her down.

Afraid to rest the plate on her velvet skirt, Emily held the cake at arms' length and prayed she'd have the strength to hold it up while the elderly Dolly took her time creeping down from the wagon seat.

"I'll take that now," Ben said, reaching up for the plate.

Emily's fingers itched with the urge to push the whole thing in his face. It would serve him right for not warning her about the barn. On the other hand, the Lindstroms were probably counting on Dolly's good baking to provide some of the refreshments, and this was supposed to be partly her contribution, too. Emily didn't want to appear an inappreciative guest. She handed the plate to Ben. He handed it back to Dolly, then helped Emily down.

She was angry with him. Why was she looking for him to place both of his hands around her waist and help her down that way? And why was she so disappointed when he only held out his hand for her to take?

Once Emily had both feet on the ground, Ben turned back to Dolly and offered, "Let me carry that for you, Ma."

Dolly clutched the cake to her as if it were her favorite child and Ben was the hangman.

"Not on your life," she said. "I know ya still like to lick the frosting off where ya think it won't show."

Ben stared at his mother. His eyes were wide with

pretended guilt, but deep inside, Emily could still see the mischief in his eyes.

"Oh, don't play Mr. Innocent with me," Dolly scolded. "And ya always thought I didn't know."

"Never could put one over on you, Ma," Ben said with a laugh.

Then Dolly leaned a bit closer to him and whispered, "Better make sure he don't go wandering off." With a nod of her head she indicated Noah, already sauntering across the farmyard at rapidly changing angles.

"Come with me, Emily," Dolly offered. "After all, it might do ya some good to talk recipes and housekeeping with the womenfolk."

It hadn't done her much good yesterday afternoon, Emily thought. She didn't believe it would do her any good now, either, especially since she didn't have much to offer on the subject. Still, Ben was off taking care of Noah, and Meggie and Frannie had pursuits of their own. There really wasn't much else Emily could do right now but follow Dolly toward the large red barn.

Emily almost gasped when they entered. The Lindstroms had cleaned it so well—why, it hardly smelled like a barn at all. The center of the floor had been swept and scrubbed until the grain of the wood stood out plainly. A score of lanterns hanging at equal intervals from the rafters lighted the dance floor. The bales of hay set around against the walls provided a touch of rustic comfort for weary dancers or those who would rather talk and eat than dance.

It wasn't so much being in a barn that disturbed Emily anymore. As a matter of fact, it sort of reminded her of Grandmama's old barn, she thought wistfully. It was the people here and what they wore that bothered Emily the most. Amidst the colorful array of calicos and ginghams, along with varying shades of blue denim and nutbrown wools, there was not a silk or satin or velvet in the crowd.

Emily turned to Meggie and, in a hoarse whisper, demanded, "Why didn't you tell me this afternoon that this dress was all wrong?"

"Well, shoot, Aunt Emily," Meggie answered. "I'm just a little girl. What do I know about what grown-ups wear?"

She tugged at one of Frannie's plaits. Their mischief apparently successfully accomplished, the two headed for the refreshment table at the other side of the barn. They wandered up and down in front of it, eyeing all the good things there.

Emily pressed her lips together with exasperation. Meggie had tricked her again, deliberately. Would she ever succeed in winning her niece's affection—or should she just stop trying? Maybe if she learned to make cookies like Mrs. Hannigan—or drink and build boats like Noah—or chew tobacco and spit like Dolly?

Emily trailed along as Dolly made her way through the crowd to the refreshments. Long planks had been laid across sawhorses. Bright red and white checkered cloths covered the rough wood, but there were so many pies, cakes, tarts, and cookies set out that Emily could barely see the top of the cloth anyway. There was barely room to squeeze Dolly's cake in.

Darn, Emily thought. I could have pushed that cake into Ben's face, and no one would have missed it after all!

"Looks mighty tasty," Mrs. Robbins said as Dolly set her cake down among the many others. She spoke to Dolly, but she never took her eyes off Emily in her blue velvet gown. "That's some gown you got there, Miss Shaw."

"Thank you," Emily replied. At least, she thought what she had heard was a compliment.

"And don't you look . . . well, like a splendid little peacock," Mrs. Hannigan said. Her voice oozed like honey, yet all the while Emily could detect the venom seething underneath.

Emily returned her smile with equal sweetness and replied, "Well, no, this isn't peacock. Actually, this shade is called royal blue."

Through narrowed eyes Mrs. Hannigan looked Emily up and down. "Somehow, I thought that's what you'd call it." She quickly changed her tone when she noticed Ben approaching. She turned as if Emily had never even been there. "Why, hello, Ben. Noah."

Noah opened his mouth to greet them but emitted a loud belch instead.

Emily hoped the ladies might think she just happened to be passing by when Noah arrived and wasn't actually here in his company.

"Evening, ladies," Ben said as he guided Noah toward the table. "They told us we could get something sweet here. I thought they were talking about the cakes till I saw all you fine-looking ladies."

Mrs. Robbins giggled and her little brown eyes began to sparkle. "Say hello to Ben, Pearl," Mrs. Robbins commanded. She prodded the short plump girl at her side.

Pearl—a pale imitation of her mother—only giggled. She clenched her yellow gingham skirt tightly in her hands and swung it back and forth at her sides.

The other ladies weren't quite as obvious as Mrs. Robbins, but their appreciation of Ben was still evident.

"What can we offer you, Ben?" Mrs. Hannigan asked.

"Oh, nothing for me, thanks," he answered. "But I thought a piece of cake and a nice hot cup of strong black coffee might be just what Noah needs tonight."

Emily pursed her lips and gave her head an imperceptible shake. She was a woman. She didn't need an interpreter to know exactly what Mrs. Hannigan had in mind to offer Ben, even though he seemed pretty dense about it. Emily couldn't believe for one moment that he was deliberately ignoring her not so subtle invitation.

"I didn't come to eat," Ben continued. Much to Emily's surprise, he turned to extend his hand to her. "I thought I might be doing some dancing tonight."

"Mrs. Hannigan! Mrs. Hannigan!" Meggie and Frannie cried in unison.

Frannie snatched her father's outstretched arm away from Emily's grasp. She began to coax him closer to the center of the barn, where they had cleared a large space for dancing. Ben apparently was having trouble deciding in which direction he wanted to go and kept tripping over his own feet as his daughter pulled him along.

Meggie reached for Mrs. Hannigan and began to pull her toward Ben. "C'mon, c'mon. Uncle Eb wants to dance with you!" she declared.

Maybe to any casual observer it looked as if Meggie were pulling a shy Mrs. Hannigan, Emily thought. In reality, anyone could plainly see that Mrs. Hannigan needed no coaxing to take Emily's place at standing close to Ben while swaying back and forth in time to the music.

Who could blame her? Emily thought. She hardly would have said no herself.

The two fiddlers that the Lindstroms had hired were already playing for all they were worth. The pair seemed to be trying to outdo each other in volume and virtuosity. Whenever it looked as if one was finished playing, the other would pick up another tune, only to be eventually joined in harmony by the other fiddler.

Emily watched Ben offer Mrs. Hannigan his arm and lead her to the dance floor. She certainly looked very pretty tonight in her pale pink calico gown with all the little ruffles around the neck and sleeves. She looked more like she belonged here than Emily, in all her finery, ever could.

No sooner had Ben finished his dance with Mrs. Hannigan than Meggie and Frannie quickly pulled another lady up to dance with him—so quickly that Ben never had the chance to return to Emily. As long as the fiddlers were playing, the girls kept Ben supplied with one dance partner after another. And never once, Emily noticed with disappointment and irritation, did he refuse a lady a dance so that he could return to her.

As the time dragged on, Emily believed Ben had danced with each and every lady in the barn. Except for one, she thought sadly as she stood alone at the side of the barn. He hasn't danced with me.

No one else seemed to want to dance with Emily, either. Oh, once or twice, out of the corner of her eye, she'd seen a man begin to approach her, only to have his wife or mother or sister or aunt—or maybe even his daughter—haul him back.

Mrs. Robbins, Mrs. Lindstrom, Pearl, even Dolly enjoyed an occasional swing around the room on the arm of several obliging gents. But no one asked Emily. Not even Noah.

Of course, Noah could be excused his rudeness, she supposed. As soon as Ben had released him to go dancing, Noah had made his way to the far corner of the barn, where he was very busy with some pretty rowdy friends and a very large jug. He'd hardly make a very desirable dance partner.

Emily was getting tired of listening to the ladies bickering about whether butter or lard made the best pie crust, or chattering behind their hands about who had worn the same dress to church three Sundays in a row. Why in the world had Ben suggested she come if he was going to ignore her like this?

She was getting tired of just standing all evening, too. But when she looked around for a seat, all she saw were people in denims and calicos perched atop bales of hay set around the sides of the barn. She certainly couldn't sit on a bale of prickly hay in a velvet gown. She sighed and shifted her weight on her aching feet.

"No, no, no," Ben declared to Meggie and Frannie as he passed in front of Emily as he was leaving the dance floor for the first time since they'd all arrived. "I've danced with every female you've managed to haul in my direction. I think the only ones you two missed were Mark Hanover's two-year-old and Mrs. Robbins's mother, who only has one leg and doesn't dance much anyhow. Now I need a rest."

"But you haven't danced with Pearl yet," Meggie protested.

Ben leaned closer to Meggie and whispered, "I don't intend to, either. Now go help Gramma clean up the cakes. Party's almost over, so we'll be leaving soon anyway. Church tomorrow morning, you know." He gave the girls a frown that sent them scurrying on their way.

As he turned, Ben almost ran into Emily. In spite of his exhaustion, a wide smile spread across his face and his pale blue eyes lit up with anticipation.

"And you!" he said. He snapped his fingers with frustration. "Darn! I haven't danced with you."

Had he just noticed? Emily thought with disgust. He hadn't forgotten the Hanover's little girl or even Mrs. Robbins's poor lame old mother—but he had forgotten her.

He motioned his arm toward the dance floor.

"Oh, I don't think so," she responded to his silent invitation.

"Are you done dancing tonight, then?" he asked.

"Not really," she answered. How could a person finish what they'd never started? How could she admit what a wallflower she'd been? Ben had certainly been enjoying himself, though. Even though he had invited her, she didn't think he cared one bit that she'd been left standing around all night—alone.

Of course, she didn't intend to give him the satisfaction of thinking that she didn't have anything better to do with her time than stand around watching him dance with every lucky lady in the place but her.

"Well, you're made of sterner stuff than me," Ben conceded. "I must be getting old. I need to sit down."

"I think I'd like that, too," Emily said. Her feet certainly were in favor of it.

Ben made a sweeping gesture toward a vacant bale of hay.

"Oh, I can't. . . ."

Suddenly seeing the problem more clearly, Ben stripped off his jacket, folded it, and placed it on the bale, just so Emily could sit down.

"Why didn't you say something earlier?" he asked.

"Wearing this fancy gown is my own fault," she admitted. "I never should have trusted Meggie. And, anyway, I didn't want to embarrass Mrs. Lindstrom."

"Or yourself?" Ben asked.

With a rueful little laugh she answered, "After all the things that have happened to me here since I arrived, I don't think I could be any more embarrassed."

"You didn't make a fool of yourself dancing," Ben reminded her cheerfully.

"I didn't dance," she quietly admitted to him.

"I wanted to dance with you, Emily. I really did."

"Oh, I'm very sure it was an oversight—on everyone's part," she said. Her voice fairly dripped with sarcasm. Good, she thought. She intended it to.

The mischievous grin faded from his face. His blue eyes looked at her with regret. "I'm sorry, Emily. I'd still love to dance with you now,'' he offered. ''If you still want to.'' He stretched his aching legs out in front of him and groaned loudly as he rose.

Emily shook her head. ''What a blatant bid for sympathy!'' she accused, trying very hard to hide her smile. ''Well, you'll get none from me. If you choose to dance yourself into exhaustion, you deserve to ache. And if you think I'll take pity on you and not claim a dance—you're right,'' she finished with a little laugh. ''Don't forget, while you were dancing, I've been standing all night.''

''That could be painful.''

''It was. Now I think my toes have gone numb.''

''Serves you right for wearing such tiny little shoes.''

''It provides a smaller target that's harder to hit when dancing with big, clumsy men,'' she said, glaring at him playfully. ''But then, I didn't dance with you.''

''I'm not clumsy,'' Ben protested. ''Just ask Mrs. Hannigan.''

''I'd rather get my information firsthand,'' she said.

Ben glanced around the barn at the thinning crowd. Then he looked at her. The playfulness had gone from his eyes. He seemed truly sorry.

''I wish I could show you now, Emily, but the party's over. See, the fiddlers are packing up.'' He rose and extended his hand to Emily. ''Of course, we don't need music to do the Shank's Mare Two-Step.''

''The what?'' she demanded, blinking with puzzlement.

''Come on. I'll walk you home.''

''Oh.'' She grinned at him. His hand was warm as she took it. She rose from her seat to stand close to him. He didn't let her go as he walked her toward the barn door, where they thanked the Lindstroms for their hospitality.

''But what about the girls?'' Emily asked as they made their way across the farmyard.

"Ma'll bring them to your house," he said.

"But you can't leave her to see herself home."

"Do you think my ma can't handle that buckboard?" he demanded.

"Well, no. Of course not." Emily felt pretty certain that Dolly could handle anything she put her mind to. "But . . ." She hesitated to bring up the subject. She lowered her voice to ask, "But what about Noah?"

"Don't worry," Ben answered with a chuckle. They were passing in front of their own buckboard. He reached out to gently tousle the horse's dark forelock. "Annabelle knows the way home."

Emily nodded. "Yes, I've seen that for myself," she answered. "I guess I can trust Annabelle with Meggie's safety."

"You can trust all of us, Emily," Ben said softly as he continued to stroll slowly down the peacefully dark country road. "We've been doing a good job for ten years now."

She supposed he was trying to impress her with the amount of seriousness in his voice. But she was not impressed.

"But you don't trust me," she countered.

"I do, Emily," Ben insisted. "I think you'll probably do a very good job of taking care of Meggie on your own. I just doubt the wisdom of your taking her away from *here*."

"Trustworthy but not wise," Emily said. "Is that supposed to sum up your opinion of me?"

"Oh, no, Emily," Ben said. He was shaking his head emphatically and at the same time chuckling almost to himself. But his eyes were watching Emily with a deep intensity that showed neither mockery nor humor. Emily almost thought it might be a deep longing.

"That just barely scratches the surface of what I think of you, Emily."

She wasn't sure what he meant by that. Were there more derogatory things he could add to his list? He didn't know her well enough to insult her a lot. And if the list was bad, why was he looking at her this way?

Deep down inside, she knew the reason very well. She might have led a very sheltered life, but she'd read more than one romantic novel. She'd seen young couples in the park. She had a pet cat once that had four kittens. She wasn't completely ignorant of what went on.

On the other hand, she'd never thought anyone would ever feel that way about her. The very thought made her shiver. She began to pull her wrap more closely around her shoulders. Ben placed a hand on each shoulder and helped pull the wrap around her.

"For instance, I think you cleaned yourself up real nice," he offered.

She turned to look up at him. Having helped her with her wrap, he was much closer to her than he had been when they first started this walk home.

"Oh, I did? Well, I'm glad my appearance meets with your approval, even if my actions don't."

"I didn't say *all* of your actions don't meet with my approval," he told her as he again took her elbow to help her up the crooked path to George's house.

Emily turned to him again, her green eyes made all the wider with her pretended astonishment. "You're becoming more selective of my behavior now? Well, just what is it you still don't like?"

Ben opened the door for her to enter. Emily turned up the wick on the small lamp she had left burning on the table in the vestibule. She waited while Ben closed the door behind them, fearful of hearing again just what he didn't like, and eager to hear what he did.

"I think we've been over—and over—the things we

don't like about each other, Emily, until I'm sick of hearing them,'' he said as he approached her across the vestibule. ''And I think you are, too.''

He stood so close to her now that she could feel his breath, warm on her flesh, which was chilled from their walk in the cool autumn night. He reached out to remove her wrap. Without even looking where it went, he tossed it back over his shoulder onto the bench by the door.

Emily's heart gave a little leap. She was breathing so heavily now that she could see her own breasts moving up and down. It was pretty obvious that Ben could see them, too. Oh, why had she let Meggie talk her into wearing this daring gown? Why had she even bought the thing in the first place? How could she have let herself be talked into walking home, all alone, with a man she felt this way about—and who obviously felt that same way about her? And how soon could she count on Dolly and the girls, or even Noah, coming through that front door? She really was counting on Annabelle now.

''I think it's time we started talking about what we like about each other instead, Emily,'' Ben said. He raised one hand and placed it on her bare arm.

Her own rapidly flowing blood had warmed her enough. But his touch burned her flesh like fire—and she wanted him never to let her go.

''You . . . you don't like anything about me,'' she said, backing away from him. She moved into the parlor. Maybe, with George's and Sarah's pictures peering down at them from the mantel, Ben would feel guilty and be able to control his lustful thoughts—and maybe she could even control hers! ''I dress all wrong for the occasion. . . .''

''I think you looked wonderful in that gown tonight. You'd look wonderful any night.'' Ben followed her into the parlor. "I think you'd look wonderful even without that gown. . . ."

"I fell into a pigsty and got my head caught in an oven," she quickly reminded him. She gave a little laugh. She wasn't sure if it was because of how silly she felt recalling these incidents, or because of how nervous Ben made her feel, following her around, saying the things he did.

Ben chuckled and moved to stand directly in front of her. "Happens all the time around here."

"I'm so stupid that little girls can trick me." She wasn't so stupid that she would allow him to come closer and closer to her. She backed away from him, moving in the direction of the mantel. Maybe he wasn't close enough to see the pictures of Sarah and George. Maybe he wasn't close enough to feel guilty doing something he shouldn't in front of them.

"That's because you're sweet, Emily," he said, coming even closer to her.

Apparently Sarah and George weren't doing their job. Maybe she should have sent George a large portrait of their stern-looking father to hang over the mantel. She moved directly next to the fireplace now and turned to face the mantel with its array of pictures. Ben could hardly *not* notice them now.

"You're always willing to believe the best about someone else," he said.

He came and stood so close behind her that he pressed his chest into her back. With both hands, she clung to the mantelpiece for support for her quaking knees. He placed both of his hands on her shoulders. He leaned his cheek against the side of her head and softly whispered into her ear, "Except me."

"That's not true," she protested. She didn't dare turn to

look him in the eye. How could she tell him that some of the best thoughts she'd ever had were about him!

His pale blue eyes grew wide. "It's not?" he asked. "You mean you do have a kind thought or two for me?"

Oh, no. Not kind, she silently contradicted him. Wild, wicked, and abandoned. But not by any stretch of the imagination simply kind.

Emily released her grip on the mantel. Slowly Ben began to turn her to face him. He moved his hand slowly up her neck, his thumb gently smoothing over the small ridge and hollow at the base of her throat. Then he slid his thumb gently up to rest under her chin, lifting so that she had to look up at him.

"Do you even think about me at all, Emily?" he asked.

Slowly she nodded.

"I think about you," he said. His thumb traveled slowly over her chin to rest at the corner of her mouth. "A lot. You're so trusting, and innocent . . ."

This was going much farther than Emily had ever imagined. She should keep quiet, but she'd never lied in her life, and she especially did not want to lie now—not to Ben. "And I'm taking your niece and your daughter's best friend away from you all."

Ben shook his head. "Do you really have to go away?" he asked. "Is there someone special waiting for you in Baltimore?"

"No," she admitted reluctantly.

Except for a slight twitch of the corners of his lips and a slight flaring of his nostrils, Emily could not have detected Ben's smile at all.

"If there's really no reason to go back to Baltimore, is there really any reason why you couldn't stay here?"

Ben's hand moved up to cradle her cheek as his thumb

continued to hold her chin lifted to his face. Slowly his lips lowered until they were within an inch of hers.

The crash on the front porch jarred the windows in their frames.

''What the—!'' Ben abruptly turned toward the door. He kept his body in front of her, his arms ready at his sides, as if to shield her from whatever might be coming to batter down the door.

Had the good people of Bidewell come to tar and feather her and run her out of town on a rail? Emily worried. Or had Iris Hannigan volunteered to do the job single-handed? Either way, it didn't matter. She felt safe and protected, snuggled between the sturdy fireplace and the warm hardness of Ben's body.

The repeated booms against the front door made Emily cling to Ben all the more tightly.

''Hey, you! Op'n up!'' came the muffled cry.

Ben turned back to Emily. Holding her two arms, he pulled himself out of her grasp.

''Stay here. It's only Noah,'' he explained. Releasing her, he headed toward the door.

If it was only Noah, why did she have to stay here?

''What's he doing here?'' She really had hoped Noah would be sleeping it off in the back of the buckboard by the time Dolly brought the girls back home.

When Ben opened the door, Noah fell on his face into the vestibule and stayed there.

''We had a great time, Uncle Eb,'' Meggie declared, stepping over Noah's supine body as if it was every day she found her uncle laying facedown on some floor. ''Didn't we?''

''Sure did,'' Frannie answered, following her cousin, as if Noah made no more of an impression on her.

Meggie stayed in the vestibule. But when Frannie saw

Emily still standing in the parlor, she ran over to her. "Did you have fun, too?"

"I've never been to a barn dance before, Frannie. It was a very interesting evening," Emily answered. She felt that was a vague enough response not to hurt any feelings unnecessarily.

"We're really looking forward to spending the night here," Frannie continued. "I haven't stayed here since . . ." She stood on tiptoe, indicating that Emily should bend down the rest of the way to meet her. When Emily bent down, Frannie whispered, "Not since Meggie's ma died."

"I hope you have an especially good time, then," Emily responded almost automatically. She really was more worried about what Ben and Noah were doing. She patted Frannie's shoulder, then moved into the vestibule.

Ben had managed to get Noah to stand beside him, holding him up under his arms. Emily wondered how Ben managed to stand the mixed smells of whiskey, straw, and whatever animal had been lying in that straw before Noah had taken up residence.

"I'll take you home now, Ma," Ben said, hauling Noah toward the door. Glancing back over his shoulder, he said to Emily, "I'll be by for you all tomorrow morning 'round eight."

"I hope Noah will be all right," Emily said.

"I expect so," Dolly answered. "He usually is."

Ben smiled at her, one eyebrow lifted. "I hope you will be, too, by tomorrow."

CHAPTER TEN

"A DRESS! YOU WANT ME TO WEAR A DRESS?" Meggie exclaimed. Her blue eyes were wide with horror.

Emily held the little blue dress up in front of her, trying to show Meggie how nice she'd look in it. Emily fluffed up the little swag of fabric at the front, carefully rearranging the row of pale blue satin pleats around the edge. She flipped the dress over so that Meggie could see the full gathering of dark blue wool and the wide, pale blue satin bow at the back, which mimicked a tiny bustle.

Meggie glared back and forth between Emily and the hated dress.

''Wow! It sure is pretty, Meggie,'' Frannie said enthusiastically.

''All the little girls in Baltimore wear dresses,'' Emily said, seizing Frannie's approval as her opportunity to impress Meggie.

''Not like that,'' Meggie pointed out.

''Well, no, not like this,'' Emily admitted. This dress had cost a good bit more than most families could afford. In fact, it had cost more to have made than she had intended to pay for a child's dress, but she had wanted it to be special for Meggie. ''But most of them wear some kind of dress.''

''Most of 'em here do, too,'' Meggie admitted, tugging at

the straps of her overalls. ''But only the little prissy ones wear dresses like that. Not us. Right, Frannie?''

Frannie had been watching the dress so intently that she'd barely heard her cousin. ''Oh, yeah. Right,'' she answered automatically.

''But you can't just wear overalls like you've done every other day,'' Emily protested. ''Not for church.''

''Course not,'' Meggie agreed. ''Today we put on clean ones. And shoes. And look. Even got a brand-new blouse.'' She tugged at the rounded white collar. ''Washed my neck, too. See?''

''But I bought this especially for you, Meggie,'' Emily said.

Her little nose curled up in a sneer. ''Hope you can get your money back.''

Emily had hoped that if Meggie thought she considered her to be special, that might make Meggie want to wear the dress. Obviously, special or not, Meggie didn't want Emily to think about her at all.

''I was really hoping you'd wear it this morning when you went to church with me—and Frannie and your Gramma and Ben,'' Emily added, just to be on the safe side. Also, just to be on the safe side, she had deliberately left out Noah.

''Can't wear it. It won't fit,'' Meggie said with absolute certainty.

''Of course it will,'' Emily said. She reached out to hold the dress up in front of Meggie, but Meggie quickly backed away, as if being touched with the little dress would poison her.

Emily turned to Frannie instead and held the dress up to her at the shoulders.

Frannie, on the other hand, actually seemed eager to try it on. Gazing longingly at the dress, she ran her fingers gently over the soft woolen fabric. "It sure is pretty, Meggie," she repeated.

Meggie shot her cousin a look that would crack a rock, much less ensure Frannie's silence.

"See," Emily said. "You two are about the same size, and it fits her perfectly."

"If she don't wear it, can I have it?" Frannie asked.

"Well, it does fit you," Emily said with hesitation, all the while watching Meggie's reaction. "And the color looks just perfect with your pretty blue eyes. It would be a shame to waste such a nice dress. . . ."

"Course you can't!" Meggie snatched the dress out of Emily's hands, away from Frannie. "It'll fit me. And . . . and I have pretty blue eyes, too. So I'll wear the darned thing—but I won't like it."

Frannie looked so disappointed that Emily decided then and there to have an identical dress made up and sent to Frannie just as soon as she and Meggie returned to Baltimore.

"Do you think I can run over home and get a dress of my own?" Frannie asked Emily.

"You don't have any dresses," Meggie reminded Frannie testily.

"Yes, I do."

"*I've* never seen 'em."

"Pa bought one for me last Christmas, but . . . well, I stuck it way in the back of the chifforobe," Frannie finally confessed. "I couldn't tell him I didn't want to wear it and hurt his feelings. So I figured if he didn't see it for a while, he'd forget all about it." She turned to Emily. "Will you wait till I put it on?"

"Certainly, but—"

"Oh, geez, Frannie," Meggie protested. "Just 'cause I have to look like a fool is no reason for you to."

"No, no, Meggie. I really want to."

Emily thought Frannie sounded a little too enthusiastic to be motivated by purely unselfish reasons. After all, Frannie might only be ten years old, but she was still woman enough not to want her cousin to outshine her.

Emily had never had much to do with children before. She'd expected to love her niece, but she was surprised at how much she cared for Frannie, too. It startled her to realize that, when she left, she would miss Frannie.

"But, Frannie, no one's home at your house," Emily said.

"Sure there is," Frannie said as she made her way out of Meggie's bedroom and started down the stairs. "Pa stayed there last night."

"Oh, he did?" Emily tried to hide her surprise, as well as her irritation. "I thought your father took Dolly and Noah home and stayed at the farm last night."

"Well, usually we do—to keep an eye on Uncle Noah. But last night he came back home." Frannie paused at the bottom of the stairs just long enough to turn back and shrug her shoulders. Then she ran out the front door in search of her dress.

The more she thought about it, the closer Emily's annoyance with Ben came to becoming genuine anger. It was bad enough that he thought her incompetent in taking care of Meggie. Did he think she was worse than Noah? Did he think she was so irresponsible that he had to stay next door just to make sure she didn't destroy the house or misplace his daughter overnight?

Emily was so angry that she had to make some sort of sound. She could hardly scream when Meggie was still in the house. A frustrated "Oh!" was as close as she could come. She did manage to stop herself from doing some childish foot stamping. She hadn't done that in years. Oh, confound Ben Cameron for having the ability to upset her so!

Then Emily noticed that Frannie had left the front door wide open behind her. No sense in even trying to call her back now, Emily thought. The child was probably already pounding up her own front steps and flinging wide her own front door.

It wasn't too chilly on this bright autumn morning. Emily decided to leave the door just as it was and wait until Frannie returned. Then she could illustrate to her how impolite it was to leave the house doors standing wide open.

On the other hand, Emily was pretty certain that Mrs. Hannigan's chickens had no scruples—religious or otherwise—about working on Sunday and might wander in, searching for food, at any moment. Better close the door herself—now, Emily decided—before further trouble could find her.

As Emily began to descend the stairs, the door opened even wider. Emily froze. It wasn't windy enough for a breeze to have caused it. It couldn't possibly be Frannie coming back again so soon. She hoped the chickens didn't have the strength to move that door. Then what a peck she could expect the next time she weeded the garden! she thought with horror.

Then Ben stuck his head cautiously into the vestibule. He raised his hand from the knob and knocked loudly on the wooden frame.

"Hello!" he called, still knocking. "Anyone home?"

"Is anyone home?" Emily repeated as she descended the stairs. "Of course someone's home."

Ben smiled as soon as he saw her. His pale blue eyes were alight with anticipation. He stepped boldly into the house.

Oh, she was the best thing he'd seen in the morning in a long, long time, Ben thought. He tried to take in as much as he possibly could of her in that pretty green Sunday-go-to-meeting dress.

Emily stood at the opposite side of the small round table, almost as if she was using it as some sort of shield. Did she really feel as if she needed protection from him? He didn't think he'd been that aggressive last night—and she had seemed willing enough then. Was she having second thoughts?

"Did you think I had run off with Meggie like a thief in the night?" she asked.

"Of course I didn't think you'd run away," he answered. Slowly, almost cautiously, he circled the table, drawing closer to Emily. "At least, I sure hope you wouldn't want to go." He took one more step, which brought him so close to her that his legs rustled her skirt. "Especially not now, Emily."

He raised his hand to place it on her arm. But when he saw the hostility in her green eyes and felt her body stiffen at his approach, he dropped his hand to his side instead.

"What's the matter, Emily?" he asked slowly.

"Nothing's the matter," she said, stepping back from him. She swung one arm out to show him the vestibule and the parlor, then the other arm to indicate the dining room. "The house is still standing in one piece. True, you might have seen your daughter running out of here, but she was going home to look for a dress to wear to church—"

"A dress?" Ben interjected. His eyes opened wide with surprise. Frannie actually *wanted* to wear a dress!

"Yes . . . and not because I was chasing her with a meat cleaver," Emily continued. "And while you haven't seen Meggie yet and can't be certain of her well-being, I assure you, she's upstairs putting on a lovely little dress I bought her in Baltimore—and not lying on the floor in a pool of blood."

"Emily, Emily, Emily," Ben repeated slowly, shaking his head sadly. "You've got to stop reading so much Edgar Allan Poe!"

"*I've* got to stop reading Poe? *You*'re the one who thinks I can't be trusted alone with two young children. Did you think I was going to put them in the oven?"

"No, no. That's the Brothers Grimm. Poe walls them up in the cellar," he corrected her with a chuckle. "And after what they've pulled on you, don't you think they deserve it?"

"Of course not! I'd never do that to a child!"

Ben laughed aloud. "Emily, I'm only joking." Then he took another step closer to her. "I know you'd only get yourself stuck in the oven." Emily couldn't help but laugh with him. Suddenly his expression grew more serious as he looked intently at her. "Don't you know by now that I trust you?"

Emily grimaced. "You don't act as if you do."

"Didn't I help bring Meggie's things here?" he asked. "Didn't I let Frannie stay, too?"

"Then why did you spend the night at your house?"

Ben's brows lowered with puzzlement. "Because it's my house."

"But you said you were going back to the farm. Why did you stay next door?" She glared up at him. "Were you trying to keep watch over me?"

"Yes."

Emily was not prepared for such a simple, straightforward response. She stood there staring at him.

"I was watching out for *you*, Emily," Ben said. He took one step toward her.

Emily's eyes searched his face, as if looking for some kind of a sign there that proclaimed him a liar. Apparently finding none, she lowered her gaze.

"Your brother let this house run down—maybe more than you realize. Sometimes things don't work so well here—the pump, the stove . . ."

"I managed to make oat porridge and toast for breakfast," Emily informed him proudly. "I've got a pot roast simmering on the back burner this very minute."

Ben sniffed the air appreciatively. "Smells good. Probably'll taste good, too."

"But you still think I can't take care of myself, don't you?"

To avoid giving an answer, Ben asked, "Who would you have gone to last night in an emergency? Mrs. Hannigan?"

"Oh, have mercy, no!"

Ben nodded sagely. "Then, am I forgiven for worrying about you and the girls?"

Emily still thought he was more concerned for the girls than he ever could be for her.

And why shouldn't he be? she scolded herself. They're his own flesh and blood, his family—and I'm just . . . just . . .

She wasn't sure what she was to Ben anymore. Certainly not a *complete* stranger. Not after the way he had approached her last night—or the way she'd almost responded. She wasn't sure what he wanted her to be to him—or what she herself was willing to be.

"Does it bother you that I want to watch over you, Emily?" he asked.

She shook her head.

Ben smiled at her. He raised his hand to her shoulder, just as he had done when he first entered. This time she was no longer angry with him. She stood completely still and allowed him to touch her.

"Are you absolutely sure Meggie is dressing upstairs?" he asked. An inviting gleam lit his eyes.

Emily shivered, then nodded in spite of the apprehension that mixed with her anticipation. "How long will it take Frannie to find that dress in the back of the chifforobe?" she asked in a very small voice, so as not to attract Meggie's attention.

"Frannie? Ages and ages," Ben answered with a little chuckle. "Depend on it."

Ben raised his other hand to her other shoulder. She looked up into his eyes. His lids were half-closed, almost as if, should he open them completely, he might sear her with the desire she saw burning there.

"How do I look, Pa?" Frannie demanded as she burst into the vestibule.

Ben quickly stepped back from Emily. "How time flies!" he murmured, rubbing his chin.

Emily swallowed hard and fidgeted with the cloth on the table.

Ben was startled at the transformation of his daughter. Even when he'd bought it, he'd never thought he'd actually see her wear that little pink dress. He'd bought it anyway, just hoping, maybe someday she'd turn out to be a lady after all. Even if the dress was badly in need of a pressing, Frannie was still more beautiful than he'd imagined any child of his could be. He couldn't help the swell of paternal pride in his chest.

"You're just beautiful, pumpkin!" Ben exclaimed.

"Beautifuller than Meggie?" Frannie demanded.

"I think so."

"Good!" Frannie dashed up the stairs and disappeared into Meggie's bedroom.

Ben watched Frannie until she had completely disappeared from sight. Then he turned to Emily and said softly, "Now, where was I?"

"Yoo-hoo!"

Emily could not mistake Dolly's shrill cry piercing the air. She peered past Ben out the front door. Dolly and Noah had just pulled up—in a handsome little yellow surrey, no less. Where had they been hiding that? she wondered, surprised and impressed. On the other hand, she noticed with returning dismay, Noah was driving. She hoped Annabelle understood that this was Sunday and knew the way to church.

"Yoo-hoo!" Dolly called again.

Disappointed, Emily watched Ben move to the doorway. He stood there, waving. Dolly continued to call several more times, each time louder and more shrill. Apparently Ben's form in the doorway was not enough to satisfy her that the people inside were almost ready for church.

"I'll go tell her we'll be right there," Ben offered. "Why don't you go up and get the girls?"

Emily made her way up the stairs. Dolly's loud calls had blotted out her footsteps, and the girls hadn't heard Emily approach.

She paused at the doorway to Meggie's room, watching them in silence. Both girls were trying to admire themselves at the same time in the long narrow mirror standing to the side of Meggie's bed.

"Think she'll let me keep this here, even when she goes back to Baltimore?" Meggie asked.

Frannie slowly shook her head. "I don't think so, Meggie. That thing looks awful expensive. Maybe she can get her money back for it."

"People like Aunt Emily don't take these kinds of things back, silly. They . . . they give them to . . . um, their servants. Yeah, that's what they do."

"Does *she* have servants?" Frannie demanded, awe-struck.

Meggie just shrugged, as if she didn't know—and really

didn't care—and continued to admire herself in the mirror.

"If you dare tell her I really like this dress, I'll . . . I'll throw your lunch in the pond for a week," Meggie warned in a hoarse whisper. "I swear."

"On one condition," Frannie boldly bargained.

Emily chuckled. Apparently, striking bargains was a family trait, too.

"Someday, before we outgrow it, you just *gotta* let me wear that dress!"

Meggie grimaced, as if thinking really hard. "Just to church." She began setting her conditions.

Frannie nodded eagerly.

"And you can't have a cold when you wear it," Meggie said as she admired the narrow blue satin ribbon bordering the long sleeves.

"Course not!"

"Or if you do, you gotta carry a handkerchief."

"Yeah, sure."

"And when you eat, you tuck up a napkin."

"Sure."

"Well, all right," Meggie agreed reluctantly.

Emily coughed and heavily retraced her steps across the carpeted hall to warn the girls of her approach.

"Your Gramma's here," she announced. She said nothing of Uncle Noah. They'd know of him soon enough.

Emily was surprised to see Meggie and Frannie—the two little tomboys—walking sedately down the stairs and out to the surrey, Meggie squeezed into the front seat between Noah and Dolly. Just to be sure she got a seat at the edge, Frannie scooted around the other side while Ben was helping Emily into the rear seat.

Emily ducked her head to be sure the fringed roof didn't dislodge her new hat. She could feel the length of Ben's strong arm pressing against her shoulder and the firmness of his thigh moving against her hip as they rode along.

She'd felt that before, on other rides. But now she wondered how Ben would feel pressed against her—face to face with no interruptions to stop them, body to body with no denim or velvet to come between them. The tingle in her arm moved to other, less accessible parts of her body.

Oh, how she wished Frannie wasn't traveling right beside her and that the front seat was empty, too. After all, Annabelle probably knew the way—and, in Emily's admittedly limited experience, she had never yet met a horse that gossiped much.

Still, something was missing, but Emily couldn't quite name it. Then the breeze picked up as Annabelle moved along. Suddenly Emily realized what it was. She no longer detected the strong scent of whiskey coming from Noah. Once she realized that, she also noticed that he was guiding Annabelle, and that he was sitting upright to do it. What in the world had happened to Noah overnight? And, without appearing *really* rude, who could she ask to find out?

''First thing Monday morning I'm getting back to work,'' Noah announced, breaking the silence that had enveloped them as they rode along.

''Good,'' Dolly agreed.

''Once again I have been snatched from the foul grip of Ol' Demon Rum,'' Noah continued. ''Once again I have seen the error of my ways. I repent in dust and ashes.''

''Good,'' Dolly repeated.

Ben leaned over and whispered in Emily's ear, ''Noah sees the error of his ways *every* Sunday morning.''

''I will return to the task which the Lord has set for me,'' Noah said.

''I hope you fix the roof on the chicken coop first,'' Dolly grumbled.

''Sure will, Ma. Then I will return to my appointed task.''

''Noah used to be an architect,'' Ben whispered.

Remembering the construction in the farmyard, Emily replied softly, ''I should have guessed.''

''No need to whisper,'' Noah called back to them. ''What happened to me is no secret, Miss Emily. I used to be a damn good . . . 'scuse me, ladies . . . a very good architect in Chicago. Then, amidst the luxury and high living, Ol' Demon Rum got hold of my soul. Ruined my career. Almost ruined my life, and I came home in disgrace. Then I went to that camp meeting. There I saw the light, and as I lay in my bed that night, I saw the true reason for my existence. I'm to build that there ark—and I sure intend to see it completed.''

Emily sat silent. It wasn't so much that she was enthralled with his tale of redemption, inspiring though it was. It was just that she'd never before met a man with a mission quite like Noah's.

''Only trouble is,'' Noah continued, ''Ol' Demon Rum still grabs hold of me sometimes. On Friday nights I get such an overpowering thirst . . .'' He shook his head with dismay. ''But I'm always sober again in time to go to meeting on Sunday morning, ain't I?''

''Yes, indeed. And I'm proud of you, Noah,'' Ben answered.

''I still wish there was something . . . some way, somehow I could shake Ol' Demon Rum for good,'' Noah added with a wistful sigh. ''I suppose I'll be battling him for the rest of my life.''

''Don't worry, Noah,'' Dolly said, patting his arm to comfort him. ''Used to be, I couldn't get no work out of ya at all. Now, at least I get four days a week. I'm real proud of ya, too.''

Emily nodded. She understood Noah a little better now

and certainly wished him the best. She was glad to see the loving support his family gave him. But it was still a difficult situation to leave her niece in. She still needed to take Meggie back home with her, where no one drank—not even for medicinal purposes.

In spite of Frannie's continual squirming, Emily enjoyed the short ride to the little white church at the edge of Winterset. The surrey pulled up in the crowded churchyard. Ben had barely helped Emily down before she heard the familiar syrupy call.

"Well, good morning, Ben," Mrs. Hannigan said. "Mrs. Cameron, Noah." She waited just the few seconds it took to indicate that greeting Emily was an afterthought. "*Miss* Shaw."

Emily nodded politely.

"Frannie, Meggie, do you want to sit with me again this morning?" Mrs. Hannigan invited.

"No."

Mrs. Hannigan could barely conceal her shock at Meggie's refusal. "Why not, dear?" she asked. She threw a venomous glance at Emily, as if everything were her fault.

"'Cause you always sit way in the back," Meggie answered.

"But you like that, dear," Mrs. Hannigan reminded her. "That way you can enjoy the goodies I always bring. Look." She pulled open the clasp of her tiny bag. In a conspiratorial whisper she said, "I brought toffees this morning."

Frannie looked tempted, but Meggie shook her head. "No, this morning I want to sit with Gramma—right up front."

With the thumb and forefinger of each hand, Meggie held out the gathered fabric of the skirt of her new dress. Frannie quickly did the same. Mrs. Hannigan blinked with surprise.

Obviously, she'd been so intent on charming the girls that she'd missed the most important thing.

This time there was no doubt in her mind as to who was to blame for their abandoning her. She directed another venomous glare at Emily.

"Well, don't you two look pretty," Mrs. Hannigan said to the girls.

"Yes, we do," Frannie answered.

Noah pulled out his pocket watch. "Got to get going," he announced. "Can't be late."

"Of course not," Mrs. Hannigan agreed, moving toward the wide red church doors. Suddenly she turned and added, "My goodness, I hope you'll all fit into one pew."

"Oh, don't worry, Mrs. Hannigan," Emily replied. "There's always room for family."

Emily wasn't sure if she was disappointed or not. She was sorry not to have Ben sit beside her in church. On the other hand, with Ben sitting in the choir loft on the other side of the pulpit, she had the opportunity to study his handsome face all sermon long.

Mother would have been appalled if she had known that Emily wasn't paying the least bit of attention to a single word the kindly old minister said. But Emily was delighted to be able to watch Ben's clear blue eyes contrasting with the vivid red and yellow stained-glass windows behind him.

She liked to watch how his firm jaw moved as he sang. Never in her life would she have expected that a man who could tote feed sacks like he did could also carry a tune. Suddenly the memory of Ben's bare torso, glistening in the sunlight as he lifted feed sacks at the train station, gave way to the tantalizing image of Ben, just as bare-chested, singing in the choir. Emily dropped her hymnal.

Emily was glad to hear the last strains of the closing hymn. The smell of warm wax and smoke permeated the air as the candles were extinguished. The lanky little organist began her somewhat shaky postlude on the creaky pump organ. She should stick to Charles Wesley hymns, Emily decided. Bach fugues just weren't this woman's—or the pump organ's—strong point.

After the service Emily stood with Dolly and Noah and the girls, waiting in front of the church.

"I know you've planned a meal for Meggie and yourself," Ben said as he came up to Emily. "But I was hoping you wouldn't mind if I came by the house later."

Emily wasn't sure what to say. Back home, when a man asked a girl if he could accompany her home from church or call later on a Sunday afternoon, with her father's permission, it meant that he was seriously considering courting the lady. Things couldn't be that different out here in Iowa, Emily thought with mixed feelings. She was glad Ben was paying her all this lovely attention. On the other hand, she couldn't help but worry about what was going to happen Monday, or Tuesday, when it was time to go back to Baltimore.

"Oh, yes, Uncle Eb," Meggie pleaded. "Oh, please come by. And bring Frannie. Please."

"Are you sure?" Ben asked.

Emily wasn't certain if Ben was asking her or Meggie.

"Oh, I'm really sure, Uncle Eb," Meggie answered before Emily could refuse. She grabbed him by the lapel and pulled him down close to her. In what was supposed to be a whisper, but in reality could probably be heard in the next county, Meggie said, "Please come. Otherwise, it's just going to be me and her and the pot roast."

Ben didn't straighten up. He only lifted his gaze to Emily, making his eyes look bigger and more blue. Oh, why did he have to do that?

"I wouldn't want to impose."

Emily had been looking forward to a quiet Sunday afternoon alone with her niece—getting to know each other better before undertaking the long train ride back to Baltimore. But when she looked into Ben's eyes, and realized that very soon she might never see him again, she couldn't refuse.

"I'll be happy to see you—and Frannie," she answered.

"Yeck! This is terrible," Meggie exclaimed. She spat the mouthful of stringy beef out into her plate.

"Meggie! Ladies do not spit!" Emily exclaimed horrified.

"Well, ladies don't have to eat your cooking."

Emily poked through her slices of beef. It hadn't been that hard to slice. How could the piece of beef she'd bought yesterday afternoon from Randall's Emporium be so tough? After all, it had smelled fresh, and Mrs. Randall had assured her it was. Maybe if she hadn't let all the juice cook off she could have tried to make gravy. Maybe gravy would have helped.

"Try the potatoes," Emily suggested. "They can't be that bad."

"Have you tried them yet?" Meggie demanded.

How could she have let the potatoes burn? Emily wondered as she scraped the black half off with her knife. She tried to chew the white half, but the burnt flavor had gone through the entire vegetable. Swallowing with difficulty, Emily decided not to even bother with the black and orange carrots.

"I'm still hungry," Meggie whined.

"Have some more cider," Emily suggested. "I'm sure that's not burnt." Maybe that would help fill her up.

"I'm hungry, not thirsty!"

"Me, too, Meggie," Emily admitted sadly.

"I want to go back to the farm," she complained. "There's always something good to eat there."

"I know," Emily answered wistfully. She remembered the taste of Dolly's chicken and johnnycakes, and the fresh-brewed coffee—not to mention the fact that Ben would be there to share them.

"I wish I'd gone there instead."

"Me, too," Emily said.

"I wish I hadn't stayed here with you."

"I'm sorry, Meggie." She didn't know what else to say. For Meggie's sake, she'd go to Dolly at the farm, to see that the child at least got a good meal. As for herself, she'd rather starve than admit to Ben that her cooking was anything less than satisfactory.

Meggie rose and carried her plate from the table. "Might as well throw this swill out," she said, heading toward the kitchen. "Pigs wouldn't even eat it."

Emily rose and picked up her own plate. "Meggie, you're absolutely right."

As Emily moved toward the kitchen, there was a tapping on the front door.

"I'll get it!" Meggie fairly flew out of the kitchen. Flinging open the door, she cried, "Oh, Frannie! I'm so glad to see you." Seizing her cousin by the hand, she pulled her up the stairs. "You didn't happen to get any of them toffees off of Mrs. Hannigan this morning, did you?"

"Afternoon, Emily," Ben said, stepping into the dining room.

Emily watched him as he came closer to her. Just by being here, he caused a tingle in her arms and a flutter in her heart.

"Just finishing up?" he asked, nodding toward the dining room table.

"I guess so."

"So that's how you keep your stylish figure?" he asked. He frowned at the full plate in her hands.

"Not usually."

He stepped closer, walking around Emily, inspecting the contents on the plate.

"Hmmm. I've never seen potatoes done like that before. Maybe you could give Ma the recipe."

"I don't think so," Emily answered, putting the plate back down on the table.

"Is it an old family recipe? Some big secret you're not allowed to tell?"

"No," she admitted with a laugh. "I was sort of . . . experimenting."

"And that's what you got?"

Emily nodded.

"Very interesting results. It could be hard to duplicate."

"I hope it'll be impossible to duplicate."

Ben lifted a fork and poked at the untouched food. "Sort of looks something like what we're having at Ma's. Sort of."

"You're just being polite," she said. "That doesn't look the least bit like anything!"

"Tell you what," he said. "I know I invited myself over here to enjoy your company. But why don't I take you and Meggie back out to the farm—just so you and Ma can . . . well, maybe swap recipes—or whatever it is you gals do."

Ben speared a black and white potato and lifted it up, turning the fork this way and that to get the full effect. "Ma just loves to figure out other people's recipes. I bet she'd really puzzle over how you did this to a potato."

"Oh, I don't think it would take her too long to figure it out," Emily admitted. Ben was still examining the burnt potato. "Do you want to take that back to the farm for

Dolly?'' she asked. ''Or keep it as a little memento for yourself.''

Ben chuckled and laid the speared potato back down on the plate. He turned to Emily. His eyes traced the form of her face, then glided over her figure as if memorizing every line and curve of her. At last his gaze returned to hers. ''I'd rather take you.''

CHAPTER ELEVEN

"NOW, THAT WAS A POT ROAST!" BEN EXclaimed. He took a deep breath and leaned back in his chair, too full to eat another bite. He stretched his long arms out at his sides. Instead of returning to his original position, he kept one hand on the back of Emily's chair.

Emily longed to stretch out comfortably just as Ben had, but decided a gesture that personal would have to wait until she was in her room alone tonight.

''Thank you very much for having us,'' Emily said to Dolly. No doubt about it, the woman was a good cook. Emily wished she knew how Dolly did it—and that she'd show her how.

''My pleasure,'' Dolly responded. She fixed Emily with an icy blue stare. ''Ya gotta learn. Young'uns need to be fed *proper*. So do menfolk.''

Ben rose. He slid his hand along the back of Emily's chair. ''Meggie and Frannie'll help with the cleaning up, Ma. Think I'll take Miss Shaw for a little stroll. Maybe explain to her about how menfolk around here like to be fed.''

Dolly watched her son through narrowed eyes. ''If ya really think that's a good idea.''

''I do, Ma.'' Slowly Ben moved his hand along the back

of Emily's chair until he found the small hollow at the base of her neck.

Dolly shrugged her bony shoulders. "Suit yourself," was all she said.

"I will." Gently he moved his thumb up and down.

Emily did her best not to shiver noticeably at his touch in front of all these people. That, too, was something personal that would have to wait until they were in her house alone . . . Emily quickly leaned forward for another sip of coffee—anything to move away from Ben's touch and to shake away the wanton thoughts she was having about what would happen if they ever were completely alone together for any length of time. Her hand shook so badly she almost spilled her coffee on the red and white checked cloth.

Dolly snorted and snatched up an empty plate. Meggie and Frannie were carrying what little food was left over into the kitchen. Noah had already retired to the parlor to read his Bible by the light of the coal oil lamp.

"I hope you enjoyed yourself here today, Emily," Ben said, holding the chair for her as she rose from the table.

"Yes, I did. It's amazing how you can look through the stereoptican with one eye closed, and it's just a plain picture. But when you see it with both eyes, the pictures just seem to pop right out at you!"

"I know it's nowhere near as exciting as a trip to some fancy museum or concert hall," Ben admitted.

"We don't always need those things to have a good time," she said. She placed her hand on his arm, trying to ease his feelings. Then she realized that he had made his point pretty well. Well, she had points to make, too. "Meggie seemed much happier to be with me today."

"Especially after she was fed," Ben said. "You know, Iowa's as good a place to be happy as Baltimore."

She wanted to argue with him about that. She'd be much

happier back in Baltimore, and she wanted to tell him so. On the other hand, although she'd be with Meggie in familiar places, Ben would still be in Iowa. Deep down inside she had the wretched foreboding that, no matter where she was or who else she was with, without Ben she wouldn't be truly happy ever again.

Ben placed his hand on her back and, with his other hand, indicated the front door.

Emily could see that it was growing dark outside. After all the things that had happened between them in the past three days, she knew that he was certainly not taking her out there to talk about pot roasts or burnt potatoes or stereopticans. But she went anyway, willingly. Almost, she felt ashamed to admit, eagerly.

But once Ben had closed the door behind them, and they were alone on the porch in the waning light, Emily's courage deserted her.

"Your mother didn't seem very interested in my potato recipe," Emily said. Maybe talking about food wasn't such a bad idea after all.

"Darned shame, too," Ben said.

He placed his hand on her shoulder again, as if he didn't want to lose the feel of her in the dark. Slowly they began to stroll the length of the porch. In the silence of the twilight their shoes padded a soft rhythm against the wood.

"I think, with a little practice, you could get really good at making those things."

Emily laughed. "I think it's going to take more than just a little practice for me to be a better cook."

"Not just a cook," Ben said. He was moving his hand over her shoulder, gently smoothing it up and down her arm as he drew her closer to him as they walked to the edge of the porch.

Here it was darker. The corner of the house shaded them

from the orange-gold rays of the setting sun. The closed draperies reduced the pale yellow gleam of Noah's coal oil lamp to a tiny sliver of light.

"With a little practice, a person can become really good at almost anything they set their mind to." His hand moved up until it rested at the base of her throat.

"So that's the secret?" Emily asked, swallowing hard. "Practice?"

"Practice. Doing the same thing over and over and over again," he said slowly. With each word he moved farther around her until he stood directly in front of her. "Until you get real good at it."

He stood so close that, in spite of her petticoat, she could feel his legs intertwined with her skirts and his knees pressing between hers.

"Does that apply to anything?" she asked. She was afraid her quaking voice would never have the strength to be heard over the violent pounding of her heart.

"Oh, yes," he assured her quietly. He began to stroke her cheek with his fingertips. They were rough and callused from work, but his touch was gentle. "But especially to physical activities."

She knew she ought to say something bright or witty, something that would relieve the tension in the air—a tension between them she had felt building since the first moment they'd met. She couldn't think of a thing to say, and was glad of it. She really didn't want this moment to end.

"Oh, hell, Emily," he said in frustration. "I'm a lawyer. People pay me for my words, and right now, I've plumb run out of them."

Suddenly he wrapped his arms about her and pulled her roughly to him. He wanted to go slowly, but there was only so much flesh and blood could bear, and he was only human, and it had been so long.

He lifted her face to his and pressed his lips down on hers. She didn't struggle. She entwined her own arms about his neck, joining them more closely now than he could have hoped.

He couldn't bring himself to separate his lips from the heated contact with hers. He continued to press kisses against the soft edges of her mouth, moving across her smooth cheeks to the warmth of the little hollow beneath her ear.

He opened his mouth. His tongue slipped over her smooth skin, flickering over her tiny earlobe. His lips drew the soft bit of flesh into his mouth. He stroked the edge with the tip of his tongue. She twitched and giggled. It must have tickled. He smiled as he realized he had discovered a tiny spot of vulnerability in her.

He let her moist earlobe slip from his mouth, pressing his cheek against it to protect even that tiny part of her from getting chilled in the night air. He moved his kisses down her neck, then traveled once again across her jawline to return to her waiting, willing lips.

His hands slid from her shoulders down her back. He moved to encircle her tiny waist with her hands, then traveled up again, moving toward her rounded breasts pressing against his chest. His palms tingled with the very thought of cupping their soft fullness.

Slowly he pulled himself away from her. Their breathing came in ragged gasps. If he continued, there would be no stopping. He'd take her on the porch right now—with Ma and the girls washing dishes in the kitchen and Noah reading in the parlor, right under their very noses. So he merely held her at arms' length and continued to study her flushed face and sparkling eyes—and continued to long for her.

"Oh, no. Oh, no," she said breathlessly, slowly drawing away. Her body still quivered.

"Emily, I'm sorry. I didn't mean any disrespect to you. Really, I didn't."

"I know," she said. She was trying to breathe normally.

"It's just . . . I've wanted to do that forever," he said.

She smiled and shook her head. "You haven't known me that long."

He reached up to stroke her cheek and twirl about her finger the wispy little tendrils that had come loose at her temple. "I've wanted to do that since the first moment I laid eyes on you."

"I can't believe you feel this way."

"You can't believe that I find you a warm and desirable woman?" he asked. Although he'd promised himself to go slow, he couldn't help but slide his hand down her cheek and neck, over her smooth shoulder and down her back, trying to draw her closer again.

"I can't believe that you actually feel for me . . . what I feel for you," she admitted at last. Then she began to shake her head and stepped away from him completely. "I . . . I can't, Ben. I just can't."

"Emily . . ."

Before he could stop her, before he could cradle her in his arms again to reassure her, Emily had slipped away from him. She stopped in front of the door, quickly pinning her disheveled hair into place and smoothing down the wrinkles in her dress.

She couldn't let anything like this happen to her . . . not now, she kept insisting to herself, no matter how much her heart—and other parts of her—kept screaming to turn back. She had other things to think about, other duties, family responsibilities. Slowly she opened the door and went inside.

With studied calmness, she thanked Dolly for Sunday dinner.

"Meggie and I need to go back home now," she said. "You will drive us, won't you, Ben?"

Ben stood watching her sadly from the doorway. "If you really want to go," he answered.

"Come along, Meggie. School tomorrow," Emily called. She hadn't answered him directly, but that was all the answer she needed to give.

"Oh, for Pete's sake! I thought you'd unpacked everything," Meggie complained. "How much more of this darned stuff do you have in those trunks?"

"Just this." Emily held up the red and green plaid dress.

"A dress for *school*?" Meggie shook her head. Reluctantly she slipped the dress over her head, then turned for Emily to button up the back.

"You wore a dress to church."

"Church is one thing. School is a whole 'nother matter," Meggie said, squirming so badly that Emily had trouble fixing the tiny buttons. "I can't wear this thing to school. All my friends'll think I'm getting prissy, just like you!"

"I am not prissy!" Emily protested.

"Well, all the boys'll make fun of me," Meggie whined. "Especially Jimmy Lindstrom."

"Oh, ten-year-old boys make fun of everything."

"Jimmy's twelve."

"That's even worse!" Emily said with a little laugh. "Don't worry. In a few more years all those nasty little boys will grow into nice young men. Then they'll be paying you all kinds of attention."

"Like what?"

"Sending you flowers. Inviting you to parties." Emily tried to remember all the things she had been invited to as a young girl—things Mother had never allowed her to go to. She pressed her lips together, then continued. "Christmas tree trimming and skating parties in the winter. Independence Day parades and picnics in the summer. Birthday parties all year long."

"Aw, we go to them now."

"And when you get older, fancy balls in real ballrooms—not barns," Emily added with a teasing scowl and a playful little poke in Meggie's ribs.

Meggie giggled.

"They'll pay you nice compliments," Emily offered.

Meggie's eyes narrowed. "Like when Uncle Eb said you looked nice in that blue gown?"

Emily blushed. She didn't think Meggie had noticed. "Well, yes. Like that."

"And you *like* that kind of stuff?" Meggie demanded, wrinkling her nose with disgust.

"Oh, yes. And you will, too—someday," Emily assured her.

"You really *liked* when Uncle Eb said you were pretty? You like him to think you're pretty? Do you think he's handsome?"

This persistent questioning regarding her feelings about Ben brought a deeper flush to her cheeks. Still, no sense in lying to the child, Emily decided. "Yes, I do," she admitted.

Meggie laughed. "Hey, Frannie, you look silly, too," she called.

Emily whirled around to see Ben and Frannie standing in the doorway to Meggie's bedroom. How long had they been standing there, listening to every word she said? And Meggie hadn't given a single clue, the little minx!

Ben was grinning at her shamelessly, his eyes blatantly ranging over her face and figure. So he knew she liked him to compliment her, and he knew that she thought he was handsome. Even if her embarrassment at being discovered didn't stop her from returning his appreciative glance—then her good sense did.

"Frannie, you look so pretty!" Emily said, specifically directing her attention to the little girl in her blue checked dress so that she could ignore the child's father. "Where did you get your dress? I thought you said you only had one."

"Pa had it hidden in the back of his chifforobe," she said. "Saving it for my birthday."

"And you thought you were the only one with a secret spot," Ben said, grinning at Emily.

Emily didn't dare answer Ben, not yet.

"Are you two about ready for school?" Ben asked.

Meggie snatched up her bookstrap. Her books thumped against the steps behind her as she and Frannie descended the stairs.

Emily moved toward the door, but Ben still stood blocking her way. As she came closer to him, he held out his arm for her.

Was she more embarrassed because she had kissed him last night, or because she had stopped? Either way, she couldn't meet his gaze. "I have to get Meggie's lunch," she said.

Ben stepped aside.

Meggie had already taken her lunch pail from the table. She and Frannie headed toward the cornfield before Emily could even wish them a good day.

Once inside the tall, sheltering stalks of corn, Meggie pulled open her lunch pail. "Geez, I hope she didn't put any of that awful pot roast in there!"

Frannie bent down to peek under the pail. "Couldn't have. Hasn't rotted through the bottom yet."

Meggie sniffed the contents cautiously, then breathed a sigh of relief. "Nope. Gramma's leftover pot roast."

"Well, at least you won't die of food poisoning," Frannie said.

"She's trying to starve me with her terrible cooking," Meggie complained, closing her pail. Then they continued on their way. "And she gets me to wear dresses that make me look stupid in front of all my friends."

"She's getting even with you for talking her into wearing that blue gown to the barn dance," Frannie said.

"No matter what I do, she *still* wants to take me back to Baltimore. Ain't that a city on the water? Geez, she'll probably try to drown me next! What am I gonna do, Frannie?" Meggie lamented.

Frannie shook her head with frustration. "Ain't no way to get rid of her."

"She's thinking too much about *me*," Meggie reasoned. "We got to get her interested in something else."

"Like what? Cooking?" Frannie asked, laughing loudly.

"No, like . . . like . . ."

"Sewing?"

"I don't think so. I don't want her around me with pointy needles and sharp scissors. No, something like . . . like a man!"

"What do you mean? Marry her off?"

"Yeah!"

"That's not going to be as easy as it sounds," Frannie warned. "Look how long Mrs. Robbins has been trying to marry off Pearl."

"Well, look at Pearl. I hate to say it, but at least Aunt Emily is pretty."

"So, who you gonna get? Uncle Noah?"

"Geez, no!" Meggie exclaimed. "I love Uncle Noah, but he drinks too much. I wouldn't wish him on my worst enemy. Not even on mean ol', ugly ol' Miss Bloom!"

Meggie laughed and gave her cousin a playful punch as they emerged from the cornfield into the rear of the schoolyard. They took off at a run to see who could reach the front steps first.

Ben came up behind Emily as she watched the two little girls disappear into the cornfield. He placed both hands on her shoulders.

Emily stood there, holding her breath, wondering what to do now. It felt so good to let him touch her again. All night long she'd imagined his kisses again pressing against her lips and neck. All night long she'd yearned for the feel of him against her breasts and longed to know the feel of him between her thighs.

Right now it was enough to feel his hands gripping her shoulders as if he never wanted to let her go. He rubbed his freshly shaved cheek against her hair. She drew in a deep breath, savoring the smell of the shaving soap he used, enjoying the scent of his body so close to hers.

She could feel his chest pressing into her back. She wanted to turn around and feel him against her breasts. She wanted to see the soft dark hairs at the open neck of his shirt. She wanted to slip her hands over the soft flannel and unfasten the thin tin buttons. She wanted to reach into his shirt and feel the strands of hair that curled about each rigid nipple and trickled over his flat stomach and thickened as they trailed down to disappear into the tops of his tight jeans. She wanted to feel his manhood as it demanded her attention.

Now that the house was empty, how easy it would be to

close the doors and draw the blinds. How tempting to take his hand and climb the stairs to her room.

"Emily."

She didn't turn immediately when he whispered her name. She leaned her head backward slightly, resting it against his shoulder.

She knew that if she turned to him, if she saw his lips parted in an inviting smile, if she saw the need for her in his blue eyes, she would never be able to resist him.

"Emily," he repeated. The pressure of his hands on her shoulders slowly and gently turned her around.

After a sleepless night spent thinking of him— Oh, she was finally prepared.

"Will a shawl do . . . ?"

She swallowed, surprised. How unusual did he think their intimacy would become? she wondered, that he expected her to wear only a shawl . . .

"Or do you think you'll need a coat this morning?" he asked.

Her mouth hung open as she realized what he was referring to.

"It's not that chilly," she managed to answer. "My shawl will do."

"Then we'd best get going," he said. "I know you're eager to settle these papers."

Emily studied the floor intently as she made her way into the vestibule to get her shawl and her bag from the bench by the door. She hoped Ben hadn't noticed what an eager fool she was—so eager that she'd forgotten he was here to take her into Winterset to see Mr. Taylor again today. Ben had to hurry to catch up to her as she made her way down the porch steps and out to the buckboard.

"I hope they've found my brother's papers by now," she said as they rode along. She hoped she sounded casual, not condescending nor condemning. She didn't want Ben to think she actually blamed him for any of this.

"Lottie's a hard worker. She'll find them," Ben assured her. "And Mr. Taylor, I know he's young, and sometimes he can be so overeager he sorely tries my patience."

Emily raised her hand to her mouth to hide her giggle. She'd only met Mr. Taylor once and had the same opinion of him. She could imagine how Ben, having known the man for much longer, would feel.

"But he's really not a bad sort of fellow," Ben continued. "And he's a very good lawyer."

Emily nodded. George had trusted Mr. Taylor. That was good enough for her. And Lottie—well, how could she distrust someone who looked so much like a baby bird?

When Ben swung the door to the law offices open, Lottie's head popped up from behind the desk. She rose, clutching a pile of bent and folded papers to her bosom.

"Honest, Mr. Cameron. I didn't drop them this time," she quickly explained. "The stack slid over."

Emily looked around the waiting room. Every table, bookcase and leather-bound chair was topped with stacks of loose papers or papers slipping out of their blue bindings.

"I didn't hear of a cyclone going through. What happened?" Ben asked.

"Oh, it's been like this since Saturday morning, Mr. Cameron," Lottie said. "Cecil—Mr. Taylor—and I, we've been searching all the files for any other papers of Mr. Shaw's."

"Obviously, you haven't found them," Ben said.

Sadly Lottie shook her head. She placed the mutilated pile of papers onto the top of her desk. Before she could catch them, they slid to the floor again.

"No, sir. But we're not done looking yet!" she proclaimed with confidence. Then she disappeared behind her desk to pick up the fallen pile.

Emily was completely overwhelmed by the vast quantities of papers and dismayed that, out of all this, apparently not a single one pertained to her brother's estate.

"Lottie, is Mr. Taylor in yet?" Ben asked, stretching his neck to try to see her over the desk.

The wispy white-blond curls at the top of her head and her pale blue eyes behind their transparent shield of spectacles was all that appeared from behind the desk.

"Yes, sir. He's in his office, waiting for you," Lottie answered, then disappeared again.

Like an owl back into a hollow tree, Emily thought.

Mr. Taylor emerged from his office, smiling a wide greeting. Emily liked the young man, for all his foolish flatteries. Still, she couldn't help but throw a wistful little look at Ben as she entered Mr. Taylor's office without him. What a pity she wouldn't be sitting for hours on end alone with him in the law office.

She felt a little more relieved, knowing that soon she would finish her business here and return to Baltimore with Meggie. Soon she would also be leaving Ben. She would never see his pale blue eyes smiling at her, or feel his rough hands gently caressing her, or feel his warm lips on hers. She felt an ache in her heart that wouldn't stop.

"I'm sorry you had to come all the way into town today, Miss Shaw," he began.

"Do you mean that you still don't have all my brother's papers in order?" she asked. After all this time and the obvious effort, it was very hard to keep the disgust and impatience out of her voice.

"Well, yes and no," Mr. Taylor answered.

"I don't suppose you could be more specific?"

"Yes, Miss Shaw," Mr. Taylor began. "We have your

brother's last will and testament. We have been over it several times. It is in good order. There is absolutely no cause for worry there."

"I knew that when I came here, Mr. Taylor," she said. So did they. If this was all the information they could give her after all this searching for all this time, there was obviously something wrong here that they weren't telling her. In a voice that grew stronger with its demands, Emily asked, "What else is there, Mr. Taylor?"

"Miss Shaw, please understand. Lottie—Miss McGregor—and I, spent Friday and Saturday searching this office for any more of your brother's papers. Now, Miss McGregor would probably be the first to admit that her secretarial abilities are—how shall I say this?—somewhat below expectations. But she truly is a good girl, Miss Shaw. We *will* find those papers, if only you could . . ."

"Stay in town for another day or two?" she finished for him. After all, she *knew* that's what he was going to say. She was afraid that's what he was going to say.

Emily sighed. "I don't see how I can avoid it." She rose quickly. Before Mr. Taylor could do the same, she leaned over the desk and glared at him. He seemed to cringe back in his chair. "But only a few more days. I want this settled, Mr. Taylor. I *have* to leave here—soon."

A few more days in this wretched town, she thought as she left the law offices. A few more days in that run-down house, eating her own wretched cooking. A very few more days to spend with Ben Cameron, fearing each time she was with him that she would do something she would regret for the rest of her life, and fearing that each time she was with him would be her last.

How much longer could this go on? She wondered which was worse—having your heart ripped quickly from your breast or cutting it away little by little.

* * *

''That's it! That finishes it!'' Meggie burst into the kitchen and slammed her books down on the table. She sent up a puff of flour and almost upset the bowl of eggs Emily had put out, in another futile attempt to make biscuits. She plopped down in the chair, crossed her arms over her breast, and hung her head down.

Frannie entered more slowly, shaking her head. ''She really did it this time,'' she announced to Emily.

''Who did what?''

''Oh, it wasn't bad enough you made me wear this bright red plaid dress to school today,'' Meggie complained loudly.

''Didn't they like it?''

Meggie looked up at Emily. She sniffed and twisted her little lips. ''Well, yeah . . . yeah, come to think of it, they did,'' she admitted more softly. Then she started shouting again. ''But that's not the point.''

''It was so bright that nobody could miss seeing her when Miss Bloom made her sit on that stool in the corner,'' Frannie explained.

''With that big stupid hat on!''

''Oh, Meggie, did you fail another test?'' Emily tried to sound as sympathetic as she could. ''I wish there was something I could do.''

''How's your aim with a shotgun?''

''Not too . . . Oh, Meggie!'' Emily said, shocked—not only that Meggie would suggest such a thing, but that, just for a moment, she had considered going along with it. ''That won't work. They'll just hire someone new to take her place—maybe someone even worse than Miss Bloom.''

Meggie sat silent for a while. Then she stood and announced, ''Well, I can read and I can cipher—as good as

Mrs. Randall, and she runs the Emporium. I've learned all I need. I'm not going back to school. Never!"

"If you think I'm going without you . . ." Frannie began, horrified at the very prospect of facing Miss Bloom alone.

"Calm down, both of you," Emily said. "There's got to be a better solution."

"I already gave you my best one," Meggie said.

Emily shook her head. "*I'll* go to the school. I'll talk to Miss Bloom. Embarrassing children is *not* the way to teach them."

She spoke with such authority that she even surprised herself. First she'd scolded Mr. Taylor; now she was intending to face down the schoolmarm. Heaven only knew what she was doing with Ben Cameron. Why, if these changes in her continued, the next time Mrs. Hannigan gave her an argument, she just might punch her in the nose!

"I'll tell Miss Bloom to stop putting you in the corner."

"You will?" Meggie was so amazed that she stood up so fast her chair fell over backward. As it clattered to the floor, one of the front legs fell off and the spindles of the back separated from the seat.

Shaken from her sudden overconfidence, Emily stared at the broken chair for just a few seconds before answering. She looked up and squared her shoulders and hoped to find that same confidence again when confronting Miss Bloom.

"Yes, I will, Meggie," Emily answered. "Now, go do your lessons, both of you."

Meggie and Frannie grabbed their books and scampered up the stairs.

Emily gathered up the pieces of the chair and put them on the back porch. This was probably just a small example of what Ben had been referring to when he said that George had let a lot of little things go around the house. She examined the pieces. She didn't know anything about carpentry, but maybe she could try to fit them back together again, somehow, before she left.

She tried to think about what she would say to Miss Bloom when she went to see her tomorrow afternoon. She wished she could just take Meggie back to Baltimore and didn't have to go to see the teacher at all.

She sighed and went back to kneading the biscuit dough. Maybe if she worked the dough more, they wouldn't be so tough. Someday she'd find the courage to ask Dolly how she got hers to rise so high and tender.

If things had turned out as she had expected, she could have gotten pompous old Mr. Ebenezer Cameron the Lawyer to talk to Miss Bloom the Dragon, and saved herself a lot of trouble. Of course, if things had turned out as she had expected, she and her niece would be back in Baltimore already.

But Ben Cameron had turned out to be more trouble than Meggie, or even Miss Bloom. She wouldn't ask for his help now. That would only continue to involve him in Meggie's upbringing—something that Emily had to put a stop to. If Ben had been doing such a good job of helping to raise Meggie in the first place, why was she in this fix now?

No, Emily thought, she'd have to take care of this herself. Sadly she acknowledged that she'd have to get used to taking care of things alone. She'd have to be doing it for the rest of her life.

CHAPTER TWELVE

"I APPRECIATE YOUR TAKING THE TIME AWAY from your . . . um, building project to do this, Noah," Emily told him as he helped her into the buckboard.

"Happy to do it, Miss Emily," he answered.

"I know how important your . . . ark is to you," she added. As strange as it seemed to her to be talking about an oceangoing vessel in the middle of Iowa, it was better than riding along, past the cornfields, in silence.

"I'm here to serve wherever I'm led, Miss Emily."

"It's really for Meggie's sake that I'm doing this," she continued.

"I know," Noah agreed. "We're all concerned about Meggie."

Emily was glad Noah had agreed to drive her to the school this afternoon. She'd felt awkward asking him at first. She knew how preoccupied he was with his ark. But she didn't think Annabelle had ever been to the school before, and Emily couldn't rely on her to know the way—and she certainly wasn't going to ask Ben for his help.

Emily was nervous enough. Teachers had always made her nervous when she was a little girl. Listening to Meggie and Frannie talk, she didn't think Miss Bloom was going to be much different. She didn't need Ben Cameron around to upset her any more.

She had always tried to be so sensible, but every time she was around Ben, she either lost her temper with him or—worse yet—forgot all her proper upbringing and turned into some kind of unbridled wanton. She certainly didn't need him around, distracting her, when she was trying to talk sensibly to Meggie's teacher!

Except for seeing Meggie and Frannie off for school this morning, she'd managed to avoid Ben the rest of the day. As she rode to see Miss Bloom this afternoon, she already felt calmer, more in control of her mental faculties. It was only when she stopped concentrating on planning what she was going to say to the teacher that she realized how much she missed seeing Ben.

How much more was she going to miss seeing him as the days rolled into weeks? Or perhaps, as the weeks passed into years, could she forget him? She'd do her best to try. Or for Meggie's sake, she could at least pretend she had. But, in her private moments, how could she ever convince herself?

Noah stopped the buckboard in front of the small white frame cottage beside the red schoolhouse. The schoolhouse doors and windows were closed. The schoolyard was empty. All the children had gone home to do their lessons and their chores before supper. At least Emily would be able to speak to the teacher in peace and quiet—and not embarrass Meggie any further in front of her friends.

"Want me to wait for you?" Noah asked.

Hesitantly Emily began, "I hate to keep you from your work. . . ."

Noah looked up at the gradually darkening sky. "No, I'd be about done for the day anyway."

"Thanks, Noah. It would be a long walk home."

''It's closer than you think.'' Noah chuckled and pointed to the cornfield. ''It's right across the way. Course, I wouldn't advise you to be going in there.''

Emily looked up at the sky, too. ''Yes, it is getting dark earlier,'' she agreed.

''No, not just this time of day,'' Noah said. ''Folks can get real lost in a cornfield any time.''

Emily looked up at the eight-foot stalks crowded close together. One row of corn looked pretty much like another, especially at eye level. Once inside, it would be hard for a person to tell in what direction they were going.

''I see your point,'' she conceded. Then she felt she ought to warn him, ''Now, I could be talking to Miss Bloom for quite a while. . . .''

''Or it could be a real short visit,'' Noah added with a wink.

''Well, that depends on how cooperative she is.''

''Can't help you on that, Miss Emily,'' Noah said. ''Not having been blessed with a wife and young'uns myself, and having other pressing concerns, I haven't really paid much mind to what the schoolmarm was doing.'' Then he screwed his face up into a scowl. ''According to Meggie, however, you probably should've brought your lance and shield against the Dragon Lady, although I don't think Annabelle here would make much of a charger.''

''That's all right,'' Emily replied with a grin. ''I don't think I'm going to make much of a Saint George.''

''You never know what you can do till you try,'' Noah told her. ''It's for Meggie, Miss Emily. Go get her!''

In spite of Noah's encouraging words, Emily was still very nervous as she walked up the white gravel pathway that led to Miss Bloom's cottage. Halfway up, she was surprised by a roly-poly little hound dog who loped up to her and immediately tripped over her feet.

"Shoo, shoo," she said, waving him away with her hand.

He not only didn't leave, he was joined by another equally clumsy puppy from under the porch. Emily stopped where she was, afraid to go any further. She'd been attacked by chickens once already. She didn't want to be tripped by puppies and go sprawling across the lawn and greet Miss Bloom on her hands and knees.

"C'mon, boys. Here, Rover. Here, Fido."

Emily heard Noah clapping his hands and whistling and calling for the puppies. With relief, she watched them bounding away from her over to him.

"How do you know their names?" she turned and asked.

He shrugged his shoulders. "Ain't all dogs named Rover and Fido?"

Emily laughed and continued on her way up the path.

"Well, well, throw me in the outhouse and call me Stinky!" Noah exclaimed. "I was wrong. What we got us here is a Rover and a Daisy instead."

Emily did her best to control her laughter before she finally knocked on Miss Bloom's front door.

She wasn't sure who or what she was expecting to greet her. Remembering her own brief experience with schoolteachers before Mother insisted she get a private tutor so that she could stay at home to keep Mother company, she imagined perhaps an aged, gaunt-bodied, whey-faced prune. On the other hand, if Meggie was to be believed, Miss Bloom should have horns, glowing eyes, smoking ears—and on a good day be able to shoot fire out of her nostrils.

As the door opened, Emily swallowed hard and prepared herself for anything.

"Miss Shaw?" asked the tiny little woman at the door.

Emily blinked. She was almost ready to ask her if her mommy was at home. "Miss Bloom? Miss Ida Bloom?"

She nodded her head, her springy auburn curls bouncing in the sunlight. "Pleased to meet you, Miss Shaw."

She glanced past Emily to Noah, who was frolicking with the two puppies in the front yard. Miss Bloom laughed. "I see your friend is already amusing himself with my little pets." She craned her neck, as if to see Noah better. "I'd ask your friend to come in, too, but I'd hate to disturb them. I do so love to see a man who enjoys the company of animals. But won't you come in and sit down, Miss Shaw?" Miss Bloom invited.

Still bewildered by Miss Bloom's unexpected appearance, Emily retained just enough presence of mind not to make a complete fool of herself. She followed the slender young woman into the tidy little pink and green parlor and seated herself on the edge of the pink chintz-covered sofa, right beside a large brass birdcage. Inside, two yellow canaries warbled and flitted from one perch to the other. Emily wondered if Miss Bloom spoke to them the way elderly Miss Vogt had spoken to hers. From across the room the canaries were answered by the chirping of two brown and red finches in their cage.

"Would you care for a cup of tea, Miss Shaw?" Miss Bloom asked.

"Thank you, no. I really only came to . . ." Emily hadn't expected Miss Bloom to look quite so crestfallen at her polite refusal.

It was then that Emily noticed just the tiniest of lines at the corners of Miss Bloom's sapphire-blue eyes. Miss Bloom was not the child she had at first appeared, but rather a woman in her late twenties, like Emily herself. Or had several years of teaching school aged the girl prematurely?

Emily quickly changed her mind about tea. "Well, actually, that would be very nice, Miss Bloom, if it wouldn't be too much trouble."

"Trouble? Oh, no trouble at all," she answered eagerly. She disappeared for only a second. She reappeared so fast that Emily supposed she'd already had the tea things prepared specifically for Emily's visit.

"Sugar?" Miss Bloom asked as she poured Emily a cup of tea.

She was a graceful little thing, Emily noted with admiration for her slender fingers and carefully manicured nails. "Yes, please," Emily answered.

"Do have a cookie," Miss Bloom encouraged Emily. "I made them myself from an old family recipe."

Emily lifted the light little confection from the pink and green patterned plate. How *did* she manage to put lumps of flour, butter, sugar, and eggs into a hot oven and then take them out just as they turned golden brown instead of coming out scorched black? Emily wondered.

"It's delicious," Emily said. It must be some sort of talent, passed down from one generation to the next—this ability to make "old family recipes" taste so good. The only "old family recipe" Emily knew was the one she had for potatoes that Ben had teased her about. She wished, somehow, she could make something for him that he would actually enjoy eating.

"I understand you come from Baltimore. I've never been to Baltimore," Miss Bloom said casually, as if there were nothing else that Emily had come here to talk about.

Emily was growing more and more restless, nervous about bringing up the subject of Meggie and her terrible schoolwork, not to mention Miss Bloom's terrible treatment of Meggie. Maybe Miss Bloom's pleasant manner was just a clever disguise, Emily began to think with foreboding. Maybe, as soon as Emily mentioned school, Miss Bloom's horns and fangs would appear. Emily smiled to herself. If

Ben could read her thoughts now, would he accuse her of reading too many gothic novels?

To add to her confusion, Emily could have sworn she just saw a fluffy white rabbit scoot out from under one chair and duck under the one Miss Bloom was sitting on.

''Have you ever been to Iowa before, Miss Shaw?''

''No, I haven't,'' Emily answered quickly, feeling guilty that, after all these years, she still hadn't been paying much attention to the teacher.

''It's a very lovely state, if I do say so myself,'' Miss Bloom continued. ''Although you will have to allow me just a little prejudice, as I've never been anywhere else.''

Emily was more than a little surprised. Miss Bloom sipped her tea as if she were sitting in the most elegant New York drawing room, not some modest little cottage in the middle of a cornfield in Iowa. Emily couldn't help wondering what had brought a lady of Miss Bloom's obvious refinement to the solitary and greatly unappreciated occupation of schoolteacher. She wanted to know more about Miss Bloom and her rather stationary life.

She also wanted to know where in the world that white rabbit had come from. She'd seen it again as it slipped out from under Miss Bloom's chair and moved under the sofa. At least she could be relieved now that it wasn't a figment of her overworked imagination.

''Never?'' was the only comment Emily could think to make.

''No, never,'' Miss Bloom answered. ''Is that so hard to believe? Although I was born in Davenport, I never had the opportunity to cross the Mississippi River—even after they built the railroad bridge.'' With a little grin she added, ''At least I haven't yet.''

''This is my first time west of the Mississippi,'' Emily said. ''My family never traveled much.''

"My father was a doctor, but he always imagined himself as some sort of pioneer. We moved about Iowa for a bit, eventually settling in Dubuque," Miss Bloom continued. "That's where I went to the university."

"You went to a university in Dubuque?" This time Emily couldn't hide her surprise.

Miss Bloom looked at her askance over her cup of tea. "What's more surprising, Miss Shaw?" she asked pointedly. "That *I* went to a university or that the university was in *Iowa*? Compared to Maryland, Iowa may be a relatively young state, but we do have quite a few very good colleges here already."

"Oh, please, Miss Bloom," Emily said quickly. "I didn't intend any insult."

"Perhaps someone like you from a big eastern city might think so, but we're not all just pigsties and cornfields out here, you know," she reproached Emily gently.

Hadn't Ben pointed out to her that very same thing? Emily scolded herself much more harshly. She really should pay more attention to the evidence of her own eyes and less attention to her own preconceived notions of what a place was like.

"I'm really very embarrassed now, Miss Bloom," Emily admitted. She wanted to look into the corners of the parlor, thinking Miss Bloom kept a spare stool in her house for stupid guests to sit on. She didn't think she'd mind that so much as long as she didn't have to wear that awful pointy hat.

"Think nothing of it, Miss Shaw." Miss Bloom dismissed Emily's embarrassment with a little laugh. "I'm a teacher. It's my job to correct misinformation—wherever I find it."

Emily would have felt enormously chastened if it weren't for the friendly smile on Miss Bloom's face.

Suddenly a large, fluffy black rabbit darted out from under the sofa and headed across the floor in plain view.

"But that rabbit was white!" Emily exclaimed, bolting upright in her seat. She clapped her hand firmly over her mouth and sank back onto the soft sofa cushions. She needed to go back home *very soon.* There were good doctors there who would tend to her mental problems.

"No, no, Bonnie's always been black." Miss Bloom slid off her seat onto her knees. She stretched her arm out under the sofa and pulled out the large white rabbit. "Benny is my white bunny."

She sat back in her chair, the white rabbit cuddled comfortably in her arms.

"I apologize for rambling on so. Except for the children, I know so few people in Bidewell that it really is a pleasure to talk to an adult for a change."

Or a human, Emily thought.

"But enough about me. Now, we really need to talk about Margaret. . . ."

"My niece prefers to be called Meggie," Emily corrected.

Miss Bloom looked surprised. "She never told me. Oh, I wish she'd mentioned . . . You know, I think that's part of our problem here, Miss Shaw."

"Oh?" Since Miss Bloom was taking the initiative, Emily decided to let her have her say first.

"Margaret . . . Meggie is very quiet in class."

"Meggie is too quiet?" Emily repeated with a surprised chuckle. "I find that very hard to believe."

"She takes no part in class discussions, never volunteers an answer . . ."

"We are talking about Margaret Shaw, aren't we?" Emily asked. "You don't have her confused with Frances Cameron, do you? They're always together. . . ."

"Oh, no. I never confuse my children," she stated confidently, still stroking the fluffy white bunny.

"But Meggie tells me you've made her sit on a stool in the corner with a hat on," Emily said. She was very nervous now that they had come to the real reason for Emily's being here.

"Once."

"But why would you punish such a quiet child in that way?" Emily demanded.

"Because she is not always quiet," Miss Bloom said. "She failed a test—again. When I reprimanded her, she responded in—how shall I put this? Loudly and in rather rude terms."

"Meggie?" Emily could hardly believe such a thing of Meggie. On the other hand . . .

Miss Bloom nodded. "It was very disturbing—to the entire school."

"I can imagine."

"I tried repeatedly to talk to her, but there comes a time when even I reach the end of my patience. You know, it's very frustrating for me, too, Miss Shaw," Miss Bloom continued, shaking her head sadly. "I want all my children to succeed. But when they don't conduct themselves properly, I have to resort to some stern discipline."

Emily almost had to laugh. Recalling George's horror stories of punishments given to his classmates, Miss Bloom's idea of discipline was hardly stern.

She was also surprised that Miss Bloom seemed to care so much for each individual student. Emily's tutors had been more concerned with collecting the sizable salary Father had paid them than with her education.

"I realize I'm new here and don't know much about my students yet," Miss Bloom continued. "But my predecessor, Miss Mueller, left some records here I have found invaluable. She seemed to think very highly of Meggie and her abilities.''

''That's what I was given to understand.'' Emily felt this was a safe answer. She really didn't think this was the time to tell Miss Bloom that Meggie had thought rather highly of Miss Mueller, and that Miss Bloom paled greatly in comparison in Meggie's estimation.

''Forgive me for broaching the subject, but I understand Meggie's father, your brother, passed away recently.''

Emily nodded.

''My condolences to both of you,'' Miss Bloom offered. ''This loss, and the resignation of a beloved teacher—could this change in Meggie's behavior and lack of satisfactory performance in school be linked somehow to these factors, Miss Shaw?''

''I wouldn't be surprised,'' Emily answered. Meggie seemed so carefree. Could this be her way of hiding her true feelings? ''What can we do for her, Miss Bloom?''

''We must do our best to console her in her grief, but we cannot spoil the child. We mustn't allow her to fall too far behind in her studies,'' Miss Bloom cautioned. She left off petting Benny just long enough to wave a warning finger in Emily's direction. ''I'll do my best to encourage her in school. Perhaps if you helped her at home?''

''I'll do my best,'' Emily promised.

Suddenly there was a loud thumping and scratching at the front door. Miss Bloom rose and placed the white rabbit carefully in her seat, then ran to the door to see what was the matter. When she opened the door, Noah rolled backward into the room.

Oh, no! He's drunk again! Emily immediately thought, springing to her feet with alarm. Maybe there was a back door she could sneak out quickly and pretend she had no connection with Noah whatsoever. Where had the man gotten the whiskey—and so quickly? Then she noticed the two puppies squirming over him as he scrambled to his feet.

Noah shooed away the rollicking puppies and pulled at his clothes to make himself more presentable. ''Excuse me, Miss . . .''

''Bloom. Ida Bloom.''

''I know,'' he answered. ''I'm Noah Cameron, Meggie's uncle.''

''Yes, Mr. Cameron, I've heard about you.''

Emily noticed, to Miss Bloom's credit, that her expression gave no hint of whether what she'd heard about Noah was good or bad.

''I must apologize for forgetting you were out there, Mr. Cameron.''

''No need to apologize,'' Noah said, still chuckling at the puppies' antics. ''I've been having quite a time with . . .''

''Rover and Daisy.'' Miss Bloom supplied the missing names at the same time Noah said them.

Emily blinked with surprise. So did Miss Bloom.

''How did you know?'' Miss Bloom managed to ask.

''Well, it . . . it seemed a logical choice,'' Noah answered with a shrug of his shoulders. He seemed as astounded as the ladies.

''Mr. Cameron, why don't you join us for tea and cookies?'' Miss Bloom invited, moving back from the doorway so that he could enter.

''Thank you, ma'am,'' Noah replied, stepping inside. ''Don't mind if I do.''

''Oh, shoo! Shoo!'' Miss Bloom bustled up to the tea tray, alternately clapping and waving her hands. A big gray cat scampered off the table. ''Oh, dear, I hope you don't mind your tea without milk. I really wouldn't drink it now.''

''Don't have much stomach for milk myself,'' Noah

answered as he seated himself in the chair beside Miss Bloom. The big, sleek gray cat jumped into his lap and settled comfortably there. "Sure do like your cat, though." He was still admiring the creature when another, slightly smaller, fluffier, black and white cat slipped past his chair.

"That's Matilda," she explained. "She's a bit timid of strangers. But Maxwell seems rather taken with you." She scooped Benny back into her arms as she sat down and continued to pet him.

"Two cats, huh? And two little puppies?" he asked. He looked about the room. "Two little canaries. Like the finches, too. Is there another rabbit?"

Miss Bloom nodded and started looking around the floor. "Oh, Bonnie's around here somewhere."

Noah leaned forward in his chair and stared at the tiny little schoolteacher. Then he broke out in a big grin. "You sort of favor animals in pairs, don't you, Miss Bloom?"

Miss Bloom nodded, then lowered her head so that no one could see the blush that colored her porcelain cheeks.

"I suppose you could say it was a little personal foible of mine," she admitted quietly. "You see, as a schoolteacher . . . a maiden lady, I expect to be spending the rest of my life alone."

"How awful!" Noah said, slowly examining Miss Bloom, from the top of her curly auburn head to the tips of her dainty black leather shoes.

"I had no intention of seeing my poor little pets do the same," she stated with firm conviction. "Every living thing needs company."

"Indeed they do, Miss Bloom," Noah heartily agreed. "*Every* living thing."

Emily reluctantly glanced at the watch pinned to her bodice. "I'm very sorry, but it's getting late," she said as she rose. "Miss Bloom, thank you for your hospitality—and for your helpful suggestions for Meggie."

Noah and Miss Bloom rose even more reluctantly.

"My pleasure, Miss Shaw. I do hope you'll keep me informed of Meggie's progress at home," Miss Bloom said, all the while never taking her eyes from Noah. "And perhaps you could come again some time—soon."

Emily nodded. She knew she wouldn't be in Bidewell much longer but she'd try to find the time to pay friendly little Miss Bloom just one more call.

"Oh, we surely will, Miss Bloom," Noah answered.

Emily had the strongest feeling that Noah's *we* had nothing to do with her.

"Evening, Emily," Ben said. He stood in the doorway, grinning at her.

Oh, she was glad to see him and talk to him again! Even two days of just watching him out of the upstairs window of her house as he went to his office in Winterset in the morning and came home after dinner at the farm at night was too long. She wanted to touch him, to kiss him. Her heart ached just to hold him again. She took a deep breath. She'd just have to get used to not having those things.

Now he stood in the doorway, smiling at her. That wasn't so unusual. What surprised Emily was seeing him standing there with a toolbox in one hand, an old lantern in the other, and a short ladder hung over his shoulder.

"What are you doing here?"

"Aren't you glad to see me?"

"Of course. I'm always glad to see you," she answered before she realized what he might infer from that. "I'm not so sure about all your . . . belongings," she added, pointing to his ladder and toolbox. "What are you doing here this time of night?"

Ben just shrugged, as if he carried these things around with him all the time. ''Oh, it's not so late,'' he said.

''Could've used you earlier, Uncle Eb,'' Meggie said sadly, poking her head between Emily and the door. ''Maybe you'd have taken us to Gramma's for dinner again.''

''You're not still hungry, are you?'' Emily asked. Oh, why did the child have to bring up her poor cooking now, in front of Ben?

''No. I don't care how much grease you tried to fry those things in, those pork chops aren't sliding down any farther than right here.'' She clutched her stomach and made a horrible grimace. ''It's the biscuits that I really had trouble with. They were so hard even the butter wouldn't sink into 'em. Sort of like water running off a rock.''

''It wasn't that bad,'' Emily tried to defend herself. It was only a halfhearted attempt. The biscuits really were pretty bad. She'd dropped one from the table. She couldn't be certain until she'd gotten down on her hands and knees and examined it in daylight tomorrow morning, but, from the sound of it, she was pretty sure she'd dented the hardwood kitchen floor.

''You bring Frannie?'' Meggie asked, craning her neck to see around Ben.

''Nope. *She*'s home doing her lessons,'' Ben answered. ''You should be studying, too.''

The brisk autumn wind whipped the leaves around behind him and swirled into the house, ruffling the cloth on the table and blowing Emily's skirt out behind her.

''You going to make me stand out on the porch all night?'' Ben asked.

''No, no.'' Emily quickly stepped back from the doorway so that Ben could enter. ''What are you doing here with that ladder?''

''Looks like rain,'' Ben said, heading for the stairs.

''I'd have thought an umbrella would have been a better choice to carry,'' Emily said. She followed him. ''Where are you going? It's not raining upstairs.''

''Not yet,'' he answered. He kept going up the steps and down the hall. He came to a door that Emily had only opened, peeked into, and had not bothered to open again.

''Why are you going into my attic this time of night?'' she asked.

''The roof leaks,'' he answered. He set the ladder against the wall and put his toolbox on the floor. ''It's one of those things George kind of let go over the years.''

''If it's been like this for years, don't you think it can wait a few more hours to repair?'' Emily suggested.

Ben cocked his head sideways. ''Hear the wind picking up? It's going to rain soon, and the roof leaks—right over Meggie's bed.''

''How could George have—?''

''You must know by now, Meggie slept over my house with Frannie or at the farm,'' Ben explained slowly. ''Now that she's staying here with you, it needs to be fixed.'' The wind whipped around the house again. More quickly, he added, ''Sounds like I'd better get to it, too.''

''Aw, Uncle Eb,'' Meggie whined. ''Can't I just stay with Frannie again tonight?''

''Nope. This is your home, Meggie,'' Ben said. ''You belong here.''

Emily stared at him, surprised. Since when had he started believing that Meggie actually belonged with her?

Meggie glared at him as if he'd just told her he was about to shoot her dog.

''You *want* me to stay here?'' she shouted. ''You want me to go with *her*?''

''I want to fix the roof,'' Ben said very slowly. ''Do you

want raindrops pattering on your head all night long? Now, hand me that lantern, please.''

''You can reach it yourself,'' Meggie snapped. She tore down the hall, ducked into her own room, and slammed the door tightly shut behind her. In the silence that followed, Emily heard the key click in the lock.

Emily watched the muscles of Ben's jaw tighten. Then he turned to her.

''Will you help me with the lamp?'' he asked. His voice was much calmer than she'd expected it to be. ''I'd like to get Meggie's roof fixed first, then I can go on to yours.''

''Mine leaks, too?'' she asked with concern as the wind continued to whistle through the slats in the windows. ''How long will it take to patch Meggie's?''

Ben glanced at Meggie's door. It was still closed tight. He chuckled and bent closer to Emily. ''Don't worry,'' he whispered in her ear. ''I'd love to make sure you were safe and warm tonight no matter what.''

Emily's face flamed as hot and red as the lantern wick. Ben chuckled. He bent down, picked up the lantern, and held it out for Emily. She took it from his hand. His fingers brushed against her as he relinquished it.

''Careful,'' Ben warned.

Emily only nodded. Oh, if only he could know how very careful she was trying to be to avoid him—and how awfully difficult he was making this for her.

He slipped his arm through one rung of the ladder and swung it around to his shoulder. Bending down, he lifted the toolbox with his other hand. All he could do now was nod toward the attic door. ''You go first.''

Emily peered up the dark stairwell. ''Why me first?''

''Because you have the lantern and I'd like to be able to see where I'm going,'' Ben answered. ''Second, I don't want to hit you in the head with the ladder while you're following me up the stairs.''

Emily gave a resigned sigh and proceeded up the gloomy stairs.

The wind whistled even louder through the attic. Emily held the lantern up high. What was it about attics that made Emily refuse to look into the shadowy corners at what the lantern light might reveal?

''Watch out!''

Emily's forehead hit the crossbeam before she could duck.

''Oh, Emily! I thought you knew. . . .'' Ben dropped his ladder and toolbox at the top of the stairs. Taking the lantern from her shaking fingers and depositing it on the floor, he swept her up into his embrace. ''Are you all right?''

Emily blinked, still a little dazed. ''I'll have a headache for a week. Why didn't you tell me?''

''I'm so sorry.'' He held her closely to him, as if by holding her he could take away the pain. ''I thought you knew how low the roof was. There's enough room for a man to stand in the center, but you still have to duck under the crossbeams.''

''I haven't been up in an attic since I was . . . well, short enough not to have to worry.''

She closed her eyes and leaned against him. Still holding her gently to him, he passed his hand over her forehead, feeling for bumps. Ben smiled with relief. She hadn't been moving that fast. It was only a tiny little bump, not a big blow to the head. She wouldn't even have a headache.

Cradled in his arms, she looked as if she were sleeping, Ben thought. Slowly he began to move his hand from her forehead over her temple and down her soft cheek. He held her more closely to him and stifled a deep sigh. How he would love to be holding her like this while she slept. And oh, the things he'd like to do with her to make her sleep like this afterward! And to smile in her sleep!

She opened her eyes and smiled up at him. Oh, what more could a man ask for? Ben slowly lifted her to meet his descending lips. She slid her arm about his waist and lifted her other arm to weave her slender fingers through his hair.

His body was warm against hers in the chilly attic. She pressed closer to him, the better to feel the strength of his body straining toward hers. He bent lower, his lips caressing the length of her neck and trailing down the fabric of her bodice as he bent down. His arm caught her behind her knees, lifting her in his arms as easily as a child. Slowly and carefully, he made his way down the steps. He needn't have carried her. She'd have gone willingly on her own.

With the toe of his boot, he nudged open the bedroom door, catching it with his heel before it could make any noise. Slowly he pushed it closed. He lowered her legs so that she could stand, still held close against him, while he locked the door.

"Emily," he whispered into her soft hair. His lips meandered over her neck. "I want you, Emily. I want you now. Don't make me wait. . . ."

His hands trailed down her arm, slowly releasing her from his firm embrace, until only his callused fingers held her fingertips. Slowly he backed toward the bed, drawing her onward with him. As she stood before him, he placed both hands about her slender waist.

He sat down, pulling her gently to stand between his legs. She reached out to cradle his head between her breasts.

He was a man, fully grown—he'd been married—he'd done this before. Why then were his hands trembling like a giddy adolescent's at the very thought of loving Emily tonight?

CHAPTER THIRTEEN

BEN SLID HIS HANDS UP EMILY'S WAIST. HE snuggled his face into the little valley between her breasts. She could feel his fingers trembling with bridled passion as his hand drew closer and closer to her breasts. Slowly he raised his eyes to hers. She slid her hand from his broad shoulders, up the back of his neck, and entwined her fingers in his gently waving hair.

His hand rose slowly up her ribs. Her heart pounded and nipples tightened as his fingers touched the outer edge of her breast. She drew in a deep breath as his entire hand at last enveloped her. She stood for a moment, absolutely still, her gaze locked with his as if he sought silent permission for this bold seizure. She hardly dared to breathe, fearful that he would think the least movement an attempt to escape his tender grasp.

Ben sat before her, just as still. It was enough for the moment that he touched her. They needed no movement for now.

His lips widened in a tender smile, which Emily returned.

He turned his face to kiss the breast he held, gently pressing it closer to him. Emily closed her eyes with the joy of the tingling passing through her entire body.

Gently he moved his thumb back and forth across her taut nipple. He raised his other hand to cup her other breast. His hand slid down slightly, easing around under her arms while his thumbs still stayed tucked beneath each breast, still stroking them. Holding her where she stood, he pulled back from her.

"Oh." She breathed a little sigh of disappointment, fearing he had suddenly changed his mind. Then he opened his hands. His palms passed lightly over her breasts, teasing both nipples, as his fingers moved to the row of small white pearl buttons down the front of her bodice. Slowly, one by one, his large, sun-browned, callused fingers wrestled to unfasten the tiny buttons.

The wind whistled through the trees, tapping the branches rudely against the windows. Raindrops began to splatter against the glass. The wind hummed through the loose panes as the storm increased. The low rumble of thunder rolled across the fields.

With only his thumb and forefinger, Ben held the end of the narrow pink ribbon that ran through the delicate lace of Emily's chemise. With a slow, smooth motion, he pulled the little ribbon until the loop was just a narrow hole at the top of the tiny knot. He paused. He raised his gaze from studying the small bow to look into her eyes with fiery desire. Then one sharp tug released the entire knot.

"For crying out loud! It's raining in here!" Meggie's voice shouted at them through the thick bedroom door. She pounded on the wood in rhythm to her cries.

Ben sprang up from his seat on the bed. He pulled roughly at the tops of his jeans, trying to loosen them just a little. It looked awfully suspicious that he had to pull his shirttail out to cover himself every time he was around Emily.

Emily darted around to the other side of the bed. Keeping her back to the door, she quickly tried to fasten the uncooperative buttons. Her hands shook so badly, she had trouble just holding onto the slippery little pearls, much less pushing them through the narrow holes in the fabric. Just when she thought she was all done, she realized that she had missed a button in the middle, and had to unfasten her bodice halfway down and do it all up again. She was so upset that Meggie would wonder about the delay that it took her twice as long to do up half as many buttons.

"For Pete's sake! I thought you were gonna fix *my* roof, Uncle Eb," Meggie complained loudly. "What the heck are you two doing in there?"

Ben threw a quick look at Emily, to make sure she was fastened securely, before opening the door.

"Aunt Emily . . ." Ben cleared his constricted throat and continued. "Aunt Emily was just showing me . . . showing me where her ceiling was leaking."

Before Ben could stop her, Meggie strode into the room. Ben took her by the shoulder and, turning her around toward the door, pointed up and then kind of vaguely all around the ceiling. Better she should look up than to notice the dent still in the edge of the mattress where he had sat, he thought with a small surge of panic.

"It's right above the door here, so we had to close it."

Meggie screwed her mouth into a tight grimace. "Looks dry in here to me, but *my* room *is* getting wet—right now!"

With one last brief glance at Emily, Ben quickly ushered Meggie out of the bedroom.

"Well, maybe if you had handed me the lantern when I asked you for it, your roof would be fixed by now," he reminded her sharply as they went down the hall toward the attic.

"All right, I get the point." Turning back, Meggie added, "C'mon and help, Aunt Emily. The sooner we get my roof done, the sooner Uncle Eb can go back to working on yours."

"I'll be right there, Meggie," Emily answered in a voice that still shook with unfulfilled desire for Ben.

The man must have nerves made of glacial ice, she thought. Otherwise, how could he have regained his composure so quickly after Meggie's interruption?

And she must have a brain made of rendered lard, she scolded herself, for once more allowing her mere animal lusts to overwhelm her.

Just because the man was so damned handsome, just because his body made her want to curl up beside him naked—that was no reason to forget everything she had ever believed about the proper conduct for ladies of good breeding, was it?

It must be, she decided as she left her room to follow Ben back up to the attic. Just holding the lantern for him as he'd asked her to do, just the thought of watching the broad muscles of his arms and back straining as he nailed a few boards into place to stop the leaking roof, was enough of an attraction for her.

She wanted to be with him. It was almost as if seeing him was so close to actually touching him that she wanted to be wherever he was. The only trouble was, she was forced to admit, just looking at him was never really enough.

"It's about time you got up here," Ben scolded her as she reached the top of the attic stairs.

Ben had placed the lantern on top of a cast-off bureau. He had propped his ladder against the side of the roof. Apparently he had climbed up it, then stepped across to balance precariously on the edge of several stacked boxes and a crossbeam.

Emily's heart leapt into her throat when she saw him perched up there. On the other hand, he appeared to know what he was doing. He even appeared quite comfortable up there as he grinned down at her. And the view of his firm thighs and buttocks in his tight jeans truly was something to be admired from this angle, she decided. She grinned back at him and drew a deep, appreciative breath.

His toolbox was at the base of the ladder, with Meggie poised over it, eagerly waiting to hand him whatever he needed.

"I can't imagine what kept you," Ben added. Through the gleaming yellow lantern light, his blue eyes glowed at her with unrelieved desire.

"Oh, I had a few things that needed to be put back in place," she replied. She tried to sound as nonchalant as he had, but her voice still quivered when she met his burning gaze.

"Are you all . . . back in place, then?" he asked. His gaze wandered down from her eyes to examine all the soft places he had caressed. Apparently finding her properly attired, he looked again into her eyes and nodded. "Good," he said. "You never know when you're going to find that what you've put in place is suddenly . . . all disarranged again."

He gave her a helpless shrug of his broad shoulders, as if what he had done—and what he would like to do again—was completely inevitable.

Emily began to believe it really was.

"Come and help me put some things into place up here now," Ben said.

Emily had climbed her share of fences and a few apple trees when she was a little girl. It had been years since she had climbed a ladder. At least it looked safer than climbing the pigsty. She took a deep breath, lifted her skirt a few inches from the floor, and took the first fateful step to place her foot on the bottom rung of the ladder.

She managed to get to the top of the ladder without

putting her foot through and falling. She felt she'd accomplished a great deal right there.

Once she reached the top, Ben leaned over and whispered in her ear, "And later on, downstairs, I have something that I need to put somewhere, and I think you know just the right place."

Emily almost fell backward off the ladder.

She wanted to slap his face for his impertinence. She wanted to scold him and stomp off highly insulted. She could hardly do that now without Meggie witnessing it all and wanting to know exactly why Aunt Emily was smacking Uncle Eb in the head with a piece of shingle. Under the circumstances, the best Emily could manage to do was glare at him in the shadowy rafters.

Again he leaned forward and whispered, "I said later, Emily. I didn't say exactly when, did I?"

Well, it was true, he hadn't, Emily was forced to admit. Was she so eager for his touch that she was making all sorts of wild suppositions and making a fool of herself in the bargain? Of course not! she reassured herself. After all, *she* hadn't picked *him* up and carried *him* down the stairs into her bedroom.

"That's still an awful thing to say," she hissed back at him.

"Why? Because it's true?" he asked, raising his eyebrow and examining her closer. "Because you know you feel the same way I do—and want me as badly as I want you?"

Emily tried to raise herself up to her full height. She tried to lift her chin to a superior angle but was afraid of bumping her head once again against the rafters. She tried to glare at him again, but knew that meeting his blazing blue eyes would only melt what small shreds were left of her reserve.

She stared at the top rung of the ladder and sternly

informed him, "This is *not* the proper time or place to be discussing . . . this."

"I agree completely," Ben said. The look on his face had turned so serious that Emily was almost disappointed. Then he gave her a wicked wink and whispered, "There is a proper place . . . downstairs. And when we find the proper time, we won't be doing any . . . discussing."

Emily turned and called down to her niece very loudly, "Meggie, I think your uncle needs a hammer." Out of the corner of her eye, she gave Ben a searing look. "Needs a hammer alongside of his head," she muttered, just loud enough for him to hear her.

"A what?" Meggie called. "What are you two talking about up there? Couldn't hear you over the thunder."

Oh, thank heavens, Emily thought. There had to be a way of getting Ben's mind away from her and back to what he had claimed was his original intention for coming here tonight. There had to be some way to keep Meggie in the conversation so that Ben couldn't continue to make these little comments which not only embarrassed her, but only made her want him all the more.

"The hammer, Meggie. The hammer," Emily repeated loudly. "H - A - M . . . You finish it," she ordered with sudden inspiration.

"What?" Meggie cried in disbelief.

"Spell hammer."

"You're joking with me, aren't you, Aunt Emily?"

"No, I'm not," Emily insisted. "And the longer you wait, the more rain is coming in, and the drippier your ceiling is getting."

"Aw, darn! H - A - M - E - R. There! Are you happy?"

"No."

"Why not?"

"You spelled it wrong."

"Well, you didn't say I had to spell it right!" Meggie complained. She stood there, shuffling the toe of her shoe around in the thick layer of dust on the attic floor.

"Your ceiling is getting wet," Emily reminded her in a singsong voice.

"H - A - M - *M* - E - R. So there!" Meggie said. She handed the hammer to Emily, who passed it along to Ben.

"Hey, pretty good, Meggie," Ben called down to her. "Now, do you think you can find a couple of nails in that box?"

Meggie grinned up at him impishly. "What do you want me to spell? Nails or box?"

"Both," Emily answered.

By the time Ben had finished patching the roof over Meggie's and Emily's bedrooms, the brief storm had blown itself out.

"Good night, Ben," Emily said. "Thank you so much for coming like you did. I think we'd have both been soaked in the morning if you hadn't."

"Are you sure there's nothing else that needs fixing while I'm here?" Ben offered. His lips were grinning at her, but his eyes held hers with an intensity that told Emily in no uncertain terms that he wouldn't be able to wait much longer.

"Good night, Ben," she repeated.

Slowly—reluctantly, he'd like to believe—she closed the door.

Ben stowed the ladder and toolbox in the shed behind the house. He darted across the rain-slicked grass into his own home. The house was dark when he entered. He made his way up the stairs quietly and peeked into Frannie's room.

Frannie was already sleeping, cuddled under the patchwork quilt Betty had made when she was expecting her. Ben walked over to Frannie's bedside and picked up an edge of the quilt. He ran the smooth fabric with its small, even stitches between his fingers.

He pressed his lips together, remembering how he and Betty had looked forward to their child's birth, never thinking she wouldn't survive. He looked up at Frannie, sleeping peacefully. She was growing into a bright, pretty young girl, he decided. He hadn't done such a bad job of raising her alone for ten years. Betty would have been proud of him.

He dropped the edge of the quilt and walked over to the fireplace. He picked up the small photograph of Betty that Frannie kept on the mantel and took it over to the window, hoping to see it better in the light of the moon that was now peeking out from between the clouds from time to time.

Funny, he thought as he looked at the pale face staring back at him, without the photographs, it was getting harder and harder all the time to remember what she looked like. And he had thought he would remember forever. When he lay in bed alone at night, it was harder and harder to remember what she had felt like laying beside him. When he tried to remember, it was the image of Emily that came to his mind.

Ben put the photograph back on the mantel where it belonged, with all the other memories. He closed the door behind him and went into his own lonely bedroom.

He peeled off his wet cotton shirt and threw it into the corner. It slapped against the wall and slithered to the floor in a soggy heap. He hadn't meant to throw it so hard, but his frustrations were building up inside him, more than he'd even realized.

He stripped off his jeans and threw them even harder into the same corner. He turned down the wick of his coal oil lamp.

He flipped back the covers and, not even bothering to put on his nightshirt, threw himself backward down on the bed. It felt good to push himself forcefully into the soft feather mattress, good to have some sort of vigorous physical outlet for all the emotions that had been building up inside him over the years, and that were now churning around, demanding to be expressed.

In the dark he stared upward, watching the patterns of light and shadows that the moon, racing with the clouds, threw against the ceiling. He stretched his long arms out to either side. A hand hung over each edge of the mattress.

It was a big bed—made for two. It had held only one for far too long. He needed someone to share this big old bed with him again. He closed his eyes against the flickering moonlight.

His palms tingled with the remembered sensations of touching Emily's soft breasts, even through the thin fabric of her dress. His fingers twitched with the desire to touch her breasts again, without anything to come between him and their pliant warmth. His body tightened and his loins ached with the need for Emily.

Ben moaned and cursed softly and rolled over, facedown, to bury his frustrations in the silence of the pillows.

He'd thought to convince her to leave Meggie in Bidewell because it was a good place to raise a child. Along with so many others in his family, he didn't want to lose his niece, too. But somewhere along the line, he'd fallen in love with Emily. He didn't want to lose her, either. Now he needed her to stay.

Was she still so determined to leave? He was afraid so. He knew he had to convince her that Iowa was a good place to raise not just any children, but children they could create together.

* * *

Emily had just sat down to eat her soup.

Meggie was still splashing the bowl of the spoon against the surface of the broth, trying to sink and drown the small pieces of potatoes and carrots and chicken—anything to keep from actually having to eat the stuff.

"I'll get it!" she cried, springing to her feet when she heard the knock on the front door.

"*I'll* get it," Emily said firmly.

Meggie sat down again, a disgusted look on her face. She rested her elbow on the edge of the table and propped her head in her hand. She continued to beat at her soup.

As soon as Emily opened the door, Ben thrust a wicker basket into her hand. "I thought maybe you could use these," he said.

"Probably can," Frannie added from behind Ben.

The basket was still warm when Emily took it.

"What's in here?" she asked.

"My share of supper," Ben answered, stepping into the vestibule. He placed the toolbox he carried in his other hand below the bench by the door.

"Your *share*?" Emily repeated. She pulled back the red and white checked napkin to reveal a fragrant pile of yellow corn muffins.

"I figure these—and some of my carpentry expertise," he added, pointing to his toolbox, "should earn me some supper."

"Did Dolly die?" Emily asked, too shocked to be polite. Given her less than sterling reputation with a pot and stove, why else would he be coming here to eat?

"No. As a matter of fact, she made these especially for me to bring here," Ben answered. He decided not to tell Emily that Ma had done no such thing—or that Ma had no idea, yet, that her corn muffins were missing. As a matter of fact, she'd given him quite an argument about even coming here again this evening.

Emily was just about to ask if Mrs. Hannigan was in some way incapable of cooking or else he'd surely be there instead, but she quickly decided that bringing up her name was not a good idea.

"I . . . I only made a pot of soup, but you're welcome to some of it," she offered.

"No, Frannie, no!" Meggie shouted from the dining room. "Escape while you can!"

"Spell it," Emily quickly turned and ordered.

"I-T," Meggie replied with a grimace. Then she turned to Frannie and snickered.

"Meggie," Emily said in a warning tone.

"E-S-C-A-P-E."

Frannie sat beside Meggie, blinking and staring bewilderedly between her friend and her friend's very strange aunt. She turned to Meggie and opened her mouth.

"Don't even ask," Meggie replied. "You don't want to know. Just go home while you can."

"We're not going home yet," Ben said, sitting across the table from Meggie while Emily arranged napkins, bowls, and spoons in front of him and Frannie. "We're rude enough to invite ourselves for supper. Then, afterward, there's a few more things that need fixing around here."

"Are any more of them in Aunt Emily's bedroom?" Meggie asked with a wry little twist to her lips.

Emily's face flared crimson. She almost choked on her soup.

Meggie turned to Frannie. "See, I told you this stuff would kill you."

Ben picked up his spoon and cautiously ate just a bit. "Emily, this really isn't bad," he said. No one had ever called him a coward, but he'd sooner sit on live coals buck naked than tell her that the vegetables were mushy and it needed salt, badly.

"Thank you. But you don't have to sound quite so surprised," she answered. "It's pretty hard to burn soup."

"Oh, I bet you could do it, Aunt Emily," Meggie proclaimed confidently.

Quite honestly, Emily was surprised that she hadn't burnt the soup. She was glad that Meggie had managed to keep her mouth shut, so far, about the biscuits that were supposed to have come with this soup that she *had* burnt.

Emily had always wanted Ben to think she could manage the home pretty well. That really didn't matter. She knew that once she and Meggie returned to her home in Baltimore, she wouldn't have to cook or clean or do laundry or dishes ever again. It had gone beyond wanting to prove her competence to him merely as Meggie's guardian. There was just some strange urge in her that wanted to show Ben that she *could* make a home that a child like Meggie—or a man like him—could be comfortable in.

"I've put some S - O - A - P in the pot the S - O - U - P was in," Meggie told Emily as they were tidying up the kitchen after the meal.

"Very good, Meggie," Emily said.

Frannie continued to eye her cousin and her Aunt Emily with a great deal of caution. Had the lady put something strange in Meggie's food? she wondered. Would she give some to Pa to put in hers? she worried.

"What do you want me to do with these black biscuits I found shoved way in the back of the stove?" Frannie asked. She was almost afraid to say anything, in case Aunt Emily tried to get her to spell it, too.

"Give 'em to Uncle Eb," Meggie said. "Maybe he can

use them to nail up some more stuff if his H - A - M - M - E - R breaks.''

''No need for that, Meggie,'' Ben said.

Emily liked to watch the way his muscles rippled under his shirt as he carried the heavy toolbox into the kitchen and set it on the floor. He opened the lid and reached in to pull out his hammer.

''I thought I'd fix those loose shelves in the pantry,'' he said.

''Oh, Uncle Eb,'' Meggie said, rushing up to him. ''Before you do that, there's something else in my bedroom you just gotta fix.''

''What's that, Meggie?''

''Well, it's . . . it's sort of hard to describe,'' Meggie said. ''I need you to see it.''

''Come on then.''

Emily began to follow them out of the kitchen.

''No, no, Aunt Emily,'' Meggie said quickly. ''It . . . won't take that long, and it'll only take Uncle Eb to do it. You . . . you stay here with Frannie.''

After everything else she'd seen, Frannie was not too happy with this arrangement. But when she saw the pleading look that Meggie gave her, Frannie reluctantly gave in.

''So, Aunt Emily,'' she said, tapping the biscuit against the cast-iron stove. The biscuit didn't even crumble. ''What all did you put in these, just in case I need something real hard some day?''

Upstairs, Meggie slammed the bedroom door shut tightly behind her and leaned against it hard, as if something horrible were chasing her and she needed to keep it out.

Ben looked around Meggie's room. ''So what else needs fixing?''

''Aunt Emily's head!''

Ben grinned. He could think of quite a few things to do

with Emily, but fixing her head wasn't one of them. Of course, it was nothing he could discuss with Meggie—and if he continued to think about how much he wanted Emily, he'd have to go pulling his shirttail out again. "What's wrong now, Meggie?" he asked.

"You saw it yourself. She's always making me spell things, cipher things," she complained. "You should have seen her making me do sums while we were trying to make those awful biscuits. No wonder they turned out so bad."

Ben grinned. "But you got them right, didn't you?"

"No, the biscuits are terrible!"

"I mean your sums."

"Oh, yeah—eventually. She wouldn't stop. She just kept making me do them until I finally did get them right." Meggie came a little closer to Ben and whispered in his ear. "She's making me crazy as a junebug! Get me out of here, Uncle Eb. Oh, please! Now!"

Ben could hardly tell her yes when he didn't want Emily to be away from Meggie. Then he'd have no excuse to keep coming to see her. When he looked down into the worried little blue eyes, he could hardly tell her no, either.

He patted her shoulder in consolation. "I'll see what I can do, Meggie," was the best answer he could think to give right now. "Come on and help me fix that pantry. Maybe if the house is in better order, Aunt Emily will be happier and won't bother you so much."

Meggie gave a skeptical sigh, but followed Ben downstairs anyway.

"Let's get to those shelves now," Ben said, a little too loudly, in order to distract Emily from any curiosity she might have had about what else had been wrong with Meggie's room.

He didn't want Meggie to think he was a complete traitor to her cause. But he could see pretty plainly what Emily was trying to do. He only hoped it worked. If it didn't, Emily was going to have to contend with an awfully irritated little girl.

Emily opened the pantry door. It had been completely empty when she first arrived. The only things on the shelves now were the few purchases she'd made at Randall's Emporium—salt, sugar, coffee, a little flour—just enough to last the few days she planned to be in Bidewell.

"They're fine, see," she told him, patting the shelves.

Ben began removing the things she had put there and placing them on the kitchen table. "They might look fine now, holding only a few things, but as soon as someone puts something heavy on them, they'll collapse."

"Geez, don't put those biscuits on 'em, Frannie!" Meggie exclaimed.

"Spell . . ." Emily ordered.

"B - I - S - C - U - I - T - S," Meggie answered automatically. Then she scooped up two handfuls of the hard, heavy biscuits. "C'mon, Frannie. Let's see how far we can skip these things across the pond."

"Don't be too long," Emily called. "It'll be getting dark soon."

"Don't worry. They'll sink really fast," Meggie answered as she and Frannie headed out the back door.

"Wait a minute." Frannie hesitated just before they disappeared around the corner of the house. "What if they poison the fish?"

Ben laid his hammer on one of the empty shelves. Grabbing Emily from behind, he pulled her into the empty pantry. Emily squealed.

"Shh!" Spinning her around to face him, he clapped his hand over her mouth. Slowly he moved toward her, forcing her to back up with each step until her back was pressed firmly against the wall. He continued to move toward her until he was so close she could barely breathe. He leaned his left forearm against the wall beside her, preventing her escape that way. Slowly he began to move his right hand away from her mouth, down her throat. He cradled the nape of her neck in his warm hand.

He gave a low, wicked laugh. "Now, my proud beauty . . ."

"If you say you have me in your power, I'll . . . I'll . . ."

He pressed closer to her. "What will you do?" he asked.

He stifled any answer she might have given with a passionate kiss. He thrust his hips against her.

"What will you do, now that I have you in my power?" he repeated.

She lifted her arms to hold him about the waist so that he stayed as close as he was. "I'll just have to surren—"

"Pa! Pa!"

"Uncle Eb!"

Ben released Emily, picked up the hammer, and began banging as loudly as he could against the nearest shelf. If he kept hammering and pretended he didn't hear them for a little while, maybe this time he wouldn't have to pull out his shirttail.

"Frannie broke her foot!" Meggie cried.

Emily hurried up to the two girls. Meggie supported a limping Frannie into the kitchen.

"How did it happen—and so soon?" Emily asked.

"She dropped one of your damned biscuits on it!"

"Meggie!" Emily cried. "Watch your language."

"Why, do you want me to spell it, too?"

"What have we got here?" Ben asked. Shirttail or no, the news of Frannie's injury had brought him rushing out of the pantry. "Did you really hurt it by dropping a biscuit on it?"

Meggie and Frannie nodded solemnly. From the looks on their faces, they had to be telling the truth.

Ben examined Frannie's foot, carefully moving her ankle this way and that, pressing here and there. Frannie didn't cry out or complain at all.

"I thought you were a lawyer, not a doctor," Emily teased.

"I am," Ben said. He looked up at Frannie and gave her a wink. "But I used to work for a real good horse doctor. I say it's broke and we gotta shoot her."

"Oh, Pa!" Frannie giggled.

"No, it looks like just a bad bump, not even a sprain," Ben pronounced.

"Aw, darn."

He lifted Frannie up in his arms. "Why don't I take you home anyway, pumpkin? That shelf can wait till another day." He turned to Emily. "At least, I hope what I was doing in the pantry will be waiting for me."

What could she say? Emily knew that she was waiting for Ben, and all the pulsing sensations he raised in her, with great anticipation. On the other hand, she knew that soon she would be taking Meggie back to Baltimore. She knew that, although she would always be missing him, she wouldn't be staying with him forever.

"Do I still have to go to school tomorrow?" Frannie asked.

"Well, nothing's broke, so I don't see why not," Ben answered, heading toward the door.

Frannie groaned.

"But we'll see."

"Aw, shoot, Frannie," Meggie said. "If you wanted to get out of school, next time, try dropping one on your head."

CHAPTER FOURTEEN

"I WON! I WON! I DID IT!" MEGGIE SQUEALED AS she burst into the kitchen Friday afternoon.

Frannie, on the other hand, came trailing along behind.

"Meggie, I've never seen you so . . . uh, happy!" Emily's breath was fairly squeezed from her as Meggie grabbed her around the waist tightly.

Emily took this rare opportunity to return her elusive niece's hug. She bent down so that she could look Meggie in the eye. She held her by the arms, trying to keep her still long enough to make some sense out of what the child was saying.

Meggie was still jumping up and down too wildly to be completely intelligible. "I won this week's spelling bee."

"That's wonderful, Meggie! I'm glad to know you can win something besides a spitting contest!"

"It's the first time I've ever won!"

"I'm so proud of you." Seeing Frannie kicking at the chair leg, Emily turned a sympathetic glance to her. "How did you do, Frannie? From the look on your face, I'd say you came in dead last."

Frannie wrinkled up her nose and shook her head. "Not that bad."

"Well, I'm still sorry you couldn't win, too."

"That's not what's bothering her," Meggie said.

"I always lose the weekly spelling bee," Frannie explained. "I mean, I come in fourth or fifth, which ain't too bad, but I never really win."

"Then what's bothering you?"

"She lost her bet with Nellie Wray," Meggie said.

"I owe her three licorice sticks," Frannie admitted. "Just 'cause Meggie won."

"I *told* you I was gonna win this time," Meggie said, punching her cousin in the ribs. "But you wouldn't listen."

Emily knew she'd been a terrible nuisance to Meggie all week, but at least their hard work had now paid off.

"This calls for a celebration," Emily announced, rising from her seat. "Why don't you two go sit in the parlor? I'll bring you some cookies."

"Yeah! We love cookies."

Meggie and Frannie eagerly headed for the parlor while Emily turned to put some cookies on a plate. "I made them myself," she called just as the girls disappeared around the corner.

Meggie grabbed Frannie by the sleeve and pulled her through the dining room and into the parlor.

"Oh, no! *She* made the cookies!" Frannie whispered, flopping back on the sofa. Meggie sprawled out beside her. "Don't eat 'em. They'll break your teeth. You'll look like Ol' Man Pendergast, with only three teeth in his head, for the rest of your life."

"*I* don't have to eat 'em 'cause *I* won," Meggie whispered back. "She's gonna make *you* eat 'em. That's your punishment for gambling."

"But I only bet licorice."

"Geez, if eating her cooking is a reward for doing good, don't tell her I got 'em all right on that math test," Meggie pleaded.

"You know, you *have* been doing better in school, Meggie," Frannie said.

"Yeah, well, for a while there, I just slipped a little . . ."

"Till she brought you back up again."

"I've always been smart," Meggie said. "It wasn't her."

"Yes, it was," Frannie insisted. "And Jimmy Lindstrom ain't nowhere near as nasty to you since your aunt's been making you wear—"

"Don't say it," Meggie warned.

"Well, he don't punch you in the arm as hard on the day you wear a dress. Maybe boys ain't so bad after all, when you get older," Frannie said, nodding her head. "Anyway, getting married has got to beat being an old maid like your Aunt Emily or Miss Bloom."

"Here we are," Emily sang as she brought the tray of cookies in and set it on the table in front of the girls. "Now, I know they're a little darker on the bottom than they should be, but . . . well, just try them."

Meggie picked up a cookie and peeked underneath. "Yeah. That's dark, all right." But it wasn't what she'd expected. She thought she'd find the cookies as hard and black as the stove they'd come from. Instead, they were just a little darker brown than Mrs. Hannigan's cookies. With her front teeth, Meggie scraped a little off the top.

Frannie just watched, squirming uneasily in her seat, while Meggie ate the rest of the cookie—dark part and all!

"Go on. Try one," Meggie urged. "It's really good."

Amazed, Frannie picked up one and peeked underneath. Too dark, she decided. She put that cookie back down and moved on to the next. Well, if she *had* to eat one, this one was as close to normal as she would get, she decided. She bit into the cookie.

"Hey, this *is* good," Frannie admitted, not even bothering to try to hide her surprise.

"I'm glad you like them," Emily said. She breathed a sigh of relief, then stood. "I'll get us some cider."

As soon as Emily was out of the room, Meggie poked Frannie in the ribs. "You know, Frannie. I've been thinking. Maybe Aunt Emily ain't so bad after all. I mean, it's not living *with* her that really bothers me," she admitted. "It's living *away* from you and Gramma and all that would be so awful."

"Yeah."

"Maybe . . . maybe I was wrong," Meggie continued. "What we really need to do is not drive her away. We need to find something that'll make her want to stay here with us."

"Like what?"

"Not like what," Meggie said, her blue eyes twinkling. "Like who."

"Who? Not Uncle Noah."

"No! Uncle Eb."

"Pa?" Frannie asked. Her eyes grew wider and her voice rose as she repeated, "*My* Pa? You can't be serious," she hissed, grabbing her cousin's arm so hard, she knocked the cookie crumbs onto the floor. "You've come up with some harebrained things in your life, Meggie, but this is *my* life you're messing with now."

"Look at it this way. If she marries Uncle Eb, then they'll probably live right here in Bidewell—right in your very own house. And I'll move in, and then we can be together all the time."

"Well . . ." Frannie was still not convinced.

"If she's your ma, she'll buy you a pretty blue dress just like mine. We won't have to share it. In fact, she'll probably buy us a whole lot of other stuff, too."

"All right, so she's real smart about school things and buys fancy clothes and is pretty nice anyway," Frannie said. She leaned close and whispered, "But your aunt's a rotten cook."

Meggie leaned even closer to Frannie, and in an even tinier whisper said, "But I think Aunt Emily's *real* rich. She don't have to be able to cook."

Frannie took another cookie. "So how do we do this?" she asked.

"No, no, Aunt Emily," Meggie protested. "We're really not trying to fool you this time."

"Really!" Frannie affirmed. She looked as if she was doing her best to appear very, very sincere.

Emily still had her doubts. From across the dining room table at Dolly's farm, she eyed the two little scamps skeptically. They'd fooled her enough times already. Should she trust them now?

They'd brought her to the farm tonight for a very good dinner. They'd told her how nice she looked in her plain brown merino dress. They'd even warned her to bring an apron and a paring knife from Sarah's kitchen.

"There really is an apple bee tonight at the Willoughbys' farm," Ben told her.

Emily glanced at him out of the corner of her eye. Could she even trust Ben? After all, while he hadn't actually been an accomplice, he certainly hadn't done much to stop the girls' shenanigans. And hadn't the man proved he had a few plans for her of his own?

"It's just a short ride from here. I think you'd enjoy coming with us," Ben continued.

"Wouldn't hurt ya none to learn to peel a couple of apples with the womenfolk 'round here," Dolly grumbled. She threw Emily a disgruntled look.

"Unless you'd rather stay home and . . . fix the roof,"

Ben offered. He raised his coffee cup to his lips. His blue eyes gleamed at her from over the edge.

Dolly raised a graying brow. ''*She* don't even know how to hold a hammer.''

''You'd be surprised, Ma, what Emily can—''

''Yeah, you'd be real surprised, Gramma,'' Meggie interrupted. ''Aunt Emily even made some cookies this afternoon. Good ones.''

Emily was grateful for Meggie's interruption.

''Really good,'' Frannie echoed. ''All by herself, too.''

''Ya darn right I'd be surprised,'' Dolly muttered. She continued to push her peas into her mashed potatoes and then scoop them up with her knife.

Emily had surprised herself. The cookies had at least been recognizable as cookies, which was a vast improvement. But she'd tasted a few and they weren't *that* good. At least, not so good that they had warranted Meggie and Frannie eating the whole batch. After eating all that, Emily wondered how the girls could sit inside, eating Dolly's meatcakes and gravy. Why weren't they outside, throwing up instead?

Ben's blue eyes were wide and he was smiling at her broadly.

''Are you surprised, too?'' she asked him.

''I'm impressed,'' he answered. ''I'm glad to see you found another use for that oven besides trying to wear it.''

Meggie and Frannie laughed. Dolly stopped, her knife poised halfway to her mouth, and stared at Emily.

Oh, what in the world was that man trying to do? Emily silently lamented. It wasn't hard for Emily to tell that Dolly didn't like her anymore. Did Ben have to make her look more and more strange in his mother's eyes?

Frannie giggled. ''Now Gramma'll think Aunt Emily's really crazy.''

Dolly glanced at Meggie and Frannie, then gave Emily a scornful look. "After what Noah's been up to all year?" She nodded in Emily's direction. "This one's a piker."

Emily didn't know whether to take that as an insult or a compliment.

"Where is Noah, anyway?" Ben asked. "I haven't seen him since breakfast."

Dolly shrugged. "It's Friday. You know how it is with him on Friday."

"Yes," Ben answered. "But usually I see him while I'm at the office in Winterset, hanging around the saloon with some of his cronies. I didn't see him there today at all."

Dolly pursed her lips. "Come to think of it, I ain't seen him working on his ark all day, neither. You girls seen him?" she asked.

Meggie and Frannie shook their heads and giggled. "We've been in school all day, Gramma. He sure wouldn't be there."

Ben leaned his chair on its two back legs far enough to see out the dining room window. He peered through the twilight toward Noah's cabin. The door was shut. The windows were dark.

"Doesn't look like he's there," he said. "Want me to check if he's passed out again?"

"No," Dolly answered. "It's only Friday. He'll turn up." She peered at the tall ribs of the half-finished boat in the yard, outlined by the rays of the setting sun. "Well, one thing's for sure. He didn't sail away."

"Dolly! We've been waiting for you," Mrs. Lindstrom called.

As soon as they arrived at the Willoughbys', several of the ladies bustled up to Dolly and hurried her into the kitchen. The ladies paid no more attention to Emily than they did to the two children. She had no choice but to follow along behind. The only bit of reassurance she had was the brief touch of Ben's hand on her back as she climbed the front steps.

Then, much to her disappointment, Ben didn't follow her. He leaned against one of the tall, square white posts and crossed his arms over his broad chest. He swung his leg up, resting his foot on the top of the rail. Emily took in a deep breath as she watched how the denim of his jeans stretched over his body.

''Iris is here tonight, Ben,'' she heard one man say. She wondered if the man always spoke that loudly, or if he was only doing it tonight for her benefit.

''Yeah, but has anybody seen Noah?'' Ben asked.

The simple fact that he had ignored any mention of Mrs. Hannigan made Emily feel just a little more reassured.

One dark, lanky man pulled at his unshaven jaw. ''Seems to me I did see him 'round here, till somebody started passing 'round the jug o' corn likker. Don't rightly recall where he went after that.''

''Don't worry, Ben. He'll show up,'' another man with only three teeth mumbled. ''Like a bad penny.''

Emily threw Ben one longing glance before she and the girls were swept along with the swirling tide of busy women, to be swallowed up in the stifling warm air of the kitchen. The Willoughbys' big cast-iron stove glowed red with the effort of keeping several large kettles bubbling.

''We thought you'd never get here,'' Mrs. Lindstrom complained.

Dolly nodded her head in Emily's direction. ''Had unexpected company for dinner,'' was all she said.

''We need your help on this, Dolly,'' Mrs. Willoughby said as she bustled up to her.

Emily didn't think Mrs. Willoughby would ever need

help—not even to lift a Clydesdale. She was as tall as Ben, Emily would have bet on that—and not just licorice sticks. She was at least twice as wide. And she had a little round nose, and pretty china blue eyes, and the tiniest little pink bow of a mouth, all stuck right in the center of an enormous round face.

"Is this bath deep enough to make sure these apples don't spoil like that one batch last year did?" Mrs. Willoughby asked. Her lips were pursed and her eyebrows were drawn down over her pretty eyes in a worried frown.

Dolly was busily knotting the ribbons of her apron behind her. "Well, let's have a look," she said, with great authority.

Emily watched with amusement as the women all followed Dolly to the stove and gathered around, as if waiting for some sacred pronouncement.

"Now, don't you little ones get near the stove," Mrs. Hannigan warned.

She moved to stand between Meggie and Frannie and the red-hot stove. She also managed to include Emily in the maneuver, leaving no doubt in Emily's mind—or anyone else's—that Emily was definitely to be relegated to a place with mere children.

"As a matter of fact, we'll put you little ones here at this table," Mrs. Hannigan continued. She spread out her arms and shooed Meggie, Frannie, and Emily along just as she had her chickens. "Let's see if you can pare and core these apples without wasting too much—or cutting yourselves."

Mrs. Hannigan motioned for several little girls to scoot down and make room for the new workers.

As they sat on the long rough-hewn bench at the even longer table, Meggie poked Frannie. "Hey, what's stuck in Mrs. Hannigan's craw tonight?"

"She knows darn good and well we can use a knife," Frannie agreed.

"Why does she keep calling us 'little ones'?" Meggie demanded, screwing up her face to show her disgust.

Frannie just shrugged.

Mrs. Hannigan glanced up at Emily as if seeing her here tonight for the very first time. "Oh, Miss Shaw, have you ever done this before?"

Emily tied on the apron she had brought. Of course she'd pared apples before. She'd just never been to a party where everyone's object was to pare as many apples as they could as quickly as they could. "Not like this," Emily answered as she took the seat beside Meggie.

"Well, let me show you how it's done," Mrs. Hannigan said.

She grabbed up a bright red apple in her left hand and a small sharp knife in the other. Starting at the stem, she began trimming away the peel so thinly that the slices looked almost as red on the inside as they did on the outside.

After several small trails of peel fell off, Mrs. Hannigan put down the half-naked apple and said, "I think even you can get the idea."

Emily picked up an apple. As she withdrew her own knife from her pocket, Mrs. Hannigan stepped back several paces. Then she clapped her hands together and admonished all the young girls seated round the table. "Now, keep busy, girls. There's so much to be done yet tonight."

Emily set to work with the rest of them. Every once in a while, one of the women would collect the peeled apples. Before long, a big pile of parings had accumulated in front of them.

"Geez, Frannie! Duck!" Meggie cried. The two quickly scooted under the table at Emily's feet.

"What in the world!" Emily exclaimed. She lifted the

tablecloth and peeked under. ''What are you two doing under there?''

''Get away—or she'll see us!'' Meggie hissed, tugging the tablecloth back down over her.

''Come out from there right now!'' Emily ordered.

''No! She'll spoil all our fun!'' Meggie whined.

''Miss Shaw, I didn't know you'd be here tonight,'' Miss Bloom said.

Emily dropped the edge of the cloth and sat erect. ''I didn't know it myself until shortly before dinner,'' she admitted. She brushed at the sides of the cloth, smoothing it down as if nothing was under there at all. ''We didn't know you'd be here, either.''

''Ordinarily, I wouldn't be,'' Miss Bloom admitted. ''I haven't been invited to too many social activities in the community. But someone told them I was a good cook—and Mrs. Willoughby invited me. I can't imagine how they found out.''

Emily had her suspicions, but it wasn't her place to reveal secrets. She just shook her head and said, ''I'm not much of a cook, myself.''

''Oh, it's a skill anyone can learn,'' Miss Bloom cheerfully assured her. ''Come on. I'll show you a trick I learned when I was just a little girl.''

Miss Bloom sat on the bench that Meggie and Frannie had just vacated. She picked up a knife and, looking about at all the children, as if instructing them were something she could not help but do, began to peel an apple. Very, very slowly the narrow red peel began to lengthen.

Hearing the ''oohs'' and ''aahs'' of the other girls, Meggie and Frannie lifted the edge of the cloth and peeked out. The apple peel was one whole piece that reached all the way to the floor.

"Wow! How'd you do that?" Frannie asked, emerging from her hiding place.

Miss Bloom just stared at them.

"Dropped my knife," Meggie offered by way of explanation as she took her seat on the bench.

Miss Bloom picked up another apple and began peeling it in the same way. "It's something you have to learn with practice—just like math, or spelling, or anything else. Why don't you try?" she invited, extending the half-peeled apple to Meggie.

Meggie took the apple from her. Before long, all the children at the table—and Emily, too—were trying their best to peel the apple in one, long piece.

"And when you've finally done it"—Miss Bloom took the long strand she had peeled off and stood up—"you must turn your back and toss it over your shoulder like this . . ."

She flipped it high into the air. It fell to the floor behind her in a twisting, tangled heap.

"Now, whichever letter of the alphabet this most resembles is the first initial of the man you will marry," Miss Bloom said.

All the little girls began to giggle. Miss Bloom turned around. Everyone focused on the pile of red peel at her feet.

"What the heck is that supposed to be?" Meggie asked.

"Well, it looks like . . ." Emily angled her head this way and that, trying desperately to find something for lonely little Miss Bloom. "It's sort of a . . ."

"Doesn't look like much of anything to me," Mrs. Hannigan said. Even though this had proved more of an attraction than she could resist, she still stayed on the other side of the girls, away from Emily and her small, sharp knife.

Miss Bloom gave a weak little laugh. "Oh, I was only

doing it so the children could have a little fun,'' she said. ''I really never expected it to look like any letter for me.''

''Well, why not?'' Frannie demanded.

''Oh, Frannie, dear,'' Miss Bloom said, giggling behind her hand. Yet somehow, Emily didn't think that Miss Bloom's sapphire blue eyes held any laughter at all at this turn of events. ''It . . . it won't look like any particular letter as I . . . I haven't planned to marry.''

''Well, it's gotta look like *something*!'' Frannie insisted.

''It's an *N*.'' The masculine voice intruded upon the feminine babble.

All eyes lifted from the peel on the floor to Noah in the doorway. His trousers were pressed and so was his white shirt. His hair was clean and neatly slicked back. His gray-blue eyes were clear, not bloodshot. He was actually standing on his own, not leaning against the doorframe for support. He stepped into the kitchen, without falling flat on his face.

''Lord have mercy!'' Mrs. Lindstrom exclaimed in a whisper that carried to the very edges of the hushed crowd. Everyone else maintained a profound silence. ''Friday night and Noah's sober.''

''Well, I had something important to do tonight,'' Noah answered. He pointed to the apple peel on the floor. ''Why, you folks never would've known that was an *N* if I hadn't come along.''

''No, it's not, Uncle Noah,'' Meggie said at last. ''It's a . . . well, it looks like a . . .''

''It's an *N*,'' Noah insisted. He circled the peel on the floor, examining it carefully from all angles, until he stood directly beside Miss Bloom.

''I'm afraid I don't quite see it,'' Miss Bloom said.

''Well, now, you're not looking at it right,'' Noah replied.

Placing one hand on her shoulder, he drew her closer to him. At the same time he placed his head directly against the side of hers, so that the two could share the same line of sight. Maybe that would help her to see the right letter.

He pointed at the apple peel, moving his finger up and down to outline the letter for her to see. "See there, Miss Bloom. That *is* an *N*," Noah insisted.

"Could that stand for 'Nobody'?" Miss Bloom wondered aloud. Her little face was turning almost the same shade of red as her hair.

"Or Nicholas," Meggie offered.

"Or Newton," Frannie said.

Noah turned to look Miss Bloom in the eye. Since he had not yet removed his hand from her shoulder, the two were standing very close together.

"Miss Bloom, there are lots of names that begin with the letter *N*. We could probably think of what they are a little better if we were outside, away from all the heat of this kitchen." Noah indicated the back door.

Miss Bloom untied her apron and handed it to Emily. Then she followed Noah out into the cool night air.

"If she can do it, I can do it," Meggie declared. She picked up her knife and another apple and began slicing.

"I'll do it before you do," Frannie challenged. "Oh, shoot!" she exclaimed as her peel broke too soon and fell to the floor.

"Hope ya didn't let the water level go down on that bath while all this foolishness was going on," Dolly complained. The women all started moving around again to their appointed tasks. Dolly walked over to the pile of apple peel.

"*N*, my eye," she muttered. Still, Emily noticed she did pause to study it just a little before scooping it up and tossing it in with the rest of the parings.

Emily continued to quietly peel her apples. Of course, she

didn't believe for one minute that old wives' tale! How could someone predict the name of their future spouse using the outer coverings of fruits? Still, it was quite a challenge to peel that apple. If she could do it, maybe Dolly and Mrs. Hannigan wouldn't think she was such a muddleheaded, fumble-fingered dope.

She was concentrating so hard on getting the apple to peel just right that she hadn't even heard Ben come up behind her.

"Not bad," he said. "For a beginner."

Emily knew that he was standing directly behind her. All she had to do, she knew, was to lean back slightly and she would feel his warm body pressing into her spine.

It was useless to try to ignore him. His very nearness made her hands begin to tremble. But she pressed her lips together more tightly so that she could concentrate on her work. She was almost done.

"I did it!" she said. She sprang to her feet, proudly holding high the long, thin piece of apple peel.

After a brief glance between them of surprised disbelief, Meggie and Frannie began to cheer. Even among the other women there, an impressed murmur rippled through the crowd.

Emily turned to Ben. "Pretty good—for a beginner."

"I always thought you had potential, Emily," he told her, holding her gaze very firmly with his pale blue eyes.

Emily was so glad she hadn't been able to see him while she was peeling that apple, or else she'd never have been able to concentrate on anything but him.

"Now you got to throw it over your shoulder, Aunt Emily," Meggie insisted.

"Oh, that's just silly. . . ."

"No, no. You got to!" Frannie insisted.

With what she felt was a very foolish grin on her face,

entirely suited to the foolish action she was about to perform, Emily stood in the center of the floor and gave the peel a toss over her shoulder.

Meggie and Frannie rushed up, bending their heads so far over the pile that Emily could hardly see for herself what it had made. Not that she was interested, she told herself. This was just foolishness, meant to entertain people out here in the country, who didn't have anything better to do to occupy their minds.

Still, she wished Meggie or Frannie would move their head just a little, so she could see.

"It's an *E*," Meggie announced.

"Is not!" Frannie said.

"*That* is an *E*."

"No, no." Frannie grabbed Emily by the hand and pulled her over to the peel. "See how those ends come 'round and almost meet," she explained, pointing with her finger. "That makes it a *B*."

"It's an *E*, Frannie," Meggie insisted. She gave her cousin a nudge in the ribs and a very significant look. "You know . . . an *E*." She turned bright eyes up to her aunt. "Who do you know has a name that starts with *E*, Aunt Emily?"

"Besides myself?" Emily replied with a nervous little laugh.

Mrs. Hannigan stood on the opposite side, staring down at the puzzle. "It could be a 3," she offered. Looking up at Emily, she asked, "Could that mean you'll have three husbands?"

"Oh, I doubt that," Emily answered. She was a little surprised. She'd have thought Mrs. Hannigan would have supported the *E*—for *Execution.* "I haven't even had one husband yet."

Mrs. Hannigan shrugged. "Maybe you're right. It's a little late for you to be starting now, isn't it?"

"It's never too late," Ben interjected. "But you'd better get started—especially since you have to find an *E* and a *B*."

"Both?" Meggie exclaimed, looking again at the apple peel. It was as if the startling thought that it might be both had never occurred to her.

"Sure looks like both to me," Ben said, nodding his head and circling the apple peel. When he came up to Emily, he wrapped his arm around her shoulder and drew her along with him. "Now, who do you know who has both initials?"

Before Emily could reply, Mrs. Hannigan suggested, "Since you're such an expert, why don't you try it, Ben?" She stood before him, ready with a knife and an apple.

Meggie and Frannie started to giggle.

"Oh, you don't think I can do it," he demanded, glaring playfully at them.

More quickly than Emily could have imagined, Ben whisked the skin off the apple. He tossed it over his shoulder, high into the air. It fell down right beside Emily's.

By now several of the other women—and a few of the men—had been drawn to watch Ben.

"It's an *E*," Ben announced softly.

"Oh, Ben, you're as bad as Meggie, thinking everything looks like an *E*," Mrs. Hannigan said with a laugh that rang with little humor.

"Looks more like an *I* to me," Mrs. Willoughby said.

"It's an *L*," one man interjected.

"Could be a *W* if you kind of look at it this way," another lady said.

"No. It's an *E*," Ben said adamantly.

He turned to look at Emily. His blue eyes searched her face, almost as if he were waiting for her to contradict him.

Well, if she'd sworn on her mother's grave to tell the truth, Emily would have had to say that it looked like an *I* to her, too—not a printed one, but one done in cursive, with lots of little curlicues. On the other hand, she didn't really believe in this silly children's game, did she? It served for a bit of fun when there was nothing better to do. Soon she'd be going back to Baltimore with Meggie, forgetting she'd ever played this ridiculous game, wouldn't she?

"Oh, well," Mrs. Hannigan declared. Clapping her hands, she shooed all the girls back to the work table. "Enough of this, children. We've still got a lot to do."

Emily began to move away from Ben, back to the table. He pulled her a little more closely to him and whispered in her ear, "Even if it doesn't, I think it *should* look like an *E*." His hand was still resting on her shoulder. Very gently he reached his thumb up to stroke the soft part under her ear. "I only know one other person whose name starts with *E*, Emily."

Emily's heart thundered in her chest. Miss Bloom had said this was supposed to be the initial of your future spouse. What more did Ben have planned for her?

She grinned at him shyly. A hot, crowded kitchen was not the place to discuss it. "I think I'd better get back to work for now," she said.

Ben released her from his grasp. He watched her rounded little bottom as she settled it again on the hard wooden bench . . . and wished she'd have been settling herself on his lap instead.

Suddenly Dolly flicked his ear with her forefinger. "I think *you* ought to go back to school and study your proper letters."

Ben reached into the back of the buckboard and lifted out a sleeping Meggie. He followed Emily up the walk to the front door. He opened the door and carried Meggie up to her room. Emily pulled back the covers while Ben gently laid the sleeping child in her bed.

"You know, it really would be a lot easier if I just carried Frannie up here, too, instead of having to take her home," Ben said.

"I'm sure the girls would have a good time," Emily told him as she tucked the quilt up under Meggie's chin. "But I think it's a good idea if everyone spends the night in his own bed."

As much as she wanted him, she knew she had to keep her distance from Ben, or all her good intentions would be gone.

Ben followed her out into the hall. He seized Emily's arm, so that she had to turn around to face him. He took both arms in his hands. Slowly he wrapped his arms around her until his hands met behind her. Then he drew her closer to him.

She raised her palms to his chest. She could feel his taut chest muscles through the thin cloth. She wanted to stand there, gently brushing her hands against him, feeling the tiny hairs under his shirt and his nipples as they tightened at her touch. She didn't want to have to leave him now.

"Do you really want to sleep alone tonight, Emily?" he asked.

How could she say yes? How could she tell him what she really wanted was to lie with him naked and hold him close? There was more to be taken into consideration here than just a few moments of pleasure—for him or for her. But how could she answer no and be a liar?

"Go home, Ben," she said. She placed her palms flat against his chest. Trying very hard to ignore the wonderful feel of the man, Emily pushed away from him. "Please. Tonight, I think it's best if you just go home."

''Is that what you really think is best?'' he asked.

He resisted her push against him. His grip on her tightened, until he crushed her against his chest. He bent over her so that she felt completely enveloped in his arms. He cradled her head in his arm as he kissed her.

There was no escape from him. Her heart pounded harder in her breast. Suppose he tried to take her right now? she wondered with a moment's panic. Suddenly it didn't seem to matter. She knew what he wanted, and she knew that she wanted it as much as he did.

Slowly Ben released her. He took a step or two back. ''You know, I'm only stopping because you said 'please.' ''

Emily watched him as he walked down the steps and out the door. For the first time in her life, she wished her mother hadn't taught her to be so damned polite.

CHAPTER FIFTEEN

EMILY SAT AT THE BREAKFAST TABLE, EXAMINING her ruined nails and the blister that the paring knife had rubbed at the middle joint of her index finger. Her nails would grow back, eventually. When the blisters went down, she'd have a nasty callus there for a while, though. Still, she'd had a good time at the apple bee. Maybe life wasn't so terrible here after all.

"You thought you worked hard last night," Meggie said with a giggle. "Wait till you see what we've got for you tonight."

Two days ago Meggie's ominous warning might have finally sent Emily running for the train station. But the change in Meggie had not only been immediate, it was almost miraculous. Emily was actually looking forward to whatever it was—short of hog butchering—that they might have planned.

"What is it?"

"A cornhusking!" Meggie said. "Everybody gets together and—"

"I think I understand." Emily looked once again at her ruined nails. She supposed, after this, they'd never again be the same.

"You'll like it. Trust me," Meggie assured her. "There's

always plenty to eat. That's Frannie's and my favorite part.''

''Are . . . are we going with Frannie . . .'' Emily was almost afraid to continue. ''And your Gramma and . . .''

''I got a feeling Uncle Noah will be there—if Miss Bloom is,'' Meggie answered. She looked up at Emily and wrinkled her nose.

The little rascal knew that Emily had wanted to ask about Ben, and she had deliberately come up with another answer.

''Can you imagine? My uncle and the schoolmarm.'' Meggie shook her head. ''I thought my friends would all make fun of me for wearing a dress. And now this! Kind of disgusting, ain't it?''

''I think it's kind of sweet,'' Emily said.

Meggie grimaced. ''I thought you would. Anyway,'' she said, jumping up from her chair, ''Frannie and I don't have to watch 'em. All we gotta do is eat.''

''What shall we bring?''

''What do you mean, 'we'?''

''We should bring something to eat,'' Emily said. ''Your Gramma brought something to the barn dance, but I should bring something of my own this time.''

''I don't think that's such a good idea, Aunt Emily,'' Meggie said. ''See, these people come here to enjoy what they eat.''

Emily rose from the table. ''I am going to make a cake,'' she announced. Then, hoping to continue the closeness that seemed to be developing between Meggie and herself, she offered, ''You can help if you'd like.''

Meggie thought about it for just a minute. ''I think I'll go over and see what Frannie's up to. Maybe we'll stop in from time to time, just to see how you're doing. And to help you get your head out of the oven if you need us.''

* * *

This time Emily was prepared. She figured the cornhusking would be in a barn. She wore a plain blue cotton dress and a crisp white apron. She entered with more assurance, proudly carrying her cake on a pretty cut-glass plate she'd found in the china closet.

"Just put it over there with the rest of the food," Dolly told her when they entered the Robbinses' barn.

Emily didn't want to put her beautiful cake with the other, ordinary cakes. She eyed the full table. Maybe she could find someplace up front, so everyone could see it.

As she searched the table for just the right spot, Ben came up beside her and placed his hand on her waist. She could only feel his fingers touching her side, but it made her happy just knowing he was near.

"Are you sure you don't need some help carrying that?" Ben asked.

"No, thank you," she said. "This is the first thing I've managed to bake that I didn't burn. I want everyone to see this—especially your mother."

She especially wanted Mrs. Hannigan to see her fine cake, too. Still, she didn't think mentioning her name right now was a good idea.

Ben's hand moved slowly up and down Emily's back, making her tingle with remembered feelings, and with the promise of all the new and wonderful things he could make her feel.

He leaned closer and whispered in her ear, "It looks almost as good as you do."

She managed to pull away from him just as his other hand made a swipe at the icing. "Shame on you!" she scolded. She found a clear spot on the table and set the cake down, for its own safety. "And I thought your mother was only teasing when she told us about how you always used to steal icing when you were a boy. You haven't grown up, have you?''

''Of course not. You should have believed her,'' he said. ''Haven't you figured out by now that I'm capable of doing almost anything to get what I want?''

''Oh, I wouldn't put anything past you, Ben Cameron,'' she told him with a knowing air.

He didn't say anything. He only looked at her with his pale blue eyes and set her heart pounding with just the thought of holding him again. Yes, indeed, the man was capable of a lot of things. And she was very glad for it.

''Hey, little lady, this cake yourn?'' the old man called to Emily.

Emily blinked with surprise. She turned to see an old man pull a huge Bowie knife from the sheath at his side and hack a big, uneven slice out of her beautiful cake. The man held the slice in one grimy hand while he wiped his knife on the side of his pants. Then, without benefit of plate or fork or napkin, he ate it in big bites. What Emily noted most, however, was the fact that the man had only three teeth.

''Yes, sir, Mr. Pendergast,'' Ben proclaimed proudly. ''Miss Shaw baked it herself this afternoon.''

''Dang, little lady, it's real tasty!'' he exclaimed, the crumbs falling out of his mouth as he spoke. Emily just hoped that none of his teeth would come out, too. He took another big bite. With his mouth still full, he continued, ''Yep. I think it's the best dang cake I et since my wife died.''

''Well, thank you very much, Mr. Pendergast,'' Emily said. She didn't know what sort of cook the late Mrs. Pendergast had been, but, judging from the looks of Mr. Pendergast, he wasn't too picky. That, coupled with the fact that he carried a large, sharp knife, made Emily decide to take his remark as a compliment. Also, when she considered the knife he had cut her cake with and the filthy hand he had touched it with, Emily decided to be generous. "You just eat as much of that cake as you'd like, Mr. Pendergast."

"Thank'ee, little lady," Mr. Pendergast said, and cut himself another slice. He spotted a friend and sauntered off toward him, calling, "Hey, Joe! You ain't gonna believe this. I ain't had a cake like this in years!"

Ben and Emily moved slowly away from the refreshments. The barn was crowded. In order to stay together, Ben placed his arm about Emily's shoulder and guided her through the throng.

His hand was firm. He moved his thumb back and forth, caressing the nape of her neck. Emily felt more secure, just knowing he was with her, knowing that he cared enough about her to stay with her.

"I was hoping you'd get a chance to taste my cake," Emily said. It was the first thing that had actually turned out right. She had wanted so badly for him to know that she could be a proper wife.

Why should that concern her when she knew she was leaving? It was the leaving that bothered her so much. Was there any real reason she couldn't stay—for Ben as well as Meggie? she began to wonder.

"Maybe someday you can make me another cake—just like this one," Ben invited her.

"Oh, I hope not," Emily said. Seeing the look of disappointment on his face, she quickly made her point clear. "I hope the next one will be better."

Just then Mr. Robbins beat on a washtub and called, "Choose up your teams."

"Teams?" Emily repeated.

Ben took her by the hand and skirted the big pile of ears of green corn in the center of the barn. Someone had placed a long broom handle directly down the center of the pile and had placed long benches in two rows on either side of it.

"Where are we going?" she asked.

"This is the lucky side," he explained as he led her to the far side of the barn. He sat her on a rough wooden bench, then sat so close beside her that their legs touched. "I always sit here."

"Why, hello, Ben," Mrs. Hannigan said as she settled down on the bench to Ben's other side. "I just thought I'd take my usual seat, like you have." She leaned forward just enough to catch a small glimpse of Emily. "Well, hello. Fancy seeing you here. I'd have thought you'd be on your way back to Baltimore by now."

"Not yet," Emily answered. She smiled with a great deal of sweetness, something that she certainly didn't feel toward Iris Hannigan. "I still have a little unfinished business in town."

"I hope you finish it soon," Mrs. Hannigan replied. She wore an equally sweet, and equally insincere, smile.

What would Ben think of her reply? Emily wondered for only a portion of a second before she looked at Ben intently and told Mrs. Hannigan, "That all depends on Ben."

Emily, an enigmatic smile on her face, turned away from Mrs. Hannigan. She could have been referring to her brother's business that the Cameron and Shaw law offices were handling for her. Or she could have been referring to other, more intimate matters which Ben alone was handling. Emily couldn't resist a smug little grin. Let Iris Hannigan worry about what she'd meant.

In all her life, Emily had not been a spiteful person. Still, she thought Mrs. Hannigan deserved to worry, just a little.

"Well, I swear," Ben muttered under his breath.

Noah had just escorted Miss Bloom into the barn. Ben stood and waved, trying to get his brother's attention.

Seizing Miss Bloom by the hand, Noah tried to pull her through the crowd. It was hard to do. Every few feet they were stopped by men who wanted to clasp Noah's hand and pump it vigorously, or to clap him heartily on the back. While they were stopped, women came up to Miss Bloom and whispered in her ear.

Noah nodded and smiled. Miss Bloom just nodded.

At last Noah managed to forge their way across the barn. He held Miss Bloom's hand until she settled herself onto the bench beside Emily. Then he bowed very politely and sat beside her.

Miss Bloom giggled and patted Noah on the arm. Then she leaned over to Emily. "Noah's such a wonderful man," she said. "I don't care what those awful gossips have to say about him."

Emily debated for a moment. The schoolteacher was such a dear little lady, Emily wouldn't want to hurt her feelings for the world. On the other hand, she did deserve to know everything.

"Miss Bloom—Ida," Emily said hesitantly. "I don't want you to think I'm an awful gossip, too. But sometimes what people gossip about . . . does contain a portion of the truth. Noah does have . . . well, a little problem. . . ."

"Emily," Miss Bloom said, looking at her as if she were another errant child in her classroom. "Do you think I've lived in this town for over a month now and not noticed? And do you think Noah himself hasn't already told me about his drinking—and about his partially successful attempts to stop?"

Emily blushed, deeply chagrined.

"It's something we'll work on," Miss Bloom said. She reached out and patted Emily's hand reassuringly. "I'm not naive. I know we'll have more than our fair share of problems, but I have faith that Noah and I can conquer this thing—together.''

For Miss Bloom's sake, Emily certainly hoped so.

''All right, folks,'' Mr. Robbins called out. ''First side done is the winners. You all know the rules?''

''Yeah!'' the crowd shouted back.

''There ain't no rules!'' Mr. Robbins howled and dived into his share of the ears of corn.

Ben showed Emily how to hook the corn shucker on her finger, and how to peel back the still-green leaves from the plump yellow kernels, and how to snap off the stem as close to the end of the cob as possible. He tried to show her how to pick out the fat green worms, too, before tossing the cob in the bin. Emily adamantly refused to have anything to do with them. Still, she was enjoying working hard, side by side with Ben.

As the people worked, and the pile grew smaller, the broomstick in the middle shifted. First it would roll down one side. Shouting their protests, the people would kick it back where it came from—or even nudge it a little farther over to the other side, as if the others wouldn't notice.

It amazed Emily that she learned to shuck the corn so quickly. It didn't amaze her at all that Mrs. Hannigan appeared not to have any idea of what she was doing. After fifteen or so, Emily lost count of the number of times Mrs. Hannigan asked Ben for help with a particularly difficult ear of corn.

''I got it!'' Noah suddenly sprang to his feet.

Emily turned to him with alarm. Had he found a jug of whiskey hidden among the ears of corn? Were all poor little Miss Bloom's hopes and dreams thrown out the window? Or had he got religion again, like the night he spent at the camp meeting? Would he run out of here, abandoning Miss Bloom, to complete the work on his ark?

"Well, you lucky dog," Ben muttered.

Emily leaned closer to Ben. She still didn't take her eyes off Noah, just in case things weren't quite as good as Ben thought they were.

Noah was waving a red ear of corn high above his head. He held out his hand to Miss Bloom, assisting her to rise. Once she was on her feet, he swept her up in his arms and bestowed a very passionate kiss on her lips.

A howl went up from the men in the crowd. The women in the group were much more subdued. Miss Bloom blushed as furiously red as her curly hair. When Noah released her, she waved her hands in front of her crimson face, trying to cool the heat of passion that still flamed there. It didn't seem to do any good.

"Miss Bloom, you appear a bit flushed," Noah said. "Why don't we get a glass of cider and take a little walk? The night air might cool you down a bit."

"Mr. Cameron, I think that would be very appropriate," Miss Bloom answered.

Emily watched them depart.

"What in the world was that all about?" she asked Ben after they were gone.

Ben looked at her askance. "Emily, you must know by now what a kiss is."

She gave him a playful poke in the ribs with her elbow. "Oh, hush. I mean the ear of corn."

"Don't you know?"

"I'm afraid not," she said, shaking her head.

"The man who finds a red ear gets to kiss the girl next to him," Ben explained.

Emily smiled with relief for Noah, and also with happiness for Miss Bloom. "How often does one find these red ears?" she asked.

''Oh, they're pretty rare,'' Ben answered. ''I wouldn't say no more than two—maybe three—a night.''

Emily wasn't sure if that was good or bad. A wanton little spark inside her bosom longed for any excuse to feel Ben's body, hard and warm against hers, while his fingers traced fire up and down her skin and his lips pressed hers in a passionate kiss. On the other hand, she preferred to be alone with him. She didn't think she'd want to be kissing Ben in front of all these people.

Of course, the opportunity might not arise, either, she told herself. Hadn't Ben said the red ears were rare? Only a little disappointed, Emily went back to shucking her section of the dwindling pile of corn.

Meggie and Frannie sat on a bale of hay in a corner of the barn, each eating a piece of cake.

''How're you doing?'' Meggie asked.

''Not bad,'' Frannie answered. ''I've had six pieces of cake and a couple of fried crullers, some of Mrs. Jessup's fruit salad. I'm really waiting for the ice cream to crank up.'' She nodded her head at Meggie's plate. ''How many does that make for you?''

Meggie swallowed a mouthful before she answered. ''I've had a piece of everything but the apple cake and Aunt Emily's cake. I'm saving hers for last. That way, if it makes me sick, I'll have already eaten all the good stuff and won't be missing out on anything decent.''

''What if it makes you so sick you throw up?'' Frannie asked.

''Well, then, I guess I'll just have room to go back and eat some more,'' Meggie answered.

''Well, if you're planning on getting any of Aunt Emily's cake, you'd better get it soon,'' Frannie warned. ''I'd never have believed people would really eat that thing up so fast.''

"You're kidding?"

Frannie slowly shook her head.

The two girls sat there eating and watching the workers for a little while.

"I'll tell you, Meggie, I'm really disappointed in Pa," Frannie said in a worried tone. "I never thought he'd go and give our red ear to Uncle Noah."

Meggie shook her head. "Me, neither. And after all our hard work trying to get that thing for him."

"I had to promise Jimmy a new penknife before he'd let us borrow the red ear his brother always used to take to the barn huskings before he got married," Frannie complained.

"Well, wait a minute," Meggie said. "Uncle Eb did take it, planning on using it. Maybe Uncle Noah found a real, honest-to-goodness one."

"Could be, I guess. But then why hasn't Pa used his yet? That pile's getting awful low. There's not much time left."

"You don't think he chickened out?"

"My pa? No! Nobody's ever called him a coward," Frannie staunchly defended Ben. "And I get the feeling he'd really like to kiss your aunt."

"Well," Meggie said, eyeing with concern the receding tide of corn, "he better use it soon, is all I got to say."

Dolly came over to where Meggie and Frannie were sitting. "Are you having fun?" she asked.

"Sure are, Gramma," Meggie answered. "Did you try any of Aunt Emily's cake yet?"

"Why? Shouldn't I?"

"No, no, Gramma," Frannie said. "I ate some. It's not bad. Neither were her cookies the other day, or her soup."

Dolly scrutinized the girls with one squinty blue eye. "You mean to say she's actually learning to cook?"

"Yeah," Meggie said.

"Who's teaching her?" Dolly demanded.

''Don't know.''

Dolly grunted with disdain. ''Won't be Wilhelmina. She don't give nobody none of her recipes—leastwise, not right. *Shouldn't* be Nola. Only thing that woman can make is pickles.''

''I think she's kind of learning on her own, Gramma,'' Meggie said. ''She's cleaned the house and worked real hard on the apple peels. And she helped me with my lessons. I won the spelling bee this week.''

Dolly frowned and looked out over the crowd toward Emily. She *was* working, just like everybody else there. They were all talking to her and making jokes with her—all except Iris Hannigan. People were actually eating the cake she'd brought!

Emily'd stopped dressing so fancy, too. Oh, anybody could tell her dresses cost a lot more than anyone else's—even Nola Lindstrom's—but Emily almost looked like every other lady there. If only she'd lose those uppity airs. If only she weren't so insistent on taking Meggie away, Dolly could almost like her.

Suddenly Mrs. Hannigan cried, ''Why, Ben, you did find one after all!''

''Oh, oh!'' Meggie and Frannie looked at each other in panic. They jumped down from the bale of hay and scrambled over to stand behind where Ben sat between Emily and Mrs. Hannigan.

The girls breathed a simultaneous sigh of relief. Ben had pulled out the red ear he had hidden in the inside pocket of his jacket. Now was his chance to use it! Then the girls held their breath. Would he be smart enough to use it on the right lady?

Emily sat to Ben's left. Out of the corner of his eye, he saw her smiling. It wasn't a completely happy smile. Did she think he was going to do more than just kiss her in public, and embarrass her in front of all these people? Oh, he had plenty of plans for Emily, but none of them included an audience.

Mrs. Hannigan sat to his right. Ben didn't want to turn to her. He would have to be blind not to notice the way her eyes gleamed with anticipation. It wasn't fair to build up her hopes. She *was* pretty, and soft, and probably made for cuddling on cold winter nights. He'd known her for years. She was a very good cook and liked Frannie. She had all the qualities any man could look for in a wife—except one thing. Ben wasn't in love with her.

Emily held her breath, waiting. Which would be worse? she wondered. Kissing Ben in front of all these people—or having him choose to kiss Mrs. Hannigan instead? He was definitely fond of her. If he chose Mrs. Hannigan, Emily decided, it would probably be best to just pack up and catch the train Monday morning back to Baltimore.

She hadn't figured on it hurting so much if he wanted someone else. There was more to her feelings about Ben than just an intense fascination with his lustrous blue eyes, or a plain and simple lusting after his incredible body. There were feelings inside that had more to do with the heart than any other part of him or her. She'd only come to Bidewell to collect her niece and be gone. Somewhere along the line, she had fallen in love with Ben Cameron. Now what was she going to do?

Suddenly Ben rose. He held out his hand to Emily, just like Noah had done for Miss Bloom. Emily gave him her hand and allowed him to assist her to rise. She wanted to smile at him, but she was too nervous to move. All she could do was gaze at him and hope that he could read what was in her eyes.

Slowly Ben raised his hand to cup her chin. Gently he lifted her face to his. As if this were their very first kiss, he lowered his lips to softly touch hers. He lingered there only a moment, his lips covering hers until she thought she'd melt from the warmth. Then he slowly drew back.

There was a hush over the crowd. Emily had expected as many cheers and catcalls as Noah and Miss Bloom had received. She never expected complete silence, as if they had witnessed something very special.

Over Ben's shoulder, Emily got a brief glimpse of Mrs. Hannigan. Mrs. Hannigan was *not* happy.

Her face was almost as red as Emily's, but her blue eyes were almost black with anger.

"I think I need some cider," Emily murmured, looking up at him.

"I think we need to talk."

Ben placed Frannie beside Meggie in the big bed. Emily drew the covers over the two sleeping children. As she stepped back, Ben placed his hand on her shoulder. He drew her closer to him.

She could feel his broad chest pressing against her back, rising and falling with his even breathing. There was something comforting about standing enveloped in the arms of the man she loved, watching two children who meant so much to her—the feeling of a complete family that she had never known before.

Oh, she'd loved her own family—and they had all loved each other, in their own way. Although he'd been much older than she, George had been a wonderful brother while he was around. Her mother had been a domineering invalid, her father too preoccupied with his business to be concerned with family matters. The closeness, the playful bantering and unconditional caring of the Camerons made Emily realize what it was like to be part of a real family.

The longer Emily stood there, the more she could relax

against Ben. The more closely she leaned against him, the quicker his breath came. He began to move his hands up and down her arms.

"Emily," he whispered. "Come on. We don't want to wake them." He stepped back, urging her to come with him.

He held her hand, gently drawing her out of the children's bedroom and across the hall toward her own room.

"I need you, Emily," was all he said as he tried to draw her closer.

"You said we needed to talk," she reminded him, holding back. "We should go down to the parlor."

When he couldn't urge her closer to him, he took a step toward her. He lifted his hand to her shoulder, then moved up to stroke her soft hair. His hand moved from her hair, down her cheek, to caress the little hollow at the base of her throat showing above the prim collar of her little blue dress.

"Why? Can't we talk in there?" he asked, nodding his head in the direction of her bedroom. The smile he gave her, and the gleam in his pale blue eyes, was almost enough to make her forget all her firm resolves. Almost.

"Probably," she conceded. "But I don't think we'd be talking about the same thing as we would in the parlor."

He began slowly circling his finger around the button at the top of Emily's dress. It was larger than the pearl buttons had been. It was easier to unfasten with one hand.

"And eventually," Emily said as she reached up to stop him, "we would end up not talking at all."

"Sure, I'll still talk to you, Emily," he said. He wrapped his large hands about hers. Raising her hand to his mouth, he began kissing each separate fingertip. "I'll tell you how beautiful you are. I'll tell you just how much I love touching each and every part of you."

Emily drew in a deep, ragged breath. Reluctantly she

pulled her hand from his grasp. She turned and headed for the stairs. Ben followed.

"I still think we need to talk, Emily," he insisted as he descended the stairs.

She was standing by the front door, as if she really expected him to leave.

"Dammit, Emily! Why are you always running away from me?" Ben demanded, shaking. Whether he shook from unrelieved passion or from frustration and anger, Emily didn't want to know. She was almost afraid to ask.

"I don't always run away from you, Ben—or have you forgotten?"

"I could never forget you, Emily," he told her softly.

She didn't want to hear that. Ben pining away for her was not the image she wanted to spring to mind whenever she thought about him if she returned to Baltimore. *If* she returned. She had been so sure of her intentions in the beginning. When had *when* turned to *if*? And what would happen if she didn't return to Baltimore?

"It's just, I have other things to do right now, Ben," she said, trying to explain to him—and to convince herself. "Other things to think about."

"You're all I think about, Emily," he said softly.

How could she admit to him that he was all she wanted to think about, too? The ugly image of herself, pining away for Ben after she had returned to Baltimore without him, sprang to her mind.

But she had a responsibility to her family, she tried to tell herself. To parents long dead, to a brother recently gone—and to a niece who was alive and well and very, very happy right here in Iowa.

"I want you to stay here—Meggie, and especially you—with me and Frannie," Ben said.

He stopped by the door to the parlor. He had no intention

of leaving yet—not until he had made it perfectly clear to Emily exactly what he had to offer her, and exactly what he wanted from her, in every way.

''Emily'' was all he said as he held out his hand to her. ''What are you afraid of? Do you think I'll take you right on your very own couch?''

Emily couldn't stop herself from smiling at the pleasurable thoughts such an idea conjured. She fought down the slight blush in her cheeks. Imagine, she, Miss Emily Shaw, harboring—and actually enjoying—such lustful thoughts. Oh, and they were enjoyable! She reached out to take his hand.

He pulled her against him—slowly, as if he were giving her a chance to change her mind. She had wanted just to talk to him. But when she looked into his eyes, burning down at her with the intensity of his passion, she knew, shamelessly, that she wanted more from Ben than just talk. She was very certain she wouldn't change her mind.

She allowed him to pull her close to him. She felt a stirring throughout her entire body as his hands tenderly slid across her shoulders, down her arms, and around her waist.

She looked up, smiling. His lips may have been smiling down on her with the sheer joy of holding her, but his eyes still flamed intensely with the desire to touch her more. She tingled with the pleasure of his caress.

She was ready and very willing to meet his demands. There was no tentative exploring. His lips were soft, yet hard in their pressing need to be satisfied.

''We shouldn't be doing this, Ben,'' she said breathlessly when he at last released her.

He drew her slowly into the parlor until they were standing in front of the sofa.

''No? Not this?'' he asked, kissing her again. ''Not even this?''

Slowly his hand slid from her waist, down her hips, until he cupped her soft bottom in his hands. He pulled her hips roughly toward him. At the same time he pressed against her. He was excited already, hard and demanding, yet gentle with her in his urging.

"Don't you know by now how much I want you, Emily? How much I need you in my life?" he whispered, his voice growing hoarse with the desire he held in check. Slowly he began to lift her light cotton skirt. "You want me as much as I want you, don't you?"

"You know I do," she whispered. She made no move to stop him as his hands slid under her petticoat. "But—"

"There are no *buts,* Emily," he told her, smoothing his palms down her slender thighs. "There's only you and me."

His hands slid up her thighs, slowly, as if he were waiting for her, any second, to stop him. She knew she wouldn't. Ben was right. There were only the two of them. She realized that she loved Ben more than anything else in the world. How could she leave him now? Their being together was all that mattered to her now and forever.

His hand slid over her hips, up to the tiny drawstring that held her drawers in place. Slowly he began to pull at the slender ribbon until it at last came undone.

He eased her back upon the cushions. Every movement he made with deliberate slowness, as if he were always allowing her the freedom to leave him at any time, if she chose. She knew she would never leave him—not now.

Slowly Ben slipped her drawers from her and let them fall carelessly to the floor. He bent over her as she lay upon the sofa looking up at him. Never in his life had he seen such love in a woman's eyes. He only hoped his own reflected what he felt for Emily.

He stretched out beside her, cradling her head in his arm.

The front door burst open, slamming against the wall and reverberating through the vestibule.

Emily jumped to her feet, sending Ben sprawling to the floor. Quickly she smoothed her skirt and petticoats down. Ben had sprung to his feet and stood ready for any intruder.

"I thought Noah was sober," Emily said nervously.

Peering intently into the half-darkness of the vestibule, Ben shook his head. "It's not Noah," he said.

"Who is it?" Emily asked, suddenly even more nervous.

"Aunt Emily, Frannie's sick," Meggie said. She stumbled into the parlor, rubbing her eyes against the light. "She ran outside to throw up."

Glancing down, Ben and Emily both noticed the thin white silk drawers lying in a heap at their feet. With the toe of his shoe, Ben quickly shoved them under the sofa. Her drawers still stuck out from beneath the legs. Emily caught an edge of the lace with the toe of her shoe and pulled them out again. Carefully inching along, she shoved them under the cloth that hung from the table in front of the sofa.

"I don't feel so good myself," Meggie complained, rubbing her stomach.

Suddenly Meggie clapped both hands over her mouth and headed out the front door. Ben quickly followed her to check on Frannie, too.

Emily took one more quick glance to make certain her drawers were well hidden until she could get them after the girls were back in bed. As she reached the door, Ben was just ushering the two little girls back into the house.

"I'll get a bucket of water for the front porch," he told her. "Why don't you put these two back in bed?"

"But they're sick," Emily said. "Shouldn't you go for the doctor?"

Ben shook his head. "Maybe a good dosing of castor oil

would do their stomachs some good. And maybe a swat on the behind.''

''It's not my fault, Pa,'' Frannie mumbled. She turned to Emily and complained, ''I ate your cake.''

''Yeah, it was your awful cake that did it,'' Meggie agreed.

''Only because you shoved it down on top of everything else you ate,'' Ben scolded. ''Don't think you can blame Emily for this.''

Meggie grimaced. Frannie had no fight left in her. She slowly and quietly made her way back up the stairs.

''Go on,'' Ben ordered Meggie. ''Back to bed.''

Meggie reluctantly followed Frannie. Emily trimmed the wick of the lamp in the vestibule.

Ben came up beside her. He bent close and placed his hands about her waist. Leaning his chin on her shoulder, he nuzzled her ear longingly. ''Oh, Emily,'' he whispered, ''when can I make love to you without interruption?''

Before she could answer, he had released her. As he headed for the door, he suddenly turned back. Giving her a wicked wink, he said, ''By the way, don't forget your drawers.''

CHAPTER SIXTEEN

EMILY SPENT ALL DAY SUNDAY NURSING A CRANKY Meggie through the colic.

Dolly stopped by with a brown bottle containing a horrible-smelling, home-brewed concoction that she swore took away the bellyache. According to Dolly, Frannie was staying at the farm, suffering the same affliction as Meggie—with about as much patience.

In spite of Meggie's protests, Dolly made her swallow a large tablespoon of the thick brown liquid in the bottle. If how bad a medicine smelled was any indication of its power, Emily believed this potion was a veritable miracle cure.

Then Dolly left the bottle on the back of the kitchen sink, with instructions for Emily to dose Meggie several more times during the day.

Emily was surprised. Dolly actually was pleasant to her and seemed to have come to believe that Emily could take care of Meggie without poisoning her or dropping her on her head.

Even while Emily was busy worrying about Meggie, and Dolly and her potions, she continued to ponder what she was going to do about Ben.

She wanted to stay with him—there was no question about that. And he wanted her to stay. There was no reason to take Meggie back to Baltimore now. She was happy here with her friends and family. Having spoken with Miss Bloom, Emily felt more reassured that Meggie would be able to receive all the education she needed right here in Iowa.

As for Emily herself, there certainly wasn't anything to keep her in Baltimore—and there were a thousand reasons why she should stay in Bidewell. But even they seemed meaningless compared with the one overpowering reason she should stay. She was in love with Ben Cameron.

She could begin the process of selling her own home in Baltimore and transferring funds from one bank to another. All she had to do was make a payment to the bank on George's house and sign the papers for her brother's estate.

If Mr. Taylor had the papers. Surely he'd been able to find them by now, Emily hoped. After all, she'd given him a week. That was certainly more than enough time. If he didn't have them by tomorrow, she'd . . . she'd tell Mr. Ebenezer Cameron, she thought with a little grin. With a sweeping feeling of relief, Emily realized that, from now on, Ben would be taking care of her.

Monday morning, Noah drove Annabelle and the buckboard from the farm to George's house. Emily allowed the little bay mare to take her into Winterset. It was so nice to again have an animal one could trust implicitly.

Emily hadn't driven a horse since she was fourteen. Sitting behind Annabelle now, she watched the reddish-brown rump bobbing up and down. She listened to her snorts and the clop of her hooves and the jingle of her harness as the mare trotted along the road beside the fields of corn. The autumn sun beat down on Emily's stylish little hat, warming her in spite of the coolness of the breeze tickling her cheek.

All this brought back to her remembrances of the happiest days of her childhood, spent on Grandmama's farm. Visiting Grandmama was her only relief from the smothering demands of her mother. It was the one place where Emily was allowed to run and laugh aloud, to climb trees and get dirty making mudpies. It was the one place she was allowed to act like a child. It all ended when Grandmama died and her father, more concerned with his business in town, sold the farm when Emily was fourteen.

Maybe, without her parents, Meggie needed the Camerons' farm as much as Emily had needed Grandmama's. Not like Emily had enjoyed it, for only a few short weeks in the summer when her mother had grudgingly allowed her to visit, but all the time.

As she rode along, Emily decided to make that same wonderful life possible for her niece. She would try to regain what she had lost, too, in the slower pace and friendlier atmosphere of a loving family in a small town. She smiled, certain that she had made the right choice.

Emily pulled Annabelle to a halt at the ornate, black cast-iron hitching post. She gave a scruffy little boy a penny to watch Annabelle. Then she entered the yellow brick building and climbed the steep, narrow steps up to Ben's law office.

She knew she was early for their appointment, but she was anxious to get her brother's troublesome business over with. She opened the heavy door to an apparently empty office.

Although they had managed to clear everything off the tables and chairs in the waiting room, Lottie's desk was still strewn with papers. But Lottie was nowhere to be seen—unless she was hiding. Emily expected to see her come popping out of one of the desk drawers like a little owl from its nest.

Ben's door was shut tight, and in spite of the bright morning sunshine streaming in the other windows, his office appeared very dark, as if the curtains were still drawn. He wasn't here yet, Emily thought with disappointment—and a bit of surprise. She'd seen him leaving his house for the office this morning. Where could he be?

There appeared to be a bit of light coming from Mr. Taylor's office. Emily pushed open the gate in the rail that separated the waiting room from the offices and walked up to Mr. Taylor's office door. As she drew closer, she could tell that he had raised his blind and she could hear someone shuffling papers on the other side of the door.

If Lottie, or even Ben, had been there, Emily would have waited for them to show her in. She disliked entering unannounced. On the other hand, who knew how long she would have to wait outside? She tapped gently before turning the doorknob.

She hadn't even gotten the chance to poke her head into the office. Mr. Taylor, his head still bent low as he studied his papers, didn't even bother to look up before he began speaking.

"Ben, Ben, I'm real sorry," he said, shaking his head. "I've been over this will again and again, just like you asked me. Miss Shaw is the legal guardian for all George's minor heirs. There's no way around it. There's just no way you can take your niece away from her—legally."

Emily's blood began to chill in her veins. After all they'd said and done, after all she thought they'd come to mean to each other, was Ben still trying to see if he could take Meggie away from her?

"Unless, of course, you could prove she's not a fit guardian."

Emily's chilled blood immediately froze. She felt so cold

she could barely breathe. She even doubted that her heart was still beating.

Mr. Taylor shuffled through the papers in his hand. Then he spread them out on his desk, hunched over them, and scratched his head.

"Now, I know you already checked into this, but I went over it again, just to be sure. She's rich enough—so you have no grounds there to claim that she can't provide for the child. I know you've checked her personal background, too. If she wasn't so damned upright, you could always try to take Meggie away from her on a charge of bad moral character." Mr. Taylor chuckled. "Have you been thinking about that? Eh, Ben? Ben?"

Emily shut the door softly before Mr. Taylor could see that it was she standing there and not Ben. She felt her heart sinking through the floor as she realized that this was exactly what Ben *had* been thinking.

She couldn't get out of the office fast enough. She wanted to be away from Ben Cameron and anything to do with that awful man. She didn't even want to breathe the same air he did.

She was so upset that she almost didn't see the gate. If it hadn't given way when she ran into it, she would have fallen over it. She was shaking so badly inside that she had trouble holding the doorknob to turn it to make her escape. She had to grip the handrail tightly to keep from tripping down the long, steep flight of stairs. All the way down, tears filled her eyes more and more until she could barely see.

Once outside, she flinched, as if struck in the face hard by the glaring morning sunlight. She stumbled along the sidewalk, unable to open her eyes completely in the brightness and unwilling to lift her head in case anyone should see her tears. She dabbed roughly at her eyes with her linen handkerchief and blinked hard so that she could see better quickly. She didn't want to run into some poor, innocent passerby and have to explain.

As she walked along the sidewalk, the fresh air cleared her head. She tried to remember everything she had heard Mr. Taylor say. The more she remembered, the more upset she became.

Ben had discovered just how rich Emily was. But he didn't need her money. He was hardly a poor man himself. His affection for her couldn't be based on her purse rather than on her heart.

Or did Ben truly hold any affection for her in the first place? Had it all been just a scheme? Did he want custody of his niece so badly that he was willing to ruin Emily's reputation just to get it? Emily shook her head as if by doing that she could shake out all these unsettling thoughts. She didn't want to believe Ben was that kind of man. And if he was that kind of man, she didn't want to think how close she had come to surrendering to him the most precious part of herself that she had to give.

"Miss Shaw. Emily, how good to see you here today," Mrs. Hannigan said.

Emily moaned. On top of everything else, she thought with disgust, a little chat with Iris Hannigan is just what I need!

She sniffled into her handkerchief, hoping to dry her eyes completely before looking up at Mrs. Hannigan. Unfortunately, there was nothing she could do to disguise how red and puffy her eyes probably looked.

Well, she couldn't hide behind her handkerchief forever, Emily decided. After all, did it really matter what any of these people thought of her? Soon she would be taking Meggie back to Baltimore and never see a one of them—not Dolly or Noah or Frannie or Ben—ever again.

Mrs. Hannigan scrutinized her. "Oh, dear, you look just

terrible. Do you have a cold?'' she asked, so sympathetically that Emily knew she couldn't possibly be sincere.

''I don't think so,'' Emily answered. ''Perhaps the street dust and straw out here in the country . . .''

''Yes, that could bother some people with weak constitutions,'' Mrs. Hannigan agreed. ''Perhaps you should get back to the city very, very soon.''

''I intend to, Mrs. Hannigan.''

Mrs. Hannigan's narrowed eyes grew brighter. She glanced over Emily's shoulder toward the door to the law offices that Emily had just left. ''Oh, then, I take it your business with Cameron and Shaw is complete.''

Emily nodded. ''Just about, Mrs. Hannigan.''

Yes, her business was almost completed, Emily thought. But there were still a few items that she needed to discuss further with Ben Cameron, personally and privately. And after she was done with him, she hoped Dolly had a good home remedy handy to stop his profuse bleeding.

''Ben has been handling my late husband's—and now my business—for many years,'' Mrs. Hannigan continued her conversation. Emily was not at all surprised that she would choose Ben as her topic. ''He's a very good lawyer and a close friend.''

''My brother thought well of him, too,'' Emily said. Of course, George had let his house fall down around his ears and allowed Dolly to teach his daughter how to become a spitting champion. That showed what kind of judgment George had.

''Ben's such a devoted family man, too,'' Mrs. Hannigan said. Emily had also been waiting for this. ''I realize you think you're doing what's best for your niece and all, but it really is a shame to just tear that child away from the bosom of her family.''

"I know, Mrs. Hannigan," Emily said. "You've told me this before."

But Mrs. Hannigan was very intent upon saying what she had to say, almost as if she had rehearsed it to herself beforehand and couldn't stop once she'd begun.

"Ben was devastated by the loss of his wife and sister. The possibility of losing his niece as well is just heartbreaking for him." Mrs. Hannigan emphasized the depths of her sympathy for Ben by placing her hand over her ample bosom. "Why, I think the man would do almost anything to keep his family together. Almost anything," she repeated for emphasis.

Her emphasis was not lost on Emily—perhaps more than Mrs. Hannigan even realized.

"Of course, a man doesn't usually show these kinds of feelings. *You*, of course, may not know this, Miss Shaw, but he would confide his concerns to an old friend like me."

"I'm sure Ben will be pleased to know he can depend on your discretion, Mrs. Hannigan," Emily replied with a forced smile. Just for sheer spite she couldn't resist adding, "And I'm sure he couldn't have an older friend. Good day."

Emily continued to walk down the sidewalk, away from Mrs. Hannigan. She had no idea where she was going in Winterset. She just wanted to get away from Mrs. Hannigan and away from Ben's office. She wanted to be somewhere she could have the time to think.

On the other hand, she really didn't want to have to think, because the only thing on her mind right now was Ben Cameron.

She still had enough of her wits about her not to take everything Mrs. Hannigan had said as gospel. Still, there was probably more than a grain of truth in what she had told

Emily. Hadn't Ben himself admitted that he would do almost anything to get what he wanted?

Well, he wasn't the only one who felt that way, Emily thought. Meggie was her niece, too. Maybe she hadn't spent the past ten years trying to raise the little girl, but she loved her all the same. She realized now that she was bold enough, and woman enough, to fight Ben Cameron tooth and nail for her niece. And maybe, someday, she'd get even with that man for what he'd tried to do to her.

First she had to sign those papers for George's estate. Then she and Meggie would be on the next train out of Bidewell—back to Baltimore, back to the lawyers who would know exactly how to ensure Meggie's future.

Emily drew in a deep breath and once again mounted the stairs to the law offices of Cameron and Shaw. It was past time for her appointment now. She hoped they were ready for her.

As soon as she entered, Lottie sprang to her feet, knocking over just a small stack of papers this time. Emily was pleased to see that Lottie was apparently improving. But she didn't even wait for the little bird-lady to show her in. She strode through the gate and up to Mr. Taylor's door. This time she knocked boldly.

"Come in, Miss Shaw," Mr. Taylor said, rising. "Please, have a seat."

"I know I'm a little late, Mr. Taylor," Emily apologized as she sat in the tall-backed leather chair. "I had . . . unexpected business elsewhere."

"Yes, things come up from time to time," Mr. Taylor said, sitting down again. He seemed almost relieved that she hadn't been here sooner.

"I can tell from the look on your face you don't have good news for me," Emily said.

"I wish I did, Miss Shaw. As you can see, it isn't for lack

of trying,'' Mr. Taylor said, gesturing at the piles of papers that still cluttered his office table and shelves. Then he began nervously shuffling the papers he held in his hands. He fidgeted in his seat and had trouble looking her in the eye.

He truly had bad news, Emily feared. So bad that he was having a hard time even bringing up the subject. But Emily had waited all week for some kind of information, and she was very tired of waiting. ''Mr. Taylor, what's the problem?''

''In searching through your brother's things . . . well, this is so hard to say that I'm afraid I'll just have to be quite blunt.''

''Please do, Mr. Taylor,'' Emily said. She hoped the nervous young man recognized the sarcasm in her voice.

Mr. Taylor pulled his handkerchief from his pocket and wiped his perspiring brow. ''We've found certain papers that indicate that your brother's estate is actually worthless. In fact, he didn't owe money on the house you now reside in because he didn't even own the house.''

Emily stared at him across the desk. ''How could George have done this?'' she demanded.

Mr. Taylor shook his head. ''Apparently, your brother made certain investments that turned out very badly.''

Mr. Taylor swallowed so hard that Emily could see his Adam's apple rise and fall. She was surprised to see him stand again and make his way to the office door. He pushed hard against it, making certain it was closed.

''Certain investments,'' he continued in a much deeper, more ominous tone as he resumed his seat, ''that he was encouraged to make by Mr. Cameron.'' Mr. Taylor laid the papers he held in his hand before her on the desk.

Emily sat very still for a moment, letting the information wash over her like the tide. She felt as if she were drowning in these facts as they swirled about her, threatening to pull her under. She put her hand out to hold the edge of the desk. Very slowly she picked up the various papers.

Emily looked, barely seeing them. Even if she had seen them better, she still would have had trouble deciphering all the legal writing, or even the things written in plain English, because of the whirling confusion in her mind. They appeared to be records of payments George had made for stocks in companies that did not even exist, and a document stating he had signed over the house for the money to make some of these speculations.

"How . . . how can you be sure Ben . . . Mr. Cameron suggested my brother do this?" she asked in a voice that shook more and more as she tried to use it, but shook worst of all when she tried to say Ben's name.

Mr. Taylor slid several other papers toward her, identical to the ones she held except for the fact that they bore the name of Ebenezer Cameron.

"Mr. Cameron has been handling your brother's affairs for many years," Mr. Taylor explained. "So he would also have access to his funds. I was only assigned this account when he heard of your arrival. Perhaps he was hoping that, my being new, I wouldn't notice something like this."

"I'm very grateful you did, Mr. Taylor." At least, she thought she ought to be. It was difficult to be properly grateful to someone who was telling her that the man she loved was an atrocious cad, a despicable thief, and an out-and-out liar.

"I'll admit, I'm pretty inexperienced with this sort of thing, Miss Shaw," Mr. Taylor said. "I haven't spoken of this to Mr. Cameron yet. I hate to admit this, but . . . well, we're still gathering evidence against him at this time."

Emily was finding it increasingly difficult to breathe in the stifling little office. "We?" she repeated in a breathless whisper. "Gathering evidence?"

"I'm not at liberty to say," Mr. Taylor continued, obviously oblivious to her pain. "But from everything we've seen so far, apparently Mr. Cameron was showing his own false stocks to trusting clients, taking substantial sums of money from these investors, and then claiming the company suffered a loss when it came time to pay dividends, pocketing the money for himself."

If Mr. Taylor had told her this yesterday, she'd have slapped him and called him a barefaced liar, at the very least. Now, after what she had discovered about how Ben had treated her, she wasn't one bit surprised to find that he had treated so many other people so badly just to get what he wanted.

What angered Emily was not the fact that Ben was capable of stealing from so many strangers, or that he had even stolen from her own brother. What infuriated her the most was that he had robbed Meggie of her inheritance. He was even prepared to ruin Emily just to get custody of Meggie, if he couldn't get her money any other way.

Through her hurt and anger, at last Emily found her voice. "I'm . . . I'm not sure what we should do about this, Mr. Taylor," she admitted. She pressed her lips tightly together. She was determined she would find out what to do.

"For the moment, may I suggest you do nothing, Miss Shaw?"

Emily was startled by this advice. She was angry, and she wanted revenge—swift and complete.

"More people than just you are involved in this, I assure you," Mr. Taylor told her with an air of authority and just a slightly enigmatic lift of his eyebrow. He pushed several long papers in front of her and offered her a pen. "Just sign these, right there, if you would. Then take your niece and return to Baltimore. Someone will contact your lawyers."

"I can't sign those things now," Emily said, shaking her head and rising abruptly from her chair. She pushed them back at Mr. Taylor. "I'm sorry. I've got too much else to worry about right now. My lawyers in Baltimore will be in touch with you."

Signing those papers was not the most important thing she had to do, Emily thought as she left the office. The most important thing she had to do now was buy two tickets back to Baltimore on the very next train. She didn't say good day to Lottie as she left the office. She barely looked in either direction as she crossed the street to the train station.

As she climbed the steps of the platform, the image of Ben, bare-chested and toting a feed sack in the afternoon sun, returned to her mind. She'd never even gotten a chance to see him close up with his shirt off. She'd never had the chance to feel his warm skin or the firm muscles underneath. Now she never would.

Emily pressed her lips more tightly together. She replaced her handkerchief in her purse. She refused to cry any more tears for that man—especially tears of regret.

Emily looked about the deserted station for Sam, but the stationmaster was nowhere to be seen. She walked over to the ticket window in the center of the small red building on the platform. It, too, appeared empty. She knocked anyway.

Suddenly Sam the Stationmaster popped his head up from under the counter. His wispy white hair waved in the breeze he created in his own wake. His watery blue eyes peered at her intently through his thick spectacles.

"Who . . . ?" he said.

"Lottie!" Emily exclaimed, suddenly struck with the likeness.

Sam shook his head. "Yer not Lottie. I think I know my own daughter by now."

Emily shook her head. How was she going to manage to get this man to give her the right number of tickets to the right place?

"I remember ya," Sam said. "Yer Miss Shaw, Mr. George's sister from Baltimore."

"Yes, and I need two tickets back to Baltimore—as soon as possible," Emily stressed.

Sam immediately ducked back under the counter and reappeared with his stationmaster's hat atop his head, prepared to do business. He consulted the tattered chart that hung on the wall beside him.

"Ya want to go by way of Chicago?" he asked.

"Is there any other way?" she countered. If he didn't know his railroad routes by now, how did he expect her to?

Sam withdrew his precious watch with a flourish, flipped it open, and examined it carefully before replacing it.

"Ever get yerself that good watch, Miss Shaw?" he asked, peering at her over the top of his gold-rimmed spectacles.

"I still have the same watch I arrived with," she answered.

Sam shook his head and turned back to his timetable. He hummed as he ran his finger up and down and over and across the chart, stopping every once in a while to tap at a particular cross-section, then moved on.

"Ya got one going outta here this afternoon at four," Sam finally said. "Ya sure yer gonna be able to make it in time?"

"I'm sure," she answered, nodding her head so emphatically that her hat almost fell off.

"Next one don't go out till six tomorrow morning," he warned.

"Don't worry, Sam. We won't miss this train."

Sam shrugged his shoulders. He started to pull out lengths of tickets and began scribbling on them and stamping them with all the theatrics of a great complicated process.

"Ya didn't stay with us very long, Miss Shaw," Sam observed as he worked.

"I stayed long enough," she answered.

"Nice town, ain't it?"

"Yes, it is, Sam." Emily really meant it, too. Bidewell, and the whole courtryside, was beautiful.

"Well, now, here ya go," Sam said. He handed her a long roll of tickets across the counter and accepted her payment in return. "Two to Baltimore. Now, mind ya don't miss that train at four—sharp!"

Ben sat in the storeroom, staring at the small bundle of papers he had found pressed way down at the bottom of a small box hidden behind a tall pile of larger boxes. He was having a hard time believing what he was seeing. After spending half the day searching, finally, there were the missing bank drafts. They were written for large sums, signed by several of his clients and made out to a company he had never heard of. He frowned. It was bad enough to think that George had been stealing from his own clients. He hated to think George had been trying to steal from his clients, too.

He felt a surge of relief when he came across several checks with George's signature. He could hardly have been stealing from himself. But if he wasn't, who was? Then Ben paused, studying the drafts more carefully. That wasn't exactly George's signature. Even when he had been drinking heavily, George's handwriting was better than that.

Ben picked up several more pages, then grasped them so hard he wrinkled the edges. What was *his* signature doing there? But it wasn't exactly his signature, no more than that was George's.

No, he shook his head. Lottie was too nervous to steal. Cecil Taylor was such a bright, eager young man. Ben hated to think he'd do such a thing.

He brushed the dust from his knees and entered the office.

"Lottie," he said, holding the papers in front of her. Before he could ask anything, Lottie took them from his hand and began to file them. "No, no, Lottie," he said, retrieving the papers. ''This is very important. Have you ever seen these before?''

Lottie pursed her lips and peered at them through her spectacles. She looked up at Ben, blinked, and shook her head.

Ben sighed and turned away. Someday he would have to hire a secretary who looked less like a bird and had more intelligence than one.

Ben knocked on Mr. Taylor's door. ''Cecil,'' he said, entering his office. ''I've found those missing . . .''

Ben stopped in his tracks. Mr. Taylor was frantically scooping up piles of paper from his desk.

''Going somewhere, Cecil?'' Ben asked.

''Ben! I thought you were out. . . .''

''I was in the storeroom.'' Ben reached out to pick up a thick, green-edged piece of paper. He turned it over in his hand, reading it carefully. ''I never heard of this company. I'll bet George Shaw never did, either.''

Mr. Taylor grimaced. ''George was usually too drunk to care.''

''But what about all these other people? What about Meggie? What about me?'' Ben demanded. ''How could you think you'd get away with this?''

Mr. Taylor shrugged his shoulders. ''I *almost* did.''

''Why?''

''I needed the money. . . .''

''Don't give me that story!'' Ben shouted, slapping the papers he held down on the desk. ''Didn't I pay you enough?''

''I needed the money to buy into the law offices here,'' Mr. Taylor continued to explain. ''I hated the way you and George were always so condescending to me.''

''I was going to make you a partner, just as soon as things got settled after George's death!'' Ben shouted with exasperation and disappointment.

''I didn't even have my own office until George died,''

Mr. Taylor complained. "I didn't want to have to wait until I was fat and bald and forty to be a partner."

"But you had such promise. We trusted you! Geez, Cecil, why couldn't you wait?"

Ben slammed the papers down on the desk so hard that several of them fell to the floor. When he bent over to pick them up, he saw George's and Emily's names on them, and an empty place for Emily's signature.

"She didn't see these, did she?" Ben demanded. More loudly, he repeated, "Did she?"

Mr. Taylor jumped. "Of course she did. I even told her you were the one who convinced George to buy this stock. She believed me, Ben. But she refused to sign the other paper, unfortunately. Otherwise, I'd have had her share of George's estate, too."

Ben strode over to Mr. Taylor so quickly that the man didn't even have time to back up. Ben grabbed him by the collar. Mr. Taylor wasn't a short man, by any means, but Ben fairly lifted him from the ground in his anger.

"Don't hit me," Mr. Taylor pleaded, holding his hands up before his face. "I can't stand the sight of blood. And I'd hate to have a scar."

"You're not worth bruising my knuckles on," Ben told him with a sneer. He pushed him back into his big leather chair. "But don't even think about leaving town," Ben warned him in an ominous whisper.

Ben stormed through the outer office. "Lottie, was Miss Shaw in here?"

"Yes, early this morning. But she left in a hurry," Lottie answered.

Ben pressed his lips together in frustration. He'd have to find her, explain to her that what had happened was none of his doing. She loved him. She'd believe him.

"Where'd she go?"

"I think I saw her go across the street, to the train station," Lottie answered, pointing in that direction.

"Of course," Ben said as he pushed open the gate and pulled open the door. Suddenly he turned back. "Oh, Lottie."

"Yes, Mr. Cameron?"

"Send one of the errand boys to tell the sheriff to come get Mr. Taylor."

Lottie's eyes popped open wide.

Ben thundered down the narrow stairs and burst out onto the sidewalk. Dodging carriages and wagons, he ran cross the street to the train station.

"Sam! Sam!" He took the platform steps two at a time as he called out for the elderly stationmaster.

"Hey, Ben," Sam said as he shuffled out of the ticket office. "Thought I might be seeing ya here. Miss Shaw was by this morning. Bought two tickets for Baltimore. Now, that's a strange place to go on a honeymoon."

"It's not a honeymoon, Sam," Ben said quickly. In the time it took him to explain everything, he could be finding Emily and explaining things to her in a much more pleasant way. "She's leaving and taking Meggie with her."

Sam stroked his white-stubbled chin with a gnarled hand. "Well, then, yer in luck. She ain't leaving till the four o'clock—if ya get my meaning." He jabbed at Ben's ribs with a bony elbow.

"Thanks, Sam. I owe you one," Ben said as he took off down the stairs.

"Well, now that ya mention it, I got another daughter in need of a job. . . ."

Ben waved as he ran back across the street. He reminded himself to try not to owe Sam any more favors again.

CHAPTER SEVENTEEN

NOAH HAD BROUGHT EMILY'S TWO BIG BLACK trunks down from the attic. He had also found two smaller suitcases up there that Emily decided she could use for some of Meggie's things. It didn't matter if she couldn't take all of her clothing. Most of it wouldn't be appropriate for her new life back in Baltimore anyway. She and Meggie would go shopping together. That could be fun, she hoped.

She looked at all her own clothing, taken from the drawers and chifforobe, and spread out on the bed, waiting to be folded neatly back into the trunks for the long journey home. It had been so much easier when the maid had packed for her.

"Are you sure you want to do this, Miss Emily?" Noah asked, lowering the last trunk onto the bedroom floor.

"No, I'm not," she answered, shaking her head.

Noah looked at her with a mixture of bewilderment and exasperation. "Now, what kind of answer is that?" he demanded, placing his knuckles on his hips. "I didn't get sober again just to come into a world where you can't get a straight answer out of a person."

"No, I don't want to leave, Noah," Emily admitted. "But I have to."

"Well, I'm real sorry you feel that way, Miss Emily. But

I guess everybody's got to do what they feel they have to do,'' Noah said philosophically.

''Thank you, Noah. I don't know who else I could have gotten to help me with these heavy things.''

''You could always get Ben,'' Noah suggested.

''No, no,'' she said quickly. ''He's . . . too busy . . . at his office.''

''Does he know you're leaving?''

Emily swallowed hard. Of course Ben didn't know. If he knew she was leaving, he'd probably be over here right now, she thought bitterly. He'd be holding her, kissing her, touching her in places that only made her want him to touch her more. She quickly shook such thoughts from her head. If Ben thought he could get the job done by tonight, he'd probably be over here in a minute. He'd have the papers drawn up and have custody of Meggie by the end of the week.

''Ben's known all along that I'd be going back with Meggie someday.'' Emily decided that was the safest explanation.

For all his faults, Noah was a nice man. He'd had a hard enough life already. Maybe he'd finally found some happiness with Miss Bloom. He didn't deserve to be disillusioned about his own brother.

''Are you ever coming back?'' Noah asked.

''I don't think that would be such a good idea, Noah,'' Emily answered slowly. ''I'm sorry. But maybe you and Miss Bloom can come visit us sometime.''

''Like for a honeymoon?'' Noah asked with a twinkle in his eye and a little grin on his face. ''That would be nice. Still, it won't be the same as having you two here all the time.''

''No, it won't,'' Emily said as she began stuffing all her clothing into one trunk.

Noah watched her in silence for a while. Then he remarked, "Miss Emily, are you in that much of a hurry?"

"Yes," she answered. She was in a hurry to get out of here. She didn't care what she did with her dresses. The blue velvet gown ended up crushed in the bottom of the trunk beneath her shoes as she threw everything in at once. "I don't want to miss my train."

Noah glanced at his pocket watch. "I'd say you could slow down just a bit. After all, it's only eleven thirty."

"I don't want to miss my train," Emily repeated, not bothering to look up from her packing.

Of course she didn't want to miss her train. The next one wasn't until six tomorrow evening. That meant she'd have to spend one more night here in Bidewell. One more night trying to fall asleep in her cold, solitary bed, remembering the warmth of Ben's lips caressing hers and the shiver of delight when he touched her body, with Ben sleeping so close in the house next door. She hoped it would be easier to forget the feel of his hands on her skin when he was much farther away.

It also meant that there was still a very good possibility that she would have to face Ben again. How could she see him without wanting to hold him close and feel his lips on hers just one more time? Or wanting to punch him in the nose, very hard?

"I'll be waiting downstairs for you," Noah told her, heading for the door. "Whenever you're ready for me to take the trunks out to the buckboard, just let me know."

It didn't take Emily long to roll everything into a big knot and shove it into her trunks. Slowly she made her way across the hall to Meggie's room.

Dolly was standing at the window, hugging Meggie's doll close to her heart. Emily paused in the doorway. When

Dolly realized that Emily was standing there, she turned and held the doll out to Emily.

"Don't ya go forgetting this now," she ordered. "It's her favorite."

"I won't." Emily took the doll from the old woman's outstretched hands. She set it on the chair by the window. "I shouldn't put her in a suitcase. I'll leave her out so Meggie has something to play with on the train."

Dolly nodded and kept staring out the window, across the cornfields. Her empty arms hung at her sides.

In the silence the buckles of Meggie's suitcase clicked against each other as Emily unfastened them and threw the straps back. She opened the lid and began to take Meggie's two dresses out of the wardrobe.

Whether it was because Dolly was there or because they were Meggie's, Emily took more care in folding and packing these clothes.

When both suitcases were full, there were still a lot of things to pack. Emily decided to leave them. Under the circumstances, it would be much easier to just buy Meggie all new things once they were back home.

"Most of her things are out at the farm," Dolly said, "if you want to come by and take them, too."

"No," Emily answered. She really didn't want to do anything that would put her at risk of seeing Ben again. "I think I'll leave them here for now. Meggie's not really going to get much use out of denim overalls where we're going. Of course, if I need them, I could always send for them."

Dolly nodded silently.

"Or I could leave them here for her to use when we come back for a visit," Emily suggested. She had no intention of coming back ever, but one could never be absolutely certain. And perhaps letting her think they might return would ease some of Dolly's pain.

Dolly laughed without humor. "Ya ain't been out here in ten years. By the time ya get 'round to coming out here again, Meggie'll be all growed, and I'll probably be dead."

Emily grimaced as she shut the lid of the suitcase. She was so glad Dolly wasn't bitter about this.

"Geez, Uncle Noah!" Meggie exclaimed as she and Frannie burst into the kitchen. "Did you have to go taking a shine to my teacher? You should see how my friends are all teasing me now."

She tossed her schoolbooks onto the table and began looking around for something to eat. Then Meggie pulled up short. She frowned when she saw Dolly standing behind Noah, and Emily standing at the pantry door with a wooden box in her hands.

"Hey, what are you doing here anyway, Uncle Noah?" she asked. "Shouldn't you be at the farm, working on that boat?"

"I . . . um . . ." Noah had trouble answering.

"Noah's been kind enough to give us a hand here, Meggie," Emily explained. She moved into the pantry and began putting the small amount of food she had bought into a wooden box.

"Did the shelves break again?" Meggie asked.

"No, I'm giving this to Dolly."

"Well, then, what are we going to eat?"

"We'll eat on the train," Emily said.

"What train?"

"Uh-oh," Frannie murmured. She dropped her books to the floor and dragged them by the bookstrap over to where Dolly stood. Her big blue eyes were even larger with apprehension. She reached up and put her hands around

Dolly's waist and cuddled close for comfort. Dolly reached down to encircle Frannie with her arms.

''We're going back to Baltimore, Meggie,'' Emily told her.

''No, we're not.''

''Yes, we are, Meggie. We have tickets. The train leaves at four.''

''Well, I hope you have a nice trip, 'cause I won't be on it.''

''Meggie . . .''

''I'm not leaving here!'' she insisted. ''Why do you want to go now? What in the world do you think we worked for, me and Frannie? We still owe Jimmy Lindstrom a new penknife. Now you tell me you're leaving anyway! What about me? What about Frannie? What about Uncle Eb?''

Emily cringed when Meggie mentioned Ben's name. She almost answered that Meggie would have to learn to live without him, but that seemed a pretty heartless thing to say to a child. She thought it was a pretty heartless thing for her to have to suffer, too. But she was older. She could endure—maybe.

Emily drew in a deep breath. She didn't want to lie to the child, but there must be some easier way to soften this blow.

''Meggie, I have to go back to Baltimore to settle some business,'' she said. ''I thought you'd like to come with me.''

''When are we coming back?'' Meggie asked immediately.

''I'm not sure,'' Emily said hesitantly.

''We're not coming back, are we?'' Meggie demanded.

''That depends on how the business goes.''

''I'm not stupid, Aunt Emily,'' Meggie said. ''We're not coming back—ever. Are we?''

Emily couldn't disguise the truth, however distasteful, anymore. She said nothing.

"Are we?" Meggie shouted. Her little face was red with anger, and her fists were clenched tightly at her side.

"Meggie," Emily began, trying to speak in a low, calm tone of voice. "Maybe when you're older, you'll understand these things. . . ."

Before Emily could say any more, Meggie turned and bolted for the back door. By the time Emily could gather enough of her wits about her to follow her to the door, Meggie was already out of sight.

Over the top of Frannie's head, Dolly glared at Emily across the kitchen. "I'm real old, and I still don't understand."

Emily stood, looking out the kitchen door. She tried to think of where Meggie could be. Ben wasn't home yet, so she couldn't have gone to his house. She hoped Meggie hadn't run into the cornfield. The little girl might be able to find her way through the tall stalks on a straight trip through to the schoolhouse, but as upset as Meggie was, she was bound to lose her way.

There was only one other place Meggie could have gone. Emily didn't want to go there. She had hoped that their meeting in Winterset would be their last. But Meggie was her niece. If she wouldn't allow Ben to take her, there was no way on earth Emily would allow Mrs. Hannigan to come between them.

As she crossed the lawns and made her way up Mrs. Hannigan's front porch steps, Emily kept a sharp eye out for chickens, just in case. She smoothed down her skirts just a little—she didn't want to appear too nervous. Taking a deep breath, she raised her hand to knock on the door.

The door flew open in her face.

"What do you want?" Mrs. Hannigan demanded.

"Oh, you must have seen me coming," Emily said,

lowering her hand. She felt pretty certain Mrs. Hannigan hadn't just happened to be passing by her front door.

"What do you want?" Mrs. Hannigan demanded.

"I was wondering if Meggie—"

"Meggie goes to your house now when she comes home from school," Mrs. Hannigan said. Her lips were drawn into a tight little frown.

"Well, yes, usually she does."

"Isn't that what she did today?" Mrs. Hannigan asked.

Emily had more than just a slight suspicion that Mrs. Hannigan knew exactly where Meggie was. But she wasn't about to tell Mrs. Hannigan that Meggie had run away from her, or why. It was bad enough when Mrs. Hannigan had discovered that Meggie was not happy with her aunt from the beginning. This would only provide more fuel for Mrs. Hannigan's gossip.

In order to avoid answering, Emily asked, "Have you seen Meggie this afternoon, Mrs. Hannigan?"

"No. No, I haven't," Mrs. Hannigan said quickly, beginning to close the door.

Emily reached out and blocked her. Then she stood there, silently waiting.

"I said I haven't seen her, Miss Shaw," Mrs. Hannigan repeated with mounting anger. "If you intend to take care of Meggie yourself, don't you think you'd better learn to keep better track of her?"

"I do, Mrs. Hannigan," Emily said. "That's why I came here, to ask if you knew where Meggie is."

"How should I know?" Mrs. Hannigan began to close the door again. Then she stopped and said, "Of course, if Meggie has run away from you, I think you should have figured out by now that she doesn't want to go with you. She wants to stay here, with people who love her."

"Is she here, Mrs. Hannigan?" Emily asked point-blank.

"No, no, she's not here!" Mrs. Hannigan shouted, slamming the door in Emily's face.

Emily knocked on the door. "Mrs. Hannigan. Mrs. Hannigan, if Meggie's in there, you can't keep her."

There was no answer.

"Mrs. Hannigan." Emily continued to knock. "I do have legal guardianship of Meggie. You can't keep her."

Still there was no answer.

"Mrs. Hannigan, do I have to get the sheriff?"

"Sheriff's busy," said the voice behind her.

Emily turned to see Ben standing at the end of Mrs. Hannigan's front walk. "How do you know?" she asked.

"Because I'm pressing charges against Mr. Taylor," Ben answered. "And the sheriff's taking him in custody right now."

"How dare you!" Emily exclaimed with horror. "Just because the man found out that you—"

"Emily!" Ben said, quietly, yet forcefully enough to stop her speech. "Do we have to shout our business all over town?"

"Why not? They'll all know soon enough anyway."

He held out his hand to her. "Come down here and we'll talk," he called to her.

Emily stayed where she was. She knew if she came down to him now, she would want nothing more than to hold him and would forget all her intentions of leaving. She would allow him to make a fool of her again and again. Emily stayed on the porch.

"Emily, I said we need to talk, and we were interrupted Saturday night." Suddenly he grinned at her, his blue eyes sparkling. "Of course, we weren't doing much talking anyway."

"Oh, all right," she said. "The town doesn't need to know all our business."

If he kept talking like that, he'd have a dozen witnesses to attest to her depraved moral character when he took her to trial for custody of Meggie. This was a terrible way to force her to come to him, but she'd learned to her sorrow not to underestimate Ben Cameron.

"What do you want?" she asked as she grudgingly came down the walk toward him.

"I came here looking for you." He held out his hand to her but she backed away. "Sam told me you and Meggie were leaving."

Emily nodded. She was waiting for some protest from him, some impassioned plea or protestation of undying love that would make her want to believe he wasn't a thief and an uncaring villain. Something that would make her want to stay.

"I don't blame you," he said.

She wasn't prepared for this.

"I also talked to Mr. Taylor about your brother's stock."

Emily recovered enough to raise her chin and glare at him. "Oh? I didn't think you'd want anyone to know about that."

Ben rubbed his chin. In a low voice he began, "Well, actually, no—for Cecil's sake—"

"For *his* sake?" Emily repeated. "I would have thought you'd be more concerned about yourself."

"No, I didn't lose that much money, not compared to others. . . ."

"*You* lost money?" She glared at him in surprise. "I thought you were making a pretty penny out of—"

"It wasn't me, Emily. How could you even believe I would do such a thing? Cecil lied to you, just like he did to a lot of other people. He forged their signatures."

"How could he?" Emily demanded. "He's only been handling the account for a few weeks. You did it all. . . ."

"I never handled George's affairs," Ben protested. "I didn't think, being family, that I should meddle in his business."

Emily stood, not saying a word, just staring at him, frowning.

"If you don't believe me, you can always ask the sheriff," he suggested.

"Good idea," Emily said at last. In a rush she continued, "I need the sheriff. Now."

"Why?"

"When Meggie found out I was taking her back to Baltimore, she . . . she ran away," Emily explained reluctantly. She threw a worried look at the immense cornfield behind the houses. "I just hope she didn't go in there. But I'm pretty sure she went to Mrs. Hannigan's. That's where she usually goes."

"And you went to talk to Iris. . . ."

"And she says she doesn't have her."

"Well, she might not."

"Ben, I *know* Meggie's in there," Emily insisted.

Ben heaved a deep sigh. "*I'll* go ask."

"Oh, I'm sure she'll be much nicer to you," Emily said.

Ben started up the walk, then turned and added, "Why don't you go back to your own house, for the time being?"

Ben was relieved when Emily actually did what he asked. He raised his hand to wipe his brow. How could falling in love cause him so much trouble? he wondered. He straightened his jeans on his lean hips, then proceeded up the walk.

Ben knocked and waited. The sheer white curtain at the side of the door opened just a bit. Ben saw Iris's blue eyes peeking out cautiously.

She opened the door just a crack, then seized Ben's hand and hauled him inside, slamming the door tightly shut behind him.

"Where's Meggie, Iris?" Ben demanded.

"Not here."

Ben shook his head. He didn't believe her for a moment. "Where's Meggie?" he repeated.

"Shh." Mrs. Hannigan placed a rounded little finger up to her pink lips. "We don't want Miss Shaw to know we have Meggie. She's hiding here until that wretched woman gets on that train and goes back to Baltimore where she belongs—alone."

"You can't do this, Iris."

"I'll only keep her here for a little while. Just until Miss Shaw leaves," Mrs. Hannigan said. "Then we can be together—Meggie and Frannie—and you and me, Ben." She laid her hand on his arm.

Ben shook his head as he pulled away. "I can't do that to Emily, Iris. And I can't let you do it, either."

"But I'm only doing this for you, Ben. Meggie belongs with her family," Mrs. Hannigan protested.

"Miss Shaw *is* her family. And *you're* not."

Mrs. Hannigan's jaw dropped open. "But . . . but . . . but I could be."

Ben said nothing, but only shook his head. Any other answer would only leave her room for argument—or hope.

The cellar door opened and Meggie poked her head out. "Is she gone? Is it safe to come out?"

Ben grabbed Meggie by the arm and pulled her into the vestibule. Releasing her, Ben crossed his arms over his broad chest and glared down at Meggie.

"No, she's not gone—yet. And no, it's not safe, because *I'm* still here, young lady," Ben growled at her. "Just what do you think you're doing?"

"Hiding, so Aunt Emily misses the train—and I don't have to leave."

"Do you know how worried your aunt is about you?" he demanded.

"Yeah." Meggie grimaced. "So worried that she wants to take me away from you all."

"I'm taking you back home, Meggie," Ben said. He held her by the scruff of the neck and directed her toward the front door.

"You can't," she protested, her arms and legs flailing. "She'll leave. She's got to stay here. . . ."

"You leave Miss Shaw to me," Ben answered with assurance, but Meggie still had her doubts.

All her life, Meggie had trusted someone grown up to take care of her. Since her mother was dead, then Gramma would. If Pa had been too drunk then Uncle Eb would. For the first time in her life, Meggie knew that not a single grown-up here cared about her, not one bit. They were all doing what they thought was best for her, but no one had asked her what she wanted.

Well, if the grown-ups weren't going to take care of her, she'd just have to take care of herself, she decided.

When they reached the bottom of Mrs. Hannigan's front steps, Meggie turned and gave Ben a sharp kick in the shins. He gave a short yelp of pain and released her. As soon as he dropped his grasp, Meggie took off at a run, straight for the cornfield.

"Oh, damn!" Ben yelled. "No, Meggie! Not in there!"

As Ben sprinted across the backyards, Emily ran out of the house.

"Where's Meggie?" she demanded.

"In the cornfield!" Ben cried.

"Can you find her?"

"I hope I can find her in time," Ben answered. He drew up to a stop in front of Emily. Resting his palms on both knees, he leaned forward, gulping in air.

"The train doesn't matter, Ben," she said.

"It's not the train," Ben told her. He pointed farther down the field. "Old Man Pendergast is harvesting this field today."

From far down the long rows of corn, Emily could hear the rattling of the harness, and the snorting of the mules, and the whirring of the blades as the harvester continued its steady progress up the field.

"She'll hear them, but in there, she won't be able to tell where they're coming from," Ben tried to explain as quickly as he could. "And they'd never be able to see her until . . . it's too late."

Uttering a desperate cry, Emily ran into the cornfield at the same place where she had seen Meggie enter. The tall stalks were turning brown but were still as thick and high as ever. How could she ever find Meggie in here?

"Meggie! Meggie!" She got no answer.

She continued to run down the rows of corn, calling Meggie's name, trying to warn her to get out of the field. The only sound she heard was the jingling of harness and the whirling blades coming closer all the time. She couldn't stop her search.

Suddenly the enormous black and brown muzzle, flanked by two limpid brown eyes, loomed ahead of her, coming closer all the time. She didn't know which way to run. Right or left could take her directly into the path of the rest of the team and send her stumbling under the slashing blades.

Emily was knocked to the ground so hard that the breath was knocked out of her. The heavy weight bore down on her. She was dead for certain! She closed her eyes, waiting for the pain that was coming and praying for a swift death.

The weight shifted off her. Lighter pressure moved across her arms and legs, searching her body. She opened her eyes.

Ben's blue eyes shone down on her like the sky above. Looming behind him was a wrinkled face with a wide smile containing only three teeth.

"Emily, Emily, are you all right?" Ben demanded. He continued exploring her body.

"What ya doing here, little lady?" Mr. Pendergast asked.

"Meggie! Where's Meggie?" Emily demanded, trying to scramble to her feet.

"She's fine, fine," Ben assured her. "I found her. I smacked her behind for pulling such a stunt and sent her home, safe. Are *you* all right?" he repeated.

Knowing that Meggie was safe, Emily was at last able to relax. It felt so good to rest, cradled in Ben's strong arms.

"Almost lost ya, little lady," Mr. Pendergast said. "Sure would've been a shame to lose the best little cake baker in Bidewell." He shook his head. Then he slapped the reins, urging the mule team into action once again. The huge harvester rumbled past, shaking the ground as it went, and leaving in its wake only a lane of decimated stubble. Emily shook to think that she might have been mowed down just like that.

"Let's get you back to the house," Ben said.

As Emily emerged from the cornfield, Meggie ran into her open arms. "Oh, Meggie!" Emily exclaimed. "How could you do such a thing to us?"

Ben enveloped them both in his arms.

Meggie looked up into Emily's eyes. "Does this mean we're going to stay together now?" she asked.

Still keeping her arm around Meggie, Emily pulled them both away from Ben's embrace. "No, Meggie," Emily said. "I still have to go back to Baltimore. You have to come with me."

"Do I?" she turned to Ben and asked.

"Just go clean yourself up. We'll talk about it later."

"Do you?" he asked Emily after Meggie had left for the house.

"You know I do," she answered quietly.

"Why, because you still think I stole from George and Meggie and all those other people?"

Emily shook her head. "It's not just that, Ben." She had a train to catch. She didn't want to waste time going over a subject that would be more painful to her than falling under the slashing blades of the harvester. The important thing now was to get Meggie away.

"I believe you didn't steal from my brother and all those other people. I can only hope you did what you did because you wanted what was best for Meggie. What's best for Meggie may be here or it may be in Baltimore. But it certainly isn't with two people who will spend their time arguing over what's right for her. I'm taking Meggie away. You're welcome to visit any time. Bring Dolly, too."

She glanced down at the watch pinned to her bodice. Then she looked at him again. She tried so hard to keep from crying. She tried to keep her gaze cool.

"Now, I have a train to catch and barely enough time to make it," she said, tapping her little watch. "Will you take me into town?"

When he didn't answer, she turned away from him. "Then I'll find someone else who will."

"Good. Because I sure as hell won't," Ben called angrily to her as she crossed the lawn toward the house.

As Emily reached the kitchen, Dolly turned away from her.

"I saw her into the world in this house," the old woman

said. Her shoulders stooped wearily. "I think I'll say my goodbyes from here, too."

Emily turned to Noah, still standing in the doorway. "You said you'd help me, Noah," she reminded him.

"I know," Noah answered. "But I sure wish I hadn't."

CHAPTER EIGHTEEN

"DO YOU REMEMBER YOUR PA?" NOAH ASKED Emily as he climbed up into the buckboard.

Meggie sat scowling silently between them.

"Certainly," Emily answered. "He only died last year."

"Do you remember your ma?"

Emily frowned, puzzled that he would continue to pursue such a morbid line of questioning.

"A little less," she confessed. "I was younger when she died, so I don't remember as much, and I have less to remember about her."

"I don't remember my pa hardly at all," Noah said.

"What . . . what happened to him? If you don't mind my asking."

"Course I don't mind you asking," Noah said, turning to stare at her as if she certainly should have known better. "Why else do you think I'd bring it up?"

In spite of her sadness at leaving, she had to smile at Noah's glowing pride in his obvious lack of subtlety.

"I was only eight when Pa was killed."

"Oh, I'm sorry," Emily said, her expression turning serious. "I didn't know."

"Sarah was ten, Ben was fourteen." He turned to her and chuckled. "Are you surprised to know I'm the baby of the family? I guess I don't look it. Whiskey might make you feel young at heart sometimes, but it sure plays hell with your face.''

Emily had to grin again.

''Pa was killed at Sayler's Creek, Virginia, April of sixty-five,'' Noah continued, as if Emily should remember the battle well.

Emily shook her head. She'd only been six years old. Battles then had just been dots her father marked with little blue or gray flags pinned to the big map on the wall of his huge, dark-paneled, smoke-filled study.

''After four years of fighting, Pa almost made it home,'' Noah continued with a sad shake of his head. ''I missed him for a while, so did Sarah. But I really didn't have a lot of memories to miss. Ben probably remembers Pa the most. I guess that's why he misses him the most.''

Emily was silent. She was sorry now she hadn't given much thought to what had happened to old Mr. Cameron, or how much it had affected Ben.

''After that, Ben helped Ma with the farm. He still managed to study law, and helped raise me and Sarah, and put me through architect training,'' Noah bragged. Then he grimaced and hung his head a little lower. ''Although I didn't turn out so well after all, I guess.''

Emily reached out and, in a spontaneous gesture, patted Noah's hand. ''I think you're going to be just fine now.''

Noah grinned and nodded his appreciation of her faith in him. ''Five years after Pa died, Ben married Betty. Then she died having Frannie.''

''Oh. I didn't know Ben's wife had been dead that long,'' Emily said slowly. A little more softly she asked, ''He never remarried?'' Of course, she wasn't really interested, she told herself. She was only talking to be polite.

''Nope,'' Noah answered with an emphatic shake of his head.

Emily knew how hard it was to lose someone you loved. She was almost ready to tell Noah to turn Annabelle around and go back to the farm, back to Ben. She understood just a little better now his intense desire to keep what was left of his family together. It still didn't excuse his despicable behavior toward her, but at least she could understand it.

Maybe she could try to visit Bidewell once in a while so that Meggie could see the Cameron family more often. If she was lucky, she could find something else to do while Meggie visited so that she didn't have to be around Ben. Or maybe she'd have gotten over him by then—if she waited a long, long time.

Much to Emily's surprise, Noah began to chuckle. "He's driven every widow, single woman, and mother with a marrying-age daughter in this town crazy for the past ten years. Course, he never paid any attention to a one of them. That's what riled them most."

Noah stopped laughing and looked at Emily intently.

"Have you ever noticed how different people seek comfort in different things when confronted with adversity?" Noah asked. "Some of us take to religion, some of us take to drink, like me and George."

"George?" Emily repeated.

"Right after Sarah died," Noah explained. "We were comrades in our cups, I guess you could say. Till I was stopped—sort of. And poor George just drank himself away," he ended with a sad shake of his head.

"Poor George," Emily murmured. "Poor Meggie."

"Ben's not one to sit and drink his troubles away. He took to working all the time instead. Kept himself busy with the farm and his law offices. Sometimes he wouldn't even come home at night, just slept right there on a sofa in the storeroom of the office."

"My father was like that," Emily said. "Confidentially, I think he did it to get away from my mother."

Noah chuckled again. Then he said, "You know, Ben was always so busy working, he never used to take time out to go to a barn dance or a cornhusking—or anything that was fun—till you came along."

Ben had told her himself that he was a man who would do anything to get what he wanted. Was taking her to a barn dance included in with all the other distasteful things a man had to do to get what he wanted out of life?

Emily let Noah continue on to Winterset.

Emily looked around as Noah pulled the buckboard up to the train station. No one was there, not even a railroad worker, or a stockman, not even Sam the Stationmaster. Noah began to unload her trunks and Meggie's suitcases.

"Noah, you know, for a town this busy, I'm amazed that the station has been empty every time I've been here," Emily remarked.

Sam came shuffling out of the office. He glanced down at his watch. "Well, yer just a tad early, Miss Shaw. Won't be nothing much going on here for a while. Tell ya what. Why don't ya have a seat here with yer baggage, and I'll take Meggie over to the general store for some penny candy to see her through to the next stop?" Sam offered. "A gal can get awful hungry on a long trip."

Meggie grabbed Sam's hand. "Thanks, Sam. Say, you wouldn't happen to know of a good place to hide nearby, would you?" she asked as she and Sam crossed the street.

"Well, everything's here, Miss Emily," Noah said. "Won't be long before the train gets in. If you don't mind, I won't wait. I'll say my goodbyes now." He looked down at his feet as he shuffled them nervously across the wooden planks. Suddenly he reached out and gave her a big hug.

"Goodbye, Noah," she said, squeezing him back. "Thank

you for everything. You know I wish the best to you and Miss Bloom."

"Thanks, Miss Shaw." Noah pursed his lips and shuffled his feet some more. Then he looked up at Emily and said, "Now, I know you've heard all this so many times before you're probably sick of it. I know you think you're doing what's right—and a person's got to do what they feel is right, so I wish you the best—but I sure wish you thought differently."

"So do I, Noah," Emily murmured.

She watched him turn, climb up into the buckboard, and ride away with Annabelle. She thought differently about a lot of things now—about Bidewell and the people who lived here. She also thought differently about Ben, and she wished with all her heart that someone could prove her wrong.

"So do I," she murmured to the wind.

Emily took a seat beside her trunks and Meggie's suitcases. She glanced down at her little watch. Ten to four. The train was due at four—sharp, Sam had said. Where was everyone? She supposed not many people were traveling east this time of day, or this time of year—or ever?

She continued to wait. Four on the dot, and not a soul in sight. Ten past and still no passengers.

The heavy suitcase thunked down beside her own. He'd packed so quickly that a white shirtsleeve stuck out from the closed suitcase. Emily looked up into Ben's eyes.

"Going somewhere?" he asked. Without waiting for an answer, he said, "Me, too."

Just seeing him again, when she thought she never would, shook her. She moistened her lips nervously. "What are you doing here?" she managed to ask.

"I hear there's a train out of here at four. Frannie and I are going to be on it."

"It's past four," Emily said.

"No, it's not," Ben contradicted. "You forgot. See, it's four o'clock down the road a ways. Here, it's not four yet."

"But Sam told me four sharp," Emily protested.

"That Sam's a crafty old coot, ain't he?" Ben said with a hearty laugh. Then he looked at her more seriously and said, "I hope the extra time he gave you let you do a little more thinking—about me, and about us. I know I did a *lot* of thinking about you, Emily."

"What did you decide?" she asked. She wasn't sure if she wanted to hear his answer.

Ben kicked at his suitcase with the toe of his boot. "What do you think?"

Emily kicked the suitcase back. "Am I supposed to believe this is really packed?"

Ben looked at her, puzzled. "Yes."

"Is this just another ploy to get me into your bed, Mr. Cameron?"

Ben reached out to stroke her cheek. "I hope I can do that without a suitcase," he whispered, although there was no one around to overhear.

"You don't have to try anymore, Ben," she said, shaking her head so that his hand no longer made contact with her skin. "It didn't work. Give up."

"What didn't work?"

"You never got the chance to seduce me like you planned," she said.

He tried reaching out for her again. "Well, give me a little more time, then."

"I'm still a virgin, moral now as I ever was," she said, raising her hand to slap his hand away. The feel of his fingers on her cheek, and the remembrance of what his hand felt like encircling her breasts and caressing her thighs, were so unsettling that she could hardly continue to speak. She knew if he continued to touch her, she would lose not only Meggie, but all her self-respect. "So you can't use that to take Meggie away from me," she finished.

Ben blinked in surprise and dropped his hand. "Why do you think I planned to do *that*? Did Mr. Taylor tell you more lies about me?"

"This wasn't a lie, Ben. I came to the office early," she tried to explain, although her voice trembled. "He thought it was you standing in the doorway. He didn't see it was me, and so he talked . . . freely."

Ben clapped his hand over his forehead in exasperation. "That's what that scoundrel always joked about although *I* didn't think it was very funny. Do you think I could do that to any woman?" He moved his hand so he could look her clearly in the eye. "Do you think I would do that to you?"

"You almost did."

"Oh, Emily," he said, reaching out to her again. He took both of her arms in his hands. "Couldn't you tell I did what I did because I love you?"

"I don't know, Ben," she answered. She tried to walk around him, just to get away from him. "I know what I feel for you, but how can I know what you feel for me?"

"By what I do," he answered.

"I know what you do," she answered. "I need to know why."

He reached out to touch her cheek again. This time, in spite of all her good intentions, she didn't move away. He held her chin so that she had to look into his eyes.

Very slowly he said, "I'm here now because I'd rather take my daughter and go with you, anywhere, than spend the rest of my life without you. If you won't stay with me here, I'm willing to leave everything I have just to come with you. But I have to be with you, Emily, or I'm nothing."

''But your law offices are in Bidewell,'' Emily protested weakly.

''Don't they have lawyers in Baltimore?'' he countered, softly stroking her cheek and meandering across her slender jaw to trickle down her throat.

''Well, yes, but there are so many of them there already.'' Emily didn't give a damn about the lawyers. It was so good just to feel Ben touching her again. She held her breath and enjoyed the roughness of his callused fingers caressing her throat. ''It'll be hard for you to establish another office.''

''I can do it,'' Ben answered confidently. He closed his hand so that only his index finger was left to wind a slender trail down the front of her dress. Very softly he said, ''With you, Emily, I can do anything.''

''But the rest of your family is here,'' she continued.

''You'll be my family, if you'll have me, Emily. You and Meggie and Frannie.''

''The farm, your home . . .''

''I want you to be my home, Emily.''

''You'd leave all this for me?'' Emily asked.

Ben nodded.

''You really do love me, don't you?''

''Don't you know by now?''

A shrill whistle split the air.

''The train's coming at last,'' Ben said. He dropped his hand and bent to pick up his suitcase. ''Time to get Meggie and Frannie.''

''No,'' she answered. She reached out her hand to stop him. ''It's a good place for Meggie. It's been a good place for me. I only did what I thought I had to do. I don't really want to leave here. I love you, and I don't want to spend the rest of my life without you, either.''

A wide smile began to spread over Ben's face as he dropped his suitcase. It fell over on its side with a thump.

"We both want to do what's best for the children. I think an aunt and uncle who love each other very much—and will raise Meggie with the rest of her family, together—are what's best." Taking only her hand in his, he asked, "Will you stay here in Bidewell with me, Emily, as my wife?"

"I'd stay with you anywhere, Ben."

As the train pulled into the station and passengers began to descend, Ben pulled Emily up into his arms and enveloped her in his strong embrace. She wrapped her arms about his neck, standing on tiptoe to lift her mouth to his. His lips met hers in a fervent kiss. He moved a second tiny kiss to one corner of her mouth and then the other.

"People are staring, Ben," Emily managed to say against his lips before he could kiss her again.

"Who cares?" he whispered. "Let everyone know this is a friendly town."

The lanky organist at the creaky pump organ churned out a stirring processional.

Meggie and Frannie proudly took their places beside Dolly in the front pew.

After a bath or two in lye soap, and a shave and a haircut and a generous sprinkling of bay rum—and after the minister had made him leave his Bowie knife at the church door—Mr. Pendergast cleaned up real well. Now if only he could keep his mouth shut at the altar, Emily hoped, as he had a rather nice face when he didn't show his three remaining teeth.

On his part, Mr. Pendergast was more than delighted to have the chance to escort his little cake lady up the aisle. Why, she was almost as pretty as the late Mrs. Pendergast, he maintained.

Miss Bloom's curly red head bobbed up and down as she

preceded Emily up the aisle. Was she so nervous, anticipating her own wedding day, that she was shaking already?

Noah and the minister stood on either side of him, but Emily saw only Ben. She heard the minister drone on, repeating their charges and their vows, but Ben's deep voice replying "I do" was all she really listened for.

She felt almost as if she floated through the service, until she felt Ben's warm hand as he took hers and placed the shining gold band on her finger. As he reached out to lift her veil, she couldn't help but quiver, anticipating his removal tonight of her other garments.

He held her shoulders, leaned slightly forward, and placed on her lips a brief, chaste kiss. Just as he was drawing away, he leaned forward again and whispered, "The real thing comes later tonight." Then he gave her a wicked wink.

The happy crowd pelted them with rice as they made a run for the carriage that was to take them back to the farm. When the others jumped into their own wagons to follow them, they discovered their harnesses were tangled. Two little boys sat on a nearby fence, laughing, until someone spotted them. Then they took off across the field at a run.

"Food sure was good, Dolly," Mr. Pendergast said, wiping his sleeve across his mouth. He turned to Emily, who was standing next to Ben at the door of the farmhouse. "Shame ya didn't get to make yer famous cake."

"Next time, Mr. Pendergast," Emily promised.

Ben leaned over and whispered in her ear, "Since when has your cooking become famous?"

Emily maintained a serene smile on her face, biding Mr. Pendergast goodbye, while she poked Ben in the stomach with her elbow.

"Well, food's all cleaned up, so ya don't have to worry

about that,'' Dolly told Emily. ''I take it ya can get breakfast for the two of ya tomorrow?''

''Oh, they won't be worrying about food for a few days, Ma,'' Noah said.

Dolly twisted her lips to hide her grin. She turned and motioned for Meggie and Frannie. ''C'mon, girls. We'll be staying in the house in Bidewell for a couple of days.''

''I'm sure Ben and Emily won't be needing us, Ma,'' Noah said.

Ben reached out a strong, sun-browned hand and closed the door. The noise of the departing guests, laughing and singing, and the sounds of the creaking wagon wheels was suddenly blotted out. The parlor and dining room, which had been ablaze with the light of every coal oil lamp Dolly owned, was now darkened.

''It's so quiet,'' Emily said. ''As if, suddenly, we were the only two people left in the world.''

''For tonight, we are,'' Ben told her. He left the doorway to come stand beside her. Placing his hand about her waist, he said, ''And forever after, Emily, you're the only one in my life.''

Pulling her more closely to him, he urged her to the foot of the stairs. He placed one foot on the bottom tread, then turned to her.

''I need you, Emily,'' he said, extending his hand to her. ''I've wanted to hold you and touch you since the first day I saw you.''

Emily smiled. She realized she had wanted him from the first moment she saw him, too. She wanted him now. She gave him her hand and followed him up the stairs.

They turned down the hall. Ben opened the door. Emily's heart beat faster as she entered the small bedroom. She moved to stand in the middle of the room. Ben followed her inside and closed the door.

The click of the latch made it all seem so final. Her heart beat so fast she could almost feel herself shaking with its pounding. She was actually married to Ben. All the times he had held her and kissed her, and the hundreds of times she had dreamed of repeating that, were now for real. He would hold her again, and kiss her, and so much more that she had only imagined. That would all come true tonight.

She wanted Ben so badly, yet now that the moment was almost here, Emily's body shook so hard with anticipation that she could barely stand up.

Ben slowly approached her from across the room. He stood in front of her. He held his arms out to enfold her in his embrace. She knew he could feel her quivering like a frightened bird.

"Don't tell me that you've suddenly turned into a timid bride," he whispered.

He rubbed his face across her hair. His breath was warm across her cheek. His chest was firm as he held her closely to him. She could hear his heart pounding almost as rapidly as hers was beating in her own breast.

She couldn't stop the nervous little giggle that escaped from her. "Just a little," she admitted. "After all, I've never done this before."

"Oh, Emily, we've done *this* before," he gently chided her. He drew her so close to him that she could feel the urgency of his need for her pressing against her own body.

He ran his hands up and down her back, crushing her breasts against his broad chest, then pulling her waist into his. His hands drifted down her ribs, diverging only slightly to caress the outer edges of her breasts, then continued downward to encircle her waist.

His hands ranged upward again, repeating the same motions. This time he paused at the nape of her neck to unfasten the tiny buttons there. Slowly easing down her back, his fingers continued to fumble with the endless row of buttons.

"Next time we get married," he whispered with a little chuckle, "I think you should wear a dress with a draw-string."

She quietly laughed, burying her face against his chest in her embarrassment. As she sank into him for comfort, he pulled her even closer and continued to unfasten her buttons.

He held the dress by the seams on either side of the back opening. Slowly stepping backward from her, he drew the dress from her shoulders and over her arms until the dress hung only from her skirt.

Ben's eyes were agleam again, the same way they had shone the first time he had seen her like this in only her chemise. Emily swallowed hard. A small part of her still felt as if she should cover herself before a man's eyes. But this man was Ben. He was her husband now, the man she loved. She stood and, barely breathing, allowed his eyes to take in the entire sight of her.

Ben came up to her again. He reached out to unfasten her petticoats. The fabric dropped to the floor with a soft rustle.

Ben looked at the heap of clothing. "Oh, look at the mess we've made," he said, shaking his head with mock dismay. "We can't stay here."

He held out his hand to her and helped her to step out of the skirt and petticoat on the floor. He led her to the side of the bed. Holding her in front of him, he sat on the edge.

He looked up into her eyes and gave her a wicked wink. "And I know we've done this before, too," he said, reaching for the drawstring on her drawers.

He gave the narrow pink ribbon a gentle tug. The bow came untied. Ben hooked his finger in the gathered silk at the top of her drawers and gave a little pull. The gathers loosened, but the drawers still hung crookedly on her softly rounded hips.

Emily drew in a deep breath, fully expecting Ben to remove her drawers as he had before. But he left them there.

He placed his palms on her stomach and slowly smoothed up the front of her chemise, untying each bow as he went until she was completely loosened from her garment. With only his thumb and forefinger, Ben held the lace edging and gently peeled it back.

Emily's heart jumped into her throat as Ben saw her for the first time. Her nipples tensed at his glance, almost as if he had caressed them with his hands. Ben pulled the chemise back over her shoulders, pushing her breasts out. Ben closed his eyes and drew in a deep breath before he opened them again. The chemise fell to the floor.

Ben placed his hands around her waist and pulled her closer to him. Burying his face against her, he kissed the little hollow between her breasts, then moved to the soft pink mounds in the center of each white swell. At first he only brushed his lips against her nipples, so gently she barely felt his touch. Then he kissed them, teasing each nipple to further hardness with the gentle pressure of his lips closing down on them. Then he finally opened his mouth and drew her nipple in.

Emily thought she would faint from the fire in her heart and the burning in the pit of her stomach.

"Oh, please, Ben," she murmured. "Don't make me wait."

Taking her arm, he urged her down on the bed beside him. She sat, but he held her in his arms and leaned her backward until she lay beside him.

Ben rose, kneeling astride her. Emily moved her arms to cover her breasts, a gesture that made Ben utter a little laugh. He bent down to kiss her on the lips, then reached over to move her arms away. As he righted himself, she could see his eyes gazing down upon her, burning with passion and love.

He reached up and began unbuttoning his own shirt. Emily swallowed hard. The image of Ben's bare chest had stayed with her from the first moment she'd seen him. She longed to see him again.

As he opened the front of his shirt, she could see his body was still tanned. His small brown nipples, with the dark hairs curling about them, were taut with desire. He slipped the white shirt off his bronzed shoulders. Then he unfastened the cuffs and discarded the shirt on the floor. His belt joined the rest of the unwanted clothing.

Then Ben reached out and seized the sides of her drawers in his fists. His desire was mounting, Emily could tell. His movements were not so leisurely but were becoming more and more demanding. In one swift movement he pulled the silken underthings from her hips and gave them a wide flip over his back.

Ben reached down to stroke her stomach, pulling his hands toward him. His forefinger dipped into her small oval navel, then out again to trail along her stomach until he reached the small triangle of softly curling hair. His fingers twitched as he ran them through the tiny curls. When Emily looked into his blue eyes, they were deepest indigo with desire.

Gently he parted her, only enough for one finger to tenderly explore that most precious part of her.

Emily held herself very still, so as not to wince. It didn't really hurt, she told herself. How could anything Ben did to her from love ever hurt her?

"I won't hurt you, Emily. I'll try not to," he corrected himself. His hands moved to the top of his trousers. She watched him unbutton the fly with fingers that visibly trembled with his pent-up desire. "I don't ever want to hurt you."

He stood to remove his trousers. Emily smiled. His back was tanned right down to the small dimples, but his buttocks were almost as white as hers. She watched the little indentations that formed just below his hips as he stood.

He turned and slid into bed beside her. He lay close against her, cupping her breast in his hand. He kissed her again, her lips and cheeks, her chin and the small hollow at the base of her throat. He kissed each breast again, gently swirling his tongue around each erect pink tip.

Emily placed her palms upon his chest. She traced the patterns of the whorls of his hairs and the tiny bumps at the outer edges of each flat nipple. She let her gaze travel down his chest and stomach until she at last saw his desire for her, pressing into the flesh of her hip.

"Touch me, Emily," he whispered.

She reached out timidly to stroke his manhood, hot and rigid with his desire for her. Ben closed his eyes. His whole body shuddered with the pleasure of her touch. She felt her own womanhood burning with the same desire to hold Ben within her.

"Emily, I want you so much," he said as he slid atop her. He kissed her softly once again. "I'll try to be gentle, but it's been so long, and I want you so much . . ."

"I want you, too, Ben," she said as she opened to welcome him. "I really do want you."

She felt his fingers parting her again. Another part of him pressed into her, deeper and deeper. She thrust her hips upward, more than ready to envelop him in her love. She closed her eyes against the searing of his hot flesh in hers. There was no pain with Ben, she tried to tell herself—she loved him and he loved her—and soon she found that this was true.

He rested on his forearms. His strong arms enclosed her in a protective shield of love from any intrusion. She felt safe in his embrace.

He began to rock her back and forth, back and forth. Their breathing became ragged and shallow, gasping for breath to fuel their thrusts. The gentle rhythm built in intensity until she cried out. Ben moaned. She felt his entire body shuddering within her. Deep within her own body, she felt a lightning tingle that spread up her stomach to her very heart.

His body collapsed on top of her. She held his head between her breasts, close to her heart where he belonged. Their breathing was ragged and deep as they began to drift into sleep.

"I love you, Emily," Ben said as he slid to her side. "For all my life, I'll love you."

She curled up beside him—naked, just like she had always wanted—and laid her head on his chest. She kissed the brown nipple that fascinated her so. The hair tickled her nose.

"I love you, too, Ben," she said.

It was raining outside, Emily supposed as she lay beside Ben, tenderly enfolded in his embrace after their passion had run its course. Thunder crashed, but it sounded more like someone beating on tin pots with wooden spoons. The gentle patter of rain on a tin roof sounded more like someone beating on a washboard.

"Ben! Ben!" she cried, shaking him awake. "What is it?"

Ben drew in a deep breath and rubbed the sleep from his eyes. "What's what?" he asked.

"Shhh. Listen," she ordered.

Ben listened. "Geez, Emily," he said with laugh. "You

don't have to be quiet to hear that. Ol' Man Pendergast's wife could hear that, and she's been dead five years."

"What is it?" she asked.

"Come and see." Ben rose from the bed and extended his hand to her.

Emily's eyes roamed appreciatively over Ben's body. Relaxed now from making love, it was every bit as wonderful as it had been—and would be again—soon, she hoped. "I can see everything I want from here," she told him.

"No, no, you got to see this," he said, urging her to rise.

Ben slipped into his trousers. He only hitched them over his hips and didn't bother to button them. Emily boldly traced the hair from his navel down into the tops of his trousers.

"Later," he said, grasping her hand and raising it to his lips to kiss her fingers.

He held out a dressing gown for her. As he draped it over her shoulders, he didn't fail to give each breast a delicate caress.

On the front lawn was just what Emily had envisioned. Dolly, Noah and Miss Bloom, Sam and Lottie, Mr. Pendergast, the Lindstroms, and so many other people that Emily had a hard time identifying them. They were beating on pots and pans with spoons. Some of the men were singing songs—with very bawdy lyrics, from what little Emily could understand amidst all the clatter. Noah was blowing loudly on a badly dented and seriously out of tune cornet.

"Dang if he didn't find Pa's old horn," Ben murmured.

"What is this?" Emily asked, peeking cautiously out from behind the curtain.

Ben laughed, drawing her back, closer to him. "Don't let them see you. It's a shivaree. Didn't you know that?"

Emily shook her head. "No. And you'd certainly think a person would have found out about anything this noisy."

"It's just their way of celebrating our wedding," Ben said. "They'll go away in a couple of hours."

"Hours?" Emily repeated, raising her hands to cover her ears.

Ben took full advantage of the opportunity this gesture afforded him to cup her soft firm breasts from behind. His fingers grasped her nipples, urging them erect.

"Come back to bed with me, my love," he whispered from behind. "I know a much better way to celebrate our wedding."